STRAYBLOOD

DRAEV GUARDIANS
BOOK TWO

E.E. RAWLS

To those who stand true,
even in the face of monsters.

ISBN: 978-0-9985569-9-4 paperback
ISBN: 979-8-9852392-0-1 hardback

[1. Fantasy. 2. Coming of Age—Fantasy. 3. Ability—Fiction.
4.Orphans—Fiction. 5. Magic—Fiction.]

www.eerawls.com
Printed in the U.S.A.
First edition, December 2021

Titles by E.E. Rawls

Earthaverse:

~⊙⊙~

Draev Guardians Series

Strayborn (1)

Storm & Choice (0.5)

Dragons & Ravens (1.5)

Strayblood (2)

Alteredverse:

~⊙⊙~

Frost, Winter's Lonely Guardian

Portal to Eartha

Beast of the Night

Madness Solver in Wonderland

Coming Soon:

Straypath (3)

Secret projects ;)

Find out when the next books are releasing, and get
exclusive content, by following my newsletter at:
eerawls.com

Prologue

It was a dark fortress made of sharp edges and foreboding gloom, seated upon a rock island at the center of a deep, hollow crater. Its black towers rose like daggers toward the storm clouds overhead.

Ellefsen stood at the crater's edge, examining the steep drop and the distance across to the island and its ominous structure. He brushed back his white bangs.

"The Morbid Dungeons," he mused. "A terrifying prison, said to be impossible to break out of, or even break *into*." He chuckled to himself. "It almost hurts my heart to have to ruin such a magnificent reputation."

He let the final piece of a log drop to the ground beside his boots. A row of more than eighty log pieces now stretched out to either side along the crater, brought there by his power.

"Yes, that should be enough." He clapped his hands together. "All right! Now for the fun part to begin…"

He squinted at the sharply tipped towers. He could just make out one of the lookout guards on a balcony. It was a nice spot situated away from the main gate and drawbridge, and less likely to draw someone's attention.

Ellefsen smirked and raised his hand.

"*Switcheroo*," he commanded, and turned his palm inward.

The guard thought he saw movement over on the crater edge, and he squinted to better see. Not that it mattered much. If it was an intruder attempting to fly across the gap, the weapons installed in the towers would shoot them down.

He was about to comment to the guard beside him about it, when the stone surfaces and tower around him suddenly vanished, and he found himself standing on bleak grass on the other side of the crater.

He stared about his new surroundings and cried out in shock.

Ellefsen reappeared at the very spot where the guard had been on the balcony, and he turned to the second guard there, who gaped at him, eyes wide. "*Burrr*, it's quite drafty up here, isn't it?" Ellefsen commented.

Before the guard could shout an alarm, Ellefsen moved the rifle-axe in the guard's hand with his power so that it swung up, striking the vempar in the head and knocking him out.

Ellefsen hurried off the balcony to the stairs, a skip in his step, and entered the tower while the guard collapsed to the floor.

The stairs ended at an indoor balcony ledge, and he paused to peer over the rails, observing the huge, hollowed-out center of the tower—a massive space of sculpted stonework and dim shafts of light, throughout which hung metal cages, rows upon rows of them, all the way down to the distant floor below.

Ellefsen hopped onto the rail, hands in his pockets, and stepped off.

He levitated down, taking his time, and peered into the cages that he passed by. Some convicts stared at him in open shock, not only because he was floating but because someone had successfully infiltrated the Morbid Dungeons. Others grinned with a malicious eagerness.

"This one, yes. That one, no. But definitely *this* one." He tapped the cage locks of the criminals he chose, and their barred doors swung open. Heads, both grisly and conniving, poked out from the openings. But it was still a steep drop to the gray floor far below.

Ellefsen grabbed each of them with his mind and lifted them out of their cages and up towards the tower ceiling. Several yelped and cried out in fear, finding themselves floating through the air with nothing to stop their fall should they suddenly drop. "Quiet," Ellefsen rebuked them. "Don't be such wimps."

A guard patrolling below heard the noise and looked up.

"See what you've done?" Ellefsen grimaced at the criminals. He splayed his palm toward the guard below.

The guard bolted through a doorway and escaped just before his power could reach him.

Ellefsen made an irritated sound in his throat and continued carrying the large criminal group up to the highest balcony. There, he shoved them through the door and outside onto one of the tower's wide balconies.

An alarm bell began sounding from somewhere beneath them, followed by more bells in the adjacent black towers. Guards outside shouted, and some pointed at them once they spotted his group.

Soon the large guns would be aimed their way.

"My, my, things just can't ever be easy, can they?" Ellefsen huffed. He turned, facing the distant logs he had set up on the other side of the crater. Then, facing each of the criminals, he motioned with his hand and said, "*Switcheroo.*"

One by one, the convicts vanished, as if into thin air—then they reappeared down at the crater's edge, where the logs had been, while the logs appeared in their place up on the balcony beside him.

A loud gun shot sounded, and Ellefsen watched as a heavy bullet came speeding through the air towards him. He flashed a smirk before he, too, vanished—just before the shot reached where his forehead had been.

"Toodles!" He waved at the towers from the crater edge.

The drawbridge lowered and guards spilled out, but Ellefsen and his new group of lackeys were already gone.

PART 1

ORACLE

1

Cyrus tried to shake off the image swimming through her head: of the human girl dying in the cemetery that dawn, her hair as red as her own. But the girl's body had disappeared; and though Cyrus had run to tell Master Nephryte about it, in the end, she hadn't been able to bring herself to say anything.

A dying human rambling about some secret group called the Impure Nights, claiming they were hunting for red-haired girls in a vempar city? How could any of that make sense?

No, Cyrus must have been so tired from the past few days that she'd started hallucinating or half-dreaming or something. That would also explain why there was no trace of the girl left, even when Cyrus went back to check.

Either way, she now shoved the incident out of her head and put the Draevensett coat-of-arms on her olive-green shirt back and headed out of her room. She rubbed her forehead, which suddenly ached.

The air in Harlow's dorm floor felt hot today...or was it just her?

Achoo!

She rubbed her nose.

"What was that? Did you sneeze?" Aken appeared behind her.

Cyrus jumped in her shoes. "Can you *not* sneak up on me all the time?" she reprimanded him.

Aken cocked his head, not understanding, since any other vempar would have heard his light footsteps.

He wore a V-neck blue shirt, the lace strings loose down his chest. The color brought out his sky-blue eyes and sun-blond hair. He peered at her closely, and she leaned away.

"What?"

"You look like you're burning up. Are you okay?" He pressed his hand to her forehead.

She blushed and pushed away. "Of course I...*ah-choo!*"

Aken flinched. "Why are you sneezing? There's no dust around."

Cyrus fanned a hand to cool her face. None of Harlow knew about her being a girl. Only Master Nephryte, Doctor Zushil and Gandif knew the truth—as far as she was aware—and a warning voice in her head told her to keep it that way. It was a real pain. But if the warning was from Lord God, then she would listen.

Just then, Bakoa came trotting past them. "Wow, Cy, you look terrible! Your nose is all red and puffy and dripping." He paused and gasped in horror. "Wait a minute, Cy's got a cold! It's that weird illness that non-vempars get, and it makes them all sweaty and red before they die."

"Die?!" Aken exclaimed.

Cyrus tried to box Bakoa's pointy ears. "That's *not* how it works."

Aken grabbed her shoulder. "We've gotta get you to the doc, *now*! Why didn't you say something sooner? I can't let you die!"

Cyrus tried to pry his hand off. "I told you, that's not—*achoo!*"

Aken and Bakoa both shouted in alarm and started shoving her towards the stairwell doorway, ignoring her angry protests.

Master Nephryte emerged from his dorm flat just then and, without bothering to ask, he grabbed both boys by their shirt collars, freeing Cyrus. "What on eartha are you panicking for? Because I am sure it has nothing to do with you about to be late for class."

"Cyrus is sick!"

"He's gonna die!"

The Master gave them both a skeptical look, and then Cyrus sneezed again.

"See, *see?*" Aken insisted.

Master Nephryte refrained from rolling his eyes. "Cyrus seems to have caught a cold. But it won't kill him. Stop being so dramatic." He released the boys and they dropped to the floor. "Cyrus, stay in bed for a few hours and rest. I'll see what medicine the doctor can bring for you," he ordered.

She complied, dragging her suddenly heavy feet back to her room...

When Cyrus woke sometime later, it was to Doctor Zushil and Master Nephryte entering her room. The doctor measured her temperature and her pulse before nodding. "A simple cold, yes," he declared, and dug through his bag of medicine bottles. "*This* should boost your immune system to fight it off." He set a bottle of yucky green tablets on the nightstand.

Cyrus's tastebuds wanted to protest, fearing what manner of green stuff might be in them. They looked like something plucked from a rotting bog.

The door to her room flung open again.

Nephryte moved to intercept whoever it was, when a shoe

showed through the doorway and kicked Aken into the room—the boy falling into the Master head-first.

"Deal with this blubbering student of yours, Master Nephryte!" demanded Professor Kotetsu, the owner of the shoe, his wing-like eyebrows flapping. "I'm normally a patient teacher, but even *this* is too much for me."

The Master straightened his blue tunic collar, embroidered in golden crescent moons. "My apologies. I will take care of..." he began, but Kotetsu had already left.

The Master looked down at Aken, only to find that the boy had dashed over to Cyrus's bedside, his face all worry lines. "Aken-Shou, he is not going to die."

Aken shook his head. "I'm staying right here anyway."

From the pillow, Cyrus squinted, irritated by all the commotion. She wasn't some fragile baby bird for everyone to fret over!

"Fine," the Master relented. "As long as you do your homework." He exhaled and left the room for a bit.

"One tablet every six hours," Zushil instructed her, and he picked up his bag of medicines to leave.

"Will he really be okay?" Aken started to ask, and Zushil looked down his nose at the boy.

"Cyrus will recover soon enough. I've treated many a human slave over the years; I am well familiar with their anatomy," he said matter-of-factly. "One would think owners would Heal their own slaves, themselves, but I suppose it's too much effort for the lordships and moneybags. Instead, they pay me to use medicine."

Aken's ears perked, and he glanced at the empty doorway. "Say, Doc, can I ask you a strange question?"

Zushil gave him a look that said he would rather him not.

Aken proceeded anyway. "Is it dangerous for a vempar to taste someone else's blood?"

Zushil's eyebrows slanted inward. "Always full of weird questions, aren't you?" he muttered under his breath. "Boy, hardly any blood is dangerous for a vempar. In fact, some say we were once created to be the Healers of the world: curing illnesses and mending all manner of injuries, though much of that knowledge has since been lost. There are limits to Healing, of course. Not every single problem can be cured—that girl, Cherish, for example." He frowned. "I'm rambling now, but the idea of blood being dangerous is absurd."

"So, let me get this straight," said Aken. "You're saying that it's completely safe for a vempar to Heal others—blood isn't dangerous to them in any way?"

Zushil nodded absently, "Yes. Exactly. Unless it's dwarf blood—that stuff *will* make you sick for a good while. But otherwise, most blood is just fine. Why do you even ask?"

"Master Nephryte told me it wasn't safe. I don't know why."

The doctor raised one wiry eyebrow. "Hm? How odd of him. You must have heard him wrong, or perhaps he was preoccupied and misspoke."

Aken frowned to himself while the doctor left.

Cyrus listened, pretending to be asleep, curious what that talk was about and what Aken could be thinking.

❧

An hour later, Master Nephryte returned to find Aken doing some history homework while Cyrus dozed, nose red and stuffed with tissue.

Aken looked up and met his gaze.

"Cyrus is sleeping well?" the Master inquired.

Aken closed the book and stared at the cat clock on the nightstand. "I asked him," he said instead, ignoring the question.

Nephryte tilted his head to the side.

"I asked Doc if blood could be dangerous. And he said no," Aken furthered.

Nephryte's mouth pressed into a grim line. "For other vempars, perhaps. But not for you."

"What is *that* supposed to mean?"

The Master regarded him, then shifted his focus to Cyrus. "Just trust me on this," he said.

"But *why*? I bet I could Heal Cy of this stupid cold in seconds, instead of waiting for some silly medicine to do the job. Don't fangs attract and draw out bad virus cells—or whatever you call them?"

"Do you know where the main artery is? Or where *any* veins are, for that matter?" Nephryte eyed him sideways.

Aken's cheeks reddened but he persisted. "I want to help Cyrus get better. You can show me how to..."

Aken's sentence trailed away, and Nephryte looked back to see why.

The bed Cyrus had been sleeping in was empty.

They both went still. No trace of the half-human was anywhere in sight.

"Uh...did my mention of fangs freak him out?"

⟿

Cyrus bolted past the entryway and down the stairwell.

Fangs? They wanted to Heal her with their *fangs*? She screamed inwardly, her feet tearing down the stairs, ignoring her pounding headache.

At the ground level, she dashed into the first-floor hallway, heading for the nearest exit.

She took out a pocket tissue to wipe the snot and blew her nose. Several students she passed by flinched away, with grossed out expressions on their faces.

"Hi, Cyrus!" Bakoa waved a cheerful hand, stepping out of a classroom, his grin stretching the cleft in his chin. "Wow, you must be feeling better. Running around so fast like a—"

She sped past him—or rather, through him—his body shifting into fine grains of colored sand and dispersing where she rammed through.

He reformed into a miniature version of himself, spinning in the air dizzily, as she kept running. "Sure, don't mind me. I'm just a sandbag that people forget has feelings," he said after her.

Cyrus tore out of an exit door and raced across Draevensett's front courtyard, her footfalls thudding against the flagstone drive and then grass and the path. She made her way down the slope to the grand front iron gate and its curling rods. Even the leafy pixit there avoided her as if she was a walking germ; its large eyes set in a head of cotton fluff glared as it ducked behind a cluster of leaves.

"Sick! Sick! Go away!" it cried.

"I'm trying to!" she growled, yanking the right gate half open. The winged lions atop their stone posts to either side seemed to be regarding her with disapproval, as well.

She made a face at them all while she hurried out into the city streets.

A half hour later, Cyrus was nestled quietly in one of the numerous blooming trees in Cherryblossom Park—high up and well-hidden amidst the branches and floral pink petals, her back propped against the trunk.

She fingered the twin metal bracelets shaped like feathers around her upper arms—a gift from Master Nephryte, so that she could use its metal in case of emergencies, instead of using the iron in her blood and making herself weak.

Tall Tim's bell gonged across the city, and she glanced to where the sun was, guessing that school must be over by now.

Aken wouldn't find her here, not for a long time, she told herself. She could hide in the trees until her cold went away. Yeah, that would work.

"Good afternoon, Cyrus."

She screeched and almost fell out of the tree.

She shifted on the bark to peer down at the ground below.

Mamoru stood at the foot of the tree, shielding his face from the sun with a hand. His ebony shirt and pants today had rips through the fabric like claw marks, showing his sap-smooth skin. He flashed a smile up at her. "Feeling better?"

"Uh..." She wasn't sure how to answer that. With a red nose, and tissues stuffed in every pocket, the answer was obvious. But if he dared to mention anything about fangs...

Mamoru gave her a knowing look, his smile tweaked in an almost laugh. "Don't worry, Cyrus." He held up a hand for her. "Come on down. I won't let anyone's fangs touch you."

She hesitated. But, well, Mamoru *was* the trustworthy sort.

Plus, a line of ants was making its way up the bark. She really didn't want to risk them crawling over her while she dozed.

She scooted down the branch, and then down part of the tree trunk, when her foot suddenly slipped out from under her. "*Ah!*"

A pair of strong arms caught her, and she found herself staring up into his mulberry-colored eyes—the red scar, edged in black down his cheek, stark against the sunlight. She felt her cheeks redden.

"They mean well, you know," Mamoru said, and he lightly set her down on her feet, as if she were a feather. "Even if they don't understand humans' fear of fangs."

"How did you know I was hiding?" she asked.

He chuckled. "Because you would still be resting in bed, otherwise—not out inspecting flowers in trees."

Cyrus pouted.

His mirthful gaze took on a distant look for a moment, as if seeing something from the past. Then he came back to himself. "That fever won't get any better until you sleep it off. You can use my dorm room for the day and rest—no one will dare look for you in there; they know my wrath would descend on them if they so much as touched anything. Will that suit you?"

She nodded reluctantly, blowing her nose again.

"I'll walk you back," he said, brushing his deep maroon bangs back with a hand.

"No, no, I'll be fine on my own," she assured. "I'm sure you have more important things to do."

He shrugged. "They can wait. The practice recital can do without me for a while."

"Recital?"

"Did I forget to mention? I've been teaching the children at Hope's Orphanage to become little puppeteers—and they're very good! They're practicing a play now: *The Magician's Flute*."

He walked alongside her up one of the park's smooth paths. She glanced sidelong at him, and at the enthusiasm clear on his face. He loved sharing his passion of puppeteering with others.

What passion could she use to help others? She wondered silently. She wasn't particularly good at anything.

"You and Harlow should come to the recital," he said. "Having a big audience would encourage the children."

She glanced up and nodded.

"Excuse me, but may I escort Cyrus Sole back?"

Ahead of them, where the path exited the main park gate, waited Hercule, his hair combed to one side, though not as neatly as it usually was, and wearing gray pants and matching silk vest over a pale lilac shirt. His hands rested casually in his pockets.

Fear needled her as she recalled his betrayal—how he had revealed her half-human identity to the entire school.

Mamoru's gaze took Hercule in for one considering moment, then he shocked Cyrus by nodding. "Very well, Hercule. I'll entrust Cyrus to you."

She gave a start, wanting to grab Mamoru's arm and make him stay with her.

Hercule bowed his head slightly in return, and Cyrus soon found herself walking through the mix of cobbled and paved streets of the city alongside the boy with dragon-gold eyes.

Passersby stared openly. Children playing in the streets and slaves tired from running errands also glanced her way. So many eyes analyzed her. She wished she could melt into the pavestones and vanish, or at least hide her attention-grabbing red hair.

"You're popular now, whether for good or for bad."

She gave a start. It was the first time Hercule had spoken during their walk.

"I kind of figured," she replied, eyes on the sidewalk beneath her feet.

"People will judge you, scrutinize you, watch every decision and movement that you make. It is the way of society," he told her. "But don't let it wear you down or make you weak. Keep being the resourceful person that you are."

Did he just give her a compliment *and* give her advice? To her, a half-human? Cold and prideful Hercule?

"Thanks. I'll keep that in mind."

He shrugged uncomfortably. "I misjudged you. I thought you were something that you're not. And I thought you couldn't be trusted." He halted then, turning to face her, and bowed—a waist-deep bow, his pearl-gray hair spilling forward to shadow his face. "Your life was put at risk because of me. I am truly sorry, Cyrus Sole. I beg for your forgiveness."

Her eyes bulged, and she waved for him to straighten up quickly. The heir to one of the twelve great Noble Houses bowing to her? Now even more people were staring! "No, don't, there's no need for that, *really*!"

"This is my punishment. Please accept it," Hercule insisted, raising his golden gaze just enough through his eyelashes to meet hers.

She froze awkwardly, then with a small sigh, nodded. "I accept your apology."

People around were whispering. Hercule rose from his bow with a pleased look on his flawless face. "Thank you."

They continued their walk. "Does this mean we're friends now?" she asked him tentatively.

"Comrades." His expression didn't change, so she wasn't sure if he meant it as something *better* than friends or not. She hoped it was the *better*.

Upon reaching Draevensett, she nodded her thanks to Hercule and then entered one of the side doors beneath the front colonnaded walkway. She went into stealth-mode, locating and creeping up the stairwell to the fifth floor.

"I can understand wanting to avoid Aken," Hercule said from beside her. "But Healing is not dangerous."

She was startled again, unaware that he had continued to follow her. She made shushing motions at him and peeked into the empty entryway. Coast clear, she hurried to the corridor.

From her room she snatched the medicine, then hurried over to Mamoru's dorm. To her relief, Aken was nowhere to be seen.

Hercule glanced away and shrugged. "I have homework to finish. When you're feeling well tomorrow, I can help you catch up with what you've missed today, if you like." Just as he lifted a hand to open his own door, the door flung wide.

A faeryn girl of honey hair, mixed with flaxen and amber streaks, came out with a basketful of laundry in her arms. Her skin was like angel cake, mottled with patches of honey freckles, and her eyes mint green, the pupils not black but a darker green shade.

Hercule gave a start. "Marigold!"

2

The Night Before

Marigold perched on the sill of the single window inside her makeshift bedroom, up in the Dragonsbane Mansion's attic—a little space all to herself. She watched as the stars unveiled their glory through the fading storm clouds, and the partial moon slowly rose to glaze its soft light over the pond and city rooftops.

She was to move into Draevensett Academy tomorrow, where she would live and serve Hercule. A part of her worried what life would be like in some place other than the mansion. She'd never lived anywhere else, except for the forest—and that was a distant memory now: a vague image of a child version of herself skipping through the lush, emerald woods, picking wildflowers, while other faeryn lingered somewhere nearby with Papá and Nonna. Then the clamor of shouts and fighting began, and a sack was thrown over her head.

That was the day she had been kidnapped.

The day her life as a forest faeryn had ended—or rather, never had a chance to begin.

Marigold subconsciously rubbed the Mark on her neck: an ink-like symbol in the shape of a dragon's wing, binding her to Hercule Dragonsbane. She watched anxiously as the moon lowered and the stars faded.

When morning finally bathed the horizon in warm pastel colors, Marigold clenched the handle of her suitcase and followed Hercule out the main entrance, ducking inside a motor carriage waiting for them, and taking the seat opposite him. She caught the rich scent of earthy lavender—the expensive shampoo that he used.

The carriage engine hummed as they turned down the driveway, and she glanced across at Hercule. Judging by his pinched forehead, it was clear that he disliked this plan of his father's: insisting that a noble heir should always have their personal slave attendant with them. In other words, that Marigold should live at the school and attend to his every need. Many noble children were following this trend now.

Hercule shifted his head to one side, not looking at her while he brooded.

Marigold knew it wasn't her he was upset with, but rather the thought of his father being in control of every aspect of his life, even when he lived away at school.

What *would* life be like for her at the elite academy? No maids hollering at her every five seconds of the day, no Lady Chatsalott determined to keep her busy cleaning *this* and scrubbing *that* just because she was a slave and shouldn't have free time to herself.

This could be a nice change. Plus, there was another perk: the half-human training to become a Draev Guardian lived there. After hearing about his victory during the Festival Duel, she really wanted to meet him.

The motor carriage swayed as it followed the paved path, and she held her suitcase closer.

～э

Marigold hurried to perform her first chores as a new maid in Draevensett. Upon their arrival, she'd been given a small room in the servants' quarters—a building sectioned off from the rest of the academy.

The school's housekeeper had taken her aside when she arrived and given her a quick tour and a schedule sheet, explaining what was to be expected of her. And just like that, she was sent off to work!

Her top priority was her role as Hercule's personal attendant, which meant tidying his room, keeping things spotless and presentable, and doing his daily laundry—as well as helping with any of the school's extra laundry needing done.

Hercule came first, the school chores second. Speaking of which, she hadn't seen Hercule since they parted ways earlier that morning, but she thought she could remember where and which dorm room was his from the tour. He'd always been good at keeping a tidy room—probably because he didn't want her or anybody else nosing through his belongings and ruining his precise organization.

She crossed the front courtyard, heading toward the servant's entrance, when a boy burst from a nearby door, his red hair fluttering as he ran.

Marigold gave a surprised gasp. His ears were *human*. Could he be the…?

She stared after the boy, her chest filling with hope.

With the famous half-human's help, maybe, one day, she and other slaves would finally be set free…

She shook herself from her daydream and hurried indoors.

It was after that, when she came to Hercule's room and began dusting, that she set about doing the laundry. She had folded and put everything away that was clean, putting the rest in a basket to carry, when she ran into Hercule just outside the door—and the redhead who was with him.

THE PRESENT

The faeryn gave a startled gasp. "Milord Hercule! Did your classes end already?" Her question trailed off when she noticed Cyrus, and her mint eyes widened.

Hercule scrubbed a hand through his hair as if embarrassed, glancing nervously at the basket she held. He leaned towards the faeryn, whispering, "I am perfectly able to do my own laundry, Marigold. You needn't bother."

But the faeryn shook her head, respectful yet blunt, "I've just returned some clean laundry to your closet, milord. Every shirt ironed and all underwear folded neatly to your liking."

Cyrus watched as Hercule's face turned uncharacteristically bright red. "I told you, I can fold my own—" he tried to whisper, but the faeryn continued, indicating the basketful under her arm: "And these, here, are the staff's shirts. But I came to put away your clean things, first, and just now finished."

"Yes," he finally managed to say. "It is appreciated, but...but at least, please, let me wash my own..." his voice lowered to a whisper near her ear, "...undergarments."

Cyrus sucked in her lips, trying not to laugh. She sneezed instead.

Hercule's face remained red. "*Ahem.* Cyrus, this is my... personal attendant, Miss Marigold. And this is my Floor comrade, Cyrus Sole," he made introductions. He avoided using the word *slave*, but she knew that's what the faeryn girl basically was—though maybe of a better status with her *personal attendant* title.

"A pleasure to meet you, sir." Marigold curtsied in her simple green dress and apron, her expression gleaming with a bit of wonder.

Cyrus dismissed the honorific with a palm wave. "Just plain Cyrus is fine."

"But, sir—"

"Please," Cyrus insisted, and the girl blinked.

Cyrus realized suddenly that they were not the only ones in the dorm corridor. She peered around Hercule's shoulder to spot Bakoa, Lykale, Zartanian and Aken eavesdropping around the corner.

The nobleson froze stiff.

Aken came out of hiding and flourished his arms dramatically. "Dost thou have trouble cleaning thy undergarments, that thou had to bring thy attendant to do it for thee?"

The others couldn't contain themselves and burst out laughing.

She didn't think Hercule's face could get any redder, but it did. Ribbons of steam curled from the insides of his ears.

As for Cyrus, she used the opportunity to escape.

Aken called out, "Ah—wait! Cy! *Cy!*"

But she was already gone…

After ten minutes of hiding, ducking behind a potted plant in the stairwell, she eluded the blond and quickly crept back into the corridor and slipped inside Mamoru's room, locking the door behind her.

She ignored the dismembered limbs of a puppet across the back table and a bowl of shiny glass eyeballs.

The bed inside the artsy room was tidy and comfortable; she stretched out across the russet embroidered bedspread. There was a pleasant scent of amber oil and wax in the air, which soothed the tension from her body.

At last, she could rest in peace without fear of Healing and fangs and…and…

Zzzzzzz…

3

Aken strode across the school grounds, kicking grass as he went, berating himself for ever bringing up the topic of fangs around a human. What a doofus he was! Why couldn't he ever keep his big mouth shut?

He wandered over by the patch of trees where he and Cyrus had eaten their stolen morning dessert that one time. He chuckled at the memory and the trouble they had gotten into.

His ears picked up a sound nearby, like someone exerting effort: "*Hah! …Haa! …Hyah!*"

He crept closer through the underbrush until he spotted the source: Zartanian, in a small clearing and practicing sword strokes with his saber against a dummy made of straw, slashing in a right arc, a left arc, then a full-circle spin. His curly mop of raven hair was tied back with a blue ribbon, his bangs damp against his forehead, his white blouse sleeves rolled up.

The dummy got sliced in three places, the cuts not deep enough to knock it over.

Zartanian panted, wiped his brow.

"How pathetic," spoke an irritating voice.

Aken quickly hopped up the nearest tree and perched on a branch to watch as Denim and his gang approached, swaggering over in Zartanian's direction—the group noticeably still lacking Doughboy. Tathom's crest on their shirts was a snake coiled around a crescent-moon axe.

Zartanian did his best to ignore them.

"That dummy's faring better than he is. I suppose we can't all be blessed with useful Abilities, though, can we?" Denim stuck his peacock nose up in the air. The other boys grouped around, snickering, as Zartanian continued the sword strokes.

"That sword looks too heavy for him."

"It matches the too-big hat. Haha!"

"Why does he wear that thing? Does he really think he's gonna become some Bladeer from the fairytales, let alone a Draev?"

"Nope. It's just to hide his antlers—he's part rehfabel."

Some of the others gasped.

The knuckles on Zartanian's hands grew white from gripping the sword hilt. He took several slow steps away, keeping a gap between himself and the bullies without them noticing. "I *will* become a Draev Guardian," he murmured, and paused his practicing.

"What's your Ability, anyway? I don't think I've ever seen you use it. Must be real lame, or non-existent, like all the other Armavis types. How is wielding a blade even considered an Ability?" Denim scoffed.

One of the lackeys spoke up, "I think it's because they have a special affinity with the weapon through their *essence* and can use it in ways that normal people can't."

"Shut it, Malfred; who asked you? Anyways, *my* Ability, on the other hand, is a weapon in and of itself!" said Denim. He held out his palm and the air above it shimmered white before freezing into a ball of ice crystals. "Yeah, everybody knows my ice power is cool. It suits me, since I'm royalty and all."

The lackeys bobbed their heads.

Aken rolled his eyes from atop his perch.

"I'm not just an Armavis," Zartanian said quietly.

"Huh? What was that?" Denim cupped a hand to his ear as if straining to hear.

Zartanian was such a kind and quiet soul, he didn't know how to handle bullies. Aken's fingernails dug angrily into the tree bark as he readied to leap down and help. But in that moment, his ears picked up a buzzing sound coming from somewhere close. It had been there since he climbed up, but he hadn't fully taken notice of it until just then.

Aken scanned the thick foliage around him and, at last, spotted a large beehive hanging from an elm branch, just above where Denim and his gang stood. And not just *any* beehive. This was a nest of spine hornets. A vicious bee with a spine made of protruding stingers, ready to pierce venom into your skin. And once their spine of needles got you, the barbs at the ends wouldn't let you just pull them out easily. The bee lived, too. It didn't die like normal bees, but instead wriggled its body back and forth to drive the stingers further in before disconnecting itself and flying away to grow a new set.

A mischievous grin spread across Aken's face.

Zartanian backed away as Denim swaggered forward, not wanting to raise his sword and start a fight. Meanwhile, high above, Aken pulled out a tiny clay bird from a back pocket, infused with bits of his *essence*. He would just tap the hive, get some of the bees angry so that they'd buzz loudly and catch Denim's attention. Then, the bullies would run away in fright like wimps!

Aken took aim…and threw.

The clay bird bumped into the hive.

But instead of just shaking the hive a little, like he intended, the stem holding the hive to the branch snapped...

The hornet hive fell, hit the ground, bounced, and rolled to a stop at Denim's feet.

"Huh? What's this——?" Denim began.

That was all he had time to say before an angry swarm of spine hornets roared out of the hive like a black cloud of doom—coming straight at the bully and his Floor Tathom lackeys.

"*AAAHH!!!*" Shrieks and screams rent the air as the boys jumped and leaped, swatted and ran. The spine hornets pursued them, stinging their spines into vempar flesh.

Denim cried as he ran, shouting curses at his followers as if they were to blame. "You idiots!! Why didn't you tell me there were spine hornets around? *Aahk!*"

"We didn't know!" they cried.

They ran towards the school, coated in writhing, wriggling bees, and shouted frantically: "Doctor Zushil!!!"

Aken had gotten himself and Zartanian a good distance clear of the fallen beehive during the commotion, and now he rolled on the grass laughing, watching the distant figures run.

Zartanian touched a hand to his mouth in dismay, also watching.

"That wasn't what I meant to happen, but still, serves them right for picking on you like that," Aken said, giving a satisfied nod.

The other boy shrugged uncomfortably and put the practice sword in his belt loop. The cries faded away. He didn't seem to know what to say. "Uh, um...do you know if Cyrus is feeling any better?" he asked out of topic, instead, his voice faint.

Aken ceased laughing, the question a reminder of his failure as a friend, and his shoulders slumped.

Zartanian cocked his head in question, his pale winter gaze

trained on him.

Aken finally gave in and explained how he had accidentally frightened the redhead earlier.

"I don't know what to do now; he runs away every time I see him," Aken told him, and tossed a handful of grass up in the air, watching the stalks as they twirled back down.

Zartanian pursed his lips in thought, tugging at the rim of his plumed hat. "It must be hard for Cyrus here, living in a world so different from where he came from. It was hard enough for me, coming from a small fishing town. I can't imagine what it's like living in an entirely different kingdom and with a different race."

Another world. So many things about vempars and their culture were different from the humans that it probably *did* feel like another world to Cyrus.

Aken squinted in thought. "We need to make Cy feel more at home, then...somehow."

"Maybe if we bring some elements of human culture here?" Zartanian suggested. "Like some human traditional food, or drink, or..."

Aken's ears perked. "Traditional food! That's a great idea. Eh, except I don't know of any traditional food for humans..."

"I know of one." Zartanian nodded. "There's a human dessert sold in specialty bakeries. It's highly craved and loved—and I've long wanted to try some, myself."

"That popular? What is it?"

"They call it..."

Aken waited expectantly.

"...Chocolate bars."

Aken's jaw slackened. "Chocolate bars? It comes in *bars*?" he exclaimed. "It's rare enough when the school serves chocolate flavored cake, the stuff's so expensive. But an entire bar of real, solid chocolate?"

"Yeah. Apparently, it's part of human culture. The bar is pure cocoa, solid and smooth. Ever since merchants started exporting it from the southern islands, it's been prized among the upper-class."

Aken jumped to his feet from his seat on the grass, a new mission gleaming brightly in his eyes. "Then what are we waiting for? Let's go get these chocolate bars and cheer Cyrus up!" He grinned, his arms akimbo. "This is the best idea we've ever had."

Zartanian blinked. "It's the *only* idea we've ever had."

⤳

Hercule grimaced. He was trying to study quietly in his room, when an annoying thumping of fists started knocking a drum beat on his door, making his head pound.

"Herrr-cule, Herrr-cule, Herrr-cuuule!"

Slamming his study book shut, he marched over to the door and flung it open. "What?" he half growled, half shouted.

Aken, and a meek Zartanian behind him, stood there, the blond wearing a mischievous expression on his face.

"Oh no you don't. I refuse to involve myself in one of your stupid schemes or pranks." Hercule tried to slam the door shut.

"It's nothing like that, promise!" Aken stopped the door with his shoe. "We just need to borrow a little of that noble wealth of yours."

Hercule huffed through his nose. "I'm not some bank account you can use whenever you feel like it. And aren't you the one who always criticizes me for being rich? Yet now you want to use me for it?"

Aken's mouth twisted to the side; he had him there. "It's not for me. It's for a gift for Cyrus—you know, our comrade, who you betrayed and almost got killed?"

Hercule's lips pressed into a thin line. "Fine. But I'm coming with you," he stated. "I refuse to hand my cashcard over to someone else—especially *you*."

"What's that supposed to mean?"

"Let it go, let it go…" Zartanian tugged at Aken's sleeve. "At least he agreed to help us."

Aken clamped his mouth shut. He was surprised that Zartanian had actually touched his arm; the quiet boy who always shied away from physical contact. But he seemed a little more open lately, ever since Cyrus had come into their lives.

Hercule went to retrieve his wallet.

A while later found Aken, Zartanian and a frowning Hercule striding down wide Main Street, following the river coursing its way through Downtown, the heart of the city and commerce. They surveyed the various bakeries dotted along the way, and Aken trotted up to the window of the first promising one, smooshing his face against the glass to better see the desserts spread out on display.

Zartanian joined him, his pale gaze filled with wonder at the numerous cakes, strawberry scones, tarts, cream-filled croissants and much more.

"What are you doing?"

Aken craned his neck sideways to see Bakoa approach; the spikey-haired boy's grin was as cheerful and eager as an otter's. "Well? What're you doing? Oh, are you gonna buy some fancy desserts? I didn't know you had that kind of money! I thought you were flat-broke since the Master halted your allowance."

Aken flinched. "Thanks a lot, Bak. Really," he muttered under his breath. "Me and Zartin are on a mission. And he *unhalted* my allowance, just so you know."

"Cool. Let me help, too! What's the mission? What're you looking for?" Bak hopped up to Aken's side, likewise smooshing his face against the window glass to see.

Hercule, standing casually off to the side and with his arms crossed, regarded all three of them. "You look like weird beggars with your faces pressed against the glass. Knock it off, will you? You're scaring people."

Aken frowned back at him. But then he noticed a mother and her children passing by, one child pointed and said, "Look, Mommy. Beggars!"

The mother hurried the children away. "Don't make eye-contact with beggars, dear."

Aken backed up from the glass, yanking Bak and Zartin by their sleeves with him. "Let's just go inside..."

The bakery wafted sweet scents over them as they entered, scents of spices and creams and flavorful breads. Aken went to the counter to ask for their finest chocolate.

The aproned woman who was managing the counter eyed their group with suspicion. "Chocolate? Is that why you smudged the window glass with your drool?" She sniffed. "Well, we have one last bar of chocolate, on the lower shelf there. But it'll cost you over a hundred dels, which I'm sure is too much for kids like you."

"A hundred?!" Bak hiccupped.

Aken looked to Hercule, who motioned them back outside.

Leaving the bakery, Hercule rounded on them. "*Chocolate* is what you came here for? Do you realize how expensive that is for such a small dessert? I refuse to spend my father's money on such frivolous things." He started to turn and leave them.

"So, you're basically saying that Cyrus isn't worth spending money on?" Aken countered.

Hercule halted in his tracks.

A sly smile tweaked Aken's lips. "We want to make Cy feel more at home here by bringing him something that humans love—and chocolate is just that."

Hercule's thumbnail dug into his palm.

"I still don't want my father seeing I spent *that* amount on chocolate. However, if you find some at a lower price..."

Aken didn't wait for him to finish; he raced down to the next bakery.

"*Tch*. At least let me finish speaking!"

Time passed as they went from shop to shop, but none of the prices were any cheaper. Bakoa groaned and plopped down on a sidewalk bench overlooking the shimmering river water. "Man...chocolate's just too high-class for us."

Across from them, Aken was pleading to the baker inside *Le Crème* bakery: a simple ocher building, barely two stories tall, and only half owned by the bakery; the other half was owned by a tailor and painted russet.

Hercule folded his arms impatiently. "If this place doesn't work out, I'm leaving. There are better things to do..."

Inside the bakery, Aken pleaded to the owner. "C'mon, mister! Mister, sir? Lower the price, just this once, pretty please?"

"*No* means *NO*, you darn brat. Now, get out of the line and let real customers through!"

Aken grimaced as the big-bellied man shooed him away from the counter, customers waiting behind him stepping forward to make their orders.

Aken leaned against a vacant round table at the back of the room, staring crossly at the glass counter full of desserts, which included delectable bars of chocolate and fudge. "Stingy people," he muttered under his breath. "They don't even care that we're Draevensett students when it comes to money." He raked a hand through his hair.

"You shoulds make the stuff."

Aken turned, for the first time noticing a child there: a boy around seven years old. Over by the shop's back door, the child stacked an order of pastry boxes, tying them together with thick string; the door was braced open and led out into a back alley.

Aken eyed the cap hat on the kid's head and the rumpled brown jacket and gray trousers with suspenders—all of it a size too large. And his shoes looked almost ready to fall apart. His skin was lake-blue and shimmered where light touched it around the baggy clothes; his wisps of hair beneath the big brown cap were a deep blue, mixed with strands of silver. The child glanced his way—his irises chestnut-red, with pupils a shade darker.

A faeryn, judging by the very long, pointed ears sticking out from either side under the cap. But a blue one, which was unlike any type of faeryn Aken had ever seen inside the city. The child must be a slave of either the head baker or the shop's owner.

"Makes it. If you don'ts have money t' buy chocolate, just makes it yorself," the child said again.

Aken chuckled at the way children couldn't fully pronounce words. This little guy had something like a lisp, adding "s" at the ends, and with a foreign accent on top. Where could he be from?

"Wait, what did you just say? You can *make* chocolate?"

The kid nodded, lifting the tied stack of pastry boxes and carrying it out the open back door.

Aken followed, while the kid placed the stack in a basket at the rear of a small bike. "All you needs is the cocoa nibs, and then grind intos a paste—I've seen the baker make it lots of times."

"This is perfect!" Aken cheered. "We'll use the kitchen and stuff back at school, and you can show us how it's done!"

"Nope," the boy cut in. "Figures it out yorself."

"Wha—?"

Before Aken could protest, the kid hopped onto the bike and peddled off.

"Hey, wait! Get back here! We need you!" Aken sprinted down the narrow alley after the child, his fast pace easily catching up to the small bike.

The child looked over his shoulder, giving a sharp gasp when he saw that Aken was gaining on him. He pulled out a pair of riding goggles, placing them over his eyes.

Aken wondered why, and then the bike gave a sudden *Vrroom* sound. The kid twisted the bike handles as some type of fuel tank came to life in the bike's rear, and the small bike became a speedy moped.

The last thing Aken saw was the child sticking out his tongue and making a face back at him as the bike zipped away, out the alley and up Main Street.

"What the heck?" Aken hissed through his teeth, and he whipped out the clay swallow from his pocket, hopping onboard and soaring after the little brat.

The child wove through the streets like a pro, experienced from his work as a pastry-delivery boy. But the swallow, Limitless, was catching up, and Aken's hand reached out, barely missing the scruff of the kid's jacket.

The child jerked his head up, spotting Aken riding the swallow just behind him. "*Yag!*" he yelped, and immediately swerved the bike into a sharp right.

Aken flew past, struggling to veer quickly.

"Leaves me alone!" the child shouted, bike rattling down a steep side alley. "I don't like clingy girls like you!"

Aken waved a fist. "You brat! My hair isn't *that* long!"

"Coulda fooled me!"

The swallow swooped low and Aken's hand came down.

Finally, he caught and lifted the child up by his jacket collar. The kid's hands clung to the handlebars, lifting the bike up with him.

"*Owah!* Stopit! Stopit!" The kid struggled.

The alley opened onto a small, flagstone clearing with a fountain. Aken plopped down the bike, and the faeryn child with it, keeping a firm hand around his arm so the faeryn couldn't take off again.

"That'll teach you not to go running off when someone older is talking to you," Aken reprimanded.

The child glared at him defiantly for one moment, before realizing there was no way of escape. And then...the kid started wailing.

Rivers of tears ran from his chestnut-red eyes and he gurgled, "You don' unnerstand! *Wuuuh.* If—if I don' makes these deliveries, I'll gets punished! Punished baaad!"

A nearby woman and an old couple looked their way, disturbed, maybe even ready to call The Guard.

Alarm shot through Aken, and he tried to calm the blubbering faeryn. "*Shhh*, it's okay! I didn't know. Stop crying, please? Let's, *um*...let's make a deal."

"*Waaaah~* Huh?" The child paused mid-cry, peeking one teary eye above a hand at him.

"I'll help you deliver all these pastry boxes, and then you'll come back with me and teach us how to make chocolate. How does that sound?"

The child sniffled and waited; clearly he wanted something more in return.

"*Grr*, fine! I'll do a whole day's worth of deliveries for you, some day this week, so you can go play or dance or fish or whatever you want to do."

The boy's lips puckered in thought. "Mm...okay!" His face changed from tears to instant smile.

'*Yeah, he got what he wanted,*' thought Aken.

Great. Now he was going to have to be a delivery boy for an entire day. But it would be worth it, seeing the look on Cy's face when they brought him a chocolate surprise.

"By the way, I'm Aken-Shou."

The child wiped his nose on a sleeve. "My name's Apfel Strudelburg."

Aken blinked and barely held in a laugh. "Like Apple Strudel? That can't really be your name."

The boy glared back, and he looked Aken up and down. "I'm no goods at remembering names." His eyes narrowed. "But you acts like a *nervensäge*, so I'll calls you that."

"A what?" Aken shook his head. "What does *that* mean?"

"Figures it out yorself. Here!" Apfel shoved the stack of pastry boxes at his stomach. "Deliver these, or I can'ts help you today."

Aken's lips thinned at the impudent child. But, he didn't have much choice.

⁓ゝ

Thanks to Limitless's speed, Aken managed to deliver the pastry boxes, despite getting lost and struggling to find most of the addresses. Once finished, he brought Apfel back with him to meet up with Bak, Zartin and Hercule. Apfel regarded them with his chin held high, the large brown cap slipping forward.

"Are you sure this child knows what he's doing?" asked Hercule, after Aken had explained the situation.

Apfel stood proudly with his arms akimbo. "Takes me to the kitchens, and I teach you."

Bakoa and Zartanian shared a look and a shrug.

The following hour, the group snuck into Draevensett's kitchen quarters, the bakery section, and took one of the side rooms farthest to the back. They closed the heavy curtain which acted as a door, so no one passing by would see it was them inside. The staff were busy enough, and Head Baker Bel wasn't around at the moment.

Rolling up their sleeves and donning aprons, the group proceeded to follow Apfel's instructions:

Bakoa and Aken were given the task of pounding and grinding the cocoa nibs, purchased by Hercule (the nibs were much cheaper), until their arms ached.

Zartanian mixed sugar into the resulting paste and further ground the mixture. He next added something called melted cocoa butter.

Lastly, Hercule tempered the resulting brown mass over a hot stove, his lilac shirtsleeves rolled up and sweat beading on his temples.

"Now, stop cooking," ordered Apfel.

Aken helped tilt the pan of liquefied chocolate while Hercule scooped the stuff out into a long, shallow pan, as Apfel directed: "That's good, *mm-hm*, goods... Now, we puts cookie-cutters in, to make shapes. You gots keep it in the cool-box for...'n hour, I thinks."

Aken and Bak shared a look. "You gots?" Aken repeated, and they both snickered.

Apfel glared at them. "Yor makings fun of me, *nervensäge?*"

"Hey," Aken waved a grinding pestle, "Don't call me weird stuff I don't know."

Hercule set the pan in the cool-box, and was about to tell them to shut up, when the curtain door suddenly *swooshed* open.

They all froze, their breath stilling in their throats.

"*Eep!* Head Cook Burly, I can explain——" Aken started.

But it wasn't the raging chef that they expected. Instead, it was Marigold, and she stared at the mess of kitchen utensils and chocolate goo, her mint-green gaze widening further when she took in Hercule's apron and unkempt appearance. His face turned shades of pink, and not from the stove heat.

Aken leaned over to Bak and Zartin, "The noble's lady-in-waiting must be finished cleaning his undergarments."

Hercule shot him a warning glare.

"You're making chocolate? How fun!" Marigold's smile flashed sweetly. "But…" Her eyebrows tilted. "If it's chocolate you wanted, a batch was just gifted to the school to be served for after-dinner dessert tomorrow. You should have waited."

The room fell into silence, and Zartanian's mixing spoon dropped. "But we just finished. And after all our hard work…" he whispered.

Aken smacked his forehead against the counter.

Hercule's hands fisted and steam rose in swirls around him. "You mean to tell me," his voice lowered, "that I spent—no, *wasted*—all of that time, and my father's money, for *nothing*?" Flames flashed from his mouth, and he focused on just one person. "Aken-Shou!" he growled.

Aken dodged the blast of fire with a yelp and vaulted himself out of the kitchen window.

Hercule pursued: vaulting out after him and trailing steam across the lawn.

"How was I supposed to know? Don't blame this all on me!" Aken shouted over a shoulder as he ran, flames nipping at his ankles.

⤳

"Cyrus…"

A soft voice spoke her name. Her eyelids fluttered open from slumber, and the room came back into focus around her. A figure materialized beside the bed.

She sat up with a start, then realized it was Mamoru.

"Sorry. I wasn't sure if I should wake you," he said with a faint grin. "But you see, the young Harlow boys have a *surprise* for you."

She rubbed her groggy head, not really comprehending what he was saying. She let the older vempar guide her out into the corridor. "I feel a lot better now…" she mumbled and yawned.

"Good," he said with a nod, leading her into Master Nephryte's dorm flat, into the kitchen.

For some reason, there were candles lit all about the table, and...

Her nose twitched. "Do I smell...chocolate?"

"SURPRISE!"

Cyrus gave a start as all the Harlow boys appeared around the table before her, and lamps brightened to life, revealing bars of chocolate laid out all across the surface like a gourmet buffet, cut into stars and moon shapes. An extra bowl brimming with chocolate fondue and ready-to-dip pretzels and apple slices lay to the side.

She didn't know what to say. It wasn't her birthday, right?

"We wanted you to feel more at home," Zartanian said in his quiet tone, a partial smile on his face. His hat was off, showing his small, sharp antlers.

Aken stepped forward, flourishing an arm to indicate the table. "Pure chocolate, straight from the cocoa bean! Trust me—we ground the darn nibs ourselves. It should be just like what you had back in Elvenstone, maybe even better!" Then he added in a whisper, "And I'm real sorry about earlier..."

It took her a second to recall what he meant. She cupped her hands to her chest. "You did all this for me? Just to make me feel at home? That's..." She felt a lump in her throat and swallowed. "That's so sweet, so thoughtful... Thank you, all of you!"

Mamoru waved a hand. "It was all *their* doing. Lykale and I weren't in on it," he admitted.

Cyrus grabbed a pretzel and dunked it into the melty chocolate. It tasted superb!

"Dig in, everybody!" she motioned to them.

And they did, like toddlers in a candy store, swooning over the rich, smooth textures.

She laughed at their enthusiasm and didn't bother to tell them that chocolate wasn't all that common in Elvenstone, either.

Bakoa pretended he was a chocolate-craving zombie, wandering the room and out into the hallway, calling out, "Chooocolaaate!" while Zartanian, Mamoru, and even Lykale, laughed.

Cyrus gave Aken a quick hug. "Thanks for thinking of me."

His cheeks pinked and he scratched the back of his head with a hand. "I just wish we could do more—make this place feel more like home and all for you…"

She shook her head. "This *is* home. You guys make it home."

He smiled and averted his gaze. "Same for me, buddy. Same for me…"

"Here!" She dunked a slice of apple in the chocolate and shoved it into his mouth.

She laughed as his face puckered from the tartness of the apple and the sweetness of the chocolate.

They ate their fill of the desserts late into the night, until they were all too sick with sugar to eat another bite, and Master Nephryte finally made them go to bed.

～ゥ

Apfel stood on his tiptoes atop the wooden crate, reaching for the shutters of the last window still left open in the back of the bakery shop, to lock them tight for the night, as he always did after his owner left.

A greyhound pup watched him curiously from the floor mat, giving a high-pitched whine now and then—Apfel's only companion in a lonely way of life.

"*Ja*, Hazfel. I'm shuttings it." He stretched his short arms as far as they could reach, finally grabbing hold of one shutter handle, pulling it closed, then reaching for the other.

Hazfel growled suddenly and his hackles rose. The dog's attention focused on the window—or something beyond it.

"Hm?" Apfel glanced at the pup, then looked back outside to where Hazfel seemed so intensely focused. "I don't see anyth—" He stopped short, hand frozen on the second shutter.

There was something in the street beyond. Something blacker than the night, which the streetlamps were unable to touch. It moved on two legs, yet crouched, animal-like. And it seemed to be searching for something…or someone.

Its hooded head slowly turned in Apfel's direction, the whiteness of bone underneath the black fabric.

Apfel gasped, and he quickly closed the shutter, locking it tight.

Trembling, he grabbed Hazfel and climbed inside the large, emptied stone oven at the shop's back, shutting the small metal door behind him. It was the only secure hiding place they had in the shop.

He hugged the puppy close to his chest.

Was the creature after him? Would it break into the shop?

His lower lip quivered.

He couldn't hear anything, so maybe the thing had left? But the rough life of a slave had taught him never to take any chances, and so he didn't move an inch from that spot for the rest of the night.

4

Master Deidreem drummed his fingers on the black table, its metallic fretwork glinting in the dim light of the hexagonal room and reflecting off the polished black walls. A tinted window took up the far wall and let in just enough light to see by.

It wasn't a long wait before Leader's silhouette appeared. Deidreem bowed his head, and others around the table rose to do the same. "The Impures greet you, Leader," they said in unison.

Leader motioned with his hand, and they took their seats again. "My dear Impures," he greeted them. He flexed his left hand, and the knuckles made a sickening series of pops. "I hear that one of our experiments escaped, and even managed to make it above ground into the city." His expression turned a shade cold towards each of them, his gaze a dagger of ice.

"There's nothing to worry about, Leader," one of the shorter members spoke up quickly. "I located the girl before anyone could see her. Though, unfortunately, it seems she was another failed experiment... I've taken care of the body."

Leader gave a slow nod. "Very well. See to it that such a mistake does not happen again." He turned to circle the table. "Time passes, and the Swan still has not been found." His tone held a weary, sharp edge to it this morning.

"You know we will not rest until we have found her," Deidreem promised.

"Even so, a new course of action may be necessary..." Leader's deep voice scratched like sand blown in the wind.

"The Corpsed Project is steadily improving. In fact, some of the creatures have just learned to sniff out unique energy, such as the Pure Light," Deidreem informed, with some pride.

"Ahh, now that is nice to hear." Leader's silhouette ran a hand along the table's edge, a collection of heavy rings glittering with the movement. "I was beginning to think that our years of experimentation had been fruitless. So many have proven to be failures."

"There are still flaws," Deidreem furthered. "Draevensett Academy gives off too much unique energy from the gifted students there and is an interference."

Leader's arms stretched forward and cracked at the elbows and his long dark hair spilled forward over his shoulders. "Continue the search, regardless," he ordered. "And in the meantime, we must devise other possible strategies of finding her. I am going to send Adelheid to the school."

Deidreem gave a start. "I assure you there is no need. I'm capable of keeping an eye on things myself."

"But you are not a student—and I want a student's perspective, someone who can monitor the younger age groups around the city."

"Surely you don't think the Swan could be in *this* city? She's human," said Deidreem.

"I will not rule out anything. She could be a slave somewhere within Draeth." His right arm leaned against the head chair at the table, his fingers curling around the metal bar frame. "Once the power of the Pure Light is in our hands, the world will suffer for what they did to us." He stroked his lower lip, as if savoring the thought.

"I am looking forward to that day, Leader," said Deidreem, lowering his head. "The day when we can finally make our revenge complete."

The circle of Impures rose. "Our revenge will come!"

Leader motioned to them, and the group soon dispersed, each member exiting the meeting room through the grand mirror which stood in place of a door.

Deidreem stepped through the glassy surface and came out the other side: back inside his office room in Draevensett, before a tall standing mirror. He replaced the cloth that covered it.

There was much work to be done. If the old empire was to rise anew under the Impures' rule, they would need the Pure Light's power. Their very existence would depend upon it.

⁓

"Aken." Mamoru gestured with his thumb back behind him. "Master wants to see you."

Aken released a breath that was more of a grumble and marched up the stairwell to Floor Harlow.

Inside the Mentor's dorm flat, Nephryte waited on a leather sofa, hand gesturing for him to come into the living room. Aken did so grudgingly.

Mentor or Master? Aken kept going back and forth with that title in his mind.

He used to blame Nephryte, the great hero, for not having saved his parents from a human attack in the Outskirts. Back then, he couldn't refer to him as a heroic Draev Master. But now...he was starting to see things differently. And the title "Master" wasn't as hard to say.

"I hear Denim and his friends had a most unfortunate run-in with a hive of spine hornets yesterday," said the Master. "You wouldn't happen to know anything about that, would you?"

Aken's mouth twisted to the side and he gripped his hands behind his back, looking away.

"I see." Nephryte exhaled. "Must you two always be in conflict?"

"He was bullying Zartin! The poor guy was alone, keeping to himself and training, when that spoiled dirtbag started threatening him," Aken said in defense.

"We should stand up for our friends, yes. I'm proud of you for that. But what I want you to realize, young Aken-Shou, is that in life you will run into *many* people you don't like—people who are rude or just plain mean—and you can't lash out and attack them, no matter how much you may want to. You need to maintain your self-control. I'm not saying you have to be friends with people like that—*you shouldn't be*—but do not be the one who starts a fight, and don't let other people's taunts influence your actions."

"So," Aken crossed his arms, "You're saying that I shouldn't fight, *ever*?"

"I'm saying you need to learn more self-control and not take revenge into your own hands." His gaze softened. "I had to learn the same thing when I wasn't much older than you. I don't want you to have to learn this the hard way."

Aken wiped under his left eye with a thumb.

"Nobody said it was easy. But it does get easier, with practice." Nephryte's river-blue gaze held him. "You don't want your Pureblood power to come out again by accident and hurt someone else, do you?"

Scourgeblood was the crude name people had given his kind, because of how hated they were, but they used to be known as Purebloods, long ago.

Aken recalled the power flooding through his veins, transforming his fist, and the red marks on Denim's shoulder that wouldn't be able to Heal for a long time. He swallowed.

"If someone died, you'd never be able to make up for something like that, Aken-Shou, and your heart would carry a regret you could never undo. So," Nephryte furthered, "don't lose your cool. If you let what people say feed your anger, you've lost the fight. You are much easier to manipulate when your emotions race out of control. Keep that in mind."

Aken let his arms drop to his sides and gave a nod that he understood.

"Good. Now that that's settled," Nephryte began, when suddenly Aken sniffed at the air.

"You got groceries? Great! I'm starving." Aken yanked open the cool-box door and took out a sandwich—turkey, cheese and tomatoes slices—stuffing it down his bottomless mouth. Then he grabbed a carton of milk, washing the food down.

"I just made that sandwich..." Nephryte tried not to groan. "It was my favorite turkey."

Aken licked his fingers. "Oh. Was it okay for me to eat that?"

Nephryte's eyebrow twitched. "Sure. Anything for my dear students."

"Thanks for the early lunch! See you later." He waved a hand back as he left.

Nephryte stared at the remaining crumbs and heaved a sigh. "The stomach of a growing boy is a curse upon the lands..."

～ͽ

At the end of another school day, Cyrus started up the wide stairwell, finally feeling back to her normal self. She glimpsed her reflection in the black-and-white patterned tiles beneath her shoes. Ugh, her hair looked a right fluffy mess today.

She rounded the stairwell corner and bumped into someone coming down.

"Oh, not again—sorry, excuse me," she said quickly and stepped back, lifting her face to see who she'd run into this time, then froze.

Master Deidreem pushed his top hat back, his gaze taking in the small student before him. "Heh? What have we here?" he mused curiously and leaned forward. "Ah, the young boy of half-human descent," he said in recognition. "I've not had the pleasure of meeting you properly."

He offered a white-gloved hand, a stark contrast to his storm cloud gray skin. "I am Master Deidreem of Floor Smart." The corners of his lips quirked upward. "I'm sure we'll get to know one another better once your training catches up to my other students. Heh, I must say, I never thought the day would come when a human was able to train as a Draev." His yellow-green eyes narrowed, their color reminding her of crystal epidote, like the pendant her stepmom sometimes wore. "But then, you're no *ordinary* human, are you?"

She stared up at him, unsure how to respond. He was a few years younger than Nephryte, and easy on the eye. But despite his charm, the hairs on the back of her neck stood on end and she felt a strong urge to back away.

His eyes flickered briefly to the right side of her neck, and he spoke as if wondering to himself aloud, "I'm surprised you were ever allowed inside the city. Most non-vempars are required to have a Mark in order to travel about; either that, or special permission."

Cyrus's palm instinctively cupped the side of her neck, a chill roving down her spine.

Mark? What did that word mean?

"Could it be that you don't know?" Deidreem said as if reading her thoughts. "A Mark is what forms a slave-bond. It lets a slave's master know roughly where they are, at all times. And if they ever misbehave, the master can use the bond to inflict pain as punishment. An excellent way of keeping lesser creatures under control, don't you think?"

Cyrus swallowed, gripping her arm at her side. "I'm not sure what you mean by *lesser creatures*, Master. Anything that needs to be under such control must be intelligent, otherwise there would be no need for *such* control."

Deidreem tilted his head in thought.

"What are you saying about my friend?"

She turned at Aken's voice. He came up the stairwell behind her and moved to her side, his glare intense up at Deidreem. "Cyrus is *not* a slave."

The Master gave a shrug that he could care less. "Of course, young Scourgeblood. But it can be a dangerous world for a human without a Mark," he replied. "Any vempar who doesn't know Cyrus might think him a spy. After all, what free human in their right mind would be here for any other reason?"

"He wears the Draevensett coat-of-arms on his shirt." Aken spat the words. "And almost everybody knows who Cy is by now, anyway."

The gray vempar's smile curled. "True, young man. True. But for a wanting vempar, Cyrus might look a nice *pet* to have."

Aken scowled.

"Maybe you, yourself, have even thought so." Deidreem said the last like a question, and Cyrus could feel Aken's anger struggling not to explode.

"I would *never* think like that. And neither should anybody else."

The Master simply smiled down at them—a cool, dark smile at tiny mice he'd had some fun toying with. "Time will tell," the man mused, and he continued on his way down the stairs. "Do take care of yourself, young human," he added back over a shoulder. "Remember, you're a mere mouse in this world of predators…"

The words echoed in Cyrus's mind, even after he left.

Aken brushed at his arms, as if to wipe off any trace of being near the Master. "*Bleah*, what a creepy snake. Glad we didn't end up in *that* Floor."

"Aken. What did he mean by a pet? Denim said something like that before, too."

Aken stopped brushing his arms. Shadows from his side bangs fell across his face. "It's…a pet is similar to a slave," he said, his mouth tight as if not wanting to speak. "They do work for their master and all, but…but their main purpose is providing fresh *essence* for their owner."

It took a moment for his meaning to dawn on her, then her expression widened. "They're like *dessert*?"

"*Shhh!*" Aken motioned her to lower her voice and glanced around. "It doesn't happen much, I don't think. But owners think they can do whatever they want." He winced at the look she gave. "It's probably just a few upper-class snobs who do that, because they can afford more slaves than they actually need."

"But why do that at all?" Her hands trembled, eyes going moist. "How can anyone be so horrible? How can they treat another person like they're something to be used then thrown away?"

He watched her face. "Don't be sad. I'll never let that happen to you." He touched her shoulder and gave an encouraging smile. "And things will be different once I become the greatest Draev Guardian the world has ever seen! You and I, we'll change the world, remember?"

She took a shaky breath and nodded.

"C'mon, me *boyo*! As our Professor Ponairi would say. Shall we do our homework 'neath the cherry blossoms and merry birdsong?" He gave her one of his bright-eyed winks.

"Don't we have E.M. Study soon?" she asked.

Aken tipped his head back and groaned. "Yep. I forgot... We get to spend another hour with the lovely Tathom bunch."

She chuckled and tried to push depressing thoughts aside. They continued up the stairwell together. "I should use the restroom first."

"Yeah, me too."

Cyrus pretended not to hear him and hurried up the stairs. "See you in a minute!"

She rounded the next corner and dove into the fourth floor. There, she sprinted over to a public restroom and hid around the open doorway.

She waited, and no one followed.

Good, she'd lost him.

Cyrus looked about the room. No one else was in there, so she hurried, and when she was finished, she paused at a mirror to fix her hair.

'A pet...'

There were moments when she felt so at ease around her friends that she completely forgot they were vempars who lived by absorbing *essence*. Even if they only absorbed it through their hands, and it didn't necessarily kill, the very thought still seemed creepy. Of course, most vempars in Draeth society didn't have to absorb *essence* from anyone, anymore, because it was already infused in their daily food...

While Cyrus stared into the mirror, she felt a strange itch, a scratch underneath her shirt.

Her eyes went wide—something was crawling on her skin.

She lifted her shirt carefully to see an earwig bug crawling across her chest.

"*Eek!*" She tried to flick it off, but the bug tumbled and vanished into the folds of her clothes.

Freaking out, she whipped her shirt off, hitting and smacking it against the wall, striving to knock the bug out.

At last, the pest fell to the floor and she stomped on it, cringing.

She backed away from the squashed smudge and breathed a shaky sigh of relief.

Readjusting her cloth bra—a makeshift wrapping that wound around her chest, keeping it securely flat and featureless, though there wasn't much there to begin with—she put her shirt back on.

And she heard a small sound.

She looked about, alarm and fear spiking in her gut.

Several feet away stood someone, across from the propped-open restroom door: Marigold, her usually calm, honey-freckled face staring at her.

She must have been doing some cleaning on this floor and heard Cyrus scream, and had come to look.

Cyrus chewed her lip. Marigold had clearly seen Cyrus's cloth bra, and the faeryn now blinked several times as if confirming that what she had seen was true.

Cyrus didn't know what to say, either, quickly pulling her shirt the rest of the way down and fumbling.

"I had no idea you were a...a..." The faeryn's airy voice faltered, then regained composure. "Does everyone know?"

"No!" Cyrus exclaimed, then shut her mouth, and spoke more calmly. "No, they don't. *Please*, you can't tell anybody. *Promise.*"

The faeryn tilted her head, considering. "Of course, milady. I was a little shocked, is all."

Milady? Cyrus shook her head frantically. "Don't call me that!"

"I'm a lowly slave. I have to address others with respect."

Cyrus wanted to groan. "Then, just whatever you call other students."

"Cyrus, sir." Marigold's tinted lips smiled, and Cyrus almost thumped her own head against the wall. Being addressed as *sir* felt even more awkward.

Marigold had a curious marking on the side of her neck, Cyrus noticed: a detailed ink drawing of a dragon's wing. Could that be a slave-bond Mark, like what Master Deidreem had mentioned?

"I have been wanting to speak with you." Marigold lifted a mop from where it had fallen on the floor. "To tell you how simply miraculous it was the way you won the Festival Duel. You have touched many lives with hope and shown vempar kind that we are equals." Gratefulness beamed from her. "Thank you."

Cyrus shuffled her feet on the smooth floor, cheeks pinking, unsure how to respond to such praise. It turned out she didn't have to say anything, though, as Aken came into the hall and spotted them just then.

"There you are! Time's ticking." He waved.

"Oh, right." Cyrus grabbed up her books off the sink. "I should get going. Um, it was nice talking to you." She nodded to Marigold, adding a look that begged for the girl to keep her secret.

Marigold smiled nonchalantly and curtsied. "Of course, sir."

Cyrus trotted down to the E.M. Study training field, at the back of Draevensett, designated for young students. The rest of Harlow were following. Black curls fell loose from Zartanian's ponytail, and he tucked them back behind his ears, still keeping the hat over his small antlers.

She glanced back up the slope to see the academy's spires gleaming like gothic spears in the sun.

Ahead of them, Floor Tathom was already at the field and waiting.

"Hello again." Cherish waved.

Cyrus stopped by her wheelchair.

"Are you well? I hear you have a cold," the girl asked.

Cyrus almost groaned. Was there anyone who didn't know?

"It's gone now; I'm fine," she answered. Her gaze took in the braces around Cherish's joints. Her snowy hair was tied back today. "You're in E.M. Study, too?" Cyrus regretted the way that sounded the moment she asked, but she was curious.

Cherish didn't seem to mind and said, "I am, though I won't be able to do every assignment, obviously. The disorder I was born with keeps my Healing from working properly and makes me weak; but even so, I still have to train and learn how to manage my Ability."

Cyrus nodded in understanding. "I wish I could Heal. It'd be nice not having to worry about getting hurt all the time... How quickly does using Ability drain our *essence*, anyway?" she asked.

"It depends on how much you're using, and for how long. For example," Cherish laid a hand across her chest, "my Ability—you could say—is too great for my body to handle, and therefore, drains up a large amount of my *essence* and leaves me frail and weak." She gestured to her legs. "I had an accident, not long ago, where I overused my Ability. I could barely move my legs for weeks."

She lifted herself out of the wheelchair, slowly, and balanced on her feet. Cyrus resisted the urge to help. "Ahhh, it's nice to get up and stand again. It feels like my legs are getting a little strength back into them. I just hope it lasts." Cherish stretched her limbs.

"C'mon, Doughboy." Denim trotted past them.

The larger boy moved at his own slow pace, chomping on a plateful of carrots and cream cheese, his body now fully recovered from the Festival Duel. He paused as he passed by Cyrus's left side, his large rotund stomach wobbling like jelly.

"Little redhead," he said, and held down a fist.

She flinched, worried what he might do and what he might be feeling after having lost the Duel. But he said, "You fought like one of us, a Draev, and fought bravely. I respect that."

Her jaw went slack. He waited until she bumped her fist against his. "Um…I appreciate that."

Did that mean there were no hard feelings, then? She wondered.

Denim rolled his eyes and made a scoffing sound. While pocketing his hands and turning his back, he spotted Aken. "Well, well, if it isn't the Golden Princess," he commented, with a chin nod Aken's way. "You should braid all that blondness up and make a dandelion crown for yourself."

Aken's shoulders tensed. "If I'm the princess, then you're the evil witch—and we know what happens to witches in the end."

Denim snarled. "You punk."

The Masters called the two Floor groups to attention, and Denim stalked off to stand with his lackeys. Master Nephryte's voice carried over the field.

"I promised to teach you how to use Touch, specifically the method used to weaken your opponent by draining their *essence*. If used on a vempar, your enemy will not be able to Heal as easily. But remember: Touch is only used for self-defense and for harvesting. It is not permitted otherwise." His gaze swept through the group. "Using your power for abuse among our kind is not tolerated. Do you understand?"

The hushed students bobbed their heads, though Cyrus noted that Zartanian looked away—staring off at something unseen, his fingers curling.

Master Nephryte had them break up into pairs, and Master Seren-Rose issued her students an extra warning: "No rude behavior during class, or *else*."

Tathom responded with stiff at-attention backs and down-turned chins.

Touch was something only a full-blooded vempar could do, not a half-blood like Cyrus, so she found a spot by herself where she could practice manipulating metal instead.

"I don't want to do this..." Zartanian was saying when he was paired with Hercule.

"What is wrong with you? Why are you so afraid of people touching you?" Hercule began losing patience.

Zartanian shook his head and clenched his hands in front of his chest. "I just...I don't know..."

"Either we do this, or we fail class. Do you want to become a Draev Guardian or not?" Hercule confronted him.

Zartanian shied back at first, but then something in what he said must have stirred up some resolve inside the boy. He faced Hercule squarely. "...Yes, I do want to be a Draev and a swordsmaster. I—I can do this."

Cyrus observed them from her spot, wondering about his strange reaction.

There was still so much she didn't know about her Harlow companions.

～～

"Place your hand on your partner's arm. Grip firmly," Master Nephryte instructed. "You're going to use the micro-receptors in the palm of your hand to channel an *essence* flow."

Aken clamped his hand on Bak's forearm.

Master Seren-Rose demonstrated by holding Nephryte's forearm in her grip. "It's easiest to picture your *essence* as a hand," she told them. "And flow that *hand* through your palm and into your opponent."

Aken had to shut his eyes to picture it.

"Use this spirit-hand—as we call it—to reach and grab the core of your opponent's *essence*. The core is like a heart, the place where *essence* is generated." The lady's head turned, searching for any students who were not paying attention. "Once you do this, imagine your spirit-hand as a conduit and soak up your opponent's *essence* through that conduit."

Aken's spirit-hand tried to reach and grab, but he felt like a blind bat reaching through darkness.

Finally, he sensed a warm, glowing energy—the core—and he grasped for it.

Essence ran from Bak's core and into him.

"Once you have managed to successfully absorb some *essence*, stop and let go. You don't want to impair your partner, after all." Master Seren-Rose released Nephryte's arm with a little smirk. "The more powerful your opponent, the stronger your Touch's draw must be in order to weaken them. In other words, the more powerful they are, the more *essence* you must take from their core." She twirled a dark, curly strand of hair around her finger. "Master Nephryte, for example, would be most difficult to weaken."

Aken forgot about Bak for a moment and focused on the interaction between the two Masters. There was definitely a special friendliness between them.

He spared a look over his shoulder at Denim, who was struggling with the Touch draw.

"Dude—*dude*—let go, you're killing me!" came Bak's strained cry.

"Huh? Oh!" He realized he'd been subconsciously drawing *essence*, and he let go.

The sand boy collapsed to the grass.

"Sorry, Bakoa!" Aken looked at his palm. "How'd I keep...? I didn't mean to keep..."

Aken moved aside as Nephryte helped Bak up and replenished his *essence* with some of his own.

"*Nnn*, I need food and a nap," Bak muttered groggily.

The resilient boy was fine, but it worried Aken how easy it had been to draw *essence* out. Did being a Scourgeblood have something to do with it? He could hurt someone without even meaning to...like a monster.

"How troublesome," one Tathom boy said.

"They shouldn't let a Scourgeblood be in this class," whispered another.

Aken shoved his hands in his pockets, his chin down, and moved to the back of the group. He leaned against the stone fence marking the training ground, near where Cyrus was practicing.

Cy was twisting pieces of metal, making them float in the air, and tried melting and combining them to form a larger chunk.

He watched for a while.

The Masters started to walk about the training field, observing the paired students' progress, and their conversation came within earshot of him and Cy.

Seren-Rose's cat-like eyes surveyed the pairs, her steps gliding across the grass, night-black hair rippling down her firm shoulders.

Her gaze darted several times to the Master beside her. "Fatalities during harvests have risen this past year. And I don't see them slowing anytime soon," she said quietly, the natural slur in her voice matching the sway of her gait.

Nephryte exhaled through his nose. "That, and a rise in slave numbers." His head jerked. "All completely unnecessary."

"Yes." Her lashes lowered halfway. "Most Draevs don't care anymore about the lives of non-vempars. There's too much bitterness between the races... If humans could find a way, I'm sure they would wipe our kind off the face of the Eartha. Only Lord God knows how many of us they've killed in death-cages."

Her gaze flicked up to Nephryte when he didn't respond. "It's great Abilities like yours that keep this kingdom safe.

I'll never forget those tornados you cast against the goblin army, years back… It's no wonder the Human Republic hesitates to start a war with us." A small smile touched her full lips, dyed deep purple today. "You're too soft-hearted, though, Nephryte. Always caring about everyone and everything—even your enemies. I worry about you."

Nephryte made a sound, like a disagreeing grunt, and his gaze fixed ahead.

"I've noticed that Aken-Shou enjoys the company of your newest student." Seren-Rose nodded their way, and Aken quickly turned around, pretending to be busy and not eavesdropping. "You still have high hopes for the boy, hm? Despite his predicament?"

"Yes. He has a long way to go—both of them do. But I'm proud of how far they've come." Nephryte tipped his head up at the clear sky. "This kingdom will need them, if it is to survive the future threats that may come our way… However, one of them does have a bad habit of eavesdropping that needs to be fixed."

Aken sucked in his lips and hurried himself back over to Bakoa.

⌒⌒

Cyrus focused, working to melt the metal into one big blob in the air. She had to touch each piece first, channeling her *essence* into the metal, before she could manipulate them.

She half listened to the E.M. Study lesson. Touch was a way to absorb *essence*, or energy—removing that energy from someone.

Removing…

An idea came to her. The irregular energy inside her—what caused her wrists pain and was slowly eating away at her—could it be drawn out, somehow?

As soon as E.M. Study ended, Cyrus raced back to the school.

"Cy? Cyrus?" Aken called out after her.

But she didn't slow until she barged into Zushil's office, under the front colonnade.

The miffed man wearing a lab coat gave her a pointed look through his glasses. "Really? Too much trouble to knock these days, is it?"

Heedless of the comment, she went straight into telling him her idea; and meanwhile, Aken caught up, also barging into the room.

Zushil threw up his hands. "Why do I even bother having a door?"

"Listen, please, doctor. This *has* to work. There must be a way!" Cyrus insisted.

Zushil regarded her, the lines of his face tight. "You want me to try and draw out the unnatural energy that's inside you through Touch?" He gave a single, sharp laugh. "Why do you assume that thought didn't already occur to me? The energy didn't like it when I tried to Heal the scars on your wrists. There's no telling what trying to remove the power from you might do to me, let alone to *you*."

Cyrus persisted anyway. "Please, just try! We won't know until we try *something*."

The doctor's features pinched.

After some more convincing, Zushil finally became irritated enough that he caved in.

"Fine! I will try, but only for a brief moment. And if something goes wrong, it's on you."

She gave a firm nod.

Aken stared back and forth between them, his mouth halfway open.

Cyrus held her arm out for Zushil to grip.

At first, she didn't feel anything, but then came the cold sensation of ice cubes sliding down her skin.

Zushil's brow wrinkled in concentration. After a moment, his wrinkles deepened and sweatdrops beaded his skin.

Zushil cried out, a flash of light suddenly appearing where his hand had touched her skin. His palm was steaming and he held it up to his face.

His hand had been burned.

Cyrus stared, slack-jawed. "What happened?"

Aken neared for a better look.

"It seems as if the well of energy inside you doesn't want to be removed." Zushil gave his damaged hand several sharp shakes, fingers flexing. "That *essence*—it felt like it would overwhelm me and... I am sorry, Cyrus, but I cannot risk someone's life to do this. And even if there was a way, I fear that removing the energy completely from you would kill you; it feels practically glued to the fibers of your being."

Cyrus's heart sank.

So much for that idea.

She turned her head to Aken, who was busy pretending to poke at a cactus plant. "I know you know, Aken," she said.

His finger paused and his face turned slightly so she could see one eye.

"You've been treating me like a porcelain teacup that's going to shatter any second. It's obvious you found out about my health predicament."

That the massive core of energy inside her was slowly spreading through her body and killing her.

Aken let his hand fall and he dropped the act. He faced her, head lowered. "Sorry. I wasn't sure how you'd feel about me knowing."

She shrugged. "Well, maybe I shouldn't keep everything to myself all the time. But don't go telling anyone else—I mean it." She pointed a finger at him.

He hand-motioned zipping his lips shut.

Zushil returned from a side room and set something in her hands: a new brown pair of fingerless gloves. The seams were flexible, different patches of material making some parts stretchy and other parts firmly secure, and they came down longer over her wrists.

"Your new gloves, as requested by Master Nephryte," he stated. "These should make daily tasks much more comfortable."

She hurried to try them on, slipping her hands through. They fit, snug and soft.

"They're beautiful. Thank you!" she said, and tried to put aside her disappointment about her failed plan.

5

The next day, their E.M. Study class was paired with Floor Tathom again, but this time for a lesson in the art of Leaping. Mamoru had helped Aken and Cyrus learn the Landing part—how to fall and land from high heights using a gathered cushion of *essence* beneath their feet. Today, they would learn how to jump to reach those high heights and vault over rooftops.

It was a basic skill necessary for every Draev squad, as they traveled over the city rooftops to go on missions, racing past the bustle of street life below, as if the rooftops were roads built just for them.

"If you're feeling dizzy or nauseous, let me or Master Seren-Rose know. But keep in mind that if you're going to become a Draev, then you had better get used to these heights. Traveling by rooftop is the fastest way for us to navigate, especially when there's an attack on the city." A steady breeze pushed Nephryte's brown hair to the side, the sort of breeze that buffets from high heights, as he and the student group stood upon a section of Draevensett's long, peaked roof.

He was wearing his official Draev Master uniform today, the dark blue shoulder cape billowing behind him, the silver fang-and-bat-wing rank pin glinting at his collar.

Aken crossed his arms, chin out. He would master this technique—he *would*! To make his dream a reality and to protect his friends.

Beside him, Cy kept one hand gripped on his sleeve.

It would be a long fall for anyone who slipped, especially for someone who couldn't Heal. The roof's slanted sides at this section weren't steep to walk on, but the drop below sure was.

"Your goal today will be to Leap from here," Nephryte tapped his foot where they stood, where the school's tallest tower soared up through the roof, "to the bell tower's balcony." He raised a hand, pointing to the decorative balcony beneath the tower's octagonal spire, very high up.

Aken could hear Zartanian and Cyrus both swallow as they tipped their heads back, wide-eyed.

"Five students at a time will try. Who's first? Come on, young men, don't you want to impress the ladies?" urged Nephryte.

Aken took note of Cherish, seated beside Lady Seren-Rose; she wasn't physically able to Leap yet.

"*He's* the one wanting to impress Seren-Rose..." Aken muttered under his breath.

"Why don't you go first, Aken-Shou? Since your goal is to become the greatest Draev Guardian," Nephryte said, and a gust of wind shoved him forward.

"W-wait, you gotta show me *how* first!"

"Remember the cloud of *essence* you created beneath your feet to Land safely? Well, instead of picturing a cloud in your mind, this time picture a coiling spring beneath your feet: gather, twist, and wrap the *essence* as tightly as you can. Then, release your hold on that spring in the same instant that you jump."

Nephryte rested his hand casually on a hip. "There, I've explained it. It's fairly simple. Now, do it."

Aken frowned, but he stepped up to the tower's wall face, flexing his arms and fingers. He readied his stance, knees bent.

"Me too!" Bakoa hopped forward to join him. "I know I can fly already with my Ability, but I'd still like to give this a try!"

Two others and a smug-faced Denim also joined. All five boys faced the smooth wall of the looming stone tower, while the rest hung back to watch.

The boys readied, knees bent…and then, they Leaped.

The coil of *essence* Aken had wrapped released before he was ready—propelling him up through the air and then *splat* into the tower wall.

Bak Leaped, and his energy-coil sent him spiraling into the sky like a bottle-rocket. The other two boys ended up nearly sailing off the roof.

Denim's Leap was just a small jump, and he landed back down, laughing as he watched the others fall.

Aken peeled himself off the tower face in pain, and, losing his grip on the wall, he fell—landing bottom-down on top of Denim's skull, crushing the noble underneath his weight. The following momentum tumbled them both down the roof's slope, sending them sailing off the edge and falling to the ground five-stories below, their panicked arms flailing uselessly.

Nephryte's ropes of air caught them before they could smash into pieces. "Did you completely forget how to Land? That's why I taught you Landing first, so you wouldn't kill yourselves while trying to learn Leaping," he reprimanded them, and set them back on the roof.

Denim stumbled dizzily and had to sit down, looking like he was going to be sick. "S-s-stupid… *mrgr*… Scourgeblood… *grff*…" he mumbled. Then he turned away and threw up a rainbow.

"*Eww!*" The group shuffled away from him, giving him space.

"Next group," Nephryte called and moved on.

The next handful of students managed to get the hang of it, Leaping high enough to grab hold of the tower's balcony ledge. Both Hercule and Zartin almost succeeded.

Cy, nervous and sweaty, waited until it was the last group's turn. Aken patted his shoulder, "You can do it, buddy! I know you can."

"Cyrus, you don't have to do this yet, if you're not ready," said Nephryte. "I can let you practice somewhere easier."

Cyrus glanced around; some students were muttering about half-humans getting special treatment.

Aken felt tempted to go over and give them some *special treatment* of his own making.

"No, I want to try," said Cy. He lifted his head, the tower looming far above.

Aken watched as the redhead closed his eyes and concentrated, brow furrowed. After a minute, Cy's lilac eyes popped open.

Hands splayed, knees bent, Cy worked to find the right balance in his feet.

And then, Cyrus jumped.

As if shot from an invisible bow, the redhead soared up through the air along the face of the tower, almost reaching the ledge.

The coil of *essence* soon died out, though, and even as his hands clawed to grab for the balcony, the redhead started to fall back down.

Cy collided against the stone, scraping up his arm, before a current of air stopped his fall and carried him back down to the roof.

"A good first try, Cyrus." Nephryte set him down. "Better than some of the other boys, at least."

Some of those others grumbled.

When E.M. Study came to an end, their homework was to keep practicing but from lower heights. Aken watched as the Floor groups dispersed, Denim ranting and muttering all the way and casting glares in Harlow's direction.

Cy rubbed his sore arm and left to get Healed.

Soon, Aken was the only one left on the roof.

He tipped his head back, frowning defiantly up at the undefeated tower, the large bells inside catching the evening light.

⌒

Nighttime approached, and Nephryte spotted a figure still up on the academy's roof, just as he had predicted. He quietly glided up to the rooftiles and observed Aken, who was still attempting to reach the balcony.

Aken fell from his latest Leap attempt and hit the tower wall, just short of the balcony, and let himself slide back down for the twentieth time.

'It's not entirely his fault. What lies dormant inside him must be making things difficult. That blood essence is probably harder to control and wield than that of average Draevs.' Nephryte's brow creased. *'I wish I knew how to make it easier for him...'*

Aken collapsed to his knees, having finally exhausted his *essence*. He leaned back and glimpsed the partial moon, which now glowed between the sharp outline of the academy's towers.

"Getting much needed sleep and rest is also a part of training."

Aken looked over his shoulder at Nephryte, gliding across the roof tiles towards him, a glass of red berry juice in hand.

He handed the glass down to the boy, who took it thirstily.

"Another Nephryte saying? You should make them into a memoir, you've got so many," said Aken between swallows.

"Uh, what did you do to this juice? It tastes so…bland. Not sweet at all."

Nephryte's eyebrows slanted inwards. "Nothing. It should taste the same as always."

Aken shrugged and finished it anyway. His back creaked when he stretched, and he covered a heavy yawn. "Maybe I do need rest…"

Nephryte took care not to let his inner thoughts show. "I believe I did tell the class to practice on their own from lower heights—not from this five-story roof, for safety reasons," he said pointedly.

Aken flashed him a weary smirk. "I knew I wouldn't be on my own for long. A certain Master has a habit of showing up and scolding me."

Nephryte couldn't stop the single chuckle that escaped him. "You smart-aleck."

After dinner, Cyrus worked through three classes worth of reading assignments she had missed. Two hours passed, and she now stifled a yawn. The bunny her mother had made her smiled at her from the nightstand, the ruby necklace still hidden inside its zipped pouch. She fingered the bunny's soft fabric arm, recalling vague memories of Mother: her long, scarlet hair and her warmth-filled love.

She peered out her bedroom window, leaning over the sill until she could spot Aken's silhouette on the roof—still determined to Leap to the top of that tower. He'd been at it for hours, even skipping dinner, and now it looked like he was finally taking a break.

His determination was attractive, she had to admit to herself. She watched his silhouette with a fond feeling.

'Stop that, stay focused!' she snapped at herself and shook her head.

She was here to train to become a Draev—not to grow complicated feelings for a boy! They were friends, and that's all she wanted it to be.

She turned back to her homework fastidiously and faced away from the window.

6

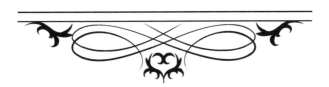

yrus glanced about the dorm corridor, the early dawn light coming in pale through the windows and across their decorative bat-wing frames. Some of the oilpowder lamps along the wall still glowed. Seeing that the coast was clear, she crept along quickly, wearing her robe.

Floor Harlow had a small, single shower room separate from the bigger restroom and its shower stalls. It was the only safe place where she could shower in peace.

She slipped inside and closed the door behind her.

Soon, she was humming a lively tune and lathering sandalwood scented shampoo in the curls of her hair; the hot water soft and comforting rolled down her skin.

Clink!

She paused.

Was that the door handle?

But she was sure she had locked it before—

"Man, you early birds. Today's Saturday, you know, the day you're supposed to sleep in."

Cyrus yelped inside her head. Aken's voice? In the shower room?!

She carefully peeked one eye around the edge of the thick shower curtain and glimpsed the door ajar.

'Great. Just great! What fine messes you get yourself into, Cyrus stupid-head!'

Aken glanced at the folded blue pajamas and robe resting on a white cabinet shelf. "Oh, it's *you*, Cy! Here I thought you were Mamoru. I didn't think you were the early type."

'I'm not,' she thought bitterly. *'But when you need to hide your identity, you can only have the shower room to yourself if you beat everybody else to it!'*

"Um, Aken, what're you doing in here?" she asked, trying to keep the tone of her voice calm.

He pulled out a toothbrush from the shower pack he set beside the sink. "You aren't gonna be in there long, are you? Because I really need a shower. This handsome magic doesn't just happen, y'know."

He began brushing his teeth. "Noble Rich Pants and Sandy Man are hogging the other shower stalls. Knowing Hercule, it'll be a good hour before he gets out. And Bak leaves soapy sand behind; *gross.*"

Cyrus quickly rinsed her hair, resisting the urge to grab a towel and run, instead trying to finish quickly and think up some excuse to make him leave.

"I tink ah'm gettn de hang o it—de Leapwing Techtique, I mwean. Ah'm keepn at it untwil I dwo! Ah'll bwe de bwest o de bwest!" he said around a mouthful of toothpaste.

"That's good news. Hard work pays off," she said distractedly.

He spat, rinsed. "Yep! You caught on pretty fast, though. I was impressed."

She paused.

A compliment. For once, it wasn't just stepsister Heily who everybody praised.

"Did I leave my soap bar in there?" Aken asked. His hand reached around the edge of the curtain, searching.

Seeing the hand, Cyrus panicked.

"I thought I—"

Before she could think, she wrapped metal around her fingers and chopped downward on the searching hand.

Crack!

Aken yelped and drew his hand back, clutching it. It looked bent the wrong way, sideways.

'*Oh no, oops!*' Cyrus thought and winced, but she used the distraction to reach out and snatch hold of her robe, quickly drawing it inside the shower and wrapping it on.

"Ow-ow-*ow*." Aken clutched the injury.

"I'm sorry! I didn't— I mean— You startled me, and I wasn't thinking!" She hopped out of the shower, grabbing up her belongings.

"Yep." His face cringed, voice tight and clipped. "It'll Heal in no time."

"Um, okay. You can...you know...take a shower now." She headed for the door.

As she closed it behind her, Aken righted his hand with a *crack* and yelped again.

She winced and hurried away. "Sorry!"

Changed into khaki pants and a collared brown shirt with batwing embroidery, Cyrus slipped out of her room. She then spotted Cherish, wheeling her sleek wheelchair into Harlow's wide entryway.

The vempar girl brightened to see her. "Cyrus, I'm glad I found you. I came to invite you and Harlow over for an outdoor picnic this afternoon, at the Cuore Mansion."

Cherish was of House Cuore, one of the twelve Noble Houses descended from the Twelve Legendary Knights. While the Dragonsbanes were at the top of society, the Cuores were among the lesser Houses, or so she had once explained.

Cyrus bobbed her head. "I'd love to come over! I'll let the others know."

Cherish clapped her hands together delightedly. "Splendid, I'll see you then!" She turned the wheelchair back around toward the door leading out onto the spiral walkway.

Cyrus glimpsed Hercule coming out of the larger restroom, wrapped in a white cotton robe, fresh from the shower, his pearly gray hair glistening. He glanced to where Cherish had left, and cast her a questioning look.

Cyrus told him about the invitation, and he looked away for a moment, brow furrowed as if conflicted.

"I'd...like to," he began regrettably. "But I have far too much homework over the weekend, and I would prefer to finish it today so that I can be free tomorrow."

"Oh. Okay."

He glided past to his dorm room.

Things must be too complicated. A Dragonsbane going on a picnic with the Cuores might spark gossip. She wondered if she, a half-human being on the same Floor as him, had caused him any social problems.

Cyrus made her way downstairs and through the school halls, the floor tiles polished and the hung tapestries and paintings colorful at the corners of her vision. She finally found her way to the principal's office and knocked on the grand mahogany doors, the woodwork bearing Draevensett's coat-of-arms.

Someone else was inside. She waited until the person—a teacher—came out.

"Cyrus," said Principal Han, spotting her through the opened door. "What brings you here?"

"Um…" She waited until the teacher had left, then came near, passing by shelves of preserved beetles, all different shapes and colors, the air in the room scented with age and musk. She asked him about the photo of her mother that he had found and left in her room, a few days back.

"Did you find anything else about my mother?" she asked. "Did she graduate as a Draev? But then, why did she leave Draethvyle? Did she make any enemies here? How did she meet my dad?"

"Whoa, whoa." Han motioned with his palms. "Slow down, little student, before my tired old brain overheats."

Cyrus sucked in her lips.

Principal Han took a seat at the big mahogany desk, its legs shaped like those of a giant insect. "Now then, all I could find on your mother was the usual information that we archive on vempars with Ability. Name, age, place of birth…that sort of thing. The reason she left Draethvyle was not stated, but if I had to guess, it must have had something to do with your father. Perhaps she ran away so she could marry him? Such a union would never have been permitted by the D.G. League." He leaned back in his chair. "*Ha*, I wonder how they met? It must have been during a mission, *hm*. It all sounds quite riveting, a forbidden romance tale, don't you think?"

When he saw her expression, he cleared his throat and stroked his long beard. "I wish I had solid answers to give you, Cyrus, but with the way the world is, mysteries like these often go unsolved. That isn't to say that something won't turn up *eventually*, in due time. Anything is possible," he added to give her some hope.

But the hope didn't reach her. Instead, she faked a smile and nodded.

Would Mother have really abandoned everything she had in Draethvyle to marry a human? An insensitive man who turned on her the moment he learned she was really a vempar in disguise?

Something in the story was missing...and the only person who knew the truth was her dad, back in Elvenstone.

She didn't want to go back there—she wasn't sure if she ever could.

Oh well, at least she had a photo of Mother here. It was a special treasure, and that would have to be enough, for now.

～๑

A small girl held a frilly, pink parasol as she stood upon a rooftop. She opened the parasol wide, gathered the skirt of her equally frilly, pink dress, and then let herself fall off the edge.

The girl covered her yawn with a gloved hand, the wind whipping at her short, curly pink hair, before the parasol slowed her fall—gently spiraling her down, down, until the soles of her shiny black shoes touched the academy's pristine front steps.

"Ahhh," she sighed, shielding her face from the sun, and gazed up at the rising walls and intricate gothic towers. "What a lovely thing! I could hold many tea parties here."

Her left eye smiled with a child-like laugh, the other covered with an eyepatch. She set down a purple leather suitcase, then once more adjusted the frills of her layered skirt, which flared out above knee-high striped stockings.

She took off a glove, the skin beneath it a storm cloud gray, and smoothed her pixie-cut curls. She adjusted the mini hat pinned in her hair: black, with a frilly rim and purple feathers, a veil of tulle above her right ear.

"It's time to have some fun." Her single parrot-green eye narrowed.

"Deeeidreem!" the girl in pink sing-songed and creaked open the door to the man's dorm flat. Skipping inside, she went into the living room of twin velvet sofas.

There, seated in one, leaning against an elbow while scanning papers in one hand, was Deidreem.

He glanced up from his work to see who had disturbed his quiet. Seeing her, his eyebrows lifted and he straightened. "Adelheid! You're here so soon?"

Before he could move, she somersaulted overhead—pink dress and all—to land both feet neatly on top of the sofa's stiff back. She wrapped skinny, flexible arms around his neck from behind.

"I am not a patient person, you know. I couldn't tolerate sitting and waiting to be accepted by the school any longer. And besides, Leader wants me to keep an eye on things around this place without delay."

Deidreem glanced back at her, muttering in mock irritation, "All these years haven't changed a thing about you, eh? I still don't see why Leader needs you here when he has *me*."

She stuck out her tongue.

He turned his face away with a smirk. "Fortunately, I just received the letter that you've been accepted as a student. So, you actually arrived on time."

"Oh? How convenient." Her eyelid half lowered. She vaulted down to the rug, arms splayed, and twirled like a ballerina, flicking a look his way. "I hear I'm to pose as your cousin, is that right?"

He nodded, setting the papers on a glass coffee table. She giggled, child-like, though she was anything but a child.

"You'll have to help me set up my room and things." She twirled, eyeing the array of boxes, mirrors, fabrics and gadgets that lined the walls of Deidreem's dorm: the artifacts of magicians. "Also, we're going on a picnic this afternoon!"

"What?" Deidreem raised a cautionary eyebrow.

"This nice amethyst-eyed girl with hair like snowflakes asked me to come—a way to get to know people better, or something like that, since I'm new. And you *know* how much I love a good tea party and picnic."

He stared at her for several seconds, then groaned. When Adelheid had her mind set on something, there was no denying her.

"There goes my Saturday, wasted on a picnic..." he muttered under his breath and rubbed his fingers down his forehead.

"Splendid! I must change into my red dress for the occasion!" She clapped her hands together and trotted off.

~~

With Bakoa and Zartanian in tow, Aken and Cyrus followed the map's directions to the Cuore Mansion. They also used the opportunity to practice their Leaping by traveling over the lower city rooftops. They kept to the less steeply angled roofs, and hopped off a chimney onto a cupola and then across to a roof terrace.

Pedestrians and motor carriages, with their oilpowder engines giving off a musty scent like wet rock, bustled about the streets below them.

Aken flexed his Healed wrist. Cy must have apologized fifty times by now. But he made an important note to self: never disturb Cyrus in the shower again—*ever.*

"Yoh!" came a shout from an alley below them.

The group paused to peer down, and there stood Apfel, waving his small arms, wearing the same rumpled brown jacket and cap. The faeryn child cupped his hands to his mouth, shouting to be heard. "Yoh, Goldilocks!"

Aken grimaced.

"You owes me a favor! Remembers? A whole day's work."

Yuck, Aken had forgotten about that deal. Why did he have to show up right *now?*

"That doesn't mean today, Apple Strudel," Aken shouted back. "Try another day!"

The child pouted.

"Hi, Apfel," Cyrus called down. "Thank you for helping these guys with the chocolate surprise. It was wonderful! Hey, if you have time, why don't you come join us for a picnic?"

"What?" Aken balked.

The child pretended to consider before nodding with the sweetest of smiles. "I've gots some time, at the moment, *ja*."

Bak stretched out his arm, shifting it into a long sand ladle that scooped the child up and lifted him to the roof.

"Cool powers," Apfel commented, and Bak gave a bashful grin. "I bets it's more useful than Akina's silly birdies."

"Akina?" Aken exclaimed. "I am *so* not going to let that slide!"

"Hurry up, or we'll be late." Cyrus motioned to them all and continued on ahead.

The others followed, Bak carrying Apfel along, and Aken threw up his hands and hurried after them.

The Cuore Mansion, when they arrived, was like a florist's garden. The encompassing front and back yards were a mini paradise of colorful foliage and flowers of every kind, neatly arranged in artistic designs and patterned hedges.

They followed the housekeeper through an arbor tunnel of flowering wisteria, a cascade of dangling lavender and pink, leading around the quaint mansion to the back gardens. It was at the opposite end that Professor Kotetsu greeted them, waving the housekeeper away so he could escort the guests himself.

His wing-like eyebrows fluttered with anticipation. "Hellooo, my little Draev students! I welcome you to the humble abode known as the Cuore residence." He bowed with a flourish.

Bakoa grinned brightly. "It's like a fairytale palace. Thanks for inviting us!"

"Not at all. It's a pleasure to have visitors! Come along, now. My Cherishy-pooh awaits on yonder hill!"

Apfel scrunched up his face. "What's yonder mean?"

Aken whispered back, "He's just being silly. Keep walking."

The backyard's hedge garden maze slopped upward to a little hilltop meadow, where the picnic was set out with a rose blanket, plates and silverware neatly spread, baskets of food ready and waiting. They followed the grass path up to the picnic, and Cherish carefully rose to her feet.

One hand on the wheelchair arm, she greeted them with an elegant smile and nod. "I'm so glad you could make it. Not everyone I invited could come; I suppose they had other obligations."

Aken had the stray thought that maybe people were avoiding her overly exuberant brother, but he wasn't about to say it out loud.

"And who is this little one?" she gestured to Apfel.

"He's a new friend of ours, Apfel," said Cy.

"Pleased to make your acquaintance, Apfel." She bowed her head.

"Uh…uh…and yors," Apfel stammered and shifted his feet, not knowing what to do.

Cherish moved away from her wheelchair, and Kotetsu rushed to her side. "Careful now, Cherishy! I'll never have another night's sleep if something happens to you! The worry, the anxiety, is a crushing whale upon my back."

Aken shut his eyes, trying to picture that.

With a somewhat annoyed sigh, Cherish let her overly-protective brother help sit her down on the floral blanket. "I never ask you to worry about me, you know." Her eyes flattened. "And besides, we have guests. It's only proper for the host to rise and greet them."

"Yes, yes!" he said cheerfully, not really listening to her.

She breathed in, then gestured for them all to have a seat. There was room for more people, even after Apfel snatched a spot. The unkempt faeryn grabbed for the food right away, piling everything in a heap on his plate, and filling a glass with orange fizzy drink made from freshly squeezed oranges; it was spilling over the rim.

"You piglet!" Aken berated the child, seated on his left. "Don't you have any manners at all? The host says when we eat."

"Host?" Apfel chewed around a roasted chicken drumstick. "Alien host? I thoughts so."

"Not *that* kind of host, you apple head."

Zartanian observed them both. "Usually Aken's the one without any manners..." he spoke his thoughts. "Oh, did I say that out loud?"

Cyrus and Bak, to Aken's right, and Cherish and Kotetsu, across from them, shook with held in laughter.

Aken felt his cheeks heat. Was that really how people saw him?

Cy tried to change the subject for him. "So, Cherish, is it just you and your brother who live here?"

Cherish sipped tea from a porcelain cup and set it on a blue rose painted saucer in her other hand. "Yes. I share the dorm flat with Lady Seren-Rose in Floor Tathom, but I still spend some time here, now and then. It helps to keep the Cuore House alive." She glanced at the faeryn child, who was busy stuffing his blue cheeks. "Perhaps we should pray and eat before little Apfel consumes the whole picnic?"

They started to laugh, and Apfel paused his eating to glance around at them, clueless.

After giving a prayer of thanks, the Cuores both swooned over how cute the little faeryn was: asking where he was from, where he lived and worked. He gave short, muffled answers in between bites, blinking those large chestnut-red eyes at them.

Aken hurried to pile desserts on their plates before the imp could dig his child fingers into it all. Crumble cake, zucchini bread, and chocolate parfait—real, expensive chocolate! He beamed.

Apfel swallowed down zucchini bread slices. "Is he, *mmph*, really yor brother? You don'ts look alike."

Aken gave him a warning look. Darn kid, saying something rude like that!

Kotetsu held a hand over his heart as if it had been struck through. "Not *alike*? Oh, my my. The heart throbs in agony..." He sniffled. "But alas, 'tis truth." He dabbed at his eyes. "Because I'm her *half*-brother, you see. Though, I do so dearly, *dearly* wish that we were full siblings." He wrapped both long arms around Cherish's shoulders in a squeeze. "But bonds of the heart are greater than bonds of the blood!"

Cherish mock rolled her eyes. "You over-doting heathen. Let go, will you?"

The brother chuckled. "I had to raise her like a parent after our father and both our mothers passed away." Kotetsu recalled the tiny, months-old baby he held wrapped in a blanket in his arms—himself a teenager, with no knowledge of how to raise a child.

He'd found baby Cherish lying in the grass beside her mother after a goblin raid had attacked their carriage train on the road. The nearby vempar town had also been ransacked.

They'd been on their way back to Draethvyle from the coast when it happened. Kotetsu hadn't been with them, but had arranged to meet them on the road halfway. Only, they never arrived at the meeting point, and he went out in search of them with a group, armed with rifle-axes.

He found the scene of devastation, littered with the dead and survivors, breaking his heart. He didn't pause until he found his father's wrecked carriage and baby Cherish inside.

At first, she looked dead, but as he held her in his arms, he felt movement, her tiny lungs still breathing. He made a promise that day to always watch over her.

With the help of House Cuore maids, he fed her, bathed her—even as she screamed and splashed water in his face—changed diapers, put together outfits, and spent all his spare time playing with her, until she was old enough to do things for herself.

But living was a challenge when her body became more fragile, and the doctor first explained her health predicament. Kotetsu had to leave her care to the maid while he was away at work, earning money to sustain them while the Cuore inheritance was being fought over. Relatives everywhere had tried to claim a piece, and until the dispute was settled, no one could touch it.

Being an illegitimate half-brother, he wasn't allowed to lay claim to the inheritance. Only Cherish could, but she had been too young. Kotetsu worked hard to graduate and make himself eligible to be Cherish's legal guardian—and become, therefore, the holder and guardian of the Cuore inheritance. With that, the Cuore wealth was finally restored to them.

When her Ability manifested, Kotetsu aimed to get a position in Draevensett. He couldn't let her go to school by herself with a disability.

"Believe it or not, he's not as much of a worry toad as he used to be," Cherish interrupted the story. "I've been going to Draevensett for over a year, now, and I'm capable of doing most things on my own." She directed the last bit at Kotetsu, but he kept grinning. It was clear that he would keep doing things for her, whether she liked it or not.

Listening, Aken wondered what it would be like to have an older brother. He glanced down at Apfel, still stuffing his face. "Stop eating so much. You'll make yourself sick," he whispered.

"Yor so bossy, Akina." The child glared. "Why don'ts you just…just…" Apfel paused, rubbed his forehead, his eyes squeezing shut as if from a piercing headache.

"You see? That's what happens after eating too much sugar. Little imp. Maybe you'll listen to me next time."

"Nnn…*hnng.*"

Aken paused mid tea sip, watching the child beside him.

Apfel's eyelids drifted open, and he slowly set his hands back down, chestnut gaze staring blankly ahead at nothing.

"Um, Apfel?" Aken asked uncertainly.

The child's head slowly turned, glazed-over eyes meeting his.

"You." Apfel looked directly at him. "You tasted what you should not have." The child's voice changed into a lifeless trance, his accent gone. "Shame on you, False Guardian."

That name. False Guardian—he had been called that before. By the old hunchback faeryn, who had also had blue skin.

He'd forgotten, but Apfel wasn't the first blue faeryn he had seen.

Aken shushed for him to stop speaking. Cy and the others were looking his way. "*Shhh!* Don't make a scene."

"It is too late, now. No turning back. No turning back!" Apfel continued.

Zartanian and Cherish were watching.

Feeling extremely uncomfortable, Aken leaned down sideways, whispering fiercely into Apfel's ear: "Will you shut it? I don't know what kind of game you're playing, saying weird stuff, but knock-it-off."

"You have weakened the cage—weakened the cage! Now, the change will begin—*Mmff!*"

Aken upended one of the empty picnic baskets over the kid's head, muffling him.

When the others stared, he tried laughing it off as a joke. "Ooookay, ha-ha-ha. That kid has quite the imagination, right?

I bet he'll grow up to be a great storyteller, some day."

They all shared looks.

Aken put his mouth close to the basket and whispered, "Are you gonna shut up now?"

Before he could hear the child answer, a new voice interrupted the picnic, calling up to them from the foot of the hilltop meadow: "Lady Cherish, Professor Kotetsu."

Aken straightened to watch as the housekeeper came up the slope with two impeccably dressed people in tow.

"Oh!" Cherish's face brightened and she stood again, Kotetsu instantly fretting.

Aken recognized Master Deidreem; but with him, arm wrapped around his, was a young girl of the same cloud-gray skin, perhaps around their age.

Her red dress was all frills, ankle shoes black and shiny, with matching gloves, bone-flower print along the sides and along her knee-high stockings. A mini hat sat in her short baby-pink hair, black raven feathers and peacock plumes spilling over the hat's side, encrusted in pearls. A skull pendant attached to the mini hat's side grinned at them. Her right eyepatch likewise had embroidered crossbones and skull. Her face was petite like a china doll, and so, too, was her chortling laugh.

Aken felt unnerved, though he didn't know why, and he noticed Cy rubbing his arms, as if something in the air had made him suddenly cold.

"Good day, Cuore family and friends. I do hope we are not *too* very late." The girl tapped a finger against her cheek, lower lip puckering. "I had *sooo* much unpacking to do, trying to fix up my new room."

"Not at all," Cherish assured. "There's plenty of food and desserts left. Come, have a seat."

While the new girl and Master Deidreem took places beside Kotetsu, Cherish made introductions.

Deidreem noticed the child, whose head was still hidden under a basket, and raised one questioning eyebrow.

"I believe we all know Master Deidreem," Cherish introduced.

"Yes, yes," he spoke, tweaking the rim of his black top hat and setting it down on the blanket beside him. "This lovely young lady, here, is my cousin: Adelheid. She'll be attending our school, starting this week."

Adelheid curtsied with a giggle before plopping down on the picnic blanket. "Which makes us classmates, for the time being. Oh?"

On her knees, she leaned forward towards Aken, her single parrot-green eye observing him curiously. Aken leaned away. "What an odd-looking girl," she said, reaching a hand to touch his hair. "But that hair—*oo*—it's as golden as the sun! You must tell me what shampoo you're using?"

Bakoa accidentally spat out a mouthful of tea. Zartanian quickly stuffed his grin inside a chunk of crumble cake. Cherish's curved lips quivered.

"G…girl…?" Aken stammered.

"Ooh! What a handsome young man sits beside you!" Adelheid had already moved on, and was now sitting across from Cyrus, leaning towards the redhead and batting her pink eyelashes. "The fabled and famous half-human, I presume? Simply marvelous! Ooh, I simply must sit beside you."

Aken yelped as Adelheid shoved him out of the way, taking his seat for herself beside Cyrus, and wrapping a cloud-gray arm around Cy's.

Cherish tightened her hand on her teacup, her gaze narrowed slightly.

"Do tell me your whole life story—*Cyrus, is it?*—I just love a good tale! And I've a feeling that you possess quite an intriguing one."

Cyrus looked ready to make a run for it. It was bad enough having the eerie viper Deidreem here, but now *this*? And that giggle of hers was creepy.

"Have you tasted the crumble cake?" Cherish tried to say. "They're home-made."

"*Hm*? Really?" Adelheid looked away from Cyrus to inspect the desserts laid out, loosening her grip but still keeping a hand around Cy's arm. She picked one dessert up, stuffed it in her rosebud mouth. Her eye smiled, and she picked up another. "Most scrumptious, indeed! Here, cute red, you have one too."

The crumble cake was stuffed into Cy's mouth before he could protest. "*Mmf*—m-m-mff!"

Cherish gasped at Adelheid's behavior, so forward with a boy she'd only just met.

Cyrus looked miserably from one girl to the other, and another cake slice was forced down.

Not to let herself be outdone by some newcomer, Cherish scooted near enough to hold out a fresh creampuff. "T-try this next, Cyrus." She shoved it in the redhead's mouth.

"Mu—*mmuph*—guff!" Cyrus tried in vain to wave away the desserts that kept on coming. Each girl held a spoonful of parfait ready, next, and eyed one another sideways in challenge.

Meanwhile, Bakoa shifted to speak to Deidreem on the opposite side of the blanket, his expression curious. "That's a cool hat, like a magician's or something, right?"

"Well, young man, that's because, in a way," Deidreem flipped the top hat in the air, catching it smoothly between thumb and forefinger, "I *am* a magician."

Three red swallowtail butterflies flew out from beneath the hat, fluttering around the young people's amazed faces, their wings glittering like sunshine.

Zartanian lifted a hand to touch one, and it vanished in a cloud of glitter.

The distraction gave Cyrus a chance to retreat, scooting in between Aken and basket-head Apfel.

Cherish and Adelheid blinked at one another.

"Oo, show us some more! I *love* magic tricks!" Bakoa begged him excitedly.

"Tricks?" Deidreem regarded them all mischievously, placing the hat back atop his head of dark curls. "The things I do can be considered almost *real*, young man." He rose from the blanket, snatching a napkin from Bak with two fingers. He flipped and snapped the napkin once, and it dissolved into a shower of rainbow dust.

Both Bak and Zartin gaped in amazement.

"But I do know tricks as well, if you're ever in need of learning a few." Deidreem's smile didn't reach his cool eyes.

Adelheid sat on her knees, trying to figure out a way past Aken to reach Cyrus. "Oh really. Do stop showing off, Cousin," she said in Deidreem's direction. To which his smile turned down.

"I wanna learn! Teach me." Bak's sandy-green eyes sparkled.

"I think it'd be fun to learn, too," Cherish piped in.

"Well, in that case." Deidreem tossed his hat into the air. It twirled like a spin-top before slowing above Cherish and landing with a plop on her snowy head. "I live but to please my audience."

Cherish turned the hat in her hands, fingering the purple ribbon circling its base.

Deidreem took from his coat pocket a single gold coin, holding it vertically with thumb and forefinger. He raised it above their heads. "Watch carefully, now, as I capture the sun."

Every gaze focused on the coin.

Deidreem moved the coin until it was in front of the afternoon sun, blotting it from their view.

Bak squinted. "The sun's still there behind the coin, right?"

Adelheid's doll-like lips smirked knowingly.

When Master Deidreem began to lower the coin, however, the sun behind it was gone. Instead, it was the coin itself shining like a miniature sun plucked from the sky.

Bakoa's jaw fell. "How did...?" He crawled forward to see the glowing orb more closely as Deidreem brought it down to their eye-level.

"Amazing." Cherish reached to touch the glowing gold with a finger, feeling heat emanating from its surface.

Aken looked back up at the sky, but the sun was nowhere to be seen.

Kotetsu's eyebrow-wings fluttered. "My goodness, that's quite a trick!"

The golden orb rolled around each finger as Deidreem flexed his hand, before letting it roll down into Bak's outstretched palm.

"Now, young man." Deidreem bent down to the boy's level. "To release the sun back into the sky, hold the coin high, covering the same gap of sky where you remember the sun last being—we don't want it placed in the wrong spot and messing up Eartha's time of day, now, do we?"

Raising the coin high with a long sand arm, as directed, Bak held it in place where the sun had shone earlier.

Instantly the golden orb that was the true sun flickered into view back in its original spot in the sky, and Bak nearly dropped the coin, the warmth and glow from it extinguished. "I-it was real! I mean, I put the sun back?"

Squinting, without staring directly at the sun, Aken glimpsed a thin sheet of something move clear of the sky. He shook his head at how gullible they all were. "It's just a trick." He smirked, crossing his arms. "Master Dei just waited for the right time when that long, thin cloud would come blot out the sun. None of us could stare *directly* at the sun, and the cloud was so pale, we didn't notice it happen." Aken tapped the side of his head with a finger, "It's all about tricking the eye. Making a person see what you want them to see, while letting them think they're still in control."

Master Deidreem watched him curiously. "Yes. You are surprisingly...*intellectual*...at times, Aken-Shou. That is exactly how most magicians work. The eye is an easy thing to deceive."

"But," Bakoa cut in, sounding confused, "the coin was glowing and felt warm."

"I channeled *essence* into the coin, making it heat up and glow. The fact that it's reflective metal made it shine all the brighter." Deidreem tapped Bak's hand, which still held the coin. "How about you try to do the same?"

Aken heard rustling beside him: Apfel trying to pry off the wicker basket. *'I should get Apple away from here, in case he starts talking crazy again,'* he thought.

He then stood and pretended to escort Apfel back to the mansion. "You know how children are, always needing the restroom," he said for an excuse, and Kotetsu waved them on.

Blinded by the basket, Apfel nearly ran into a conical-trimmed hedge and a marble bench. Aken steered the child along by the shoulders from behind. The picnic chatter continued, fading behind them: "What a lovely place you have here! You could throw *many* tea parties," Adelheid's voice giggled.

"Kotetsu, you are truly blessed to have such an intelligent and kind sister."

Cherish sounded bashful, "Master Deidreem, you flatter me. But I'm not that wonderful of a sister."

"The most bestest of blessings, she is!" Kotetsu proudly agreed.

Aken took Apfel indoors through a door in the back, and then yanked the basket off his head.

"Are you gonna act normal now? What's up with you today?"

Apfel shook his mop of night-blue and silver hair, and blinked several times before glancing about at his surroundings. They were inside a large, meticulous kitchen, beside a wide pewter sink. "Well?" Aken crossed his arms, waiting.

Slowly the child raised his gaze to his, chestnut irises glittering eerily. "You…"

"What?"

"…You're a bad person, False Guardian."

Aken facepalmed. He shoved a glass of water into the child's hands, commanding him to be quiet and drink. "What the heck is a *False Guardian*, anyway? Stop calling me weird stuff." He tapped the faeryn's head to knock some sense into it. But the child continued staring up at him, trance-like.

The rustle of footsteps approached.

Aken's pulse quickened and a strange unease came over him. *'I can't let anyone see Apfel acting like this!'*

He turned this way and that for a place to hide the child, but there wasn't enough time as Master Deidreem appeared through the kitchen doorway. With a backward kick, Aken pushed Apfel inside a cabinet under the sink, slapping the cabinet door shut behind him just in time before Deidreem caught sight of him.

Deidreem raised a suspicious eyebrow, halting before the tall cool-box.

Aken grinned back, leaning casually against the sink, arms crossed, blocking the sink cabinet behind him with his legs. He silently prayed the imp would keep still and not make a sound.

Deidreem took out a bottle of strawberry fizz wine, pouring out a glass while again glancing sideways at Aken.

Sweatdrops clung to the side of Aken's face. "Nice day, isn't it?" he said casually.

Deidreem's epidote gaze scrutinized him up and down.

Aken leaned back, grinning like a fool.

"I suppose," the vempar man agreed slowly. He then turned to face Aken with a more easy-going tone, "Say, young man. I didn't get a good look at that little blue faeryn who was with you. Who does he belong to?"

Aken gave a shrug. "Don't know. What's it to you?"

A muscle in Deidreem's jaw twitched. "He hasn't been behaving...oddly, has he? There's a certain disease that blue faeryn tend to catch. It makes their behavior unusual."

Aken gave him a strange look. "Like yourself?"

Deidreem coughed on the wine, then chuckled lightly; the laugh didn't touch the soul behind his gaze. "Always trying to be funny, aren't you?" He tapped his foot.

Aken's expression narrowed. Could Apfel really be sick...?

No. Something in his gut didn't trust whatever this Master was saying.

"The faeryn's fine," Aken stated.

"Where is he?"

"...He had to leave—busy with work and stuff."

Deidreem's gaze slitted.

Something *thumped* from inside the sink cabinet behind Aken's legs.

Aken coughed, trying to mask the sound. *'That little twerp!'*

Deidreem stepped towards him. "What was that sound? Is there something in—?"

Just then, like a blessing from above, Cyrus and Adelheid came skipping into the room. Well, Adelheid was the one doing the skipping, and trying to get Cy to join in.

Cy caught sight of Aken and mouthed the words "Help me!"

Aken waved at them. "Miss Adelheid," he said.

"Oh? Yes, ugly girl with pretty hair?"

He swallowed back a retort. "You must have sooo much shopping to do, just moving into Draevensett and all. Are you *absolutely sure* you've got everything you need?" He shrugged a hand. "Everybody knows the best shop deals are on weekends. Oh wait, isn't that *today*?"

In the background, Deidreem frantically waved his palms, gesturing for him to shut up. "No-no-no! No more shopping—I can't afford it!"

"*Hmm*, so I should stock up on supplies *now* while I have the chance?" Adelheid considered. "Aken, was it? Thank you, Aken. I can count on you for all my needed shopping advice!" Releasing her hold on Cyrus, the doll-like girl pranced to the door. "I do wish I could stay longer, but shopping bargains call! Come along, Cousin Deidreem! Won't you lend me some more charity?" She didn't wait for an answer.

"*Charity*, ha, as in my hard-earned cash," Deidreem grumbled to himself. More loudly he said, "Oh yes, thank you *indeed*, Aken-Shou. Thank you for encouraging her to spend the rest of what little money I have left from this morning's shopping excursion. I have to keep her happy, don't I?" Emptying the glass of wine down his throat, he quickly marched off after his cousin.

Cyrus leaned against the sink beside Aken with a sigh.

Finally, they were alone.

"Smart thinking. I owe you one," Cy said.

Aken tried to shrug off the lingering, unnerving chill.

"Where's Apfel?"

He moved and let the child shove his way out of the cabinet.

"Aken! You locked him up? How could you?" Cy started to scold him. But the child rose to his feet, eyes open and glazed over. His face turned to each of them.

Cy's brow furrowed. "Hey, what's wrong with him?"

Before Aken could answer, Apfel pointed a blue finger up at Cyrus.

"The Swan must beware," he said.

Aken and Cy shared a look.

"You, False Guardian, must keep the Swan safe. They are searching for her. Beware." Apfel looked to Cyrus. "The Impure Nights are after you. They want what's in here." His finger pointed to Cy's chest.

The redhead cupped his hands over the spot, lilac eyes suddenly wide. "The Impure Nights... Who are they?" Cy asked, sounding almost desperate, and grabbed Apfel by the shoulders. "Tell me!"

Apfel gazed blankly at the redhead for one long moment, then closed his eyes.

The child's head drooped forward.

Aken placed his hand on the kid's back before he could fall. "Apfel?"

After a while, the child blinked, looked back up at them. "What're yous doing? My head hurts..."

Aken and Cy shared another uneasy look.

Whatever had happened, Apfel was back to normal.

Picnic over, Harlow left the Cuore Mansion, and Apfel was his usual, energetic self again. He ignored Aken's whispered words that he'd been acting strange; the child had no memory of any of it.

Cherish and Kotetsu waved their goodbyes. "Visit anytime! Harlow will always be friends of the Cuores," the girl called after them. It made Aken wonder—just an afterthought—if she had any friends, and if she ever felt lonely in that mansion.

Apfel hurried ahead of them down the sidewalk, to get back to the bakery.

Aken recalled the old hunchback faeryn again. He fingered his pocket, but he had left the starlight orb back in his room.

"The False Guardian, whose destiny is tied with the Swan Princess..." the old faeryn had said.

False Guardian. What did that name even mean?

And why had Apfel pointed at Cyrus, as if the redhead was the Swan?

Ha! The Swan was a human princess—a girl. Not a half-vempar boy.

"My time as Oracle is done, my part to play in this world finished. My gift will pass on to another, soon—a young moonlight faeryn, like me."

Could it be...?

He wondered and watched as Apfel hurried away.

⁓

"Leader, I have good news!" Deidreem entered the hexagonal meeting room.

Leader was there, and he turned from the wall-sized window, his folded hands encircled in dark lace.

"I have found one of the *mondschein* faeryn survivors, here within this city." Deidreem tried to control his excitement.

Leader mused over the news, his attention focused on something distant beyond the glass. "A most pleasant surprise, indeed," he spoke slowly.

"Yes. He's young, but there is still the possibility that he could be—or become—the next Oracle," Deidreem furthered.

"Long has the gift of foresight evaded my grasp," said Leader, lifting his palm, his curved nails dyed black. "With the Oracle in our possession, he will lead us to the Swan. We will find her at last."

Deidreem bowed his head. "I will begin preparations for capturing him. The new Corpsed should be able to track down the feather of Pure Light inside the child if he is, in fact, the new Oracle."

7

"**A**pfel."

      "*Ja*, Papa?"

The old memory came into focus. He was back in Bergvolk, with the scent of pine trees in the air around him, and his father, sitting on the floor of their makeshift home, beckoned him over. "Come here."

Little Apfel waddled across the wood shack's dirt floor.

"I have to tell you something very important, so you need to pay attention." Papa drew him close, perching him on his lap, his gray pants drab and worn. "You remember me telling you about the Mondburg Kingdom, *ja*? The place where our kind once ruled and thrived?"

Apfel nodded his head on his small neck.

"There is more to the story, which you must know," he began. "A long time ago, the Mondburg royals were gifted with a Pure Light feather from the Swan Princess, as a thank you for their dedicated friendship and allegiance to her. This feather of power granted wisdom to the person who held it, making them into what we called the Oracle, and their wisdom helped the kingdom to prosper.

"For generations, the Oracle feather was passed down through the royal bloodline, with it itself choosing who would inherit the power next. But when the goblins invaded south, during the Goblin Shadow War, and our kingdom was destroyed, the Oracle went into hiding and disappeared, and was never seen again. The survivors of our people fled to other lands, greatly diminished in number, with no one to lead them and no place to call home… That leads us up to where we are today." Papa paused, wiping his eyes. "I believe someone out there is searching for the Oracle feather—and that it's the true reason why we were attacked. The goblins, or someone behind them, wanted to steal it from us."

Apfel tried to listen and understand, gazing up at his papa.

"But the reason I'm telling you this, Apfel, is because your great uncle may still be alive, somewhere—and he was the last person to possess the Oracle power. When he passes away from this life, that power might transfer to you. Only you and I are left of the royal bloodline."

He stared intensely into Apfel's chubby-child face. "Listen, ja? If that power does come to you, you must be very careful. The Oracle is a great responsibility, and the power cannot fall into the wrong hands."

"I bees careful, Papa. I'll punch de bad guys so they go away."

Papa shook his head, half chuckling. "Nein, Apfel. You need to keep yorself hidden." He held his small hands in his palms. "Promise me you will?"

Promise me you will…

…

Apfel woke up as the door to the back of the bakery squealed open, and the owner and hired bakers made their way inside at the break of dawn.

His memory of Papa… It felt so long since they had last been together. Was he looking for him? Would he and Papa ever find each other again?

Was the story about the Pure Light feather true?

Apfel wiped his nose and got up off the floor mat.

Puppy Hazfel, curled beside him, protested.

"C'mon, Hazfel, wakes up."

He let the memory fade away, regretful, and made his way over to the windows to open the shutters.

It was time to begin a new day's work.

～っ

The morning sun blazed through the clear sky, heating the sculpted academy towers and city rooftops, promising a warm day. Aken yawned widely and rubbed at his sagging eyelids. Faint music from the little ballroom's organ drifted up through his dorm window.

The sides of his head ached. It had been one of those nights when he couldn't fall asleep but just laid there with his eyes closed.

A strange feeling had kept him awake. No, more of a *craving*. A craving for something, only he didn't know for *what*.

"For coffee, that's what. I have zero energy," he spoke to the ceiling.

He grumbled and tossed the bed sheets aside. "Does Zartin really have to play music this early?" He let his body slide off the bed and plop onto the rug.

He vaguely wondered what the life of a slug would be like…

Oh well, no point lying here on the floor for a sleep that refused to come!

He hoisted himself onto his feet and coughed; his throat felt parched and scratchy. He grabbed a cup of water off the nightstand, but the scratchy feeling remained.

"*Hnn*. Feels like I caught that cold from Cyrus, if that's even possible."

⸺ᵔ

"Very good, very good. *Mm-hm*. Your timing has greatly improved." Sir Swornyte evaluated Zartanian's morning practice, as his fingers skimmed agilely from note to note across the grand organ's ivory and ebony keys.

Zartanian closed his eyes to better feel the notes and the music swirling around him. "I've practiced every morning I could, before sword practice, as you suggested, Sir."

The gray-skinned man—who was both his music teacher and swordsmaster instructor—nodded gravely. His harsh features gave him a perpetually serious look, and his precise tone of voice furthered that impression. His title "Sir" was for his being a knight in service to the king. He was a talented swordsmaster, as well as a music professor at Draevensett.

Back when Zartanian had lost so much, Swornyte was one of the few people who had helped him find purpose again and pursue his dream of becoming a great swordsmaster.

He owed him a debt of gratitude for that.

"Zartanian, are you feeling unwell?"

He paused at the professor's unexpected question and the music slowly faded. "What do you mean?"

Only then did Zartanian feel the light pressure down his cheek: a tear. Without a word, he wiped it away with the cuff of his blue, collared coat.

Sir Swornyte inclined his head knowingly; there was no need for him to explain the reason out loud. Parents Day was tomorrow at Draevensett, he had overheard from a chatty upper classman. And the reminder was a spear through the hole already bleeding in his heart—a bleeding that would never stop.

'*Mother... Elijob...*' His fingers lay still on the keys, remembering their warmth, their faint smiles.

A light tap on his shoulder brought him back.

Normally he would have shrunk away from the touch, but ever since he'd befriended Cyrus and grown closer to Harlow, it was getting easier. Little by little.

"I am well enough, Sir," he reassured the instructor.

Swornyte's expression remained as stiff as stone, but he acknowledged his words with a nod.

Kaw-kaw! A raven came and perched on the nearest windowsill, peering in through the glass at them. The raven he had since named Corben wanted a treat.

The teacher observed him from down the length of his nose. "Do you remember your goal, Zartanian?" he asked.

Zartanian looked his way timidly at first. Sometimes it was like looking through a mirror at a reflection of himself. From somewhere in the past, Swornyte must have known the same suffering as him. A suffering that was different from those who lost dear ones because of war or illness. A suffering far darker.

"Become what we always dreamed of... Lord God will take care of you." His twin brother's words still dwelled inside his heart.

'Yes, I have a goal. My promise to Elijob.'

He waved a hand at the raven, and it cocked its head at him curiously. "Yes, Sir. I do."

Sir Swornyte inclined his head. "Very good. Come along." He motioned briskly for him to follow. "I want to see how well you are handling the five saber forms that I taught you, and determine if you are ready for the next five."

Zartanian rose, quelling a spark of anxiousness in his chest.

They made their way to the practice grounds. And there, Zartanian noticed another boy, waiting by an array of straw dummies.

"Zartanian, this is one of my other apprentices also pursuing the career of swordsmaster: Mathias Turner," the instructor introduced.

Mathias bowed his head in greeting. Zartanian copied the gesture awkwardly.

"Mathias, run through the first ten sword forms of the saber," Swornyte commanded.

The boy, wearing Floor Earnest's crest, bent his stance and held the sword point down at his side, facing one of the dummies.

When he drew the saber blade up—a real one, not a practice sword—he sliced and curved the blade through the air with grace and ease, flowing through the ten forms, his footfalls moving in precise patterns.

When he finished, sheathing the saber, the dummy's head tumbled off along with its straw hands and limbs.

Zartanian swallowed. That was what he wanted—he needed to move with grace and precision like that.

Zartanian took his turn next, running through the first five forms he'd been taught. He felt clumsy compared to the other student, and was sweating by the end, but he didn't make any mistakes.

"Much improved," said Sir Swornyte, with a crisp nod. He took up his own saber. "You are ready to be shown the next five forms."

Zartanian wiped his forehead with a sleeve, trying not to show his relief that he'd passed the test.

⌒

"Master Nephryte!" Aken whined. "You didn't tell us anything about Parents Day being tomorrow."

He and the other Harlow boys had found the Master, later that day, at one of the iron lattice benches in the school's front courtyard, shuffling through papers in a folder.

"Oh. It is, isn't it? Must have slipped my mind," Nephryte said absently. One of the nearby fountains burbled, water splashing down the green marble depiction of a winged warrior.

"Slipped your mind?" Aken exclaimed. "Since when does *anything* slip your mind?" He slapped the folder away, which flopped to the ground.

Nephryte eyed him levelly. "This is another lesson about life that you must learn, Aken-Shou. Every day's path does not always run smoothly into the next. What you do not expect may come to happen, and tomorrow's plan can crumble in an instant. Situations may arise before you have had time to prepare. That is the way life works."

"You made that up on the spot! You just wanted to stress us out so you could teach us some lame life lesson—*waah!*"

Aken suddenly found himself hanging upside down in the air above the bench.

"Parents Day is for parents. I don't have to remind you that you are orphans. What do you have to be stressed out about?" Nephryte rebuked.

Hercule fixed his golden stare on the Master and spoke three words. Three ominous and emphasized words: "Mother will come."

Aken paused his struggle in the air. Nephryte's features froze. Even the water in the fountain seemed to go still.

"Ah, yes." Nephryte breathed, failing to hide a look of dread building inside him.

Lady Chatsalott was the horror of all male kind.

He released Aken, who fell with a yelp, and he rose from the bench, sending a draft of air to lift and bring the folder back to his hand. "Excuse me, but I must go and...prepare myself."

Bakoa gave a sudden shudder. "I think we all need to..."

8

Parents Day had arrived, and the day's last three classes were canceled for the event. They would have to be careful to avoid Hercule's mother, at all costs. Lord Renald most likely wouldn't show, but the lady would not dare miss out on a chance to feast her eyes upon the handsome men of the academy.

Aken sincerely pitied Hercule in that.

"You, False Guardian, must keep the Swan safe. They are searching for her. Beware."

Apfel's strange words circled his thoughts. He had studied the starlight orb again, but no image of the scarlet haired princess had surfaced.

Instead, his throat continued feeling parched and scratchy. He'd already downed two glasses of milk and a cup of honey tea. Nothing was helping.

'I need… I really need…'

What? What was it he needed?

He growled at himself, wanting to focus during History class.

Yet that craving for *something* wouldn't go away. It was wrecking his concentration.

When he tried to refocus his thoughts again, for the fifteenth time, he found his gaze lingering on Cyrus at the desk next to his.

Cy wore a pale blue shirt today, the color cold against light-peach skin. The fabric curved up and around, bordering the neck, the sleeves short around delicate arm veins...

"Um, Aken?" came Cy's voice.

"*Sotaire!* Sit back doown in your seat!" roared Professor Ponairi's northern accent.

What were they getting so upset about? He *was* sitting in his—

Aken's vision came into focus, and he realized he was standing beside Cy's chair, leaning towards the redhead's left arm.

Aken jerked upright so fast that he nearly fell backwards. *'What am I doing? What was I...? I don't even remember moving.'*

The whole class was staring at him, and Ponairi's glare burned like hot coals.

Aken swallowed before faking a nervous laugh. "Thought I saw a bug. One of those...big beetle things."

Cy tucked in his legs and looked around in alarm.

"Stupid prankster..." someone murmured.

Denim folded his arms in mock pity and shook his head. "Commoners get so easily distracted, don't they? No wonder they can't get a decent education."

Embarrassed, Aken went back to his seat and hid his face behind his history book.

⁓ꝰ

At the end of the shortened school day, Cyrus yawned and carried her schoolbooks up the spiral walkway with Aken. They passed the Floor banner and were about to enter Harlow's main door—emblazoned with the Harlow crest of a small falcon flying into a beaming sun—and put away their books, when a sultry, drawling voice spoke from just beyond the door: "My daaarling! I just haaad to stop by and see how my little angel crumpet is faring, living so far away from home."

Cyrus felt Aken's hand on her arm, halting her. "It's *that* woman," he said in an urgent whisper.

Hercule's dreaded mother—here, so soon? And wandering around on *their* Floor?

They both quickly dropped their books by the door. There was no going inside, not now.

"Great. How do we get away?" she began to ask.

Aken's arms suddenly scooped her legs up off the floor, and she yelped.

"The fastest way!" he told her. And then he launched them both over the walkway's balustrade.

They plunged five-stories to the moon courtyard below—the open, circular garden at the heart of Draevensett, rising to meet them—and she held her breath in a silent scream.

Their fall slowed and Aken managed a Landing on both feet upon the cultivated grass patches. She blinked up at him, her pulse spiking near death.

She almost slapped him for that, but he continued running with her to the nearest exit door.

It felt strange to be carried in someone's arms. For some reason, her face kept heating up.

"What do you say we escape for the day, hide out in Downtown?" he asked her.

"O-okay," was all she managed to reply.

～৩

Hercule tried not to let his embarrassment show as he gave Mother the tour of Draevensett. She was insistent upon seeing every inch of the place, even though she barely paid attention to the school history that he recited from memory.

Instead, her focus drifted to every young man and teacher who passed by.

"Mother…" he groaned.

If only Marigold were here for emotional support! But she was busy with preparations for the Parents Day Ball this evening, and he didn't want to bother her.

It was nice having her around again. A part of him had missed her presence—and Butler Lynk's, too—since moving out of the mansion.

"Oh! Is that Kotetsu Cuore, one of your teachers? My, even if he is of a lowly House such as Cuore, his shape is good-looking," Mother said, at his side. "The eyebrows are a bit much, though."

Hercule wanted to go bury himself.

When they came down the hall which led past the library, he spotted two older students coming from the opposite direction. The boy he recognized as Tyomnii of House Sivortsova, the king's stepson, with night-brown locks and rose-blood eyes. Hercule only let his gaze follow, not shifting his head an inch.

The other student, a kitsune personal slave attendant, gave them a polite nod. Tyomnii faced forward, his countenance dark, his gaze turning ever so slightly to deliver an imperious look towards the members of his rival House.

A trail of attendants followed the woman behind Tyomnii, regally dressed in purple: his mother, the queen by marriage, and also touring the school.

Each woman spared a brief glance at the other in a silent challenge, their eyes narrowed icily.

Lady Chatsalott's hair, shaped like a massive geranium flower today with sprouting lace, was far more extravagant than the other woman's—which was probably why Hercule's mother flashed a proud smirk.

To Hercule, it looked more like a trimmed bush had been plucked from the ground and wrapped around her head with lace—not something to be proud of. He was sure the queen was laughing at her inside.

Once they'd passed by one another, Mother tilted her head and muttered quietly, "Insufferable woman," for only his ears to hear. "And that purple dress is absolutely hideous on her! But I suppose with her drab skin tone, anything would look horrid, wouldn't it?"

Hercule frowned in thought, ignoring his mother's remarks. *They want me to make House Dragonsbane surpass all of the Houses. But how can I be expected to surpass the prince, even if he is only the king's stepson?'* The very notion felt ridiculous. In his mind, the Sivortsova's had already won this round. What more could Father possibly expect?

Mother squealed at the sight of another teacher and went trotting after the man in her high-heels.

Hercule hunched his shoulders. This was going to be a very long day...

⁓

Master Nephryte hurried past the library—away from the woman whose voice rang loud and clear as a giggling gong. Lady Chatsalott was headed his way. There had to be an escape route, somewhere!

The patter of high-heels was closing in on him.

He turned into another hallway and came across a wide recess of indoor trees and plants, like a miniature garden, with wide bay windows and twin benches.

Perfect—just what he needed!

He crept into the tall plants to hide, and abruptly bumped into something.

Something that spoke:

"Shoo, shoo away!"

"Is that *you*, Deidreem?" Nephryte exclaimed, and a black velvet top hat poked up from the foliage, followed by a pair of epidote eyes. "Why are you—?"

"*Shush!*" Deidreem's hand shot up, covering Nephryte's mouth. "Or you'll lead her right to us!"

Nephryte blinked. "Us?"

Mullet hair rose from the bush beside Deidreem.

"Not you too, Eletor," Nephryte groaned. "Hiding like children in a game of hide-and-seek...really, what has become of us?"

More heads poked up from the leaves.

"Kotetsu! Sir Swornyte? Even *you*, Zushil?"

A head of gray hair also rose.

"Principal Han?!"

The principal flashed him a brief smile. "Hello."

"What are *you* doing here?"

"Well, um..."

Just then, the woman's gonging, melodious voice came echoing down the hall: "I thought for certain that I spotted someone handsome come this way."

With a yelp, Eletor dove back under the safety of the leaves, followed by the others.

"If you're too proud to admit that you were trying to *hide*," Deidreem gave a forceful shove to Nephryte's back, shoving him out of the little garden, "Then go play *seek!*"

The woman's voice echoed: "Ooo, I do wonder where that handsome, cutie-wootie Master of yours is, Hercule daaarling. That hottie, Master Nephryte."

Nephryte scrambled to dive back inside the foliage. "Let me back in! *Let me back in!*" But Deidreem stood blocking him, his outstretched palms warding him off.

"*Tsk-tsk*, you're the Master of her dear-and-only son. You'll have to face the woman eventually, whether you like it or not.

So, go do us all a favor and lure her away!"

"Exactly!" Eletor piped up. "Keep her occupied!"

With that, he and Deidreem both shoved a frantic Nephryte out into the open hallway.

"*Hum?* Did I hear something? Hercule, sweetie, did you hear that? I feel as if I am sensing your Master's presence nearby."

Nephryte shook a fist at his coworkers. "You betrayers. I won't forget this!"

He raced down the hallway, desperate to find another hiding place.

Adelheid daintily plopped down in a narrow-backed chair at one of the many tables dotting the academy's cafeteria. A nice and quaint dining area, she supposed, though plain to her taste; it needed flowers and pink. She should speak with Principal Han, next time she saw him, and Deidreem too—wherever they had both gone running off to.

Today her dress was a mix of greens, a bit eastern-style, but flaring with frills below the waist and out. Snug green lace spilled from her elbows to wrists matching the small, green arrow-shaped hat with black feathers pinned in the side of her pink hair.

Taking a bite out of a plum and blackberry cake slice on her plate, she sighed, resting her cheek in a hand. *'I'm so utterly bored. I thought school life was supposed to be exciting.'*

She tried the whole "making friends" routine, as a good spy should, but so many students were avoiding her because she was related to Master Deidreem. Maybe they feared getting into trouble? Deidreem wasn't exactly the most likeable person. And Floor Smart, governed by him, had a cunning reputation— the very Floor they had placed her in.

Idiot Deidreem, didn't he know he was making her investigation harder? "*Hmph!*"

Students were whispering. She could hear them chatting about how petite she was, like a doll, and others snickered that she dressed funny.

'Meh, it's not like I need to make friends. I can do my job just fine without them.' She could care less, either way, though it might have been fun. *'After so many centuries, the world's ways have not changed one single bit.'* Her fingers tightened around the fork.

A small group passed by her table, chatting animatedly about some popular new play they'd seen; she didn't bother to listen. The only thing she took notice of, out the corner of her one eye, was a boy among them with a peculiar face.

Something about him felt oddly familiar. Tall and skinny build, ordinary brown hair in a layered cut and tied back in a short ponytail at the nape of the neck. An overall simple boy. He slowly followed the others, and he was the only one to glance back in her direction.

She looked away with a distasteful frown and busied herself eating cake.

The group claimed a wide table several rows down, digging into today's lunch of cheese pasta and garlic bread. "What do you keep looking at, Mathias?" one boy questioned the ordinary boy; they all wore Floor Earnest's crest: a flying gryphon with claws out and wings outspread.

"Is it that girl?" Eyes flickered her way. "She sure looks strange. Why do you think she has an eyepatch?"

"Every time I see her, I'm afraid I'm gonna drown in frills and girliness."

A cackle of laughter followed.

Only Mathias remained quiet, glancing back at the reclusive girl content to sit all by herself.

"Stupid boys," Adelheid huffed to herself, shoving down a large spoonful of cake icing.

Suddenly a voice spoke beside her, "Is this seat taken?"

Startled, her face whipped around. It was the ordinary boy, and he bowed his head.

'Hm? What is he up to?'

"I suppose not," she said after a moment, sizing him up suspiciously.

He took the narrow chair opposite her. She watched every move while he set a napkin on his lap, took up a fork and began eating pasta.

'Well, at least he seems to have manners when it comes to food. But why is he here, bothering me?'

He glanced at the cake and other desserts on her plate as she daintily ate. "You really like sweets, don't you?"

Her skin prickled. "And why shouldn't I? They are made to be eaten, are they not?"

"Hm?" He swallowed. "I didn't mean it as an insult. Desserts are some of the most splendid creations. I enjoy them very much."

He brushed loose hair strands back behind a pointed ear. "But it's healthy to eat a wide variety of food, not just sweets."

"I know that." Her nose turned up. "I'm not a child, contradictory to what everyone has been saying."

"Oh, sorry." He brushed back more strands. "I'm actually a practicing chef. Well, leaning more towards pastry chef, now. I'm in training to be a swordsmaster, but my hobby joy is making desserts." He flashed her a smile.

Another spoonful of cake shoved into her petite mouth. "Is that so? You should bring me one of your creations, then, and prove to me how skillful you are."

She meant it sarcastically, but the boy's face brightened like it was a challenge. She grumbled. "Do you have a name, or should I call you *boy?*"

"Oh, right." He blushed in flustered apology. "Mathias. *Ahem.* I am Mathias Turner the Third."

"Oh? A little aristocracy blood in you? Who would have guessed," she mused, patting her lips with a napkin.

House Turner, she knew that name. That's why he looked so familiar, like *him*... But this Mathias was most likely nothing more than a distant relative, and not someone of great importance.

"I'm Adelheid." She didn't give a last name, and he waited before realizing she wasn't going to. Everybody knew by now that she was a relative of Deidreem's, from someplace far away, but no one knew more than that.

The toll of Draevensett's bells signaled noon meal's end. She stood to take her leave. Mathias stumbled to stand, as well, and give a courteous bow.

"It has been a pleasure to make your acquaintance, Miss Adel—"

Then he realized she was already gone. "—heid."

Aken half groaned, half yawned, seated tiredly on the edge of a large fountain basin, the stonework depicting merfolk as they chased one another. Overhead, the blue of the sky had deepened into dusk around the chimneys and fanciful roof grotesques.

His throat still scratched, and now the back of his head pounded with a headache. He watched as Cyrus and a cutely smiling Apfel strolled up the plaza towards him.

"Did you finish? Or are yous slacking on the job?" Apfel asked him. Both were licking ice cream cones, cookie dough and coffee flavors; the sight made Aken's vision water. Even Apfel's companion, Hazfel, had a dog treat in its teeth.

"Darn brat. Making me work the day away so you could go off and have fun without me. It was such a pretty day, too." Aken sniffled and raised a hand to the sky. "So warm and bright...but did I get to enjoy it? No. I had to fly around playing delivery-boy for wealthy snobs."

Apfel faced him with no sympathy whatsoever. "It was the promise you mades me, to do a full day's work. So, blame yorself."

"Insensitive, unsympathetic little..." Aken grumbled under his breath. "Well, I hope you had a good time."

"We hads *wonderful* time!" Apfel grinned.

Yap-yap! Hazfel's puppy face wore something like a grin, tail wagging.

Cy nodded, and then from behind his back pulled out a cone piled high with hazelnut ice cream, whip cream and caramel syrup. "And we didn't forget you."

Aken's eyes went wide with delight and he took the cone eagerly. "Oh wow! You're the best, Cy! The best ever!"

Apfel licked his cookie dough cone, watching the two of them interact. "And heres I used to think vempars were scary—not big crybabies. I was taughts a lie my whole life."

Aken made a face at him.

They left the fountain and started to make their way back through the streets to the bakery shop. Apfel finished his cone and cheerfully said, "You still owes me a morning's work."

"Huh?"

"You promised me a *full* day's work. Today, yous only worked from the afternoon to now. You didn't works the morning! You owes me a morning, Goldilocks."

Aken made a sound in his throat and finished off more ice cream. "I thought my nickname was *nerven-something.*"

"Too much effort to say." Apfel shrugged. "Goldilocks's more fun."

Aken rolled his eyes.

The first stars were twinkling overhead now, and a soft breeze swirled through the city streets, ruffling their clothes and hair.

A perfect night for a hunting sabercat to be out, he thought, thinking idly of Sabe.

Ffsssh!

He heard the whisper of movement—something fast—and a black shadow streaked above their heads, crossing the narrow cobblestone street from the rooftops.

"What the—?" Cy jerked his head up, but the shadow was gone.

Aken only just made out a form shrouded in black before it disappeared. He stilled, listening.

Apfel hunkered down and clutched Hazfel to him.

He could feel fear pouring out of the child. He touched the little faeryn's shoulder. It was as if Apfel had experienced this before.

"Don't worry, guys," Aken reassured them. "If it comes back to bother us, I'll deal with it."

"But...who was it?" The redhead scanned the narrow street and buildings around them and every gargoyle at the gutters of roofs. "Or *what?*"

Aken didn't answer, hoping that his guess was wrong.

There was no one else around on this stretch of street, not a soul going for a walk, no bikes or motor carriages.

Nothing. They were alone in the deepening night...

Except for *it*.

9

A lavish feast was spread throughout Draevensett's dining hall. Red and pink flowers of the season filled vases, and every utensil and gold chandelier glistened. The furniture had been rearranged and divider screens removed to create a clear floor space for ballroom dancing. An orchestra at the back played string and woodwind instruments, led by Sir Swornyte. The colorful birds, dragons and warriors in the ceiling paintwork and sculptures gazed down at the glamorous assembly below.

Bakoa, Zartanian, Mamoru and Lykale—dressed in fine suits and jabot neckties—sat at Harlow's table, squished together at the far end. On the opposite end were Master Nephryte, Hercule and his overbearing, chatter-box mother.

Poor Master was having a rough time. He had managed to avoid the woman for most of the day, but now, at the ball, he was cornered. He fidgeted with the silver buttons on the cuffs of his indigo, silver-trim tailcoat.

Bakoa sweated nervously in his brown suit, tugging at his yellow ocher necktie. The lady kept getting up and correcting how they held their forks, their glasses, and straightening their ties. And the talking—her voice went on and on and *on*.

Hercule gave them apologetic glances whenever she wasn't looking. Aken and Cyrus were both lucky not to be stuck here—wherever they were.

After an hour in, the lights shifted and the music changed.

The ballroom dance had begun. The student choir now accompanied the music, and clusters of parents, Masters, and students took to the floor.

Hercule's mother insisted Nephryte accompany her, and he tried in vain to make an excuse and refuse. But she wouldn't hear of it and practically dragged him by the arm. For a while, the Harlow boys lost sight of them in the crowd.

Hercule rose. "I need to…clear my head," he said, and he made his way towards the farthest wall and the table booths full of pastries there.

Mamoru and Lykale both stood, as well, and went to mingle with the crowd.

"Bakoa, Zartanian."

Still at the table, and unsure what to do with themselves, both boys looked up when Master Nephryte called to them. He had managed to escape Lady Chatsalott's grasp on the dance floor—tossing her off to Master Eletor before disappearing, the poor guy now frantically flailing about for any excuse to get away, as the lady batted her eyelashes and squeezed his arms in a dance hold.

"Do you know where Aken and Cyrus are?" Master Nephryte asked them.

Both boys shook their heads. "They sort of disappeared once classes ended," Bakoa told him.

The Master straightened, tapping a finger against his chin.

"Are you gonna dance at all, Master Nephryte?" Bakoa grinned.

"Mm…" He gave a fearful glance in Lady Dragonsbane's direction. "I think not. A task such as dancing can be far more deadly than doing battle with Argos."

The Harlow boys twitched, trying not to laugh.

"I wish there were more girls our age to dance with. I really wanna dance." Bakoa bounced on his heels. "Hey, look! There's Master Seren-Rose. And Cherish and Adelheid!" He bounded towards them, waving.

Zartanian shuddered and hid behind Nephryte. When Cherish's wheelchair steered their way, the shy boy ducked behind the table, no doubt fearing they might ask him to dance.

"Lady Seren-Rose." Master Nephryte bowed. "You look as lovely as a rose this evening."

Bakoa muffled a giggle behind his hand.

Nephryte flashed him a sidelong look.

Seren-Rose wore a burgundy dress, the knee-high slit slanting down in rippling waves to her ankles; the dress sandals shimmered with silver accents and they matched her silver gloves and the silver threads woven through her night-black hair. A small topaz jewel dangled down her forehead.

Cherish's dress was honey gold and peach, pleated and layered with long lace sleeves; honey flowers were pinned in her wavy hair. Adelheid wore a crimson dress with puffy skirt and short sleeves, black lace trimming, matching black elbow-length gloves and high stockings. A corsage of crimson roses on a black headband nestled in her baby-pink hair.

Bakoa stood mesmerized by them all.

"Charming as ever, Master Nephryte." Seren-Rose's full red lips tweaked a smile.

"You should dance with her!" Bakoa whispered up to him, cupping a hand to his mouth.

Nephryte glanced off to the side. Was he nervous?

"Cherish, do you wanna dance with me?" Bakoa asked.

Cherish lowered her hand from her grin, watching the Masters. "My legs aren't quite strong enough for that, yet. But perhaps another time."

"Aw, shucks. I'm sorry."

"It's okay, Bakoa. I'm glad you thought to ask." She nudged Adelheid beside her. "You should take my place, Adel. Didn't you just tell me how much you love to dance?"

"Hm? Oh, I suppose." Her single eye regarded him, her eyepatch purple this evening.

With a wide grin, Bakoa took Adelheid's gloved hand and led her onto the dance floor.

Lady Seren-Rose chuckled, tapping her silver glove against her collarbone. "He's wise, that student of yours. Straightforward, not wasting time to say what's on his mind. Perhaps we should take a lesson from him?"

Nephryte sighed through his nose. "Only the young and innocent can be so carefree. Darkness has not yet stained their souls."

"Darkness, hm…" she repeated to herself, then lifted her chin to meet his far-off gaze. "Each of us has had a stain on our soul, at some point in our lives, Nephryte. But we do not live to punish ourselves for it," she told him. "God has already washed those stains away."

Off to the side, resting in her wheelchair, Cherish listened. What darkness were they referring to? What had happened in the past?

The words brought a sad smile to Nephryte's lips, and he held out a hand for her to take, asking her formally, "May I have this dance, fair lady?"

"Always." Seren-Rose's slender hand placed in his.

Cherish watched as they danced a slow waltz; his hand on the small of her back, her hand on his shoulder. The way they looked at each other, the soft glow in their eyes, it seemed as if they longed to be more than just childhood friends. And yet, something was there keeping them apart. Some invisible wall that the vempar man had built around himself.

'*Why? Why would you keep at bay someone you loved?*' Cherish silently wondered.

⁓

Adelheid refused to dance a second round, claiming she'd had enough for one evening, and sent Bakoa skipping toward a pack of girls that she'd spotted: sisters of students. She had asked him questions about Harlow and the half-human, working to pry something useful out of him. But he barely gave any answers at all, instead spinning her about and giving her a headache. He strutted away now, all cheerful grins, over to the girls, and she went to sit and recuperate.

"Uh…"

She heard a noise. Did someone speak? She turned her neck, looking this way and that.

"I…"

There it was again. Were they talking to her or not?

"I was wondering if…"

She followed the voice's trail up, tipping her head back to see the tall, well-dressed figure suddenly before her. The ordinary boy, Mathias. Her single eye blinked.

"Miss Adelheid." He gave a simple smile with an awkward bow. "Would you give me the honor of a dance?"

Really. He wanted to dance?

Her eye narrowed. What was he up to? Asking the girl his friends had laughed at to dance?

She turned her nose haughtily. "*You* are asking *me* to dance? Someone as plain, and clearly not very rich, as you? *Hmph.*" She sniffed, rising from her seat and turning away on pump heels, the skirt of her crimson dress twirling with her. "Ask me again once you've got some wealth on you and your appearance doesn't remind me of a chipmunk." She marched away, shoes clacking against the marble floor, face cool while her hands clenched her skirt.

Mathias had frozen mid-bow while she spoke, and now he slowly straightened, watching her go, letting his hand fall back to his side.

Adelheid made her way through the dining hall until she spotted Deidreem, over at a punch bowl. She waited until he glanced her way, and then nodded her chin—the signal for him to leave and take care of business, while she made sure to distract anyone who might look for him.

Deidreem made his way to the arched doorway leading outside, onto the veranda, the least conspicuous way for him to leave the ball.

⤙

Finished helping to serve the many dinner courses, Marigold's next task was to stand behind the table booths of heaping desserts to serve guests.

Her feet ached while she stood in stiff pumps, and her stomach growled, not having had a bite to eat yet. Servants and slaves ate their meals after everyone else, and the day had been far too busy for her to catch an earlier snack. She groaned as her nose smelled all the delicious food and her stomach gurgled in angry protest.

"Excuse me, Miss Marigold."

She jumped to attention, but there was no one on the other side of the booth waiting to be served.

A light shoulder tap brought her head around to find Hercule behind the table booth with her and holding a plateful of caramelized vegetables and pastries. His hair was slicked back, and he wore his finest red suit and waistcoat.

"I'm in quite a predicament," he began, his expression serious. "I took all of this delicious food, thinking I would eat it, but after having such a full dinner, and then dancing with my tiresome mother…" he heaved an exasperated sigh, "I find that I cannot make room in my stomach for *this*. As my personal attendant, it is now your job to dispose of the food for me. But don't throw it away! I hate the thought of wasting food when there are people in the world going hungry." His hand casually held the plate out to her. "Can you solve my…*predicament?*"

She blinked for a moment and then with a grateful look took the plate. "I think I might be able to do something with it, milord."

"I thank you, miss."

She downed a thick, creamy cannoli, feeling her tired spirit slowly begin to revive.

Hercule stayed with her behind the booth, avoiding the crowd and bothersome guests. She was grateful for the company. And he looked more handsome tonight than ever.

Her cheeks wanted to blush, but she was careful to let nothing show. After all, she was nothing more than a slave attendant.

Hercule whispered to her about how awful his mother had been throughout the entire day, and she gave him sympathetic looks, though a small grin did slip out. He noticed and mock chided her for finding humor in his misery.

She tried to bite back her mirth, and Hercule shook his head. Together they spied Lady Chatsalott, over in a circle of women a ways off, her expression as sulky as a wet cat.

"What's made her bitter this time?" Marigold whispered.

"Mother heard through some conversation that the half-human is on my Floor. I have no doubt she'll try to change Master Nephryte's mind about keeping Cyrus."

"Oh my."

"Exactly. Thankfully, our Master is not a pushover. She won't get her way."

"And that will make her very unhappy once she's back home."

"Yes. Let's be glad we live *here* and won't be going back to the mansion tonight."

"Indeed."

As they continued to watch, Tyomnii's mother came into view, and Chatsalott instantly changed her sulky tune and became her boisterous, proud self again, bragging about some recent accomplishment with her husband's silk farms.

The queen barely gave her a moment's notice, instead gliding in her rich velvet skirts past her.

The other women quickly abandoned Chatsalott to follow and speak with the queen, leaving the lady fuming and pulling out a black lace fan to fan herself.

Hercule and Marigold shared a look, holding in chuckles which threatened to spill out.

~∂

Cherish quietly wheeled her way out of the dining hall and onto the veranda, open to the night air and overlooking a portion of the school grounds and a row of cypresses. The stars and partial moon shone brightly, a silver wisp of cloud here and there caressing the darkness like silver scarves.

She sighed, resting her elbows on the white balustrade, chin in hands, staring off at nothing in particular. It was a lonely night. A beautiful and lonely night.

'*I thought Cyrus would be here…*' she thought.

She liked the redhead boy. He was thoughtful and carried himself with dignity; and even though they'd just met, she sensed a kindred spirit in him. But maybe some things just weren't meant to be.

Who could ever like Cherish, anyway? An invalid, she would grow old and die alone.

Moving her chin, she let her forehead drop in her hands instead and exhaled. *'If I had just one person in my life, just one, who really understood me...I wouldn't feel alone. So stupidly alone.'*

Footsteps clacked on the veranda, and she lifted her head quickly, pretending she wasn't doing anything—that she hadn't been talking to herself and acting pathetic.

Through the mix of shadow and light cast by the tall dining hall windows, Master Deidreem strode past her, his top hat in hand. The filtered light gave a purple tinge to the curls of his dark hair. "There's a fine breeze tonight," he commented when he noticed her there, and he made a show of breathing in the air. "Cool and fresh from the mountains."

She took her arms off the handrail and turned in her wheelchair.

"But what's this, now?" His stride paused. "A fair maiden who has yet to dance?"

"Oh..." Her gaze averted, her fingers fiddling with a bit of lace on the skirt of her dress. "I'm not sure that I could."

"Nonsense. Every lady can dance." He bowed, holding out a hand.

"I said, I cannot." She stated more firmly.

"Oh?" The vempar man kept his offered hand out. "Is the noble little dove becoming too proud? Not willing to take a risk and push beyond her limits? That's not the sort of person Master Seren-Rose describes you to be."

Her Master had been talking about her? Cherish chewed the inside of her cheek. Maybe it was true, she was acting like the spoiled rich girl she strived not to be.

She considered his outstretched hand, then carefully placed her hand in his.

His smile tweaked. "A slow dance should be easy enough." He let her lean on him for support as she stood, legs wobbling a little. Once she was steady on her feet, he took her hand in his and placed the other around her back, under the shoulders for support, and they followed the echoing music through a simple waltz.

Dancing…it was nice to dance again. Though he did most of the work, practically carrying her. Her spirits felt lifted, the gloom of earlier gradually fading.

"You see, little dove?" Deidreem slowly twirled with her. "Learn to spread your wings, and I bet you can fly."

That unwittingly brought a small smile to her lips.

Deidreem was a mystery. He was the youngest Master, with hardly anything known about his past, except that he was distantly related to Assistant Principal Pueginn and a few others—they all shared the same storm cloud skin.

"Is there a boy catching your attention of late?" His question took her by surprise. "At the picnic, I noticed you chatting with the half-human for quite a while."

She panicked. "*Crud,* am I that obvious?"

He smiled, though it never seemed like those smiles reached the soul behind his eyes.

She cleared her throat; that wasn't very ladylike of her. "I liked him a little. But I don't think he notices me in that way," she replied, and she stepped away to rest against the balustrade, leaning her weight off her legs. "Perhaps I'm not his type? I don't know… What do you think I should do?"

Deidreem looked from her up to the starry sky. "To be honest, I'm the wrong person to ask when it comes to matters of the heart. I don't care much for it."

Somehow, that didn't surprise her. But she still asked, "How can that be, Master? Didn't you have feelings for the first girl you kissed?"

His expression became clouded, his lips parted. "There wasn't time for such things where I…grew up." He stopped himself short of saying something more, the invisible walls thickening behind his yellow-green eyes. "Do keep that a secret for me, will you?" He pressed a finger to his lips in gesture of silence and winked.

She inclined her head, baffled.

"Treasure your first, Lady Cherish," he told her. "And make sure the boy truly deserves you before you give it away." He stepped back with a bow. "Sadly, I must leave and attend to a personal matter. But do enjoy the rest of the ball tonight with your friends."

She curtsied, and he made his way to the veranda steps, leaving the ballroom music and her alone with her thoughts.

For the first time, she felt like he had been honest and not playacting, and she had caught sight of something dark brooding deep inside him.

Where did he grow up? What secret could he be hiding?

Cherish brushed out a hair tangle with her fingers.

The night didn't seem so lonely anymore.

A distance away, and out of sight of the veranda, Deidreem placed the top hat firmly on his head, cursing at himself.

How could he allow himself to slip and say that? And to a student, no less! He let down his guard when he should have known better. But for some reason, seeing the girl so sad and alone, he couldn't stop himself—it reminded him too much of the past, of his younger self and the innocent life that had been stolen away from him…

"*Tch!* Since when have I ever cared about a Draev's feelings?" The bitterness inside him roiled. "I suppose this Master job does require that I help students when they are in distress. I was just playing my role, that's all," he reassured himself.

He quickened his pace across the path towards the academy's front. "But now, it is time for me to do my *real* job." His lips curled up. "There's a moonlight faeryn to catch."

10

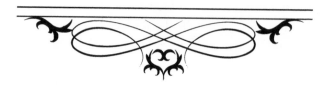

Huntter inhaled and exhaled slowly, calming the rush of his beating heart.

He kept the hood of his camouflage cloak up as he made his way through Draethvyle's Outskirts—the poor district, located outside the eastern city wall, where structures were wood and the marketplaces low quality. And where it was easier for an intruder like him to sneak through into the city—hopefully.

This was daring, even for him, but it was also the only way that he could locate Cyrus and see how she was doing.

The last time he had seen her—his betrothed—she was disguised as a vempar and had made friends at the Draevs' academy. Some idiot blond vempar was with her, too.

But what was her situation now?

Had she been found out, or was she still continuing to train as a Draev?

The questions ate away at him, fueling his resolve to find her.

Once she did decide to give up on becoming a Draev, he would be there waiting for her, and they would travel south together, far from the kingdom of vempars and away from the *life-suckers'* reach.

Now, Huntter followed the dirt paths all the way to the city wall. The arch of the gateway leading into the city came into view, and he stopped to crouch behind a parked cart beside a blacksmith stall, closed for the night.

Huntter tried not to breathe in the dusty air, still calming down from his earlier sprint across the grasslands. He had reached the Outskirts unnoticed, but there had been several close encounters. He'd had to lay flat against the ground with his camouflage cloak when a Draev appeared nearby, patrolling the area.

But here, hood up, he looked like any other homeless vempar wandering the streets in the late dusk.

Pulling out a tiny mirror from his inner coat pocket, he used it to look around behind him at the gateway—still open, if it ever closed.

Three armed guards and one Draev were visible, the Draev keeping watch from the overlooking wall top.

Huntter tilted the mirror about, searching. There was no blind spot, no place to sneak along without any of them noticing him. The partial moon shone brightly, and few people were walking about to distract the guards.

He frowned, his nails digging into the ground.

'I have to check in on Cyrus—I have to see how she's doing,' he thought desperately. *'Please, make a way for me to get through!'*

While his mind raced for ideas how to get past the guards, something started to rattle.

As Huntter waited, the sound grew louder, drawing near.

He craned his neck carefully for a look: There was a mule-drawn cart coming up the dirt street, full of repair tools, and it was headed straight for the gate.

This was his chance.

Huntter waited, until the very moment when the cart crossed the moon shadow of the blacksmith stall, before he smoothly rolled into the street, arms across his chest—his body hidden by the shadows.

The mule stepped around him, but the cart itself still passed over him, wheels barely missing his elbows. Underneath the cart, he dug his fingers and shoe tips into cracks and gaps in the wood-planking underside.

The cart continued to move along, with him clinging underneath.

After the driver exchanged conversation and paperwork with a female guard at the gate, her rifle-axe blade glinting in the moonlight, the cart soon continued its journey through and into the city.

～ゎ

"Hide! We gots to get away," said Apfel in a fervent whisper, his features wide in terror, his arms clutching Hazfel tightly to him. He hunkered between Aken and Cyrus like a trembling fawn.

Cyrus craned her neck back to tell the small faeryn that everything would be okay, but then her ears picked up another swishing sound.

Aken shifted into a ready stance, facing the noise. "Keep behind me," he told them.

Cyrus concentrated, manipulating the metal from her feather bracelets to wrap around both her arms. She was about to tell him she could help, when *something* from the rooftop shadows lunged down.

A gaping mouth with rows of dagger teeth opened wide, blacker than the night, and calcite eyes within a mask of bone focused on them. The creature landed on the street and moved with unnatural speed towards them.

It was the Corpsed—the same one that had come after her before!

Cyrus raised her metal arms in defense. Apfel screamed, clinging to Hazfel behind her.

"Don't even try it, creep!" shouted Aken.

A piece of street before Cyrus erupted in a fiery spout of lava, striking the Corpsed in the gut before its clawed hands could reach them.

Kreeeea! came its high-pitch screech, like the sound of fingernails scraping down chalkboard. It hopped backwards from the lava.

This part of the street had few streetlamps, making it difficult to see the Corpsed. The oval orbs that were its eyes glowed faintly, and black silver claws glinted along multi-jointed, corpse-like limbs. Tattered black fabric rustled about its body, a hood only partially concealing its leather and bone head. A second pair of skeletal arms burst free from its chest beneath the cloak.

Black silver—she remembered the metal was dangerous to vempars. Wounds couldn't Heal properly; a stab in the right spot could kill.

Her hand grabbed Aken's shoulder as he stood in front of them, facing the creature. "Watch out, the black silver—"

Wait. Was that *blood* smeared along the creature's skeletal fingers?

Aken let out a choked sound.

She turned at his pained cough; his left hand now clutched his side, though he kept both his feet planted firmly on the cobblestones.

"Aken!"

A red trickle was running down the leg of his pants.

The Corpsed had somehow stabbed him before the lava sent it back. It had happened so fast, she didn't even see it.

"*Nng*—I'll bring that sucker down," Aken reassured her, a surge of anger rising over the sharp, burning pain he must now be feeling.

The creature moved silently, sideways like a crawling spider, circling them, its bloody claws waiting.

Aken stepped with its steps, circling to keep in front of Cyrus and Apfel. It would charge soon. He sent out five small clay birds beneath its sight.

Circling them both, the Corpsed sprang forward with a sudden hiss.

Aken channeled *essence*, and the waiting clay birds swooped up, one after another, exploding in the creature's face.

Kreeee! It crawled sideways to evade the explosions. Several hit, but they could see the damage wasn't great. It continued forward in a circling, sideways shamble, very angry.

Aken had to admit the creature could move faster than him. But its attention kept focusing on Cyrus and Apfel. Why?

Circling and circling, Aken hurried to keep up with it, to keep himself between it and them. It desperately wanted them, trying to lose Aken and attack their backs. "I can't keep up with it, Cy! Turn your full body metal!" he shouted.

"*All* metal?" Cyrus exclaimed. She didn't know how to do that yet!

She concentrated, keeping Apfel and the dog sandwiched between her and Aken.

The silent skeletal form circled closer, *closer*; fear welled inside her, ruining her focus.

How bad was Aken's injury? She couldn't tell in the dark. He was tough, but black silver could make that meaningless. He could bleed to death before his body Healed.

'*Why does this creature keep showing up around me?*'

Clay birds circled in the opposite direction, catching the black fabric's fringes on fire. The Corpsed hissed and, in a sudden burst of speed, closed the distance between them—the claws of three hands poised to pierce Aken through, while its fourth clawed hand slashed in a downward arc to rip Cyrus's chest open.

Spouts of lava exploded all around them, a brief wall of searing yellow, forcing the creature back. The Corpsed evaded the lava attacks swiftly and kept coming when the spouts died down.

They were outmatched. They were going to die. And neither she nor Aken could move fast enough to do anything about it.

Aken turned his back to the oncoming Corpsed and pushed Cyrus and Apfel out of harm's way. Her eyes widened in horror as she fell backwards, her hand outstretched yet unable to reach him.

Aken waited for the impact, when he would feel claws ripping through his back, ending his life.

And then...

K-blam!

Was that...a gun shot?

Aken whirled back around to face the Corpsed, and watched as it stumbled several steps backwards, a black silver bullet through the head. Liquid thick like oil dripped down its leathery flesh and bone mask from the hole.

A new figure materialized from the shadows and night mist.

Another shot fired, and another, into the creature's arm and left leg. "Don't just stand there, you dunce vempar! It's not dead. Get Cyrus to safety!"

They both recognized that commanding voice.

Aken gaped. "The bossy, lone wolf human?"

"Idiot vempar," Huntter retorted. His teeth gritted, and he held the gun poised to fire again.

Aken spared a look over his shoulder at Cyrus, who held Apfel protectively, and Hazfel growling before their feet.

"I'll ask later what on eartha you're doing here," said Aken. "But right now, cover me as I rain lava down on that thing! If we don't finish it now, it'll never leave us alone."

"I don't take orders from—" Huntter growled, but the vempar wasn't listening, already charging forward and setting off spout after spout of lava up from the cobblestones, trying to herd and corner the skeletal being.

Huntter let out an irritated breath, then fired off shots when the Corpsed opened its mouth to release a black beam of energy—the bullets forcing the beam to miss.

The patch of street where the dark energy hit shriveled to dust, as if the darkness had swallowed every bit of life even from the stones.

He then fired again when it tried to circle Aken.

Together, they were managing to back the creature up against a laundry shop's brick wall.

"Now, vempar!" Huntter shouted, and Aken summoned the biggest lava spout he could muster.

Aken pressed his palms to the ground, with a shout, and the stonework beneath the creature exploded in a shower of brilliant red and yellow.

It took a moment for the air to clear before they could see. The Corpsed rose from where it had fallen and hissed from its bone mask face, now even more determined and hungry for the kill.

"*Still* not dead?" Aken exclaimed.

A shower of metal needles flew past and into the creature's ribbed sides. Aken flashed Cyrus a grin, Cy's hand on a metal waterspout.

The creature hissed, glaring at Cy, and swiveled its head about as if trying to see the little faeryn.

Aken's teeth gritted and his hand clutched the stab wound in his side.

"There's no point in wasting more bullets," Huntter voiced, now standing beside Aken and facing the Corpsed.

"Destroy the bone mask!" Cyrus called out, recalling how the Master and other Draevs had worked together to destroy the first Corpsed.

With Huntter's help, they might be able to pull it off.

"I'll come at it from the left and aim for the head with my gun's attached blade," Huntter told Aken. "You come at it from the right and take off any limbs you can. Cyrus, keep it busy with those needles!"

"Who made *you* boss?" Aken retorted.

"Just do what I said. Go!" Huntter started off, curving left, without checking to see if he would follow.

Aken did follow suit, curving right. Together they formed a pincer-move, closing in on either side of the skeletal being. The blade on Huntter's gun clicked out, ready to slice. Aken's palms filled with clay birds, ready to hit its limbs.

Cyrus released volley after volley of metal arrows, careful not to hit them.

The Corpsed snarled as Huntter came close, and his blade curved in an upward slice at the neck; Aken dodged its black silver claws and sent clay birds to blast its elbows.

FWoom!

The world turned upside down suddenly, and air rushed past Aken's ears. He found himself falling through the sky, legs splayed, and the rooftops below.

What the...? It had happened so fast that he didn't even feel when his body was grabbed and thrown into the air.

The Corpsed's bone mask grinned horribly up at him from below.

'I don't have any more clay birds,' he realized.

And Limitless wasn't in his pocket—he must have misplaced the bird somewhere earlier. "I can't fly!" His arms flapped frantically.

Off to his right, Huntter was also falling, and he glared across at Aken. "You really are the stupidest vempar ever," he shouted against the wind.

"You're seriously picking a fight *now?*" Aken could barely speak, let alone breathe!

"You're a Draev, you idiot! Use your *essence* and slow our fall," Huntter barked.

"Uh—I was going to!"

"Then shut your mouth and do it; we're about to *die!*"

Essence gathered in Aken's feet, becoming a cushioning cloud and slowing his fall. "Sounds like someone needs some anger management," he muttered, grabbing hold of Huntter's coat and wrapping an arm around the human's chest while slowing their descent.

They landed roughly on the street.

"Get off," Huntter shoved him away and hoisted himself to his feet.

With Apfel and Hazfel in her metal-strengthened arms, Cyrus ran. The metal attack wasn't doing much, and the Corpsed was now coming after *her* while the boys were falling.

She used Leaping and Landing, jumping back and forth between the street and the rooftops, doing anything she could to keep ahead of the creature.

One of the claws on its long, double-jointed arms caught the back of her pants, yanking her down so that she hit the cobblestones. She rolled, landing on her back instead of on Apfel, the air knocked out of her lungs.

The Corpsed grinned, towering over her like a wraith of death.

It raised a third clawed hand from its torso, drawing it back, ready to stab into her chest.

"*Grah!*" Aken slammed into the Corpsed from the side, knocking it off balance.

It screeched angrily and shot all four of its clawed arms out at him.

Aken dodged two, and Huntter's bullet knocked the third hand aside. But with all of the fast movements, Huntter's next bullet missed the fourth arm—and its set of black silver claws caught Aken and ripped into his chest.

"Aken!" Cyrus screamed.

Huntter made a futile attempt to reach him, his handgun raised.

Aken stared at his chest.

The Corpsed rasped something like a laugh.

In that moment, the blade of Huntter's gun struck from behind—slicing clean through the creature's bone mask.

The Corpsed gave a shudder. Then the mask cracked in half, and its head began to disintegrate.

A smaller skull behind the mask became visible, briefly, before the skin, body and limbs all folded in on itself.

Nothing was left afterwards but fabric and black silver parts...

Cyrus briefly wondered how Huntter's blade could dispose of the bone mask in one blow, unless the gun blade was special in some way. She was too busy to ponder, instead running to Aken's side as he slumped down to the ground.

Meanwhile, Huntter vanished into the shadows of a dark space between two buildings.

Cyrus reached her fallen friend, on her knees. "Aken..." Unbidden tears welled in her eyes.

Aken's hand shakily lifted from the ground to rest on top of hers, his features pale. Blood blossomed his shirt.

Apfel remained frozen where he sat on the bumpy street with Hazfel. "What was that evil?" he whimpered to the air.

"I have to get Aken help," cried Cyrus. "Huntter? Where are you?" She looked around, but for some reason he had vanished.

The street was empty, except for the Corpsed's remains.

"Huntt...?" she carefully asked the darkness.

Out of the night came a voice, but it wasn't Huntter's:

"Oh? What have we here?"

Cyrus looked up at the charming tone.

From the rooftop overhead, a man leaped down, gliding gracefully until the soles of his polished shoes touched the cobblestones. Moonlight framed his coattails, top hat and white gloves. "Seems you've been in a fight with something. That's a nasty wound he has there."

Master Deidreem. He knelt at Aken's side, placing a hand on either side of the bloody wounds. A purple glow enveloped the injuries, working to stop the bleeding. "Injuries from black silver need outside assistance," he said, the note in his tone regarding them like bothersome children. "I'm honestly surprised you're still alive. I do not think many other students would still be breathing this world's air, right now." His brief smile didn't reach his eyes. "You're a tough little monster, Aken-Shou, thanks to your Pureblood."

Aken coughed against the pain, digging his nails into the cobblestones beneath him.

"Master Deidreem, it was a Corpsed—the same one that we saw at school," Cyrus spoke up. A part of her wondered why the Master was out on the streets and not at the academy's ball.

Deidreem's attention shifted to her, then across to Apfel. The greyhound was licking the child's hands. His gaze lingered.

"Master?"

The glow from his hands faded, and the bleeding slowed to a stop.

Aken mustered enough strength to sit up. "The Draev patrols must be seriously slacking off, letting this creature through *twice*."

"Yes, I'll have to look into that." Deidreem rose from his knees. "It's nearly past curfew. What are you doing out here so late, and during the Parents Day Ball, may I ask and wonder?"

Crud, if Master Nephryte found out...

While Aken tried to mutter some excuse, Deidreem stopped by the Corpsed's remains. He deftly pulled from his sleeve a wide, black cloth: letting it spread and rest over the remains. With a whispered word, he whisked the cloth away and the remains were gone.

Cyrus blinked several times. Was that really Elemental Manipulation?

"Aken-SHOU!"

Uh-oh. They recognized that shout.

Aken cast his head about for a place to hide, though his body couldn't much move.

Master Nephryte landed on the street with a thunderous stomp. His blue-river eyes glowed fiercely and fixed upon each one of them. Even Deidreem flinched back.

"I—I was...we were just..." Aken stammered.

"—Going for a walk!" Deidreem cut in. "We couldn't handle the school's claustrophobic atmosphere—the crowd, the noise, and Lady Chatsalott. We simply had to escape for a breath of fresh air."

Nephryte's eyelid twitched involuntarily at the mentioned name. "I suppose *that* I could understand. But neither of you even showed up to the ball, while the rest of Harlow did! And why is there blood on your shirt, Aken-Shou?" His gaze narrowed.

"It was that same Corpsed—it came after us again." Aken tried to stand but fell back.

Nephryte's brow furrowed, and he approached for a closer look. "You were attacked?"

Aken nodded, wincing.

"Are you sure that's what it was?"

Cyrus pointed. "It had black silver and a bone mask. Its remains were right over there."

Nephryte looked to where she pointed, yet nothing remained.

"That creature wasn't a Corpsed, young students," Deidreem interrupted them. "I saw the figure as it ran off, clearly a thief wearing a mask, and he had on hand dagger claws."

Cyrus frowned, turning her puzzled face to him.

"Thieves walk about this time of night, and you looked like easy targets," Deidreem surmised.

Cyrus turned back to Master Nephryte. "No, it was a *Corpsed*. We saw it up close! And Huntt—" She stopped short. They couldn't know about Huntter, an Argos-in-training, being in the city.

Deidreem shook his head. "In the dark, I suppose anything can look like a scary monster to a kid."

"We're not kids," Aken growled.

Nephryte slashed his arm through the air. "Enough! I've had a rotten day, as it is, without you adding more trouble to it. We're going back. Deidreem, don't pester my students." Ropes of air moved around Cyrus and Aken, lifting them up.

Deidreem made a face.

"Wait, Master!" Cyrus pleaded. "We have to bring Apfel. *Please!* He needs a place to stay."

She didn't want to risk another creature coming after the child tonight.

Nephryte paused and considered the faeryn.

"Very well. He can remain with us for a little while. But you had better do some explaining."

From the shadows, Huntter watched the Masters and somber students depart, disappearing over the city rooftops. He holstered his gun *Bloody Thistle*.

He didn't even get a chance to speak with Cyrus...

She seemed well, at least. But she no longer wore false fangs or hid her ears, which meant that a lot of things had changed since he last spoke with her.

She wasn't hiding her race anymore. A human training to become a Draev... His hands fisted at the thought.

'They accepted her? I wasn't expecting that... And that idiot vempar is still by her side.'

He had seen the metal coating her arms—she was mastering her Ability, just like she wanted. At least *that* was a good thing.

But what was a Corpsed doing here?

And why had that one Master lied about it?

Master Nephryte laid the injured boy on a sofa in his dorm flat, and Cyrus followed. The school's atmosphere was mostly silent now, with most everyone asleep or in their dorms.

The Master assessed the damage, feeling around the scabbed-over wounds.

"Ouch! Would you stop that? You're worse than a fussy mother hen!" Aken complained.

"And you're louder than a howler monkey. I just want to make sure that you're—"

"I'm fine." Aken sat up, pushing his hands away. Too quickly, though, as he clutched his head.

"Dizzy?" Nephryte's fingers pressed against Aken's brow.

Cyrus simply watched, guessing that he was helping to lessen the headache somehow.

"You're dehydrated." Nephryte handed him a glass of

berry juice. "Here. Drink."

Too exhausted to protest, Aken took the glass.

"Will he be okay?" Bakoa sounded worried, from beside Cyrus, and he fidgeted his toes on the fancy rug. He had spotted them when they entered the Floor and had followed, fretting and asking questions.

"Yes," Master Nephryte reassured. "Though, it is a miracle. The stab wounds didn't penetrate deep enough, as they're curved. And Aken-Shou has exceptional Healing capability." The Master looked from Aken to Cyrus. "Are you sure it couldn't have been anything else but a Corpsed?"

They both nodded.

"Well, the injuries do resemble claw marks; but they could be from a set of hand dagger claws, too, black silver ones... There's never been a Corpsed in the city before. I don't even see how it would be possible." His expression clouded over while he thought.

She felt that he believed them, but was trying and failing to make any sense of it.

"Can I have some of that berry juice, too? I'm thirsty." Bakoa moved to the cool-box.

"I'm sorry, Bakoa, but it's for Aken-Shou. He needs the vitamins." Nephryte patted the blond on the shoulder with a firm hand. He rose, and wind-levitated the boy up off the sofa. "You'll be more comfortable sleeping in your own room. Bed rest should do you good."

"Stop, put me down! Let me keep my dignity!"

Aken's pleas fell on deaf ears, however, as the Master carried him away.

Giving a tired yawn, Bak left too, with Apfel and the nervous puppy tagging along after him.

Alone now, hand on her hip, Cyrus shook her head in disbelief over how the day had turned out.

How Aken could survive being stabbed *twice* by black silver was beyond her. Scourgebloods really were different creatures.

She turned to a biology book whose cover stared up at her. With so much going on lately, she still hadn't finished the two chapters of reading due tomorrow. She had better get it done, or at least try.

Opening the book to chapter ten, she moved to sit on the sofa and spotted the glass Aken had set on a side table, some leftover juice still inside. Her throat felt a little thirsty, so she picked it up, admiring the pretty red hue of the berries and the way lamplight glowed through the juice, before holding the glass to her lips.

She took a sip.

Her hand froze, and she almost dropped the glass.

'This isn't berry juice.'

Her grip tightened. Fear flared in her gut.

'It tastes like…'

The door quietly opened behind her.

'…blood.'

She whirled around at the door to see Master Nephryte there, his expression cool.

She barely noticed when the glass slipped from her hand to shatter on the carpet. Had she stumbled upon something that no one was supposed to know? Just what the heck was going on?

Master Nephryte raised a hand, and as he did, a gust of wind closed her eyes.

11

Cyrus jolted upright, forcing air into her lungs.

"What..." The word faded from her lips.

She was in her room, in bed, the covers around her...just as if she had gone to sleep.

She rubbed her forehead in confusion. Wasn't she just in the Master's dorm flat? Reading a book. Lifting a glass, only to find that it contained...

Had it been a dream?

She noted the biology book lying open on the bedside table— at the exact place she would have put it had she been reading... Maybe she *had* dozed off and dreamed it. Nothing else made sense.

Vempars needed *essence*, not blood. Aken wouldn't be drinking...

She shook the thought away. Morning light was already coming in through the window, so she got out of bed.

Cyrus followed the scent of breakfast into the Master's dorm kitchen. The Harlow boys were there, bickering and chatting, and waiting for food—which was what they did on many mornings, instead of eating in the cafeteria. Mamoru stood frying pancakes on the stove. Aken, his features still pale, hovered at his shoulder, asking: "Are they done yet?"

Apfel tugged at the older boy's apron, untying the strings and laughing at the frilly trim. "Why do you haves a girly apron?"

The greyhound puppy yapped as if laughing with his master.

Bakoa glided around the room, his legs formed into a sand tail that propelled him. "I need food, my stomach is dying. I need food!" he chanted.

Mamoru finally reached his wits' end and yelled at them all: "Shut up, and sit down! It will be *ready* when it's *ready*."

Zartanian sat quietly at the kitchen table, well-mannered as usual. Cyrus was surprised to see a juvenile raven perched on his right shoulder, its feathers a mix of fluffy patches and sleek pinions, which gave it a scruffy look. It was enjoying the bits of bread he fed it. The boy's winter-ice gaze seemed brighter and more relaxed today, which was good to see.

At the table-end, Lykale held a book to his face, ignoring everyone's existence and fingering the lock he always wore around his neck. Across from Zartanian, Hercule was busy reviewing notes for a possible surprise quiz.

Master Nephryte trudged out from his tower study room, massaging the back of his neck. He ignored the commotion and managed a smile her way, "Feeling well, Cyrus? You seemed very tired yesterday. The aftereffects of that cold, perhaps."

Skeptical, she nodded slowly.

"Here." He picked up a glass full of red. "Berries are an excellent source of antioxidants and vitamins."

She almost shrank away from the glass, the red color of it. But when he insisted, she gingerly wrapped her fingers around the glass. He continued speaking to the others as if everything was normal, making her wonder. She dipped the tip of her tongue in the juice.

The flavor was tangy berries...

Relief and confusion flooded through her.

Nephryte flashed her another smile. "Glad you like it."

She only half returned the smile. Had the glass with blood really been a dream?

Mamoru turned from the stove, pancakes done and piled high on a platter.

"Oh goodie!" Bakoa cheered. He landed on the floor, accidentally bumping Hercule against the table. The sound spooked the raven, and it took flight, heading for the platter.

Mamoru drew the platter out of the way, narrowly avoiding a collision, and the raven cawed.

Hercule glared at Bakoa and the raven, each, before putting away his study notes. "Can't you all just sit still and be normal for one decent second?"

Bakoa sucked in his lips and made himself small.

Kaw! The scruffy raven landed back on Zartanian's shoulder.

"Perhaps the bird can be kept *outside* while we're eating?" Mamoru suggested.

The boy nodded meekly.

Lykale took several sips from his coffee mug, the words painted on it reading: *I'm smart, & I know it.*

Cyrus stabbed one of the golden, crispy pancakes with a fork, observing the commotion. Apfel was already helping himself to two and got sticky syrup on his fingers. An inked mark showed on the skin of his neck when his shirt collar moved. She regarded the circular shape.

A slave Mark, like what Marigold had.

"The Hunters Race is coming soon!" Bakoa spoke up suddenly, while sprinkling salt on his pancakes.

"And what is that?" asked Cyrus.

Hercule answered for him, "It's a yearly competition between the five Floors. The Floor team who wins gets an added bonus to their grade—"

"—And gets to rub it in everybody's faces!" Bakoa added. "Harlow could sure use that."

Hercule tilted his head. "For once, I agree with you on something."

"But what sort of race is it?" Cyrus persisted.

"It's a race to see which Floor can catch the golden pixit first," answered Mamoru, busy cleaning the pan in the sink.

"A pixit?" She thought of the fluffy one at the school gate that always seemed to have an attitude. "Are they hard to catch?"

There was a pause, then they all started to laugh.

She glanced around at the boys.

"Let's just say, it's easier to hunt an anteleer in the dense jungles than to catch the golden pixit," Mamoru said with a smirk. He paused in his cleaning to fork a pancake into his mouth.

Cyrus considered that comparison. Was Harlow really going to be ready for a big race like that?

⁓ᴏ

"Doctor Zushil?"

In a side room, full of shelves and collected botanical and biological specimens, the doctor raised his narrow head, busy examining a box of contents. He blinked when a large vial was thrust in his face, and distaste creased his forehead. "Master Nephryte. I would *greatly* appreciate it if you would *knock* first."

Nephryte shrugged. "The way you obsess over your specimens, I didn't think you would hear the knocking. There is a world beyond this room, you know. It has trees and something called a sky."

Zushil grimaced. "You enjoy getting on my nerves too much." He wrinkled his narrow nose. "One more insult out of you, and I shall refuse to assist you with whatever request it is that you're about to trouble me with."

Nephryte held the triangular vial full of red liquid before Zushil's glasses. "Come now, Zushil," he smiled wryly, "Am I not the one who made it possible for you to have such a great and diverse collection, as this?" He waved a hand to indicate the room's stocked shelves. "Plant specimens I gathered *specially* for you during my travels?"

Zushil grumbled. As much as he hated to admit it, he *was* indebted to Nephryte—just as the crafty guy had no doubt intended.

"And now, in my hour of need, you would refuse me help?" The Master swirled the red liquid slowly while waiting for his reply, feigning a pitiful expression.

Zushil's fingers tightened on the box of contents he had been reorganizing. "You did it on purpose. You made me feel eternally indebted to you so that you could use me whenever you like. But I am not your scientist lackey!" He tapped a foot irritatedly. "Both you and Gandif—I'm sick and tired of being used by you people! *Stop* doing things for me, so I can *stop* being in debt."

The smirk on Nephryte's lips was infuriating. "Will you help me or not?" Nephryte dangled the vial alluringly. "I need this substance made into dissolvable tablets." He placed the vial inside the box Zushil was holding, and before the doctor could answer, Nephryte glided out of the room and was gone.

"At least ask me if it's something I'm able to do or not, first!" Zushil said between grinding teeth.

～

"What a bothersome assignment." Hercule muttered under his breath, then sipped at a latte macchiato layered in froth.

The younger Harlow boys were treating themselves at the *Piancavallo Café* after school.

Professor Ponairi had given them a rotten assignment: to write a paper on the homeland and culture of an upperclassman assigned to them.

Aken stirred his tea latte with a metal straw while Apfel tugged at his sleeve. He glared sideways at the child who sat between him and Cyrus.

He touched his pocket again, just to make sure Limitless was still there—he'd searched and finally found the clay bird at the fountain where he had met up with Cyrus and Apfel yesterday. It was a relief to have it back.

"Who were you assigned to, Hercule?" asked Bak from the opposite side of their curved booth.

"Someone from Floor Earnest: Mathias of House Turner," Hercule replied uncaringly. "Their House runs the spices industry, and they have a long heritage of knights in service to the king." He took another sip. "I can hardly consider him an upperclassman, he's only one year older than us."

Beside him, Zartanian quietly munched on a cream-filled croissant.

Aken watched as Cy let Apfel have the last bite of a red velvet cheesecake slice, even though the faeryn had already gobbled two slices of his own—the little piglet.

Another wave of fatigue washed over Aken. He rubbed his forehead and downed the rest of the latte, hoping to rid the dry thirst clawing at his throat. The mostly Healed wounds on his chest and left side began to throb. He tried to slow his breathing and fight the pain.

"Why do you looks so tired?" Apfel's finger poked him in the ribs. "Yor hands are shaped weird. So is yor face." *Poke—poke—poke.* "Maybe if you stick yor head in boiling water it'll melt and looks better."

Aken's jaw clenched. "*You little...* Start pronouncing your words better. It's *your*, not *yor*."

Hercule lifted his eyebrows. "Grammar advice coming from Aken, of all people?"

Aken made a face at him.

"I can'ts help my accent. Shame on yous for making fun of me!" Apfel pouted.

Aken was about to say something back, when he felt a tremor in his hands. It felt like an oven was burning under his skin, and his arms shuddered. *'What the...?'* He rose awkwardly, using the edge of the table to hoist himself up, and attempted to walk toward the café door. "I think I'll...nng...head back."

"Aken?" Cy sounded worried and stood up after him. "Are you okay?"

Aken reached the glass doors and leaned hard against one, pushing it open, stepping out into the warm air. He took no more than three steps on the street before he felt himself collapse on the rough pavestones.

"Aken!"

He heard shouts echo as if they were from far away.

His vision focused on the gray stone pressed against his cheek; the world looked like it was tilting sideways.

"I'll find Doctor Zushil." That was Zartanian, his footsteps running at a quick pace.

The feel of hands wrapped around his arms and chest before the rest of his senses shut down.

━○

Zartanian didn't slow until he passed underneath the arch of the twin connected towers before Draevensett, and he reached the academy's front, barely taking time to breathe. "Doctor! *Doctor!*" He tried to remember where the office was located beneath the colonnaded walkway, hoping the man would be there.

A hand on his shoulder stopped him short. He turned his neck.

"Something happened?" Master Nephryte, a hint of worry behind the calm mask he often wore.

Zartanian took a breath then quickly explained.

Master Nephryte stared off into the distance, seeming agitated, and muttered something under his breath.

Zartanian glanced up at him, his brow furrowed with a question. But when the Master didn't say anything more, he turned to head for Zushil's office again.

"—Wait."

The firm tone froze Zartanian in his footsteps; he half turned back. "But Master…?"

"There's no need to get Doctor Zushil involved. I can take care of this." The Master gave him a reassuring nod.

Zartanian's mouth hung open, his thoughts confused and unsure.

"I know how to handle this." The Master lightly patted the top of his raven hair. "His injury last night must have weakened him more than I realized. He needs rest and vitamins, which I can provide for him."

Zartanian's mouth slowly closed, though his expression remained uncertain. After one last glance in the colonnade's direction, he nodded and hurried to lead the way back.

Once they arrived on scene, Cyrus tried to explain to the Master in a flood of words how Aken had passed out. "I could tell he wasn't feeling like himself, but he didn't complain. And then he just…" the redhead trailed off.

Master Nephryte lifted Aken's unconscious form into his arms. The group stood out of the way, watching, and little Apfel released a flood of questions, not understanding the situation. "Dids he faint? Why dids he faint? I tolds him his face looked weird today."

The Master kept silent, securing the blond in his arms. A swift Leap landed him on the nearest rooftop, and then the wind carried him back towards Draevensett.

Placing Aken on the bed, drawing the sheets up to his chest, Nephryte took a seat in the room's single chair. The boy was shuddering with hunger chills, unconscious and groaning softly.

"I'm sorry, Aken-Shou..." His left hand pushed the hair back from the boy's pale face.

Propping an elbow against the bed, Nephryte let his forehead rest against the palm of his hand. "I knew this could happen. I'm a *fool*. I should have watched over you more closely...and explained to you the risks concerning blood."

His knuckles whitened. "I was too naïve, hoping that everything would just work out if you remained ignorant. But Purebloods are not the same as us..."

At least he had thought ahead and given that vial to Zushil to make into tablets, as a precaution. They should be ready soon.

12

"*S* *ooo sweet. Sooo lovely.*"

A voice spoke from somewhere, and Aken rose to his feet in the darkness.

Where was he?

"*How I wish there was more.*"

A dull light without any source came into existence, and a path became visible stretching before him, hedged in thorns. The voice sounded like it was coming from up ahead, wherever the path led.

Aken started to walk. The thorns moved and rustled upon thick, green vine branches on either side of him, and more vines curled in an arch overhead, creating a tunnel of menacing green. They scratched against his bare arms and snagged at his pants.

The path eventually curved and opened onto a circular pavestone space, and at its center stood a large golden cage.

The bars gleamed in the dull light.

"Where is this?" he wondered aloud.

"*You could call it your subconscious,*" spoke the same voice.

It came from inside the cage.

Aken took a step nearer, peering into the shadows behind the golden bars.

Red eyes glowed, and the thing inside came near, letting the dull light make itself visible.

Aken drew back with a start. His own face stared back at him: a perfect replica of himself, except for the glowing red eyes.

"You! You're the madman, the one who talks in my head, aren't you?" Aken demanded to know. "Who are you? *What* are you?"

His replica regarded him for a moment, then barked a laugh. *"So pathetic. But so entertaining."*

Aken growled. "Get out of my head!"

"You're telling me to get out? I should be telling you to get out and let me have this mind."

"I don't know what you are, but I'm in control here. So leave me the heck alone!"

The replica laughed again, and his hands wrapped around the bars. Aken took a step back. *"Feeling thirsty for something, are you? Throat parched, body faint. I can sense it."* He sneered. *"Our power is waking up, and it's hungry—as am I. It must have been that half-human's blood that triggered it. And you've had to Heal yourself quite a bit, recently."*

Half-human? Cyrus?

He recalled Healing the redhead's finger a while back, and the impossibly sweet taste.

"I don't understand what you're saying, but stop it. I will never use that Scourgeblood power!"

"Haha! It's in your very nature, little me. You can't escape it, just as a bird cannot resist using its wings to take flight."

"I *will* stop it. And you'll help me. Because if I get kicked out of Draevensett and locked up in the Morbid Dungeons, it'll be the end for both of us."

The replica shrugged. *"I suppose it would make things rather difficult. But who knows? We might have some fun."*

The replica leaned closer, pressing against the bars and the large lock which held the cage door shut. *"You're bonded to that Cyrus, now. That's what happens to Purebloods. Did no one ever tell you? You live off of the blood of others, until you come across someone special—and then, it's only their blood that can sustain you. That's why you passed out—you needed a drink."* His grin twisted. *"Did you honestly think you were drinking berry juice this whole time? That that's what your parents were feeding you? That that's what Nephryte gives you? This is really quite funny."*

"Shut up!" Aken threw his fist at the bars, causing the replica to lean back.

"You're a monster. And you always will be."

"Shut up and leave my head!" Aken screamed. "Leave my head!!"

Aken sat up, panting.

The thorns and golden cage faded away, replaced by walls and a familiar room.

His chest heaved, his brow covered in sweat.

"What are you shouting at?"

He blinked to see against the glowing lamplight. Master Nephryte eyed him from the chair at the side of the bed. "Feeling more yourself?" he asked him.

Aken was back inside his room, and he tasted something on his tongue—something sweet.

Nephryte indicated with a nod the bottle of tablets sitting on the bedside table. "It turns out you have a rare form of anemia," he answered his questioning look. "You'll be taking two of these tablets every day, from now on. I know, I know—don't give me that look." He waved a hand. "Taking medicine is the last thing you want to do, but that's just how things are. Life won't always go your way. Be grateful you're not in a sorry state, like Lady Cherish."

Aken wasn't sure how to respond, still reorienting his brain from the dream—or whatever it had been.

Berry juice. Was it really not...?

A shudder passed through him.

"I gave you one tablet already." Nephryte gestured. "It's best we keep your anemia condition a secret." Aken looked back up at Nephryte sharply. "No one needs to know about this, outside of Harlow."

Anemia?

"That's why you passed out—you needed a drink."

"How did that happen, out of the blue?" Aken managed to ask.

"It wasn't out of the blue. When you were injured by black silver, your anemic symptoms became more pronounced, enough for us to notice. This was bound to happen at some point."

Aken frowned, still unconvinced. How did the Master always have such logical explanations for everything?

"Haha, I told you. You're a monster."

Aken squeezed his eyes shut.

"Are you feeling any better?"

Aken smoothed the upset from his face, shifted his shoulders and stretched his arms. "Yeah, just fine, nurse."

Nephryte pinched his arm. "Keep those tablets with you."

Aken glanced to the bottle. The tablets behind the glass were a pale shade of red...

⌒

It was late, and Cyrus scratched the side of her head, staring down at the blue faeryn and his dog, wondering what to do. "Apfel, I know you're afraid another creature will come after you, but you're asking to move into the dorms with us? Won't your owner be angry?"

"Only for the nights. Please! No one cares wheres I am at night. I won't cause trouble. I'll be busy ats the bakery during daytime." Apfel begged, clasping his hands together and making sad puppy eyes.

It was too cute; she couldn't say no to a child in need. And to be honest, she didn't like the thought of him staying alone anywhere else at night.

"I guess it wouldn't hurt," she said slowly. "Just for the nights. But not in *my* room. I'm—I need my own space. You'll have to bunk with Aken or one of the other boys."

Apfel raised his small arms in victory and dashed down the moonlit corridor.

She sighed and went to her room to change into pajamas.

The old black-and-white photograph of her mother— younger and here at the academy—stood on the nightstand. She touched the photo for a moment.

Before Cyrus finished changing, the door to her room flung open and Aken strode inside.

"Don't barge in without knocking!" She quickly pulled the pajama shirt the rest of the way down.

"Huh?" he mumbled, not paying attention as he plopped down on the edge of her bed, a stack of picture books in his hands.

She blinked at him for a long minute until he finally noticed. "What?" he said.

"You're awake. Are you…feeling better now? Master said something about you having anemia."

Aken idly pinched the fabric of the olive-green bed cover. "Yeah, I'm fine."

He didn't seem like he wanted to talk about it, so she moved on. "New picture books?" She indicated the stack.

He cheered up. "I haggled these a few days ago off a Floor Earnest peer. Look: special editions of *The Twelve Legendary Knights*! Cool, right? Let's read them tonight!"

The thought crossed her mind that he should be sleeping, not reading. But his eager smile and begging blue eyes swayed her; after all he had been through, she didn't feel right saying no.

The door swung open again, and a bundle of faeryn and puppy landed on the bed.

"Apfel, go bug somebody else! You should be asleep; it's *way* past a child's bedtime," Aken told him.

Apfel stuck out his tongue. "I'm gonna tells yor Master what yor doing, that yous staying up late."

Aken's teeth ground together. "Fine, you little brat. You can stay, as long as you keep quiet."

"Reads the book to me. I can't read words well."

Aken rolled his eyes skyward.

Cyrus lifted the first book and began reading aloud the *special edition* winter adventure of the Legendary Knights.

Not even ten minutes of reading had passed before the child fell fast asleep.

Aken tsked, observing him.

"What do you think about that crazy stuff Apfel was saying at the picnic?" he asked her. "Calling you the Swan, and me the False Guardian. It's nonsense, right? A princess can't come back from the dead—and not as a boy. And who are these Impure Nights that are supposedly after you?"

Cyrus had been wondering some of those same things. Was the overwhelming energy inside her somehow linked to it all? Is that what the Impure Nights were after?

"Aken, something…weird…happened the morning after the Festival Duel. And I haven't told anyone about it."

He watched her intensely, the lamplight tracing down his nose and across his cheek. She began telling him about the strange scene in the cemetery: the redhead girl in broken chains, dying, and the warning she gave before her body disappeared without a trace.

"That's…wow, really creepy," he said finally. "I don't think that was a dream or hallucination, Cy. And that means there really is a group called the Impure Nights. Apfel was right…" He stayed deep in thought for a moment, then added, "You know, the Swan was said to have scarlet hair, like yours. Maybe these Impure guys really believe she's come back, and they're looking for her."

"Do you think they sent that Corpsed?"

He thought it over. "I don't know. It did look different from that ancient Corpsed Nephryte had battled. Maybe they did something to that one, to control it?"

She shuddered. "How are we supposed to keep Apfel safe?"

"The Corpsed was after *you*, Cy. It's what, the second time it tried to attack you?"

Third, actually. But still, she felt like it had been targeting Apfel just as much, this time.

"He's in a bakery during the day, and with us at night. He'll be fine," Aken said with certainty. "We can't exactly skip school and stuff to watch over him every hour of the day."

She exhaled. Apfel's sleeping form was a peaceful bundle beside them, wrapped up in a blanket and sucking on his thumb.

"I guess you're right," she finally said.

13

Finn looked back over his shoulder again, waiting for the slaver and his wagon cage of products rumbling slowly over the uneven terrain of the woods. "Will you hurry up?" he snapped at the pudgy vempar, walking alongside the wagon in the dead of night. "I don't fancy getting caught out here."

"Hey, don't get cocky with me, Draev," warned the slaver. "I paid you good money for this job."

"Paid me to help catch your supply of faeryn, you mean. And *that* part's done." Finn indicated the barred cage in the wagon with a thumb. He turned his attention back to watching the trees warily. A shifting breeze rustled the woods around their path.

Catching humanoids for slavers paid well, but it wasn't legal—unless you were convincing enough and could cover it up as harvesting work. Or better yet, pay off the right people.

The breeze felt unnaturally damp this night, chilling the skin beneath his cloak. Something about the atmosphere had him on edge, despite the guiding moonlight, as if there were eyes watching them from the shadows behind tree trunks.

"You've got to escort me back t' the grasslands, at least, for protection," complained the crude slaver. "We have t' drive slow, and can't use any lights to see by either. Any light or sounds could give us away. Don't know about you, but I'd rather not have faeryn warriors sticking my hide full of arrows."

Five hired workmen walked along behind them quietly. The vempar who sat in the motor wagon driving looked sweaty and kept nervously glancing at the sides of the path.

The handful of faeryn they had captured sat huddled in the cage portion of the wagon, their mouths gagged, now and then a head lifting up to glare hatred at their captors.

"Just hurry up," Finn growled again.

The path rounded a bend, and something sprinted across in front of them, vanishing into the bushes.

Finn halted. The wagon slowed to a stop behind him.

"W-what is it?" asked the slaver, peering around, rubbing his hands together.

Finn scanned the area. Some of the shadows were too deep to gaze into. The movement could have been anything—an anteleer, maybe.

"Keep going," he finally said.

The wagon wheels started to turn again. And that was when one of the workmen screamed—and a blade glinted from his abdomen as he fell backwards.

The silent woods erupted with armed figures charging the workmen and the slaver who cried out and ran for cover.

Finn channeled his *essence* through the ground and into nearby rocks, lifting them from the soil to fling at their attackers.

"Ah-ah-ah, that's naughty," spoke a reprimanding male voice.

The rocks Finn threw halted in mid-air, stopped by some invisible force. He struggled and strained against whatever power held them, sweat beading his brow.

A shape emerged from the shadows before him, floating over the underbrush to land upon the path. His hair glowed white under the moonlight, and a blue cape shifted in the breeze.

"Didn't your mother ever teach you not to throw rocks at people? My, what ill manners you vempars have."

To either side workmen screamed, and the wagon driver fled into the underbrush. Judging by what the moonlight made visible, the attackers were a tough and grisly lot—neither guards nor soldiers.

"The escaped criminals from Morbid Dungeons?" Finn exclaimed. "You're the one who let them out?"

The rocks flung back with sudden force, striking Finn and the wagon and anyone else in the way. Finn hit the ground, his chest bleeding. "Who—who are you?" he choked. He tried to get up, but more rocks fell over him, pinning him down.

He saw the workmen, lying dead, and the wagon being wrenched open: setting the caged faeryn free.

"Who am I?" the man said. The silhouette of his ears were like backward crescent moons. This was no vempar or Ability wielder.

"I am the rescuer of the weak. The hope of those who have none. And the executioner of vempar kind," the man declared. The corners of his lips drew into a dark smirk. "I am the White Ghost—and your worst nightmare."

Finn struggled to get up.

The White Ghost slashed his hand through the air—and that was the last thing Finn saw before the rocks crushed him.

PART 2
THE
WHITE
GHOST

14

Once the school faculty meeting for that morning had ended, Deidreem rose from the chair, and the group filtered out of the principal's office. The topic had been about recent attacks occurring in the Vemparic Kingdom, specifically those by someone called the White Ghost, who was also most likely the same culprit responsible for the Morbid Dungeons escape—a feat thought to have been impossible.

The incident had little to do with the school, or even their city, except that Principal Han wanted them all to be aware and keep vigilant.

Deidreem snorted. Whatever this new troublemaker was up to, they had better not interfere with the Impure Nights' plans.

He entered his own office and found Assistant Principal Pueginn already there and waiting.

"You called, Deidreem?" the pot-bellied vempar asked, bobbing his bird-like head.

"Yes. I have a job for you."

"*Hm*, did things not work out so well the night of the ball?

I thought you had everything under control." He wheezed through his nose.

Deidreem slammed a hand down on the desk, the sound making Pueginn jump. "There were...*unexpected interferences.* Some Draev students and that blasted Nephryte showed up and got in my way."

Pueginn's lips curled wide.

"Don't be so smug. It's *your* turn to go out and catch the little blue faeryn, now that I'm swamped with school obligations. And if you fail, Leader will be just as displeased with you," Deidreem snapped.

"Of course, of course." Pueginn head-bobbed. "Simply give me the address, and it will be done."

~

Apfel grunted as he hoisted a stack of wide pastry boxes up onto one of the back tables inside the bakery, next looping thick string around them to hold everything in place. The shop was a bit more crowded than usual this morning, which meant more work for him.

He huffed through his nose and peered into the adjacent room where Hazfel scuttled about: cleaning the floors of crumbs and sweet stuff with his pink tongue. "Lucky *you* havings such an easy job," he mock glared, child-cheeks pouting.

A sudden unease clouded the air, as if something had just entered the shop, and Apfel brought his head around to search for the source, his long ears tilting back.

Someone with a nasally voice strode up to the counter: a vempar man with cloud-gray skin and a curved beak nose, his body shaped like a chunky penguin in a fine suit. He took off a bowler hat and asked the server something about breads and parfaits.

Apfel didn't know why, but a whisper in the back of his head began urging him to run. He called Hazfel to his side, stroking the puppy's ears while peering around the stack of pastry boxes, watching.

"Is there a lad to carry this for me?" the man asked, once the server had finished filling up a box of freshly baked bread for him, the wafting scent delicious.

"Sure do, Mr. Pueginn. But he can't be goin' far with you; he's got other work to do," said the server.

"It's not far at all, not at all—right around the corner! I simply do not wish to grease my fine suit carrying this myself," Pueginn explained.

"Apfel!" the woman called. "Get over here and carry this for the gentleman."

A jolt of fear sent Apfel's heart racing. The man's beady eyes slid to him, intense as a predatory hawk.

Run! warned the voice louder inside him. *Run!!*

The man's steps approached him, and a growl began in the greyhound pup's throat.

"Come here, little slave." Pueginn's lips curled into a sneer. His hand extended, ready to grab him. "You'll help me, won't you?"

RUN!

Apfel smacked the man's reaching fingers away with one of the boxes and hurried around the table, Hazfel at his heels. He dashed out the back door leading into a narrow alley, where his small bike stood waiting.

Ignoring Pueginn's shout, he threw a leg over the bike seat and fast pedaled away, Hazfel leaping into the rear basket behind him.

He had dropped one of the pastry boxes on the alley doorstep, and Pueginn stepped right into it, slipping on the cream that oozed out and stumbling nose-first into the opposite alley wall.

Apfel managed a satisfied smirk and activated the bike's small engine, propelling him and Hazfel away, weaving through Downtown's streets.

After a long while, once he was sure he had lost the man, he switched off the engine and pedaled down a cobblestone alley.

There, he stopped to catch his breath.

Who was that creepy guy? First a Corpsed, and now this? Why was everybody after him?!

"Listen, ja. If that power does come to you, you must be very careful. The Oracle is a great responsibility, and it can't fall into the wrong hands."

Papa's words. But Apfel didn't feel like he had any special power inside him…did he?

The sound of clapping hands echoed in the alley around him, and Apfel lifted his head in alarm, searching for the source.

From the shadows emerged a slender man: his hair pure white and ears crescent shapes. He wore a turquoise, high-collared cape that came down to a point at his chest, the back of it a swallowtail-split trailing to behind his knees; his white tunic with black accents accentuated his ghostly skin. The man's hands clapped together while he observed Apfel with a look of amusement.

"Well done escaping that vempar penguin. I'm impressed," the young man said. "You've saved me the trouble of having to fight him."

The man came near without lifting his feet. Apfel watched as he floated across the cobblestones. The pupils of his tropical-aqua eyes were vertical slits. "Now, I can simply take you with me," he said. "One of the rare *mondschein* faeryn… Please, allow me to get you out of this filthy vempar city."

Alarm flooded through Apfel. He set his feet back to the bike peddles and wheeled around, ready to speed off.

Or he would have, if the bike hadn't slowed to a groaning halt.

"What the?" Apfel slammed his foot down harder on the pedals, twisting the lever to rev the engine. But nothing responded.

"Oh, so sorry about that. But I can't have you running away."

Apfel looked back to where the oilpowder fuel that had been in his bike now lay splattered on the ground. The gears in the wheels wouldn't turn, either.

Hazfel growled and barked, backing away from the man.

Apfel hopped off the bike and started to dash away on his own two feet.

A hand suddenly grabbed his shoulder.

"There's some important information that I need from you. And you're going to give it to me," the man said in his ear. "You can call me Ellefsen. Let's get acquainted, shall we?"

Before Apfel could cry out, the alley and walls around him disappeared...

Hazfel barked, and then whined pitifully, circling the empty space where his friend had just been.

⌒

Apfel coughed in the dust of the old attic around him. There were no windows or anything else to let him see where in Draeth he now was. All he knew was that his wrists were tied and there was no escape.

"Tell me, what do you know of the Swan Princess?" asked a voice.

Apfel struggled against the rope even though it was futile. The strange man circled the chair he was forced to sit in.

"For starters, where is she?" Ellefsen probed.

Apfel tossed his head to the side. "I don't knows! Why're yous asking me strange questions? Let me go!"

Pain zapped up his legs and he gasped.

"Please! My owner's angry—the Mark's hurting me!"

Ellefsen paused his pacing and looked down at him with sympathy. "You poor child. If only I could erase that barbaric thing from you...but unfortunately, I cannot. I suggest you hurry and tell me what I want to know, then I can take you back to your little bakery shop. How does that sound?"

Pain shocked Apfel again, up his back like a whip. His owner was warning him to get back to the shop.

"I...I don't knows what yor asking," he panted.

"Hmm." Ellefsen seemed to contemplate the matter, clasping his hands behind his back. "There must be a way to access the Oracle power, if it's inside you." He knelt before Apfel, his aqua gaze drilling into him. "We will find a way..."

15

"**A**pfel?"

Cyrus walked around Draevensett's front courtyard, then searched about the paved path and lawn beyond the twin towers' arch. Apfel should have been back from work by now; the sky was already sunset rose behind the city rooftops and darkening.

An uneasy feeling turned in her gut.

She went down to the main gate and waited by the roaring, horned and winged lion statues, perched like guards atop their posts.

The pixit's head of cotton fluff watched her from its nest in the wall, as if debating whether or not she was still sick and if it should risk coming close to yell at her.

What if another Corpsed had come after Apfel? She didn't think one would attack in daylight hours inside the city—not with so many people around—and yet...

She spotted Aken crossing the lawn and called him over.

"What's up?"

"It's Apfel. He was supposed to come straight here after work, but he hasn't shown up. And now it's getting late…" She pinched a strand of her curly hair. "We have to go look for him!" she decided and grabbed his arm suddenly, pulling him along with her out the gate.

"Wait, what? Maybe he's just running late," he tried to say.

She didn't listen; she Leaped up to the nearest rooftop.

Aken hurried to follow her, practicing his Leaping, and they traveled rooftop to rooftop towards Downtown and the small bakery, bypassing the tram and the pedestrians below.

The bakery's lights were on when they arrived, despite the late hour. They Landed on the street, and she felt a flurry of trepidation. Through the windows, the owner appeared to be in an angry mood, bustling about the space and cleaning.

Cyrus sucked in a breath, and they both strode into the shop. The owner halted his work upon seeing them, and Aken quickly asked him if the little blue faeryn was around.

The owner gripped his broom handle and told them what she feared to hear: that Apfel had been missing since early morning. Now, he busied himself doing the cleaning chores that Apfel usually did.

Cyrus sank into the nearest chair, a cold chill running up her arms.

Little Apfel. Someone really had been after him.

And now, they were too late.

She thought he would be safe during the day, while they were in school. She'd been wrong.

Cyrus glanced sidelong at Aken, who seemed just as upset as she was, his foot tapping as if to hold back the frustration.

Hazfel lay on the ground, his puppy eyes full of sorrow.

"Do you have any clue what could have happened to him?" Aken pressed.

Based on the owner's expression, he was ready to crack a fist on something. "The Mark I placed on him tells me he's no longer in the city but up towards the north." He took out a scrap of paper, tossing it to them. "Found this on a table: addressed to a half-human, which I now assume must be you."

Cyrus stood and read the note.

> *To the half-human:*
> *If you want the child back, come to Pearlset Town tomorrow afternoon. He'll be waiting for you in the piazza next to the westside dock 2.*

The bakery owner's throat rumbled in a growl, "Whatever it is you've gotten my slave mixed up in, you had better make it right, y'hear me? Bring him back, or I'll take this up with the Draev Guardian League myself!"

His rotund, jutting stomach forced her a step back.

"We're not doing this for you, but for Apfel," Aken retorted. He followed Cyrus back outside, the sky already the muted colors of dusk above them. Tall Tim gonged the hour across all of Downtown, the note full of melancholy to her ears.

Aken kicked at the pavestones. "I'm sorry, Cy. I thought for sure the little guy would be safe...but you were right. Somebody *was* out to get him."

She gripped the hem of her shirt. She hoped that *somebody* wasn't connected to the Impure Nights. If what happened to that redhead girl happened to Apfel...

"We have to tell the Master," she decided.

Back at the dorms, Cyrus showed the note to Master Nephryte in the study room and then attempted to persuade him.

"We have to go save Apfel, *please*," she pleaded. "If something happens to him, I'll never forgive myself."

Aken clasped her shoulder. "We'll get him back, no matter what."

The Master considered the note, studying it, tapping a curved finger against his chin. "What would someone want with a faeryn child? Unless it's because he's your friend, or…because he's a moonlight faeryn," he murmured the last bit.

"What's so special about a blue faeryn?" asked Aken.

"His kind once made up the Mondburg Kingdom, across the Diviso Sea. They were a prosperous people, until goblins invaded and destroyed their homeland. The few survivors scattered and never returned," the Master explained.

Aken crossed his arms and paced the study room's grape red rug, the pattern swirls and petals of pink, white and gray. "Don't know if it's connected or not, but I met a blue faeryn once," he told them. "An old guy. Said he was the Oracle, and that the power would soon pass on to another."

The Master looked up sharply. "The Oracle?"

Aken paused his steps. "Yeah. Why?"

"Old texts speak of Mondburg as the home of the Oracle, a power that made their kingdom prosper. Do you know where this faeryn went?"

Aken shook his head.

Cyrus silently wondered why he hadn't mentioned this earlier. "Apfel's been saying strange things," she added. "Almost as if he were in some sort of trance. Do you think he has this Oracle power?"

Master Nephryte walked around the sofa and chair in thought, tapping his chin. "Possibly. But I don't like the sound of this note. Why was it addressed to *you*? It is clearly a trap."

"Even if it is, we still have to save him!" Cyrus insisted.

The Master stood in place, finger tapping. "The Oracle is important. He needs to be brought back. Hopefully, the kidnapper isn't aware of what Apfel is and is only using him as bait to get to you. Not many people now know of the Oracle's existence."

Aken started for the door. "Great, now let's get going!"

"But I don't want to draw too much attention to this. If anyone were to discover he is the Oracle, the child would be hunted for the rest of his life," the Master continued. "I can't send a request for an official Draev squad to rescue him, and I can't neglect my own Draev work, without drawing suspicion…"

"We'll get him back! We can do it on our own," Aken said and slapped his chest.

The Master snorted. "As if. I'll assign this to an older student group, one with more experience in missions, and have you be their backup."

"Backup?" Aken's chest deflated.

Before Master Nephryte left the room, he assured them, "I'll get back to you in the morning about this."

16

M orning couldn't come fast enough for Cyrus. And when it did, Harlow gathered for breakfast, and she and Aken told them about Apfel's kidnapping.

The group got ready to leave, but it wasn't until an hour later that they finally got the permission they were waiting for.

"Your mission has been approved," Master Nephryte announced to Floor Harlow in the study. "You will locate and rescue the child, Apfel. The kidnapper is most likely a vempar who bears a grudge against Cyrus being allowed to live and train here, and Apfel was the easiest of your friends to target—that is what I and Principal Han are guessing, based on the current evidence. But you will still need to be careful. You've been given permission to skip the rest of your classes today to carry out this mission."

"Yes!" Bakoa bounced on his heels.

"Your role is to be the backup for another Floor squad. You will be following their orders."

Hercule snorted. "Playing backup?"

"Yes. For an upperclassmen squad from Floor Smart."

Hercule grimaced, and Bakoa flinched. "Floor Smart? They're kinda…intimidating," Bakoa whispered.

"They are among the best of student squads. This will be good training for you. Learn all that you can from them, and watch how they work as a team," Master Nephryte advised.

Cyrus glanced around. "Where are Mamoru and Lykale?"

"They won't be joining you this time—they have school obligations that cannot be missed, and I can't make this mission look any more unusual than it already does. It has to seem like a training exercise."

"Why?"

"Because Draevs don't normally go around rescuing kidnapped slaves for bakers."

"…Oh."

<hr>

Cyrus waited by the city's arched northern gates, where the river canal snaked its way past on a course from Lake Doroth through into the city. Small boats bobbed against their rope ties, and ruby-throated swallows in flight dipped to the water for a drink.

Aken was pacing, while Bakoa and Zartanian kicked a pebble back and forth. Hercule leaned against the rough wall face, his arms folded, a crease between his eyebrows, watching the stream of light traffic go by, mostly five-wheeled rumblers and wagons.

"Is something bothering you?" she asked him casually.

His gaze slid sideways to her, then back. "I fear Prince Tyomnii might be in the Floor Smart squad we're joining," he finally said. "He's of House Sivortsova: the main rival of House Dragonsbane. They managed to get a step above us when his mother married the king—Tyomnii's blood father had passed away during the Goblin Shadow War."

He made an irritated sound with his tongue. "My father wants me to surpass the Sivortsovas, and make Dragonsbane the wealthiest House." He ran a hand down his face. "It's an added stress that I don't need."

Cyrus flashed him a sympathetic look. His position was one she would never envy—no amount of wealth would be worth that.

"Hercule, why are you in Harlow? I mean, why did you choose to stay?" she asked. "Surely your dad could've used his status to get you into any Floor you wanted."

Hercule's golden eyes took on a far-off gaze. "Because, even though they're idiots half the time…" he glanced to Aken and Bakoa, "…and shy or wrapped up in secrets…" he looked to Zartanian, "…they were the first group to treat me like a normal person. No sugar-coated words, no secret plots running through their heads to derail me. They simply *were* who they *were*, and thought of *me* as simply *me*." Hercule smirked, almost fondly.

She looked from him to the Harlow group. She understood what he meant.

She felt accepted for who and what she was, with no strings of the past attached. You couldn't put a price tag on something like that.

It was only a few minutes later, while they were waiting, when a pair of unfamiliar voices suddenly called out to them:

"Hi there, chaps!"

"You must be the young Harlows who will be tagging along with us."

A pair of twins came striding over to their group: older boys wearing identical green vests over checkered shirts and green pants; their identical hair, a brownish burgundy, cast bangs over their right eyes. Even their gestures and manner of speaking were the same.

Wait, she had seen them once before—back when she snuck through Downtown on her way to leave the city and go see Huntter, before the whole Duel thing.

"We're the Holsome twins," they introduced as one, each sweeping an arm out. Their opposite movements reflected one another like a mirror, and they gave a dramatic bow in greeting.

"I'm Twiddle-doo!" said one, teasingly.

"And I'm Twiddle-dum!" said the other.

"And you…" The first twin leaned forward, until his face was inches from hers, and pointed a finger to flick her forehead. "*You* must be the half-human everybody's been talking about."

Cyrus turned pink.

"Get some personal space manners." Aken threw an arm between her and the twin, forcing him back.

"Ahh," Twiddle-dum eyed Aken up and down. "This must be the well-known troublemaker of Harlow, Aken-Shou."

"Who dyed the hair of Draev students, teachers and Masters all green in one day," said the other.

"That was the best, was it not, dear Brother?"

"Indeed, it was, dear Brother! A wonderful moment in prank history."

Aken puffed out his chest. "That's right! And I can do worse if you don't treat us nicely."

The twins turned to each other, their gazes flat. "You don't suppose, dear Brother, that *that* was a threat?"

The other nodded. "I do think it was, my twin. Though a very weak and plain *boring* one, if you ask me."

"Should we pin him down and braid that too-gorgeous blond hair up as punishment?"

"Ah, and add a few ribbons too. Pink, perhaps?"

"I dare you to try!" Aken fumed.

But they both merely grinned. "What a rude little punk he is. Makes me want to antagonize him all the more."

"Quite so, dear Brother. Shall we use the *Taco Chain Wrap* move on him?"

"Yes, I rather think we should."

Aken readied his stance for a fight. "Bring it on!"

They smirked down at him in unison. They took the first step forward, hands reaching inside their vests for something, and then...

"Can you never cease to cause trouble?" another new voice came, firm yet graceful as a breeze.

The twins grunted, crossing their arms over their chests and scrunching up their faces.

"As students of an older age, it is our responsibility to care for and nourish those younger than ourselves." The voice sounded almost feminine, bringing Cyrus's head around.

The person approached, wearing split-toe shoes and a long, red haori jacket—pink flower petals patterned across the front and shoulders—and matching hakama pants; a sash tied the outfit at the waist. She was kitsune, with reddish fox ears and a fluffy tail swaying back and forth behind her. Her hair, a gradient from silver to the same reddish hue at the ends, was pulled back in a ponytail, with loose strands falling about her yellow tinted skin.

A sheathed katana glinted in her sash, a pretty thing with emblazoned flower decorations, the hilt crafted to resemble a branch of cherry blossoms.

"You must be the Harlow group who is joining us." Her slanted, tranquil golden-brown eyes took note of Cyrus and the other boys. Hands together, she gave a bow. "I am Heion Yasuraka, personal guard and slave attendant of Prince Tyomnii. These twins," she indicated with a palm, "are the no-good rascals Victor and Jack."

Cyrus regarded the kitsune, a slave who clearly had high privileges.

The twins gasped in protest. "And we were having such fun using fake names! You've gone and ruined it, Heion," one twin mumbled.

"But you'll never guess which one of us is *which*," the other twin said. They laughed, switching places and making faces at Harlow.

Cyrus studied them: Victor had more of a dimple than his twin.

Heion slapped the backs of their heads. "What did I just say? Don't antagonize the youngers!"

The twins rubbed their heads morosely. "Bully Heion, waving that ridiculous strength around."

"She doesn't care if she permanently damages our handsome features…"

"*Ja*, there's no reason why she should care about that," another new, yet monotone voice stated.

A boy walked into view: short, with sea-green wispy hair and ocher-green eyes. Instead of regular clothes, he wore a full bodysuit of greenish brown fabric, with two snail antennae sticking up from a thick hood, and a brown shell backpack stuck on his back.

"Yes, there is a reason! Losing my handsomeness would be the equivalent of the world losing one of its greatest treasures," whined Victor, and Jack fanned him with a hand.

"Calm down, dear Brother, calm down."

Aken looked the snail boy up and down. "What are you supposed to be: their escar-mascot?"

The boy opened his mouth and something like a laugh, monotone and slow, came out, his face lacking any hint of emotion. "Ha…ha…ha… That was funny. Because I am dressed like a snail, you called me 'escar-mascot,' instead of 'escargot'—which is a food dish made of snails."

Aken gave him an odd look. "Uh…yeah."

The snail boy extended a hand for them to shake. "You can call me Schnel."

His hands were clothed in the same fabric, and when Aken gingerly shook it, a sliminess rubbed onto his skin. He made a face and tried to wash his hand in the nearest wall fountain.

"Sorry about that," Schnel said. "It's my Ability. My skin secretes a slug-like fluid. That's why I wear this, to help keep things from getting slimed." He tugged at the fuzzy neckline of his bodysuit. "I've been learning to control it, but sometimes my Ability gets out of hand. Ha, *out of hand*, get it? Slime came out of my hand. Ha...ha...ha..."

Aken wiped his hand on Hercule's expensive charcoal jacket, and the noble's foot kicked him in the shin.

"Your accent, I've heard it before," Cyrus voiced, thinking of Apfel.

"Really? It's Bergsprach. I'm from Bergvolk."

Bergvolk was on the western continent. How did Apfel end up all the way over here, in the east? What had become of his family after the war? She'd never taken the time to ask him. Then again, it might be too painful.

"Vhat are you blokeheads doing?" shouted a deep voice.

The twins cringed and backed away, and Heion's fox ears flattened back at the shout.

Cyrus noticed Hercule quietly edge his way to the back of the group.

Before they could see the owner of the deep voice, the lethal head of a long black scythe struck into the pavestones before them. The curved blade edge gleamed darkly with a reddish tint, and the black shaft stretched tall above their heads. It was a terrifying yet beautiful weapon, with a sculpted skull and bat filigree design.

"Whoa, is that one of the Legendary Weapons?" Bakoa exclaimed.

Cyrus looked again. The twelve Weapons were said to be among the most powerful weapons in the world: forged of blood silver, and once wielded by the Twelve Legendary Knights themselves.

"That is *Tyrving* the scythe," informed Heion. "My blade is *Sakura* the katana."

A gloved hand reached to grasp the dark shaft of the scythe. The owner, tall and long limbed, stared down his nose at them all, an aura of darkness emanating from around him. Cyrus recognized him as the grim reaper-like student who had entered the Festival Duel Tests.

He carried himself with a regal air. His fingers curled around the shaft beneath the deadly blade head and its decorative skull, his reflection mirrored in its metallic surface. Brown hair dark as night lay about his head and brow; his eyes, the deep shades of a red rose, regarded them each from beneath dark eyebrows.

The tail ends of his long, black jacket swayed about his legs, the cuffs and open collar a mane of black feathers around his neck and wrists; underneath it a white ruffle shirt, black pants belted at the waist, and knee-high black boots that laced up his shins. His fingers, in wine-colored gloves, tapped idly against the blade as he glared at the inferior Harlow students and his own annoying companions—who wisely kept silent.

"Your Highness, these are the young students who will be supporting us on the mission," said Heion, indicating them with a hand sweep.

"Support." Prince Tyomnii sniffed. His gaze scanned over them, lingering for a moment on Hercule. "As eef vee need support."

Hercule bristled but kept his arms at his sides and wore an indifferent mask.

"Tyomnii-sama, be nice. They are fellow Draev students." Heion turned back around and introduced him, "This is Tyomnii

Sivortsova Magnovska, of the north-eastern province, heir of the Noble House of Sivortsova and stepson to the king, the royal family Magnovska."

"In other words," Schnel raised an index finger, "he's a prince by marriage, but not actually the king's son. Really just a nobleman's son—the Sivortsova nobles. I think they must be bad-tempered people; and unfortunately, he inherited that —*ouch*."

The scythe shaft thunked his skull.

The prince effortlessly lifted the scythe again, propping the heavy blade against his shoulder. "Don't slov us down on thees mission," he stated directly at Harlow.

Aken blinked. "Slov? What's slov?"

"He means *slow*," Schnel explained. "He's got a particularly strong Răsărit accent, our prince does. Something about the cold and snow up there must ruin their vocal cords. His *W*'s are *V*'s, and *I*'s become *ee*. He can't pronounce *O*'s well, either: today becomes toe-day."

Vwooosh! The scythe swung close to Schnel, halting at the side of his hooded head.

"Don't antagonize me anymore tohday, Schnel!"

Schnel gave them a look. "See what I mean?"

Aken burst out laughing. "No wonder our prince never gives any speeches." The prince's red gaze cut to him.

The scythe moved to Aken's neck faster than Cyrus's vision could follow, the edge halting a mere inch from his skin.

"Vatch yourself, Scourgeblood. Don't think highly of yourself because you von een the Duel Tests. Tohday, you follov my orders."

A breath of a moment passed, and then Aken looked to Schnel. "What did he just say?"

Schnel raised a finger. "Allow me to translate—"

"Shut up!" Tyomnii attached the scythe to his back, via

magnetic pads which held it in place, and he stormed off towards the city gates, his jacket tails swishing. "Time ees vasting! Vee leave now!"

Heion heaved a sigh before turning back to Harlow and putting on a smile. "Forgive the rudeness. He's not always in such a rotten mood."

"Yes, he is," Schnel cut in frankly, earning a sideways glare from the kitsune.

The twins nodded their agreement, "His temper is as sharp as that scythe."

"Quite so, dear Brother. And we'd better hurry along before he uses said scythe on *us*!"

Cyrus shared a look with the others. Already this mission was off to a rocky start.

Harlow followed the Floor Smart squad through the northern gates. The center stone in the grand archway bore the kingdom's crest: two hands, palms up, beneath a crown in the shape of a fang and bat wings—the same symbol that was in the Draev's coat-of-arms.

They passed the gatekeepers, who recognized the prince and waved them on, and passed by a pair of grand statues to either side of the archway guarding the way to the north: twenty-foot-tall representations of two of the Legendary Knights in robes and armor, one holding a halberd, the other a scythe.

Cyrus glanced from the stone scythe to the real one on the prince's back.

A smooth dirt road stretched onward before them, and off to the side of the road stood a group of bladecycles, ready and waiting.

Cyrus studied the two-seater bike, the look of it sleeker than the Argos Corps model.

"Whoa, we're riding bladecycles?" Bakoa exclaimed, an obvious thrill bubbling inside him.

"Hop aboard, desert boy!" Victor swung into a bladecycle's seat and patted the space behind him.

Bakoa took the offer eagerly.

Aken sniffed. "My clay bird can move faster than these things."

"Just do as we're told," Cyrus whispered to him, "then the faster we can rescue Apfel."

She took the seat behind Heion, and Zartanian took the one behind Jack, leaving Tyomnii's as the only one left. No one wanted to ride with Schnel and risk getting slimed.

Hercule had his own bladecycle, brought from his mansion, and he glared a warning when Aken stepped towards him.

Cyrus tried not to grin as Aken relented and awkwardly slid into the seat behind the prince, trying not to touch him or the dark blade.

"Stop squeeggling around," Tyomnii warned over his shoulder. "And hold tight."

Aken started to mutter something, when the bladecycle suddenly jolted to life and the whirring fans propelled them forward. He yelped and grabbed onto the prince's jacket.

The bladecycle Cyrus was on moved forward, and she tightened her arms around Heion's waist. She tried not to sit on the kitsune's fluffy red tail.

The vehicles sped across the ground, fans whirring over the dirt road, headed north. She heard Zartanian yelp and looked back to see the shy boy clinging to Jack for dear life, while Bakoa whooped and hollered with glee behind Victor.

Tall grasses and wildflowers swayed in the fields that they passed, speckled with flittering butterflies and buzzing bees. Grasshoppers leaped away from the sides of the road, and gusts of warm air rolled over them, hinting at a hot summer soon to come.

Lake Doroth came into view, and the road curved to travel

along its eastern border. After a long while of riding, they came across a fishing town, a grim and ramshackle-like place.

"I'm hungry. Can we stop and get some food?" asked Bakoa over the humming of the bladecycle fans.

Before the twins could answer, Zartanian spoke. "You can wait for the next town. I don't want to stop here," he snapped.

Cyrus, Aken and Hercule turned to look over their shoulders at him. It wasn't like Zartanian to snap, let alone show a temper. What was it that had him so agitated?

With all their eyes suddenly on him, Zartanian's cheeks went red, and he ducked behind the twin's back.

Victor handed Bakoa a little box of crackers from his pocket. "This'll have to suffice, desert boy. We can't be late for our appointment!"

17

The sun lowered into early afternoon by the time they crested a hill and reached the large lake town of Pearlset. It rose like a glistening pearl from the lake waters, all pinnacled white towers and shiny, silvery domes. Sunlight slanted through the clouds and cut a shimmering path down over the rooftops and across the surface of the lake.

Tyomnii steered them off the dirt path and out onto the open waters. Waves splashed to either side as the bladecycle fans glided them across the lake. Cyrus squinted against the bright path of sunlight glinting off the gray-blue waters.

Lake Doroth stretched far and wide towards the horizon, green mountains making up the coastline in the distance. Boats with triangular sails were hard at work, fishermen casting nets or hauling in crayfish traps.

Tyomnii headed for one of the town's white stone docks. Giant wheels slowly rotated in the waters throughout the lake town, feeding a series of pipelines. Boats of various sizes bobbed at the docks, water lapping against their painted hulls.

The prince raised his fist, signaling them to stop. The bladecycles slowed, fan blades drifting to a halt upon the dock.

They dismounted. Cyrus slid off the seat, too short to step down, and stumbled.

They all grouped behind Tyomnii as he analyzed their surroundings.

"Should we use our classic ambush tactic?" Heion asked him quietly.

Tyomnii's gaze scanned the dock and silvery rooftops slowly. "Yes, that ees vhat I'm thinking. Heion, take the north. Holsome tvins, take the south. The rest of you lot are veeth me."

Cyrus noticed both Aken and Hercule bristle, but the group did as instructed and followed the dark prince along the stone docks circling the town, while Heion and the twins disappeared into the white streets.

They soon reached the meeting place described on the note: dock 2 on the westside, and turned from there to enter the adjoining small piazza.

A large waterwheel rose from the stone tile floor on the piazza's left, rotating languidly. There were no people around here, and no sounds, not even bees buzzing at the purple flower windowsill boxes. It set her nerves on edge.

Venturing farther in, Cyrus gasped when she suddenly spotted Apfel: standing near the piazza's center. She almost ran to him.

Tyomnii's arm blocked her, his hand resting the shaft end of the scythe upon the stone tiles.

With Apfel stood an armed vempar, gripping his arm. Scruff covered his face as if he hadn't bothered with a clean shave in years, and belts holding all manner of blades were strapped over his ragged clothes. He grinned toothily at them and gestured for them to come near.

"Prince, he doesn't look like an ordinary kidnapper," whispered Schnel. "Something's off."

Tyomnii acknowledged his words with a quick glance. He stayed his ground as he demanded of the criminal, "Hand over the child, now, or there veell be consequences." His voice carried across the piazza, full of authority.

Apfel was trembling, the brim of his cap pulled down. His eyes lifted just a bit to see Cyrus and Aken, an unspoken plea for help in them.

Aken looked ready to lunge forward.

"That's what I'm doing," answered the man. "One of you boys can come and get him. Send that redhead, over there."

Cyrus's pulse pounded.

But Tyomnii thudded the end of the scythe against the tiles again. "Release the faeryn, and he veell valk to us." His tone brooked no argument.

The scruffy man scoffed and shook his head. "Just can't be any fun, can you? Well, in that case…"

P-tm!

Cyrus barely had time to hear the gun shot before the bullet struck.

Tyomnii's scythe moved like lightning—striking the bullet out of the air and sending it bouncing back, the blood silver undamaged.

She looked to where the shot came from: another man, perched on a rooftop with an aimed axe-rifle.

"There're more where that came from, boy." The man spat, and little Apfel cringed.

Aken and Hercule lifted their gazes to the rooftops, where more men lay in wait. "I see now," said Hercule quietly. "These are no mere kidnappers—they're the convicts reported to have escaped the Morbid Dungeons, not long ago. It was in the city papers."

Morbid Dungeons? They were facing off against criminals—the very *worst* of criminals?

"I veell tell you one more time. Release the child," Tyomnii demanded again, his resolve not wavering even an inch.

The scruffy criminal barked a laugh at him. "Come and make us, Highness. I'd be more than thrilled to severe your head from your fancy neck."

Tyomnii shifted both hands to grip the scythe and launched himself forward in one fluid motion. "Schnel, move them!" he called out.

"On it." The snail boy saluted as the prince charged the criminal head-on, blocking several more bullets with the scythe.

Schnel ushered the Harlow boys back into the space of an alley, out of the way of flying bullets.

A man on the rooftop suddenly cried out, blocking a blow from Heion, who had suddenly appeared behind him. She slashed the axe-rifle in two with the blood silver katana.

Other shouts rang from the opposite rooftops, where the Holsome twins had appeared. They wielded a glowing length of chain between them, lassoing and knocking out attackers.

"Let us at 'em!" Aken said, watching from the alley while Schnel kept them there.

"Just wait," urged Schnel. He peeked around the stone corner.

The scruffy criminal met Tyomnii's blade with a cutlass, taking care not to let the scythe break the sword but deflect the blows instead. He was surprisingly quick on his feet, dodging.

Apfel had scurried off to the side, out of the way. The criminals didn't seem so focused on keeping the child hostage anymore. But if so, then what was their true intention?

"I'll go get him," whispered Schnel, eyeing the battle. "Wait here until you're called for backup," he added.

Cyrus watched as he slipped out from the alley and skated

along the piazza's perimeter, ducking low and headed for Apfel. He skated as if on ice, but she realized it was slime, and he left a trail of it in his wake. He was almost to Apfel, when Bakoa shouted from behind her.

She only had time to turn partway around before a hand seized around her arm and yanked her up into the air.

"Cyrus!" Aken cried out.

The grip was strong. She craned her neck to see the greasy criminal who had her, his grin speckled with gold teeth.

Hercule released a stream of fire, the flames curling upwards after the man. But her captor soared high, reaching the nearest rooftop.

Aken came flying in on Limitless, rage in his eyes.

The gold-toothed man ran along the roof, pulling her along with him like a sack of potatoes. Clay birds exploded at the man's right side, but it wasn't enough damage to stop him. Aken couldn't really hit him without hurting her in the process.

Cyrus tried to grab onto something with her free hand, but the man's strength pulled her at a fast pace. She cast about for something that was metal, but the roofs were silvery ceramic tiles and painted chimneys.

Okay. She would have to use her metal reserve.

The metal bracelets shifted from her arms, forming needle points, and stabbed into the arm and hand that gripped her.

The man cried out in pain. But instead of just letting go, he threw her across a street and onto the next rooftop, where another man—green skinned like a goblin—caught her.

She tried playing deadweight, but since she was small it didn't really matter, and the guy dragged her along. She summoned the bracelets, filled with her *essence*, and the metal came flying back to her. The needles made their way into the half-goblin's limbs.

He yelped and dropped her.

She rolled to her feet on the rooftiles and turned around to run back towards Aken.

Aken stretched out his hand for her.

A force suddenly halted Cyrus mid-run, and she felt her body being pulled sideways like a magnet off the roof.

Aken called out, his hand just missing hers, as she was wrenched through the air and across the piazza, towards the giant rotating waterwheel on the other side.

"Tut-tut," said a voice. "Stabbing people isn't a very princess-like thing to do."

A handsome young man floated above the waterwheel, his ears curved and hair pure white, a blue high-collared cape rustling about his shoulders, the rest of his clothing white with black accents.

Cyrus couldn't control her body as she floated towards him. Who was this? What strange power was he using? She struggled and fought to make her muscles obey, yet the pull kept dragging her through the air.

A dark shape crossed the corner of her vision—the scythe. It sliced at the man as Tyomnii came vaulting up the waterwheel.

The man took a step back, dodging the slice with ease upon the waterwheel's rim.

"Oh really now. Don't you royals have anything better to do? Like host another meaningless banquet?" he rebuked.

Tyomnii made a series of fast slashes with his blade, all of which the man evaded with slight steps and leaning just out of reach. The prince growled in frustration.

Cyrus's body stopped being pulled, and she now hung suspended in the air, close by.

"You," Tyomnii said through clenched teeth. "You are the Vheete Ghost who's been causing trouble?"

The man's gaze flattened. "I think you mean White Ghost. And yes, that's me. How very shrewd of you." He sidestepped, then thrust out his left palm.

Tyomnii's torso stopped moving. He grunted, struggling to push forward and reach the White Ghost.

"So arrogant, you vempars. Perhaps I should teach you how to kneel?" His hand lowered, and Tyomnii's body started to lower with it into a kneel on the edge of the waterwheel.

Tyomnii cursed, his teeth gritting against the strain of fighting the invisible force. "Vhat sorcery ees thees?" His features contorted.

The White Ghost sniffed. "Why do you people always assume that what you don't understand must be sorcery? Oh well. At least I have my prize, and I'll be able to get rid of the prince and a few young Draevs."

Heion leaped from the nearby roof and onto the waterwheel, her katana slashing through the Ghost's torso and cutting him in half...

Or it would have. The man vanished, and in his place stood a potted plant from the piazza below, the katana slicing it clean through.

Heion blinked, startled, the pottery pieces falling away from her sword.

Tyomnii stumbled, released from the force that was holding him.

"*Haha*, that was a nice try," said the White Ghost from the piazza floor. He slowly levitated himself back up to the top of the giant waterwheel. "But you really should just make this easier on yourselves and let me kill you."

The bits of bracelet metal had finally come back to Cyrus, and though she couldn't move, she willed the metal to fly at the Ghost.

He turned his head in time, lifting a hand, and the metal bits halted and fell to the distant ground.

In that moment, Tyomnii and Heion lunged forward as one,

coming at him from two angles, and a blizzard of flower petals summoned by Heion blinded the Ghost. Their blades slashed, trapping him in between them.

But the White Ghost vanished again, this time a pile of bricks appearing in his place. When the air cleared, he waved at them from the adjacent rooftop, then he cast out his palms and sent a rain of bricks from nearby chimneys flying at them.

The prince and kitsune dodged aside, hopping down the paddle boards of the waterwheel as bricks smashed into them.

Cyrus took a moment to glance around her: Schnel had Apfel but was busy evading a criminal. The twins were still on the rooftops, battling more men. Hercule's fire and Bakoa's sand hammers struck left and right from the ground, while Zartanian's saber struggled to block the blows raining down on him from a vempar twice his size.

They were outnumbered...and losing fast.

⌒ට

Aken watched in dismay as Cyrus was wrenched through the air away from him. And then the half-goblin and the other criminal were attacking him, tumbling him off of Limitless.

Aken flung out a handful of birds, exploding them in the criminals' faces.

"So weak," the voice spoke in his head. *"We can do so much more than this."*

Aken summoned Limitless back, trying to ignore the voice.

"Ignoring me will cost you. Are you okay with that?"

The golden cage appeared in his mind, hedged in thorns.

"What do you mean?"

"Look around you: your friends are going to die. They cannot fight the power that this humanoid wields."

Aken did look around. His friends were struggling. Even the older Smart boys were being worn down. And that power—the White Ghost—if someone as skilled as the prince, with a

Legendary Weapon, couldn't even land a blow on him, then what hope did any of them have?

Cyrus. Harlow. He couldn't let this happen. He couldn't lose what was precious to him again!

"You know what you have to do," said his replica from the cage. He extended one hand, just between the bars. *"Be what we were born to be."*

Fear coursed through him as he stared at the hand, the power.

He could either save his friends and possibly lose himself...or run and save himself.

It wasn't hard to choose which.

He grabbed the hand.

Power coursed through him, glowing his veins the hot colors of lava.

He didn't need a mirror to know his eyes had gone from blue to fiery red as a new energy filled his being and tried to take over his mind.

The half-goblin came at him, and Aken lifted a leg, kicking him solidly and sending him flying backwards into the other criminal.

Aken leaped onto Limitless.

"Enough games," the White Ghost was saying. He lifted his hands, and Tyomnii and Heion floated up towards him, their shoulders twitching, trying in vain to break free. With a hand motion, he smashed their bodies into the roof, then lifted them high again.

Blood streamed down the sides of their faces.

He readied to smash them down again, when he suddenly turned his gaze to see Aken flying at him—his fist a glowing obsidian gauntlet.

The Ghost raised one hand, the same move that somehow halted people in their tracks.

But Aken kept coming. His body didn't halt in the air like

everyone else's had.

The Ghost's eyes widened, just before Aken's fist plowed into his head.

The punch sent the man soaring backwards across the roof and over a street and onto the next roof over.

Aken veered, catching Cyrus out of the air. They landed by the prince and kitsune, and Cy hurried to check on them.

Aken planted his feet on the tiles and watched as the White Ghost lifted himself slowly upright. The man felt at his jaw, moving it around.

"Well, that smarted. Good thing I kept a force field around myself, or that would have left a nasty scar."

Shock jolted through Aken. It still wasn't enough? Even with this power?

"You're not using your full potential. You have to release me," tempted the voice. *"Come on. Release me."*

Cyrus looked to him. "Aken, we have to escape."

"But..." Aken watched the Ghost stand.

Escape where? How?

Tyomnii rose with effort, gripping the scythe. "Vee must retreat, much as I hate to say eet."

"How?" Cy asked, helping Heion stand.

"Can you make that bird any beegger?" Tyomnii nodded his chin to Limitless.

The power in Aken's veins called to him, urging him to let go of all restraints and become something else. He struggled to hold it back. "I..." He gripped the sides of his head.

Unable to wait for an answer, Tyomnii lifted Heion in his arms and jumped down to the waterwheel, quickly using the paddles like steps to reach the ground below.

Still up on the roof, Cyrus got on Limitless. "Aken!"

Aken made himself move, and he tried to focus as he got on and steered the bird downward.

They all regrouped with Schnel and Apfel in the piazza below. Hercule blasted flames to keep the criminals at bay, while Aken landed the bird and he and Cyrus hopped off.

"Oh no you don't," said the White Ghost from above, his hand still rubbing his jaw. "I'm not letting *you* get away." He looked directly at Cyrus.

Aken roared and plowed his fist into the nearest criminal—delivering a punch and shockwave of power that sent him flying into the other criminals and knocking them all backwards into one another.

"Go!" Aken told his friends. "Run!"

Cyrus protested and grabbed up the metal bracelets. But Tyomnii took note of Aken's glowing veins and armored fist. "Victor, take Cyrus! Vee're getting out of here."

"No!"

The twin grabbed Cyrus up. Bakoa hesitated too, but the White Ghost was coming.

Aken leaped back onto Limitless and came at the man, while his friends escaped from the piazza and headed for the docks. A swirling cloud of petals rose behind the Draev students, coming from Heion's katana, masking their retreat.

"Get out of my way!" The Ghost's hand stretched to the side then swung forward, and a mass of bricks and tiles came flying at Aken.

Aken shielded his head with his forearms, grunting. But he continued riding on Limitless towards the Ghost, and he leveled his armored fist forward.

The Ghost levitated to the side just in time, Aken and his lava armored fist sailing by.

"What's your real name?" Aken demanded.

"Why should I tell you, you little nuisance?" He floated towards the alley where the Draev students had disappeared out of the piazza, but Aken swung the bird back around and caught the edge of his cape, yanking it and him backwards.

The Ghost cursed and tore the cape free.

Aken circled Limitless around, again putting himself between the Ghost and the path of his friends. "It's only fair to know the name of your opponent."

The man regarded him while levitating above the silvery rooftops. "Opponent? Ha! You're nothing but a fly that's in my way." The Ghost's palms thrust upward, and a fountain below them ripped free of the piazza floor, water spewing from its broken pipes.

The Ghost motioned, and the entire fountain basin and statue came sailing up at Aken.

"Kill them all!" the voice urged, clawing to take over Aken's mind.

Aken roared, and as the fountain came, he smashed his gauntlet fist through the stone basin.

Shattered pieces flew past his ears and tumbled to the far ground below.

The Ghost's lips drew into a smirk. "Ellefsen. That's my real name." His arms stretched wide, and the ground below them began to rumble.

There was a loud creak and groaning as the massive waterwheel began to be wrenched free of the piazza's stone tiles.

The sight caused Aken to hesitate.

"Let me free. Let me free!" cried the voice, tearing at him, clawing its way through his thoughts. He clenched the sides of his head, trying to keep his sanity.

❧

"How could you just leave him behind?" Cyrus exclaimed as they ran.

"I deedn't," said Tyomnii, as they reached the bladecycles. "I already called for backup."

The prince tapped the comm device at his belt.

The waterwheel stopped moving. Ellefsen squinted into the distance at a group of figures that were headed their way.

"Oh *seriously?*" he half groaned, half growled.

Aken turned his gaze to see what the man meant and why his tone had become so irritated. Were those figures Draevs?

"You wasted my small window of time," Ellefsen growled across at him.

His power let go of the waterwheel, and the giant object groaned as it sank back into place and fractured. "Aken, is that what your friends called you? Sadly, it's time for me to leave. Though, I am sure another opportunity will present itself for us to cross paths again."

Ellefsen floated swiftly down to the ground and called his lackeys over to him.

Aken watched as he and the criminals stepped through a shimmering gap that appeared in the air—and then, they were gone.

Exhausted, and with no one left to fight, Aken's emotions calmed, and he drew his hand away from the replica in the cage in his mind.

His reflection snarled. *"You will need me again."*

Aken drifted down on Limitless to the ground, just as a squad of adult Draev Guardians arrived.

18

Cyrus sat in the room with Apfel, the child's blue skin stark against the white sheets of the bed. Dr. Zushil had his hands full at the infirmary building, checking over everyone who had been on the mission.

The kitsune was being Healed in another room while the prince stalked through the hallway, ignoring the nurses who urged him to rest and let his body Heal. She could still hear his accented voice fuming beyond the curtain door.

She understood. She had felt so helpless, like a weak doll thrown about who could do nothing but watch as the people she cared for were being hurt. Her Ability, all that practice, had meant nothing against the White Ghost.

The curtain rustled as a hand pushed it aside and Aken entered.

"How is the little tyke?" he asked her, nodding to Apfel in the bed.

The child glanced up at him, then back down at the sheets.

"Physically he's fine," she answered. "Are *you* okay?"

She glanced pointedly at Aken's hands, recalling the power he'd wielded.

He pocketed them. "Yeah. Pretty much. Sorry if I...scared you all." His chin lowered.

Cyrus shook her head. "You were the only reason we got away. Don't apologize for that."

"But—"

"I was useless!" she said, louder than she meant to, then paused to suck in a breath. "Be glad you weren't," she added more quietly.

A shadow passed over Aken's features, and she wondered for a moment what it was that he was so hesitant and worried about.

"Apfel, do you know why that man kidnapped you?" she asked.

Apfel's small chin sunk to his chest. "Because I'm the new Oracle, *ja?*" he said almost mournfully.

She shared a look with Aken.

"He mades me go into a trance," Apfel continued with his child lisp. "I don't knows what all I said... M' sorry."

"It's not your fault, Apfel." She patted the top of his hand. "Can you remember anything at all he asked you?"

He shook his head. Without the cap on, his dark blue hair with silver streaks was wispy about his long, pointed ears. "But..." his hands fisted the sheets, "someone else cames after me first, before he did."

Cyrus stiffened, and Aken visibly tensed.

"Gave me the chills. He tried to kidnaps me at the bakery. I think they calleds him...Pueginn."

Cyrus gave a start. Pueginn? The principal's assistant? "Why on eartha would he do that?"

Aken shook his head, creases now showing between his eyebrows.

"There's too much going on here. It's like the whole world is out to get you two."

She gave him a questioning look.

"The White Ghost wanted *you*, Cy. I saw the way he looked at you."

She swallowed. That man had also referred to her as a princess.

"Apfel called you the Swan, earlier. Maybe that guy thinks you have the Swan's power, and..." his gaze met hers, "maybe you actually do." His gaze pointed to her chest—the mass of *essence* that dwelled somewhere inside her, slowly eating away at her body.

"But—but that's crazy talk!" She tried to laugh. "I'm not some reborn hero from ages past. I'm just *me*. A little nobody from Elvenstone Town."

They both kept staring at her.

She clenched her arms. "I'm not the Swan—and I don't even want that to be a possibility!"

Aken leaned back against the wall and bent his left knee. "The old Oracle told me my life would be connected to the Swan's... I didn't know what he meant then, but if you really *are* the Swan, that would explain some things." He ran a hand through his bangs and glanced down. "Like why ever since I met you, I've felt a connection."

Cyrus blinked at him.

His face went pink. "I mean, not like that! More like we share a destiny, are fated or something."

She narrowed her eyes.

"Not in *that* way. I just—you know what I mean!" He scrubbed furiously at his head with a hand. "Besides, you're a boy Swan now. Even if you were, in the past, a...a..."

Cyrus sighed. Good thing Aken wasn't smart enough to connect the dots. It wasn't that she didn't want him to know about her being female, but if he found out, he might accidentally let it slip—and what if the wrong person heard?

A voice in her head still warned she keep quiet about her gender, and the words of the redhead girl in the cemetery echoed in her mind: *"Red hair…female…human… Don't let them find you…"*

Whoever the Impure Nights were, they were looking for a female to be the Swan.

"If Pueginn is in league with the Impure Nights in some way, that would explain why he would want Apfel," she said.

"Yeah…I don't trust that Deidreem guy, either. Why did he lie and cover up the Corpsed?" Aken furthered.

Cyrus shuddered. "If I am the Swan—*which I'm not*—I don't think the Impure Nights suspect me yet, or they wouldn't have bothered to target Apfel. Maybe they believe the Oracle knows who the Swan is, and that's why everyone's been after him?"

Aken gave a nod. "And that Ellefsen guy found out."

"Ellefsen?"

"That's the White Ghost's name."

She rubbed at her scarred wrists. They were aching again, more so than usual. "Anyway, I'm not the Swan of legend. The energy inside me is a strange power, and that must be what they want the Oracle to find. Simple as that."

She refused to believe she was some princess with a tragic past.

Aken shrugged.

Either way, if the White Ghost was after her…

She paled.

That was when Master Nephryte entered the room.

⌒

'How could I have been so foolish?' Nephryte reprimanded himself.

A simple mission to retrieve a kidnapped slave. Of course it was a trap. But he never would have imagined that the White Ghost was behind it. So far, the man's group had only attacked traveling slavers in the dark of night and set slaves free.

Instead, Nephryte had expected the trap to be some petty group of vempars who held a grudge against a half-human living freely in Draethvyle. That would have been more than easy for Floor Smart's team to deal with.

Why would the White Ghost want to lure Harlow out?

The Ghost had kidnapped the Oracle successfully, yet for some reason hadn't been satisfied with that?

Unless there was something the Ghost had learned from the Oracle—something about one of his students...

Nephryte entered the infirmary room to check in on Apfel, and found both Cyrus and Aken were there. He noted the somber atmosphere of the room.

He nodded to each of them in greeting.

"Apfel, how are you feeling?" He lightly patted the faeryn's shoulder.

The child didn't lift his head. "Okay," was all he mumbled.

"I've explained to your owner that you'll be staying with us for a while longer, to help with the investigation of the White Ghost. It's a good excuse, so we can keep an eye on you," Nephryte explained. "Don't worry. Nothing more is going to come after you."

Apfel's whole body shuddered involuntarily.

"Master, there's something you should know," Cyrus began. "Someone else was after Apfel, too—someone from Draevensett."

She explained about Pueginn, and Nephryte felt a cold brush of unease. The trusted assistant himself had tried to kidnap Apfel? He was aware of the existence of the Oracle power?

"I haven't seen Pueginn anywhere today." Nephryte tapped

his chin. "I should go and discuss this with Principal Han. But without solid proof, we won't be able to bring criminal charges against him."

"That Deidreem is just as suspicious," Aken added. "He lied about that Corpsed we defeated and covered it up."

Nephryte considered that. "Again, we would need actual physical proof. Masters cannot be charged for something without solid evidence. But that does not mean we have to trust him, either. In fact, I think it would be best if we keep our guard up and remain vigilant. And if you happen to see Pueginn, come straight to me—don't engage him."

He then glanced at a ticking wall clock. "It's getting late… Come on, the doctor says you are all well enough to be back at the dorms. I'll escort you."

〜꒰

Adelheid kicked her dainty feet back and forth, perched on the back of Deidreem's chair inside his office. Her grin was as pretty as it was heartless, and the principal's assistant couldn't calm the shaking of his knees before her.

"Master Deidreem isn't here at the moment, as you can obviously see. But you can talk to *me*." The eerie note of her giggle made Pueginn shake all the more. "You do have a plan, don't you? To steal away that little Oracle?"

"He's no longer at the bakery but here, under Nephryte's watchful eye," Pueginn complained, and he rubbed a finger under his large, beaked nose. "What if it turns out that he isn't the Oracle? I—erm, *we*—will have wasted our time. There is no way to know for sure if he's the one."

"Sure there is!" She gracefully flipped backwards down off the chair, landing smoothly on both her stockinged feet. "We keep the child locked up until he starts speaking in prophecy, or some such gibberish. Even if it takes a few years."

Sweat beaded on Pueginn's temples. It was a good thing they

were on the same side; he would not want to be her enemy.

"I don't know when I'll be able to snatch him," he said in his nasally voice. "Thanks to that blasted White Ghost, Floor Harlow won't leave the child alone for even a second!"

"Be patient, and don't slip up when a chance does happen to come." She bopped his long beak of a nose with her finger. "You wouldn't want to disappoint Leader, or me."

⤙

The next morning, Mamoru poured waffle batter into molded fryers, while Harlow waited around the kitchen table for breakfast. Cyrus made soft-boiled eggs and handed them out, the yolk inside a delicious molten gold.

The boys were somber and many brows furrowed. Bakoa rested his chin on the table, stomach growling, yet not bothering to beg Mamoru to hurry up. And Hercule glared at his coffee mug to the point that Cyrus feared it might catch on fire.

She knew just how they felt.

Inadequate. Nearly defeated. Too weak to ever become real Draevs.

Mamoru brought the finished waffles on a platter, setting them in the center of the table. No one was fast to grab them, not even little Apfel.

The scarred older boy shared a look with her, then planted his hands on his aproned hips. "If you all don't stop sulking, these waffles will get cold. And if that happens, don't expect me to make them for you again," he warned.

Muttering to themselves, they slowly stabbed their forks at the food.

Mamoru shook his head in disbelief. "You're all acting as if you failed the mission. When the truth is, you kept each other alive and rescued Apfel, despite going up against a foe that even official Draevs are having trouble with." His palm smacked the table. "So, enough moping. Wipe those miserable frowns off your faces and think of ways to improve your Abilities."

Bakoa straightened in his chair. He pounded a fist on the table, determination setting the lines of his shoulders and his cleft chin. "You're right! I need to improve my sand attacks." He stuffed half a waffle in his mouth, now in a hurry to eat.

Zartanian nodded, his winter-blue gaze hardening, and he started to eat faster.

"Yes, you should all improve," spoke Lykale, while thumbing through a copy of this morning's city papers. "The Hunters Race is coming up, and I'd rather not look like a fool on a losing team."

Mamoru sent him a look, to which he ignored.

Hercule finished his plate, stood, and downed the rest of his coffee. The mug *thunked* down on the table. "We won't be a losing team—not if I can help it. I'm going to use every spare hour to hone my skills." His thumbnail dug into his palm, and he marched out the door of the dorm flat without another word.

"Right, me too!" Bakoa's chair screeched back, and he headed out.

Zartanian followed next.

Cyrus noticed Aken over in a chair in the connected living room, quietly forking a waffle Mamoru had handed him. She didn't have time to wonder why he was acting so strange, though. The academy's bells gonged out the hour and the start of class.

She swallowed her last bit of waffle, almost choking, and hurried out. She refused to just sit back and let herself be useless—not without working her backside off and sweating blood and tears, first!

19

"**W**e should finish this assignment now. That way, we'll have the rest of the day free to work on our Ability training," Cy was telling Aken, once the day's classes were finally finished.

Aken rubbed at his aching forehead while Cy talked, and he peered down at the name he'd been handed for Professor Ponairi's cultural homework assignment: *Tyomnii Sivortsova*.

He groaned.

Cyrus stole a look at the name on his document. "Hey, this works out perfectly! I got Heion, so how about we go look for them together? I heard they're back from the infirmary."

Aken felt reluctant to see the Smart students again, but he agreed and followed the redhead out onto the spiral walkway. Maybe Cy was right—it would be best to get this over with quickly.

They navigated to Floor Smart's wing of the school, their crest emblazoned on the entry door: a smug-looking fox with its tail curled around a book.

The furnishings inside the dorm floor were a color scheme of rich purples and browns. The hallways were wide, with checkered floor tiles and decorative purple rugs. Lamps hung along the wood paneled walls, and the whole atmosphere gave off a feeling of mystery. Smart's floor was much bigger than Harlow's, and many students bustled about the corridors.

"So…where are their rooms?" Aken turned in place.

Students walking ahead of them suddenly moved to the side, getting out of the way of a dark figure striding down the corridor.

"Well, speak of the Grim Reaper himself," Aken whispered out the side of his mouth.

The prince strode forward until he bumped into Aken. Then his forehead furrowed and he looked down, as if surprised that something had dared to block his path.

"Oh, hello again." Heion waved from beside him.

Tyomnii regarded them both, then lifted his smooth chin. "Vhat are Harlov boys doing here?"

"Now, Prince, be nice. We're supposed to be role models for the younger ones," Heion rebuked.

Cyrus hurried to explain the homework assignment to them, not giving Aken a chance.

"Yes, we can certainly help with that! Right, Tyomnii-sama? I remember when we had that assignment; I was so shy." Heion chuckled into her fist.

The prince rolled his eyes. "Just get thees over veeth."

"*With*. You need to start pronouncing your W's more," Heion chided.

Aken followed the prince into his gothic furnished dorm room—a replica of what he probably had back in the palace, only smaller.

"Read thees." Tyomnii shoved a thick book into his open

hands, making Aken stumble backwards into a leather plush chair. The prince then proceeded to ignore him, gliding over to a neatly situated desk, where he began to write a letter or something, his handwriting exquisite enough to make anyone jealous.

Aken's lips thinned. The room's dark atmosphere matched Tyomnii. The black bed posts were snarling bats, wings outspread, and the curtains and rugs were a deep red, and the lamps shaped like gargoyles.

Aken looked down at the book forced into his hands: *Răsărit's Traveling Guide for Idiots*.

His brow furrowed. He flipped through several pages until the words all seemed to blur together. "Hey, Tyrant?" he began.

"Prince Tyomnii." The prince looked up with a red glare from his writing at the desk.

"Yeah. Well. I think the assignment's supposed to be something about *you*—not the land you're from in general. So, maybe if you could tell me a story from your time in Răsărit? Like a tradition or special holiday that you remember?" He waited as the rose-red eyes bore into him like thorns.

"No," Tyomnii replied bluntly, and his focus returned to his writing, ignoring Aken once more and clearly severing the conversation.

Aken gave an irritated sigh through his teeth before he settled back into the chair and pulled out a blank sheet of paper. "Fine," he muttered quietly to himself, "I'll work on my art assignment *first* and draw a portrait of your moody self."

As the minutes ticked by, he drew a good likeness of the prince distorted into a long-necked animal with angry eyes and snarling mouth, wearing a fancy cape. "There. *Heheh*, my masterpiece of the Tyrant Gioraf Prince," he chuckled to himself.

He wouldn't be able to turn in such a ridiculous drawing for his art assignment. Plus, it would be a death wish if the prince saw it. He would have to draw someone else later.

The prince still wasn't paying him any attention, and so Aken finally decided to bring the book back to his room for further study and leave the ominous dorm and its ill-tempered ruler. "I'll return this later, then," he said and rose.

"You must stop hating yourself."

Aken halted in surprise at the sudden words and half turned towards the prince. "What do you mean?" he asked uneasily.

"I can see eet een your eyes. I know that look." Tyomnii's thorny gaze cut to him. "That feeling vhen your own power frightens you."

Aken's mouth opened and closed.

"Pureblood ees dangerous, but ees also a part of you. Learn to control eet first, before eet controls you."

"But…I was told never to use it, or else…"

"Thees ees not something everyone can understand, leettle blond." Tyomnii pointed his pen across at Aken's chest. "Power does not lie dormant and quiet. Eet veell find a vay out. You must gain control."

"How would you know?" Aken asked with a waver in his voice.

Tyomnii did not trouble himself to explain but turned his back, pen to the desk again. "Leave and do your homevork."

❧

"My homeland, *mm*?" Heion motioned for Cyrus to have a seat at the little table inside her room. The kitsune offered her tea and sat on a chest at the foot of her bed. "I was born in Higashi, the eastern lands. But as a child, I was transported along with many other kitsune to the north: to a slave workhouse near Sivortska City in Răsărit," Heion chattered. "You probably don't know much about those lands, do you?"

Cyrus shook her head.

"Tyomnii-sama's House practically rules the city. The Sivortsova House is its founder, after all." Heion's gaze took on a faraway, nostalgic look.

"Are there many cities in Răsărit?" Cyrus asked, though what she really wanted to know was how a kitsune had come to be the prince's personal bodyguard and attendant. The girl even had her own dorm room, not in the servants' quarters, and could attend classes alongside Tyomnii.

The kitsune blinked, her mind returning from distant memories. "No. It is a cold land, though beautiful and untamed." Her voice sounded almost fond. "Also, the land of Eldfjöll borders Răsărit, and its residents don't like us one bit. Keeping hold of vempar territory there has been difficult because of them. But I think some vempars enjoy the challenge, you know?"

Cyrus glanced at the katana leaning against the chest. The flower designs on the crossguard and scabbard were so lifelike, delicate, like the petals of cherry blossoms. "How are you allowed to…?" she began, then trailed off, worried that such a question might offend the kitsune.

"Have such a valuable weapon?" Heion guessed at her question. "It's…complicated, to say the least. My situation is unique. But you know, you don't have to be a vempar to wield a Legendary Weapon." Her fingertip brushed down the patterned, silk-wrapped hilt. "Strange, isn't it? You would think the blade's power wouldn't work for other races, and yet it does. Almost as if…" Heion halted herself. "*Wari*, I am sorry, Cyrus-san. Here I am ranting on and on about nonsense, when you have a paper to write."

"No, it's fine," Cyrus tried to say. She glanced at a wooden clock on the wall, its sides made to look like bamboo leaves.

"I have an idea for your paper, though!" Heion brightened,

and then she dove into telling Cyrus about her first experience celebrating a winter holiday in Răsărit. "It was so cold— freezing the tip of your tail off, cold! Oh, but the snow was a sight to behold, it truly was, especially for someone like me coming from a land that rarely had any…"

Cyrus busied herself jotting down notes during the monologue. By the end, she had to edge her way to the door while Heion kept on talking, as the day was getting late.

She finally managed to step out and wave goodbye. "Thank you for your help! I hate to rush, but I have Ability exercises to do," she said and hurried off before the kitsune could find anything more to say or offer her more tea.

She still had to work on her art portrait assignment, but she would do that later; she didn't want to waste any more of the day.

~ϱ

"That's the assignment?"

"Seems to be, dear Brother. I recall we had to do the same, at their age."

The Holsome twins peered down their sleek noses, like two ferrets eyeing their small Zartanian prey. The shy boy was mustering all the courage that he could.

"Let's get to it then, shall we?" chimed one.

"Indeed, jolly brother o' mine!" agreed the other.

The first twin plopped Zartanian down on a stool in their shared room and snatched his Bladeer hat off. He fingered his exposed antlers, suddenly feeling self-conscious.

"A fine hero-wannabe he makes, does he not?"

"Quite so, with that lush dark hair!"

"But he's too pale. You'd think the poor thing was a ghost."

Zartanian glanced back and forth between the twins warily.

"I say, the poor chap is trembling like an iceberg in May.

Do you think he's allergic to us?"

"To *you*, maybe, but my charm is irresistible! Didn't you notice the cleaning maid swoon at the mere sight of me, the other day?"

Victor crossed his arms. "Not swooning, dear Brother. She was gagging and trying to get away from that horrid cologne you've been wearing! I feel like fainting myself." He waved a hand over his nose. "Wear it tomorrow, and I shall replace it with skunk oil."

"Brother, you are too cruel!"

Zartanian waited silently; why did his assignment have to be on *them*? And why twins? As if he hadn't had enough reminders of Elijob this past week, already. "I just want to f-finish my assignment..." he stammered.

The back-and-forth banter ceased, and the ferret twins' attention swiveled back to him. "Eh? What was that?"

"I think he wants to draw a portrait of us for his art class homework," said Victor.

Jack clapped his hands together. "Splendid idea! Make my head into a giant steak, and have me floating among the clouds like an angel, will you?"

Zartanian blinked. "Pardon?"

"No no no, ignore my younger sibling. You can make him into a seahorse, and I'll be the Mer King of the Seas, with a coral crown on top of my luscious head." Victor posed.

"What?" Jack butted in. "Why am I a silly seahorse? I should be the merman!"

"Because I am both older *and* smarter than you, dear Brother. But don't be offended; seahorses are intelligent creatures, you know. I did a paper on them last year. They have their own body language and everything. They even mate for life; and if their lover dies, they remain single and wither away to the grave... Isn't that simply romantic?" Victor cupped his hands together.

"Another tedious fact that I did not need to know," Jack stated flatly. "And stop calling me younger—I'm only younger than you by three minutes!"

"And what a huge difference those three minutes have made," tsked Victor.

Jack lunged to strangle him, and Victor in turn tried to hook his arm around him in a headlock. They fought and roughhoused around the dorm room, bumping into furniture.

Zartanian gave up, took out his sketchbook and started to draw.

"Hey, you've gone and drawn us while we were discussing important matters," exclaimed Victor, once he had finally pried himself free of his twin. "How rude!"

"Very rude. We didn't even get to pose." Jack sprinted forward and slyly snatched the sketchbook from Zartanian's fingers, and he peered closely at the work. "Let's see. Within a few minutes, you've…" Jack blinked. "I say, this is quite good."

"Really?" Victor smoothly snatched the sketchbook from his younger twin to see. "A masterpiece. We look even *more* stunning on paper than we do in real life—which I did not think was possible!" He clapped a hand on Zartanian's shoulder. "Well done! We would give you a medal if we had one!"

Zartanian coughed from the impact and rubbed his shoulder. "Will you tell me about your homeland, now, so I can write my paper?"

"Of course, but what's the rush? We've got all day!" Victor placed the sketchbook out of reach on a high shelf.

"All day to work on your personality make-over!" Jack's fingers pinched Zartanian's cheeks, stretching them wide. "You're so quiet and shy, you won't last long as a Draev. We have to fix that!"

Zartanian pushed his hands away and tried to escape the room. "I don't need you to. Leave me alone!"

"Tut-tut-tut." Victor caught him by the collar like a fish on a hook. "It's rude for guests to eat and run."

"But I didn't eat anything!"

"That's beside the point." Jack waved an index finger back and forth. "Guests only leave when allowed to."

The twin plopped Zartanian back onto the stool and looped a glowing chain around his arm to keep him in place, and they both grinned down at him.

Anger pinched Zartanian's forehead. This was the last straw—his tolerance level had finally reached its peak. He scrunched his shoulders, filled with tension, and then released it all with a shout: "I said, leave me *alone!*"

And then, there were two Zartanians: one behind the other.

The twins' ferret grins slowly fell.

A third Zartanian appeared from behind his other shoulder.

Both twins rubbed at their eyes, dizzy and wondering if they were imagining things. It was just enough of a distraction for the real Zartanian to unwind the chain, which glowed of *essence*.

Free, Zartanian snatched back his hat, and with an agile leap up one shelf, retrieved the sketchbook. He bolted out the room, rebuking them over his shoulder, "Quiet people are smarter and tougher than you think! I won't let you bully me."

The Holsome twins stared after him, confused how there had been *three* of him, now melting back into *one* again.

"I feel as if an extreme wave of dizziness has befallen me."

"Indeed, it has, dear Brother."

Zartanian had almost reached the Floor Smart entryway exit, when a web of glowing chains spread across the hallway before him, making him stop.

"Steady on, chap!" spoke one twin. "He's got spunk hidden behind that quiet façade, doesn't he?"

"I believe he does, indeed, dear Brother."

"But what sort of trick was it that he used?"

"What indeed? I'm not sure I quite know what your Ability is. I had assumed you were just an Armavis."

The twins, now in front of him, leaned forward and waited for Zartanian to give them an answer.

He swallowed. "I'm also Electrovis class. I just...I don't know, use my *essence* to paint duplicates of things...shifting light and color..."

"So, it's like creating an illusion?"

"I can only make duplicates of things that are around me, and it's limited by how much *essence* I have..."

"Hm, very interesting."

"Very interesting, indeed!"

"I...don't like to use it all that much..." Zartanian fingered the lacy cuffs of his sleeves.

"In this world, you must use your given gifts, and yet remain as humble as a peanut," Jack stated philosophically, and upraised his palms like a saint. "It is a fine balance that one must achieve."

"Perhaps you should turn yourself into a peanut, then." Victor slapped the back of Jack's head. But to Zartanian, he said, "That illusion was splendid work! Zartanian, is it? Interesting name." Victor's smirk tweaked upwards. "I think we will get along splendidly."

Zartanian regarded them both. "If you tease me again, I *will* get serious."

The twins feigned a step back from his intensity and raised their hands in surrender. "We won't, we won't!"

"That's the fierce warrior we wanted to see! We were just waiting for you to show it. You'll make a fine opponent, one day," added Jack.

"Come on." Victor took Zartanian by the shoulders and steered him out towards the spiral walkway, shoes skidding across the floor. "We'll tell you all about ourselves and get that homework of yours done in no time!"

"We'll tell you everything, even what you don't want to know!" added Jack.

Zartanian sweated, trying not to let his nervousness show.

Outdoors on the lawn, the twins proceeded to play a game of shuttleball while they chattered about their previous home and life, and Zartanian took a seat against a tree, patiently scribbling down notes.

They were from the Lake Doroth region, specifically the expanse of hills spread around the lake's north-eastern shore. Zartanian's old hometown was on the edge of those waters, too, but farther south—they had passed by it on their way to Pearlset Town. The mere memory of it sent a spike of pain through his chest.

The Holsome twins had grown up on a farm, sheering sheep and farming goat's milk, they were saying.

"Ahh, we played many a prank on the poor villagers forced to be our neighbors," Victor recalled fondly.

"*Haaha!*" Jack crowed, his racket whacking the ball hard over the net. "I dare say they threw a region-wide party when we were dragged off to the academy!"

"So glad they were to be rid of us—mostly of *you*, I think." Victor flung his arm wide to strike the ball back over.

"What? Don't jest, dear Brother." Jack hit the ball over the net with ease.

"I'm not. You caused the most trouble. Spilling a pail of swamp water on poor Missus Gowter's head every early morning… Why, if not for the pay, she would've high-tailed it out of that farm." Victor smirked, nearly whacking Jack upside the head with a retaliating shuttleball.

"You're the one who kept putting snakes in dear Uncle's bed."

"Oh? What about the time—*no, many times*—when you scared Mother half to death with frogs in her shoes?"

"And you helped!"

Zartanian looked back and forth between the two as they bantered on. He was reminded of the fun he used to have with Elijob, his twin—not the pranks, but the times when they were able to sneak away from home for an hour or two. Just the two of them, having little adventures on the lakeshore, rowing an old boat they had found across the waters and pretending they were Bladeers off on a perilous journey to rescue a fair maiden...

His lips curved in a fond smile.

⤳

"Wow," Schnel exclaimed, with as much effort and gusto as a sleepy snail could muster. "That's quite a costume you have on there, Bakoa."

"I know, right?" Bakoa flicked the tail of his full-body scorpion costume. "Since you're my assignment, I thought I would dress up like an insect, too!"

"*Ja*, but..." Schnel lazily eyed him up and down, "A snail is a shell creature, a mollusk, *not* a deadly insect."

"Oh. Well, there wasn't much I could find in the theater club room; and being from the west coast, I like scorpions."

Schnel stifled a shudder. "Anyway, you wanted to draw a portrait of me, too, you said?"

"Yeah, I have to draw someone for Art class. And since I'm already here to learn about your background for the other assignment, I might as well draw *you*!"

Schnel scratched under his snail hood. "Well, if that's what you want. Let's see, where should I begin..."

While Bakoa sketched him, he began by describing his homeland, Bergvolk: a mountainous and beautiful region, where towns nestled within steep valleys, and lookout posts and castles crowned secluded cliffs and hilltops. A land of pine trees, hidden turquoise pools, and snowy peak horizons. And there were many animals, including fluffy black squirrels.

"I want one!" Bakoa interjected.

Schnel shook his head. "Bergvolk is a risky country, ruled by the rehfabel, and bordered to the north by goblin territory. Raids were a regular threat where I was," he said. "*Ja*, we had to hide in shelters every time the alarms sounded. The village Guard would blow their horns and set bon fires alight to warn nearby villages."

Bakoa gaped, but Schnel waved his fabric-covered hand. "You get used to it."

Bakoa shook his head. "Why were you living way out there?"

"My family's in the trading business with the rehfabel," he said languidly. "So, *ja*, besides the risk of being slaughtered by goblins, it's a beautiful place to live. You should all visit."

Bakoa swallowed. "Um…no thanks…"

Bakoa finally held up his finished sketch with pride. "It's done! Here you are. Pretty good resemblance, huh?"

Schnel peered closely at the paper and frowned. The drawing was of an actual snail, no humanoid body. But to be fair, it was a nice-looking shell. "Uh…I seem to have lost my arms and legs," he pointed out.

"Oh. Do I have to add those?" Bakoa took the drawing back and added squiggly lines for limbs. "Hey, what did your mom think when she gave birth to a snail?" He smirked.

Schnel stared at him blankly. "Ha…ha…you are so funny, my ribs are breaking from laughter."

"I try." Bakoa grinned. "Someone has to maintain a sense of humor in this school."

Schnel bobbed his head. "You certainly do just that." He held out his fist. "Keep up the good work."

They fist-bumped.

"You got slime on my hand."

"Oh. Sorry."

20

Cyrus stood in one of Draevensett's training fields, metal wrapped around her gloved wrists. They were hurting more and more with each passing day, sharp stabs of pain where the white scars circled her skin. The new fingerless gloves were the only thing making it bearable.

She rubbed at them while facing a pile of metal scrap pans from the kitchens. She lightly touched the metal with her bare fingertips, channeling *essence*, then stepped back. She willed the metal to come to her.

The metal pans lifted and changed shape like a thick liquid.

She drew them to her and willed them to do as she imagined—wrapping into plates of armor around her arms and torso. It wasn't easy trying to control so much metal at once, and having each piece do something different.

The pieces wrapped around her awkwardly, overlapping into uneven folds.

She looked down at the resulting sad work, then huffed.

Off to the side, a distance left and right of her, the Harlow boys were also busy practicing techniques with their Abilities. That is, everyone except for Lykale, wherever he was. They had all been at it for hours, now.

Zartanian slashed at a mechanical sword dummy, its dull blades and limbs moving with each strike that he made and forcing him to block.

A large spout of lava thrust into the air where Aken was.

"Hey there!" Mamoru's voice called to them all. He came trotting down the slope, and they paused their training. "Just wanted you to know that Hope's Orphanage is having their first puppet show tonight: *The Magician's Flute*, and you're all invited. The kids have been working hard at it for months. Will you come cheer them on with me?"

A show; that did sound nice and relaxing, a good way to forget the past two days.

Cyrus nodded. "Definitely!"

Mamoru's grin tugged at the red-black scar down his cheek. "Excellent. See you there! I'll have seats reserved for Harlow."

Aken wiped his sweaty brow and gave Mamoru a thumbs-up.

"Time for a break?" she asked him.

Aken nodded. "Yeah. I think I sweated out every cup of water that I drank today."

"Ew, gross."

Aken thought over the prince's words to him, while he and Cy walked back to the castle-mansion school to get more water. Was he right? Was this power something he would have to learn to control? Was it *even* possible to control?

He had been so afraid that someone in Floor Smart would tattle about how he'd used his Pureblood power during the mission. But, so far, it seemed no one had said anything—much to his relief. Tyomnii's squad really were an unusual bunch.

Aken pushed open a back door into Draevensett, and a piece of paper fell on his head. He grumbled, snatching it off, and took a look: it was his gioraf drawing of Tyomnii.

"What the— How did *this* get here?" he exclaimed.

"Um, Aken?" Cyrus poked his shoulder until he looked up, and then Aken's jaw dropped.

Hundreds of photocopies of his drawing were stuck to the walls, and many more floated down from the ceiling, littering the floor of the school hallway.

Students were looking at the sketch and laughing.

"Oh no."

Whoever did this—making copies of his private sketch—was going to pay dearly! But, right now...

"Quick, help me get rid of these!" he shouted to Cy, scurrying around and grabbing what papers he could, tearing them off the walls. "Hurry! Before that prince guy sees—"

A door opened, and he and Cyrus both froze in place.

"*Honto*, sometimes you really get on my nerves, Tyomnii-sama," mumbled Heion, as she and the prince came in from the sun-warmed school grounds through one of the other back doors.

"*Hmph*. Ees that anyvay to talk to your preence—?"

Tyomnii's words were cut short when a swirl of papers met them in the hallway, tossed about by a breeze from the door opening. Irritated, Tyomnii grabbed at the first paper to land on his shoulder, staring down at the drawing: a drawing labeled *Tyrant Gioraf Prince* and signed by Aken.

He stared down at the offensive likeness of himself, and Aken could swear the dark aura around him thickened into a purple-black fog.

Heion covered her snicker and turned away.

Lykale also happened to enter the hallway just then, and he burst out laughing uncharacteristically at the sight.

Aken tried to use the moment to sneak away into a side room, as he felt the prince's aura boil to rage.

Tyomnii reared his head back and roared, "Death to the leettle blond!"

The blood silver scythe was in his hands, its dark blade gleaming with menace, and the prince turned and looked right at him.

Aken ran for his life.

Papers swirled like snow as Tyomnii charged forward, swiping the scythe to cut him in two, narrowly missing, and shredding papers into confetti.

"Tyomnii-sama, don't!" Heion cried, hurrying after them. "You can't kill young students!!"

⁓

That evening, inside a small yet festive auditorium, Cyrus took a seat in the row Mamoru had reserved for Harlow. Apfel sat on her right, and she saved the left seat for Aken. She urged Apfel to keep the small greyhound puppy in his backpack quiet.

"I am. *Shhh*, Hazfel! Behaves yorself," he whispered loudly.

Bakoa, Zartanian and Hercule hurried to their seats before the show started. Marigold waved cheerfully to Cyrus from beside Hercule, looking pretty in a leaf-green dress.

Cherish arrived with her brother, rolling the wheelchair into a space near the front. Mamoru was somewhere backstage, where he would remain to assist the children and make sure everything ran smoothly.

Lamps around the auditorium dimmed, and the stage lanterns lit up. The first puppet made its appearance on stage: a funny character with a long, pointed nose and a cape made of feathers.

From the corner of her eye, she saw Aken slip into his seat—somehow having escaped the prince.

"You better not have led Tyomnii in here," Cyrus warned out the side of her mouth.

"Hey, have a little faith in your friend; I'm smarter than that," he said back. But he did glance around a few times, as if to make sure.

They watched the stage as the magician puppet began his adventure. There were songs and duets by the puppet friends he met along the way, and Cyrus chuckled when the youngest of the orphans forgot her lines.

Still, it was clear how much work they had all put into the performance. Their words were in sync with the puppets' mouths and hand motions. And those who played the background music for scenes barely missed a beat.

Then a new puppet came on stage: a girl with red hair, long and wavy, and a pair of white wings on her back, matching her flowing white dress.

"Swan Princess." The magician puppet bowed to her. "May I request your assistance in aiding me to banish the darkness that has enveloped my homeland?"

The princess motioned to the flute that he carried with him, and he removed it from his pack and held it before her.

She waved her hands over the instrument, and the background music changed to something mysterious, with a sound effect of twinkling magic.

A flash of light came from her hands, and then the ordinary flute transformed into a magical flute with a fancy design.

"Use the power I have placed in this flute to banish the darkness and save your home, oh brave magician," spoke the princess. "The light shall overcome the darkness, so long as you remain true."

During the scene, Cyrus sat upright in her seat.

The Swan... Cyrus couldn't be *her*. She didn't have any such power as that. And she definitely wasn't graceful or wise, like this one appeared to be.

Her hands made fists without her realizing it, and Aken gave her a sideways look. She did her best to ignore his knowing glance during the rest of the play.

When the show came to an end, everyone rose and clapped as the orphan performers came out and bowed on stage. The play was a success, and the proceeds would go to help support the orphanages across Draeth.

Cyrus followed the line down the aisle to the exit doors, and glimpsed Masters Nephryte and Seren-Rose a ways back.

They bumped into each other afterwards, in the foyer, while the audience was still filing out.

"I'm glad to see you all came. It was kind of you to support them," Master Nephryte said.

He and Harlow waited for Mamoru to come out, and complimented him on all his hard work. Mamoru waved the praise aside, "It's all thanks to how dedicated our little puppeteers and musicians were."

While everyone chatted, Cyrus was still thinking about the play and its odd story. The part with the Swan troubled her, and she finally asked him, "Did the Swan Princess really create a magical flute? Was that story true?"

Mamoru shrugged his shoulders. "It could just be a story. The Swan Princess is often used in fairy tales and folklore—to add to the wonder and mysteriousness of the tale, I suppose." He waved to the gathered orphans again, "Great work! I hear you have an ice cream surprise waiting for you back at the house? Hurry and enjoy it, before it all melts!"

The children giggled and cheered, scampering outdoors and following their orphan keepers back to the orphanage.

Cyrus frowned to herself in thought, and she absently touched a hand to her chest, feeling the beat of her heart—or the great well of untamed energy pulsing inside it.

"Whatever this energy is, it's slowly killing you," were Dr. Zushil's words, after she had won the Festival Duel and was put in the

infirmary. *"Currently it only affects your wrists, but with time it will spread and affect more of you. I don't know how long this will take— could be until you reach adulthood, if you're lucky; but your organs will eventually shut down, and you'll..."*

Die. She might die young because of this.

She knew death wasn't something to fear, not when she had Lord God with her. But she still wanted to live, to experience things in this world, be here for her friends, and...

Aken nudged her arm. "You okay?"

She came out of her thoughts, and after a breath, gave him an unconvincing nod.

The Master walked with Harlow back to Draevensett. Cyrus could understand he didn't want to leave them out of his sight much, not after all that had just happened.

When they entered the academy doors, a paper blew out.

Catching the paper—which bore the tyrant gioraf drawing— Nephryte looked sidelong down at Aken. "Do I *need* to know what this is about?"

Aken sucked in his lips. "Um, not really."

21

The dawn's clouds were rosy pink beyond the windows when Cyrus made her way down the corridor to the Master's dorm flat. Inside, she took a seat at the kitchen table, the smell of cinnamon toast already wafting past her nose.

"Today's the Hunters Race!" Bakoa whooped from the chair beside her, pumping a fist in the air.

Hercule's left hand was gripping his head, while the right clung to his usual mug of coffee. "Will you stop bouncing around like that, Bakoa?" he finally snapped. He turned to Zartanian next, who was feeding his raven, Corben, bread. "And shut that bird up! Didn't you agree to keep it outside? Can I not have any peace and quiet around here?"

Zartanian visibly flinched and made a shushing sound to the raven to quiet it.

"Lykale, get your nose out of books and work on your chemistry Ability! Aren't there any new poison darts you could make? Harlow's reputation is at stake in this race." Hercule's glaring dragon eyes turned on Aken next.

"As for you, Aken—where should I even begin?"

Aken munched on a piece of toast. "Drink some raspberry juice. I think fiber would do wonders for your mood."

Hercule's foot kicked him under the table.

"Hercule," Mamoru interjected, "you know we will all do our best in the race. Don't let your father's high expectations rule your attitude."

Hercule's hands on his head and mug gradually unclenched, and he shut his eyes, massaging his left temple.

"I came across some good news this morning," Mamoru continued, addressing the whole group. "The White Ghost has been captured. It happened sometime last night."

They all lifted their heads in surprise, including Cyrus.

"A Draev squad led by Master Eletor had set up a trap: staging as vempar slavers, and the White Ghost appeared. They're taking him to a secure location now, until his sentencing."

Apfel and Zartanian let out relieved breaths.

Aken stared into his glass of milk in silence.

Cyrus wanted to feel relieved, too, but there was an uneasy feeling in her gut. Could a powerful being like Ellefsen really be held captive?

She tried to shake off the unease and finish breakfast. Right now, it was the race they had to focus on.

❧

Out in the school's moon courtyard, Adelheid perched herself on an ornamental tree branch and puckered her rosebud lips. Students bustled about the surrounding colonnade and the looping spiral walk, all youthfully eager for some event called the Hunters Race.

Such carefree youngsters, she sniffed. Oh how things would change once the Impure Nights took over!

She twirled her green slipper-like shoes. She chose a green skort for today, as a dress would be highly impractical during a race; her pale green stockings and a frilly green blouse matched.

Earlier, Heion had kindly emphasized that she didn't need to participate much in the race, if it would be too difficult for her, what with Adelheid being new and all. The kitsune had meant well, of course, but the very suggestion still irked her.

She could win this whole silly race on her own, if she wanted to! But all anyone could see was a frail, prissy doll.

'Well, I am a bit prissy,' she had to admit to herself. *'Still, I ought to snatch the prize and spank their bums with it...'*

"Hello, Miss Adelheid," a voice greeted her, interrupting her thoughts.

She shifted her single eye to Mathias, who was once more trying to be friendly. Honestly, why wouldn't the kid leave her alone? He was worse than the honeybee that kept buzzing around her pink hair, mistaking it for a flower.

She sighed. "Are you truly so bored, Mathias Turner the Third, that you take pleasure in grieving my astute and stoic-hearted countenance?"

The ordinary boy paused mid-bow, a loose hair strand slipping forward, his forehead creasing.

A chuckle played across her lips. Simple-minded people were so easy to confuse.

"Oh, silly me!" She set a hand to her cheek. "Did I baffle you with my high vocabulary? Did you think a small girl couldn't be so intelligent?" She leaned forward from her perch on the branch, nearing close enough to tap his nose. "Or *am* I a little girl," she asked with a smirk, "Mathias Turner?"

He stared up at her for several heartbeats. She thought he might scamper away, but instead he took a small bag from behind his back. He held it up for her to take. "As promised, I baked some of my specialty desserts for you. Please give them a try."

Now it was her turn to stare in silence. Puzzled by the boy, she finally took the paper bag that he so proudly offered. Inside were various custard tarts and croissants, golden and delicious. Her mouth began to water, the sweet aroma bringing back warm memories from a distant past, and from a long-departed friend…

She forced herself to resist temptation and placed the bag beside the tree for later. "Perhaps I'll sample some, when I'm bored."

Mathias grinned, that single, out of place strand of hair flopping against his forehead again. She looked away. Ugh, what an annoying buzzing bee.

"Good luck in the Hunters Race." He beamed over his shoulder and trotted back toward the colonnade. "Try not to win it too quickly!"

Her mouth opened. Was that an attempted flirt?

She shook herself. Preposterous!

Without thinking, she pulled out a croissant from the bag and began chewing.

He really did remind her too much of *that person*. And the croissant was delicious…

❧

The Backbone Mountains rose in grandeur before them, filling the horizon with steep green sides and sharp, craggy tops. Harlow hiked north-west through the fields along with the other competing Floor groups, and when they finally came to a halt, they faced a dark line of trees: the beginning of Greater Magica Forest. The Hunters Race would take place within the fringes, away from the more dangerous inner depths.

The Floors separated into smaller team groups, except for Harlow, which was already small enough. Cyrus spotted the prince's team, and off to the left, Denim's.

Morning light reflected on the dew drops still clinging to the leaves and grass, the dew dampening her brown shoes. A breeze tousled her hair and the sun warmed her back.

Principal Han, in his decorative red stole, and the five Floor Masters stood before the many clusters of eager students. A willowy man lurked off to the side of them, the sleeves of his dark tunic layered in black lace, his hair a straight black curtain. Cyrus recognized him from the Festival Duel: Viceroy Deciet, his eyes hollow and cheekbones deeply shadowed.

In the principal's hands sat a bird cage. He held it up high, and Cyrus tried to see over the heads of all the taller students.

Aken lifted her up by the knees and sat her on his shoulders so she could see. She tried not to lose her balance, nor let her face redden. "Uh, thanks."

Inside the bird cage, she saw a golden creature flutter about, glowing, its petal limbs as luminous as liquified sunlight.

"The team who catches the golden pixit and brings her back first, wins, and will be given privileges until the next Hunters Race, including an added bonus to their grade," declared the principal to the groups. "I will go over the rules once more: You may use your Abilities and battle, so long as you do not severely injure nor permanently impair another student. Our goal is not to maim one another, as I hope you already know. And secondly, do not harm the pixit—I will be very cross with you if you do." He made cooing sounds to the pixit, and gave them all a stern look from under his bushy eyebrows. "Heed these rules, and be sure to make your Floor and your Master proud today!"

The principal then strode ahead of the gathering and approached the edge of the trees, carrying the cage. The Masters followed.

The viceroy hung back and passed near to Floor Smart's teams. "I wish you the best of luck, My Prince," he addressed the grim royal and bowed his head.

The prince acknowledged him with a brief look.

Cyrus shook off the sudden chill she felt and drew her gaze away from them. Aken set her back down on the ground. The laces of his maroon shirt were undone, she pointed out for him to fix.

"Let's win this," Aken told her and held out his fist.

She bumped his fist with hers, not feeling nearly as confident as he seemed to.

Something poked them each in the back, and they both jumped and turned around to see the roguish faces of the Holsome twins.

"Twiddle Dee and Dum-dum," Aken growled.

The twins grinned from ear to ear. One had an arm hanging around poor Zartanian's shoulders.

"How touching." Victor placed a hand over his heart. "You remembered our soul names."

"Indeed, so touching, dear Brother." Jack nodded, and gave a slap to Aken's shoulder that made him wince. "What a good little pal you are! Just like our shy friend, here."

A look of dread crossed Zartanian's features.

"But we'll be winning this race," said Victor. "Our prince doesn't like to lose, see, so we wanted to come and warn you before you tried getting in his way."

"Quite so! He can be a right gnarly chap. But then, so can we." They both smirked.

Heion appeared behind them, grabbing a twin's ear in each hand and twisting until they squealed.

"*Baka* twins!" she scolded, and she dragged them back to where their team waited, the heels of their shoes dragging in the grass.

"Cruel damsel! You're cruel with that crazy strength of yours!"

"There's nothing damsel about her. My ear's about to tear off!"

"Call me damsel one more time, and it *will*," Heion warned.

While leaders were busy readying their teams before the race's start, Mamoru motioned for Harlow to gather close, and they formed a tight circle, blocking out all other noise.

"What's the strategy, Mamoru?" asked Bakoa.

"First is the obvious: stay focused and keep calm, no matter what happens," he told them. "And secondly...our Master told me to let Aken take the lead in this."

Aken's jaw dropped.

Hercule slapped a hand to his forehead. "Great. We've lost before we've even begun."

Lykale groaned.

Aken shook his head. "Why would he say that? I'm no good at this. I've no clue what we should do or what plan to make." He sweated.

Mamoru offered an encouraging nudge. "Being the leader doesn't mean you have to be good at *every* single thing, Aken. Our talents and power are *your* talents and power."

Cyrus still cringed. What was the Master thinking?

Aken's brow furrowed. "Okay, then you're going to have to help me. Mamoru, what's the best strategy for us to win this race?"

Mamoru smirked, a gleam in his eye.

A Draev squad leader met with Master Brangor, and after a brief conversation, the Master reported back to the principal, trotting over on his stocky legs that were meant more for battle than for running. "Squads have finished scouting the forested area—no enemies or dragons in sight. Everything's a go for the race!"

Han acknowledged the news with a nod.

"So then, shall we begin?" said Deidreem. He rolled "shall" across his tongue and tweaked the rim of his top hat.

Nephryte conjured a wisp of wind, knocking the hat off and sending it rolling, while pretending to look the other way. Deidreem hurried after it, stumbling.

Han lifted the cage high for all the groups to see. "Go, little friend," he whispered, and opened the latch.

The golden pixit flew out, beating its sunbeam wings. It sped into the forest like a streak of light and vanished within the shadowed depths.

Students waited tensely as Han's arm slowly rose...then sliced down through the air—signaling the start of the Hunters Race.

There was a great surge forward as every team raced to enter the forest before the rest, rushing in the direction of where the pixit had vanished. Master Nephryte trained his gaze on Harlow—they had entered the forest nearly first.

Good. He hoped they would stay in the lead.

"Thank goodness the White Ghost was put away in chains before today," Seren-Rose was saying. "We would've had to postpone the race otherwise, for safety reasons."

Burly Brangor stroked his red beard, agreeing with her. "Aye, well done on trapping that wicked rascal, Eletor!"

Eletor held his head high, running a hand through his mullet hair with an exaggerated gesture of pride.

Deidreem finally caught his hat, and he marched back to them, looking sour.

"Masters! Draev Masters!"

A puffing and gasping Draev in uniform came from the direction of the city and halted before them, catching his breath. Giving a quick head bow, he said, "The Draev Grandmaster is calling for an audience with you—all of you, right now! He said the matter cannot wait." The man breathed in and out.

"The Grandmaster?" Deidreem frowned, clearly baffled. "Right now? He can't wait even ten minutes?"

"Those were his words," the man replied.

"Whatever for?" Seren-Rose questioned.

The man shrugged up his shoulders. "He told me nothing more. I'm only the messenger."

Eletor made a vexed sound. He slapped one hand on Nephryte's shoulder and the other on Deidreem's. "Best we hurry and answer his Grandmasterlyness, before his tirade falls on us."

"But during the race..." Seren-Rose's head turned back to the trees, her gaze lingering on Tathom and their progress.

Brangor grumbled and started marching across the grass. "Come on. The sooner we go, the sooner it'll be done with and we'll be back!"

Nephryte formed whirling wind currents to carry them back towards the city, and left Principal Han and the viceroy behind.

"I should return, as well, and see to the king's itinerary," Viceroy Deciet spoke after a moment. He dipped his head to the principal and departed.

22

Mamoru plunged into the forest first, while Aken and Cy followed close behind him. The rips in Mamoru's clothing flapped as he ran with speed and ease.

"Out of the seven of us, I have the best chance at catching the golden pixit. I'll use my dragonfly puppet, Flitter, to maneuver through the foliage and grab it," Mamoru had told the group, just minutes before. "The best strategy is for Harlow to fan out behind me and keep any rival teams off my back. If a fight breaks out, some of you might get separated or lost, so I suggest each of you pair up with a partner."

Now, Harlow was spread out behind Mamoru in pairs. Bakoa with Zartanian, and Hercule with Lykale, fanned out to either side, just behind Aken and Cyrus.

Beams of golden sunlight pierced down through the thick green canopy overhead, making it harder to catch a glimpse of the pixit, its body blending in and vanishing with each bit of light that it passed through.

Mamoru sprinted after the pixit, and released the winged,

grasshopper-like puppet from its amber rock prison. Flitter's human-shaped hands unfolded, poised and ready to grab.

It was a struggle for Cy's human legs to keep up with them, so Aken slowed his pace down to match.

Other Floor teams materialized through the ferns and trees, left and right of them, each in pursuit of where they guessed the pixit to be heading. The creature left nothing more than a sunspot glimmer in the air to mark where it had passed, darting swiftly around moss-ridden boulders, trunks and leafy branches.

The deeper they went into the forest, the larger the trees grew, and sunshine shrunk into narrow, solid streaks penetrating a darker atmosphere. Instead of making it easier, the shift made tracking the pixit even harder. The creature flitted from sunlight patch to sunlight patch in a dizzying, zigzag pattern, and Aken lost track of it several times; but Mamoru kept on ahead of them, not once slowing down or wavering. It was the right decision to leave the catching to him.

Aken skirted around a stubby boulder. Hollers from the other teams running parallel to them echoed:

"Where are you going? I thought you saw the pixit go *this* way."

"I lost sight of it. It's gone! All these stupid sunbeams keep confusing me!"

"So help me, Malfred, you had better get your eyes back on that thing!"

"I'm tryin', I'm tryin'! Hitting me in the back won't help."

"Yeah, don't get him all stressed out, Denim."

"Shut it, Doughboy!"

Aken couldn't help but snicker.

"Well, if it isn't the loser team." Denim noticed them. "You misfits really think you stand a chance?" He angled in his run to cross paths with them.

Before Aken could comment back, a Tathom boy shouted:

"Another team's coming after Malfred! Hurry! Without him, we can't keep track of the pixit!"

Denim's teeth made a grinding sound and he veered away, running over to where Malfred was being cornered.

Each team's tracker had to be ahead at the front, but that also made them vulnerable to attacks. A team without a decent tracker would quickly become a losing team.

Aken's attention darted to Mamoru. Sure enough, out the corner of his eye he spotted three Harcourt students running low and silently, blending in with the high ferns and shrubbery—their path headed straight for the puppeteer. They looked older, lean and tough. The first one came within reach of Mamoru.

If he got distracted and lost sight of the golden pixit…

Fwip! Fwip! The first Harcourt student collapsed to the loamy floor with a dart-like syringe in his neck.

The second and third fell quickly next.

Aken squinted and spotted Lykale's white hair peeking out among the ferns. The older boy followed them at a distance, just close enough to strike enemies without being seen, sedative darts glinting in his ready hands.

Perfect! Inwardly he cheered Lykale on. Maybe they really could win this race!

"Oh my *my*! What a terrible thing!" spoke a voice.

"And very likely to be used against our teammates, if we ignore this."

"Quite right, and quite so, dear Brother. We'll have to bind him, won't we?"

"Yes, indeed. Such nightmares as scientists running loose with needles must be put to a stop."

The Holsome twins materialized around a wide lichen-speckled boulder, headed for Lykale's unprotected back.

Hearing their chatter and Aken's shout of alarm, Lykale had just enough time to dodge one of their glowing chains. But dodging it made him blind to a web of other chains already set up cunningly between the twins—and when they ran in a circle around him, a spiderweb of chain caught and wrapped him up.

"Allow us to bind these crazy needle-throwing arms," said Jack with a laugh.

"It's our classic *Taco Chain Wrap* move. Sorry we don't have any sauce to go with it." Victor winked.

There came a flash of hot yellow, just then, as Hercule's fire-breath blazed towards the twins.

They twirled out of the way, surprisingly agile.

"Sorry, but this is the way of the game, kiddies," said one twin.

"No harm meant, and all that," said the other.

Laughing, the devious twins left and continued their pursuit of Mamoru and the other teams' trackers. Hercule made as if to stop and help Lykale get free of the chains, but he didn't get a chance to: members from other teams were coming onto the scene, one after another, and all of them battling each other and getting Harlow caught up in the mix.

"We're so far behind—we'll lose track of Mamoru completely if we stop and fight!" Cy said from beside Aken; they dodged several falling branches, knocked loose by various battling Abilities.

Aken's teeth gritted, and he reached inside his pocket. "Take this, you pests!" He threw small clay birds out in a wide arc; the birds exploded in a circle around them, knocking enemy students off their feet.

Hercule's fire-blasts, Zartanian's scabbard strikes, and Bakoa's smashing sand-hammer arms furthered the damage. Finally breaking free of the chaos, Harlow continued forward, leaving the turmoil in their wake.

Lykale's brow twitched, vexed that he had been left behind, and he squirmed and wriggled to get free of the chains.

Aken sprinted across the loamy forest floor in his thick-tread shoes. "I can barely see Maru: past that boulder and up the slope." He pointed. "Nobody's been able to stop him yet, Cy. We're gonna win this thing!"

"Hate to burst your bubble," Cy's tone disagreed, "but I think it's because nobody considers Harlow worth their time yet. Their strategy is probably to save the weakest teams for last."

He cast Cy a frown, but the redhead was probably right. Even if Mamoru did manage to catch the golden pixit, he would still have to make his way back out of the forest with it—and that would be when all teams would attack them.

"You!"

A sudden, reverberating shout made Aken almost lose his footing and face-plant into a pile of anteleer dung.

"Leettle blond boy!"

Aken nervously glanced back.

There, several yards from him and headed his way, came the prince, with an aura of doom trailing behind him, his blood-rose eyes fixated upon Aken's destruction.

Tyomnii whirled the Legendary scythe in his nimble, long-fingered hands, caressing the blade as he did so. "For those gioraf drawings...thees ees payback time!"

Aken yelped. "Can't we wait until after the race?"

Ignoring his plea, the prince charged forward. "I veell make you lose thees race!" he roared.

Forced to abandon Harlow, Aken ran as fast as his legs could carry him, rounding tree trunks and leaping high over obstacles. He struggled to keep ahead of the scythe-wielding royal, and soon lost his bearings.

～◦

Cyrus halted, unsure whether to stick with her paired

partner, Aken, or continue after Mamoru.

Hercule blazed past her, followed by Zartanian and Bakoa, who nodded her way. Good, they could take care of things here, while she went to get Aken back on track.

She headed off towards the prince's distant form, when another Floor team came suddenly across her path. She halted as three of the members paused to circle her.

"Hey, isn't this the half-human?" said one.

She made metal wrap around her arms and hands, ready for a fight, though that was the last thing she wanted.

"Yeah. He doesn't look so tough, does he?"

"Let's tie him up."

Fear shook her breath, but she stood firm and tried to put her back to a tree so they couldn't jump her from behind.

Then she felt a light tap on her left shoulder, and she whirled around.

"Hi there, cute red." Adelheid waved a petite hand as she passed by on her left. The girl flipped smoothly up in the air and over a boy who stood in her way, and delivered a kick to his back while her other foot touched ground, sending him flying into the dirt. She leaped high again to deliver round-house kicks to the other two boys. Their hands, which were ready to attack with objects related to their Abilities, fell limp as they collapsed.

"Watch yourself." Adelheid winked her way, the enemy team members all unconscious.

"Whoa...thanks," Cyrus said in quiet amazement.

The petite girl flipped forward, used the surrounding tree limbs for handlebars, and took off in the direction of a distant team, her unnerving giggle echoing after her.

That nickname, cute red, *ugh*. But now Cyrus was free to continue on...if only she could be sure of which way Aken and the prince had gone.

Mamoru's footfalls were light as he raced across the uneven forest terrain, the atmosphere around him a dark emerald with stray beams of sunlight slanting through. His vision kept trained on the golden glimmers of the elusive pixit, just several yards ahead of him.

Heion was keeping up, off to his far right, with the ease and grace of a fox, and four other trackers came on his left, each working to close the gap between themselves and the target.

But the pixit was fast; Mamoru's quick pace had not been able to lessen the distance between them.

His fingers deftly steered and guided puppet Flitter around stray limbs, seeking to close the gap.

An uneasy feeling hit Mamoru like a sudden wave.

Up ahead, in a small clearing, the golden pixit rounded a low, leaf-littered hill.

He stopped in his tracks so quickly that his treads cast up a spray of loam.

Something wasn't right. There were no bird trills or common crickets singing here, and patches along the ground up ahead looked like they'd been disturbed.

Almost as if...

He whirled around and shouted at the other trackers, "Stop! There's a trap!"

Startled, several of the trackers slowed to a stop, including Heion, but two did not—racing on ahead, and both climbed the low hill.

Uncertainty held Heion and the others in place, each one scanning the area for signs of the trap. Mamoru pulled out more of his puppets sealed in amber rocks; but before he could activate them and grab the two boys who had raced ahead, there came a flash of light, followed by a string of explosions.

Heion and the others threw themselves to the ground, leaves

and debris blowing over them. Mamoru rolled behind a tree trunk.

Soon the forest fell into silence again, and he peered around the tree to see the two boys tumble down to a stop at the base of the hill, unmoving, their clothing and bodies charred.

Heion lifted her head, fox ears tilted back.

Men materialized from around the hill: a mix of vempars and half-breeds, casting off leaf and brush disguises, each of them armed with an assortment of weapons—including black silver. They grinned and sneered with wicked eagerness, coming towards them.

"The escaped convicts from the Morbid Dungeons—it's them again!" cried Heion. Only this time, there were many more criminals in the mix.

Expressions wide with fear, the students turned to backtrack and flee.

Mamoru tried to make sense of how this could be. Wasn't their ringleader, the White Ghost, imprisoned? Then what were they doing out here, ambushing Draev students in the forest?

Unless…

Crud—this was all a part of the Ghost's plan!

Where were Cyrus and Aken? He had to find them before it was too late.

Mamoru glanced back at the two fallen students one last time, both motionless, then followed after Heion. He would retreat and find a better vantage point from which he could battle as many of the criminals as possible. Experience had molded him into a fearless warrior long ago. He had to protect these students, still so young and full of potential, the future of Draeth Kingdom.

He removed rocks of amber from his pockets, activating the puppets trapped within each one.

A sharp scream, followed by shouts and confusion, brought Aken and Tyomnii's chase to a stand-still. Other Floor teams were up ahead and scattered about the forest from having clashed with rival teams, and in so doing had lost the golden pixit's trail. But none of that was the reason for the scream. Something was wrong, and a student far ahead, who Aken couldn't see, cried out: "The escaped criminals are here!"

It took Aken a moment to make sense of what was happening. Tyomnii, however, wasted no time and launched himself into the commotion.

Before Aken's eyes, the criminals from their battle in Pearlset Town, and many more, came storming through the trees and down a mound of tangled roots towards them. Students both young and old turned from fighting each other to face the new oncoming threat. There was no time to feel fear or run for cover; this was an ambush aimed to slaughter them all.

Weapons clashed as armed Armavis students defended themselves, metal squealing against metal, a resounding cacophony through the forest.

One bald criminal wielded a mace and chains—three spiked balls slamming into students and tree trunks. Others, rough and grimy, hacked and sliced with ugly saw-toothed and hooked blades.

The prince wielded the long shaft of his weapon, its dark metal blocking attacks while he twirled, side-stepped, and lunged in wide sweeps, the scythe's blood silver blade cutting cleanly through the foes in his path—a deadly dance as he and the scythe moved as one.

Other students were not as skilled, and they were failing against the onslaught.

Aken channeled *essence* under the ground through his feet, casting up high spouts of dirt-turned-lava.

The lava sprayed across one of the criminals. But instead of getting the reaction he expected, the criminal didn't cry out in pain or even flinch. Instead, the lava hit against something like a bubble shield around the man and fizzled out.

The same thing was happening with other Draev students, left and right of him: their Abilities were hitting against *something* and fizzing out of existence. Only physical weapons, like blades, made it through.

Aken backed up, a cold sweat on his brow.

The criminals. The White Ghost. Cyrus—where was his friend?

He veered to the right, hurrying in the direction he believed, and hoped, the redhead to be.

23

Downward stroke. Swift upper swipe. Zartanian swung his sheathed saber, battling a blond Harcourt student, who countered his moves with twin batons.

Harlow had gotten separated, just as Mamoru predicted.

The student blocked his next cut, and was about to hit Zartanian's left side, when he seemed to spot something behind Zartanian and gave a panicked cry. The student backed away and turned to flee.

That was when Zartanian heard the commotion.

Fear threatened to paralyze him, but he made himself turn around and look.

A scene of armed figures spilled down the tree-covered slope before him, booted-feet smashing down ferns and undergrowth and crushing spring flowers.

Criminals, like those they'd fought at the lake town—the White Ghost's army.

With a startled yelp of his own, Zartanian quickly unsheathed the saber, a blade Sir Swornyte let him use for more serious practice—a real weapon. He'd brought it but didn't expect to actually use the bare blade during the Hunters Race.

As the criminals leered and cackled and headed their way, for a split second he almost doubted what his eyes were showing him. "Bakoa!" was the only word he could force his wavering throat to shout. It didn't carry far, but Bakoa's ears picked it up.

Yards away, battling another student, Bakoa signaled that he'd heard and he fixed his gaze on the oncoming attack. Zartanian likewise shifted to face it, his legs trembling in his high laced boots. Both of his hands shook, gripping around the saber's hilt, white-knuckled and holding the blade up in a ready stance; he wished he felt as ready on the inside, calm like Bakoa seemed to be.

The nearest criminal reached him: a half-goblin with a spiky blade. Three others went for Bakoa.

Zartanian fought to keep his shaking knees from buckling underneath him. *"A shaken person, even with a sword in hand, is as good as dead"*—he recalled one of the teachings Sir Swornyte had drilled into his head. *"You cannot let fear overtake you, nor the enemy daunt you, or else they will have already won the battle in your mind."*

So much easier said than done, especially when his opponent was heads taller than him.

He'd failed to protect anyone back at the lake town. What if that happened here, now?

"What is it we do when we're afraid, Zartanian?" Master Nephryte had once asked him, years ago, after he had lost Elijob, when he was afraid of everything and everyone, and nightmares terrorized the nights.

Zartanian sucked in a deep breath now, slowly exhaling. *'Please, Lord God, give me the strength to make it through this, and keep everyone safe,'* he prayed quickly. *'I will fight to protect others, not only myself. I want to save them!'*

A gradual calm fell about him, like a warm blanket wrapping around his body, relaxing the tension, steadying the tremors in his hands and knees. Thoughts of fear faded as thoughts of protecting his friends and those around him took hold. Lowering to one knee, as the goblin came within several feet of him, he imagined his training exercises.

The sword and he were one.

He let his *essence* seep into the air and take shape, creating a duplicate of himself, which caused the criminal to pause.

Black Feather Pierces, a straightforward plunge with the sword perfectly horizontal.

A look of surprise crossed the half-goblin's face as he staggered. Zartanian pulled his sword free and rolled aside from a jagged blade that attempted to swipe down at him, before the half-goblin finally fell dead.

Rolling up onto his feet, Zartanian shifted his focus to the next nearest criminal, who was fighting the same Harcourt blond he had battled earlier. The boy struggled to find an escape, fear wiping his mind clear of all his training.

Zartanian focused, approaching from behind. *Raven's Wing Parts the Air,* a slanted downward stroke, slicing through an area of softer leather across the man's back.

The man toppled in pain and his body rolled down the slope of the terrain, and the boy looked up at Zartanian from where he had fallen, his jaw slack.

Leaving the gawking student behind, Zartanian hurried on.

Bakoa's brow furrowed deeply. He hated violence, and the sad truth that it sometimes took violence to end it. Reaching a crest where the forest terrain leveled out, he re-formed his arms into twin long hammers of churning sand. The hammers thrust blows into the enemies, shattering ribcages—or would have. There was a glow, some sort of bubble encasing the criminals, protecting them, and the sand couldn't get through.

Another group of criminals had surrounded an older Earnest student up ahead, the Draev boy already injured and holding a limp right arm at his side.

Bakoa leaped into the air, dissolving his body into sand and, fast as the wind, he flew to his rescue.

A whirlwind of sand rose around the criminals' legs. Both they and the boy glanced about in sudden confusion. The whirring sand spun around faster and then hoisted the armed men up into the air—lifting them higher and higher, bursting through the green canopy of the forest and up to the blue sky overhead.

Then the whirling sand—which was Bakoa's body—left, and the criminals dropped like stones, the bubble shields failing to protect them against a high fall, and their thudding impacts echoed.

Bakoa's form rematerialized beside the roots of a tall oak. The injured Draev boy nodded to him in thanks.

Bakoa began scanning for more students in need, when the sharp end of a spear started to grow out of his chest—piercing him from behind and out the other side.

The spear's wielder crouched behind him with a satisfied sneer.

Bakoa stood frozen in that lingering moment, then turned with the spear still inside him. He turned all the way around until his face and the craggy face of the criminal met. The scraggly man gave a startled yelp, and Bakoa's chest rippled— his torso fine crystals of sand, even though it appeared like skin and vest fabric.

"How many times do I have to tell people, I can't be attacked while in this form?" Bakoa exhaled.

And then he punched the criminal, knocking him out.

Adelheid lazily backflipped, catching a criminal's head between her crossed feet and flipping him through the air with her.

As she released him, he slammed into the ground, head-first, and ceased to move. She alighted daintily on her slippered feet atop his chest.

She hopped off, strolling onward as if it were an ordinary day in the forest and not an ambush turned battlefield. "I do hope I have time to get my nails re-polished after this." She scrutinized her fingers.

A twig cracked behind her.

She let a sigh escape from her pouting doll lips, and her left-hand fingers drummed on her hip. She was fed up with this cat-and-mouse game! And where had all these ruffians come from, in the first place?

Preparing herself to deal a side kick to the stalker's head, she twisted her neck back—and saw that it was just Mathias.

Her nose wrinkled. "Were you *following* me?"

Mathias stumbled over her frankness. "No! It—I just—ah..."

Her eye narrowed. "Stalker."

"No, it's not like that! I was just worried about you..."

A heavy and armored half-goblin charged around a pine tree, interrupting them, his raised hands holding a broad, spiked blade. He stood three heads taller than Mathias, the boy already taller than most in his class.

She frowned, watching Mathias turn quickly and hold his weapon ready: a halberd with a curved axe blade. He blocked the first blow—impressively, she had to admit.

Mathias then wielded it sideways to block two more blows from the towering green beast threatening to cleave him in two with a single stroke. But he managed to keep up, despite his lanky arms.

That blade...

Her eyelid rose as she recognized the halberd.

"*Thunderous*," she murmured, "one of the twelve Legendary Weapons."

She recalled another man who had once wielded the spear-like weapon, in what seemed another lifetime ago—and long since gone, because of her. A Legendary Knight, also with the last name Turner.

This kid appeared to wield *Thunderous* decently enough. She sniffed. Well enough for a simpleton, though nothing like its original owner.

"I'll defend you, Miss Adelheid." Mathias thrust the spike head, buckling a leg out from underneath the towering enemy.

"And who, pray-tell, says I need defending?"

The thug's spiky blade hacked down, forcing Mathias to his knees as he raised *Thunderous's* blood silver shaft and blocked several powerful blows; the force rattled his bones, jarred his clenched teeth.

A wart-skinned fist let go of the blade's hilt to punch Mathias in the side—knocking the air out of his lungs and landing him on his back, skidding him a yard away.

Green lips sneered, savoring his pain.

With a trickle of red down the edge of his mouth, Mathias heaved himself up in time to duck beneath the next swing that came. In the same movement, he thrust the spike blade up into the huge half-goblin's ribs—the blood silver cutting through armor and the bubble shield. There was little that a Legendary Weapon could not cut through.

Adelheid observed, her bored eyelid half lowered, and tapped a finger against her hip.

The tall criminal collapsed with a thud, and she continued her stroll through the dappled trees.

"Wait!" She heard Mathias struggle to recover his breath and follow her. When he did catch up, she whirled around, dangling by a hand from an overhanging branch, and caught his neck in a lock hold with her feet.

"What," she began, "makes you think I need some knight-in-shining-armor? Tell me, do I really look so weak to you?"

Her feet against his neck threatened to twist and break it. She felt him swallow. Silence reigned except for the echoes of battle. Her left eye didn't blink while he sweated, and yet, she could sense no fear of her in him.

That stray strand of hair still fell across his face, and it again reminded her of *him*.

"I never doubted you, miss," he breathed. "But I didn't want you to dirty your hands. The hands of a lady should always be clean, don't you think?"

Her eye blinked in surprise.

"Hm." One corner of her lips quirked up. "You're a strange boy, Mathias. Very strange... But I suppose I could allow you to tag along."

She released him, and he massaged around his neck. Maybe this boy could be of use to her someday? If she couldn't be rid of him, she may as well use him.

~~

All seven of his battle puppets were out: Mamoru's arsenal, which he referred to as his Justice Team. His fingers moved and flicked the thin sap strings attached from his fingertips to each puppet, his hands moving faster than the eye could follow; the liquid-like sap strings passed through the foliage with ease, not getting tangled. He commanded the puppets into the fray from his stance on a low hill.

Goliathon, a giant with spikes for hair and a green scaly surface as tough as a reptile, covered in armored plates, stomped across the forest floor—bashing criminals within reach of its fist and cutting down others with a giant, spiked mace and chain.

The Twin Dead Kings puppets worked together as a pair, cutting down foes with curved swords, their skeletal frames garbed to resemble ancient royalty. The flexible Scurro whipped itself about like a rubberband, one slap from it sending a criminal careening into a boulder. The giant tortoise, Tortuga, snapped its thick jaws, cleanly biting through whatever weapon or person came near, and the men stumbled in their haste to keep away from it.

Flitter rushed to students who were farther away, distracting criminals who tried to cut the young boys down. And at an even farther distance was Sting, shaped like a spin-top beehive, with holes dotting its body. Sting flew silently and lowered behind a cluster of unsuspecting criminals, then released a volley of needle darts shot from the holes. The men felt pricks and stings, and before they could pull the darts out, they collapsed, paralyzed by a poison strong enough to impair even vempars.

Almost every criminal had a bubble shield protecting them from *essence* attacks. But the attacks from his puppets were not of *essence*, and so made it through their shields. Even if he used *essence* to move and control the puppets, the puppets themselves were not made from any energy—they were solid sap-wax materials.

Most students only knew how to fight using their Abilities with *essence*, and that made them vulnerable to attack without Mamoru's protection.

But Cyrus, Aken—so far, he hadn't been able to find either one of them. And if he stopped battling now to go and search for them, more students would die.

⌒つ

Denim tried once more flinging spears of ice at the criminals, but the ice spears shattered harmlessly before reaching them. Even the long ice spear he wielded and used to jab at them couldn't pierce through whatever the see-through force field was. Only Armavis types were having any success dealing damage; meanwhile, the enemy thugs cut and bashed other students down.

Denim glowered. "How am I supposed to fight then, eh? Hey, Doughboy!" he hollered over at the giant ball of bouncing dough quaking the ground with every thumping bounce, attempting to flatten a thickly armored vempar thug. Two students several yards to the left had already fallen, lifeless, and several more were close to doing the same. His own Tathom team were beaten ragged and near to collapsing, even as they tried to keep together and cover each other's backs.

"Yeah-huh?" he heard Doughboy's heavy reply reverberate.

"Smashing them with your body isn't working, is it?" Denim shouted to him.

Doughboy grunted a "No."

"So use something else! What's the point of you being big if you can't deal damage? I'll bake your dough-hide if you don't think of something fast. We're dying here!"

Doughboy halted his bounces for a pondering moment, chubby facial features all scrunched up. Then his face lit up with an idea.

Puffing himself out and growing bigger, Doughboy stretched out thick hands the size of wheels, and grabbed and yanked the nearest tree out of the ground, roots and all. With dirt flinging and branches crackling, he held the tree trunk and swung it down like a club. *WhaMM!*

The energy shields didn't protect against a crazed giant swinging a tree trunk, and the thug's body was crushed into the soil. Doughboy bashed and crushed more enemies like acorns, a triumphant roar splitting his face.

"*Heh*, not bad." Denim smirked.

Something tumbled off to his right, and he jerked his head sideways to look. "Malfred!" Denim saw his teammate collapse with three stab wounds to the thigh and something protruding below the left collarbone. Everyone was too busy fighting to stay alive that no one ran to Malfred's side.

With a frustrated grunt, Denim left Doughboy to carry on while he reached Malfred. "Mal! C'mon, you gotta be okay. Don't you dare die on me!"

Hoping his threat would evoke some sort of response from Malfred, he tried to stop the bleeding, channeling Healing cells through his hands into the boy to lessen the damage. But injuries dealt by black silver needed stronger medical treatment, and fast. His outside help wasn't enough.

The boy stared blankly up at nothing, eyes glazing over.

"Malfred... Mal..."

He continued giving first-aid, but Malfred's fate grew more grim by the second.

❧

"My, my, what a pickle we're in!"

"A fine pickle, indeed, dear Brother. Our *essence* chains are quite useless."

"Whatever shall we do?"

The Holsome twins pondered in unison, ducking a thrown spear here, side-stepping from a broadsword swing there, the battle raging on around them. They caught sight of Schnel: sliding along the forest floor on slug slimed feet, leaving a glossy trail through the loam.

"Oi, Schnel!" Victor waved from amidst the chaos.

"Mind giving us fine chaps a slippery helping hand?" Jack cheerfully hollered, dodging an axe throw.

Schnel turned his hooded head around and flashed them a lazy smile. "*Ja*, I can slip up some baddies for you. Hold tight."

Schnel twisted his torso around mid-slide, and his fabric hands grabbed a tree limb. Using the limb, he turned the rest of his body around and propelled himself in the twins' direction.

He made a dive onto his stomach, sliding slug-slime across the forest floor. Upon reaching Victor and Jack, he turned and slid this way and that, the slime trails tripping up and felling the criminals around them. With the enemy down, the twins pulled hidden coils of chain from their boots and inner-vest pockets.

"Thanks a million, snaily chap! You sure pulled our buttocks out of the frying pan."

"What Jack means to say is that you gave us enough time to face these thugs properly," Victor clarified.

"And face these fiendish fiends we shall!"

They wielded the chains in unison, chains made of black silver this time, without needing *essence*.

While Schnel tripped up criminals, the chains tangled legs and arms and wrapped around necks, choking the men into unconsciousness.

～っ

"Tyomnii-sama!"

At last, Heion had found him. The prince's night-brown hair was slick with sweat, and the scythe swung in far-reaching arcs, slicing in half an enemy rifle-axe and broadsword that got in the way.

Tyomnii didn't bother with words of greeting, but gave a signal; and without pause, Heion moved to his side, back-to-back, facing the enemies who encircled them.

She unsheathed the Legendary katana from the sash around her waist, the handguard shaped like cherry blossoms, petals etched down the red-tinged blade.

"*Blossom Dance*," she whispered, and sliced the blade through the air.

Petals swirled to life from the katana, creating a blizzard around them and blinding the criminals.

And Tyomnii's scythe took full advantage.

～੭

Cherish had moved her wheelchair into a clearing at the forest's edge. Her plan was to circle around the designated forest area of the race and enter in from the opposite side where, hopefully, her team would herd the golden pixit. If they managed to herd it in her direction, she would catch the pixit by surprise.

She grinned to herself; the rules didn't say *where* or *when* you had to enter the forest for the race. And so, she waited expectantly, fingers tapping a tune on the armrests, and shifted in her black and pink protective suit.

She heard the rustle and slap of leaves and cracking twigs. Something was coming.

Cherish readied.

But it wasn't the golden pixit that burst through the trees. Instead, it was Draev students, and moving in a mad rush past her like a herd of frightened anteleer.

Unease coiled in her gut as she watched them hurry by, ignoring her completely. What on eartha had them so spooked?

Cherish started to turn the wheelchair around to follow after them, when one of the students abruptly collapsed, a spearhead sticking out of his chest.

Ten figures stepped out from the forest shadows: a mix of races with varying amounts of vempar traits, all of them armed and all of them eager to destroy.

She stifled a scream.

One student used his Ability to make and launch wooden spears, which bounced off a transparent force field surrounding the thugs. He turned and fled.

Cherish pressed a button, and the thick wheels of her chair rumbled over the ground until she reached the student who'd fallen. Leaning out of her seat, she felt for a pulse.

There was none; the spear had gone through his heart.

Dead. One of her fellow classmates was...

No, she had to remain calm; this was no time to lose her self-control.

She exhaled, deep and slow.

A spear *thunked* the ground, barely missing her right foot. The escaped convicts—that's who they must be—were coming her way. The few students who attempted to fight back now lay injured or limped away at a hobbled run.

Cherish's resolve hardened. Gripping the arms of her chair, she lifted herself up off the seat and stood, chin high, facing the enemy.

She would end this. No matter the price she would have to pay for it afterwards.

A teal glow enveloped her, a translucent aura wrapping around her body, her limbs, her face. The glow expanded and took on the shape of large, clawed paws around her fists and feet, the shape of a large tiger head over her own head, with massive jaws and dagger teeth, its tufted ears turned back in a snarl, and a tail streaming behind her. The glowing power whipped her snow-white hair back and filled her eyes with ghostly light. Her *essence* transformed into a tiger beast, an armor of glowing energy that she stood within.

Her right hand moved, and the tiger's huge right paw moved with it; one leg stepped forward, and the tiger's followed suit. In this form, she could do anything: walk, run, fight. She felt alive again.

The criminals' approach slowed, uncertain of the tiger beast and its towering, seven-foot tall shoulders. The fair girl within stalked towards them, the beast moving with her. But these men were still shielded, and so, they decided their prey was no match for them and charged forward.

'*We'll see which is stronger: your shields or my essence!*'

A paw the size of a barrel and claws the length of knives

swung into their ranks, the blow sending some careening and thudding into trees.

Her claws tore gashes in them, and she leaped high with a roar and smashed down more when she landed. Then she balanced on one foot and twirled, her outstretched claws on both hands slashing all in her path like a whirlwind.

The enemy fell left and right. One snake-like man tried to block her paw, but the force knocked him flat and shredded his vest.

Injured students hurried past her, casting grateful glances her way.

A searing pain in her left leg pulsed suddenly, threatening to bring her down.

'No,' she growled against the pain, forcing it aside for as long as possible. 'Not yet! I must finish this…must defeat them all, first…!'

24

The jagged blade slashed down. Cyrus's metal forearms rose and blocked it, but the force of the blow still shoved her down to her knees.

She grunted. Her metal attacks wouldn't work against the force fields. All she could do was keep on the defensive and shield herself.

'Stop fretting—I can do this!' her thoughts yelled.

In her search for Aken, she'd gotten lost, and had tried to steer clear of other battling teams. But then, the White Ghost's criminals had suddenly appeared.

The criminal, with snake-like scales along his skin, raised his blade again to strike her.

Then strangely, his motions paused, and he peered down at her and cocked his head to the side. "Red half-human… You're the one he wants, aren't you?" his voice rasped.

A chill raced down Cyrus's spine.

She aimed a punch to break his knee, but the force field bounced her metal fist back.

The snake man raised a horn to his lips and blew; the sound echoed low and undulated through the forest.

Cyrus gave a start, looking this way and that.

The horn's call died out and a new sound replaced it: the thudding of footsteps coming over the forested hills and dips in the land.

More criminals. They were after her. The White Ghost was after *her*.

A scaly hand grabbed her neck from behind. She cried out, her metal fingers digging to pry it off, and she heard a grunt behind her head.

A second criminal arrived nearby and sneered, as if the scene was fun to watch.

She needed air. She needed to get away before they all gathered around her and cut off all escape.

Breathe…get free…before they—

Something fluttered past, followed by a *thunk*, and the snake man behind her slumped with an arrow through the neck. Prying the hand off and freeing herself, she turned around to see.

A Floor Earnest student stood several yards off to her right, a ruddy boy with bow and arrows poised; he nodded a brief smile her way.

She silently thanked him. He released more arrows, each finding their mark, as she moved to get away.

He was reaching for a fourth arrow, when a spear took him through the chest from behind—thrown from an enemy concealed in the patches of ferns.

Cyrus's breath hitched, her mouth open. She watched the boy as he fell back, flecks of blood painting the air, and collapsed against the soft moss and loam of the forest floor. He no longer moved.

Tears welled in her eyes. He'd tried to save her, and now,

because of her, he…he was…

Anger flared inside her like a firestorm.

She lunged at the nearest criminal, a hairy half-vempar, her metal fists pummeling against his energy shield, anger blurring the pain in her wrists.

He grabbed her elbow in an iron grip, and the shield wouldn't let her hurt him. He pulled her away across the forest floor, and her struggle kicked up dirt and moss.

After a while, when his stride finally came to a halt, he tossed her into a clearing: a half-circle space within the forest.

Cyrus staggered upright inside the clearing, her back facing a crescent wall of boulder rock. There was no one around now but the hairy criminal. Or so she thought.

"It's about time you brought her to me," said a voice.

The hairy man shuffled back out of the way in a hurry, and the White Ghost glided down to land upon the ground before her, his turquoise cape fluttering.

Fear jolted through her like a lightning bolt. He was here. He came for *her*.

The young man's smirk dimpled his cheeks, framed by layers of white hair. "Please do me a favor and cooperate this time, will you?" he directed at her.

Cyrus hopped backwards several steps, and in the same motion flung metal knives at his chest. They bounced off an invisible shield wrapping the man's skin. She called the knives back, channeling more *essence* in and throwing them again.

Ellefsen covered a yawn. "You'll start to sweat if you keep that up. And, no offense, but I'd rather not kidnap someone who smells."

Cyrus halted, breathing hard.

The young man took a step forward. She moved back, the crescent wall behind her.

"How are you here? We heard you'd been captured," she said

in a tone that demanded he answer.

Ellefsen snorted a laugh. "You really thought someone like *me* could be captured? Ha! What those buffoons caught was a decoy meant to look like me. All so that Draevensett would feel at ease today." He spread his arms wide, his smirking face self-satisfied.

She tried to forestall him some more. "Why are you doing this?" she asked. "What do you have against me? Do you hate me, is that why?" Her mind raced to think of some way to escape.

Ellefsen hesitated, a flash of something, maybe regret, crossing his gaze briefly. "Hate you? Never. You are the one who saved this world, long ago. I owe you my gratitude, as do we all."

She swallowed. "Then why...?"

"Didn't the Oracle tell you who you are? Swan Princess, I came to you because you have another chance to save this world." Ellefsen held out his hand, an unnatural shade of white. "Lend me your power, and together we will rid the world of vempar kind and bring peace and unity to all the peoples."

She stared at the hand, at him, for a silent moment. "You want to wipe out an entire race?" She gaped, incredulous. "You do realize I'm half-vempar, right?"

His features winced. "An unfortunate birth, and not one you could control," he replied. "Vempars have been the root of Eartha's problems since the very beginning. I don't need to remind you that it was *their* emperor who almost destroyed the world and caused you to sacrifice your life."

This man—he really did believe she was the princess reborn. But she wasn't. She couldn't be!

"Vempars continue to kill and kidnap innocent people. Ruining lives, breaking families apart, separating loved ones..." His left hand clenched into a shaking fist. "You see what they do, don't you? Well, I'm going to put an end to all of that. And I need your power to do so." He took a step closer. "I would rather you help me of your own free will."

Cyrus backed away. She gave no answer and let the silence pass between them.

He finally gave a regretful sigh. "They've corrupted your mind, I see... You leave me with no choice but to use force."

Ellefsen's hand darted forward and grabbed her right arm.

She fought back, clawing, kicking, but that energy shield coating his skin held firm.

"I'm not the Swan! Whatever Apfel said, it's not true! I'm a nobody half-blood!" she cried out.

Ellefsen tutted. "Poor thing. You've suffered so much that you can't even accept the truth." He leaned his head forward. "But you feel the power that's hidden inside you. The radiant Pure Light, the burning energy. You cannot deny that, can you?"

She swallowed.

A spot in the air shifted, glimmered, and something like a teleportal opened. Ellefsen's hand on her arm pulled her towards it.

"No!" She pulled back.

If she went through, there was no telling where she would be taken; Harlow and the Draev Guardians might never be able to find her.

Again, she was weak. Again, she was useless. And now this genocidal maniac wanted to use her to destroy her friends and their kingdom.

Emotion built up inside her, a whirring torrent that willed to roar free from her chest. The energy of it shot down her arm and it struck Ellefsen's hand.

The skin of his hand started to burn and peel away—just as it had with Dr. Zushil.

Ellefsen bit off a cry and released her, clutching his reddened hand to his chest. It trembled as he looked down at the burnt work of his palm. "I see..." he said. "This is going to be harder than I thought."

He stretched his other hand out, and she felt an invisible force grab her body and pull her towards the teleportal. The same force that she could do nothing against.

He would steal her away, and her friends would never be able to find her...

A sudden blast of fire passed between her and Ellefsen, the burning heat forcing him back.

She suddenly found she was able to move again, and she looked to see Hercule rounding the boulder wall behind her. Another blast of searing fire from him forced the man back.

"Leave my comrade alone, you miserable coward!" Hercule shouted.

"How annoying," muttered Ellefsen. "If that fire were simply *essence*, it wouldn't be able to touch me. But it has something more to it, doesn't it? Real dragon fire." He said the last bit with a knowing smirk.

Hercule roared and charged at him, shooting flames from his hands and open mouth.

Ellefsen levitated up and out of the way.

As Hercule tried to halt his momentum, Ellefsen stretched out his palm.

Hercule's body stopped in place.

"Even so, you are no match for me." Ellefsen motioned with his hand, and Hercule lifted off the ground. At his motion, Hercule's body slammed down into the ground, lifted again, and was thrown into the boulder wall, where he hit and crumpled.

Bloodied, Hercule's unconscious form slumped against the rock.

"Hercule!" Cyrus cried out. It had happened so fast.

Her gaze went back to Ellefsen.

"If you try to run, you can kiss Hercule's life goodbye," he warned her.

Cyrus rubbed her wrists, the pain now spiking. She couldn't put someone else's life at risk because of her, and so, she willed the metal back into bracelets around her arms.

Ellefsen stalked forward, his hand raised.

~⌐

Vines wrapped around Aken as he gripped the hand reaching through the gilded cage in his mind.

"Yes, let me free! Let's get rid of them all!" the dark replica of himself crooned.

His veins glowed like molten lava and obsidian armor wrapped around his right fist.

He came at Ellefsen from behind.

The man turned just in time to dodge, but the punch still caught him in the side, sending him skidding backwards.

"Cy, get out of here!" Aken shouted.

But Cy instead hurried over to someone slumped on the ground: It was Hercule.

A cold wave of fear washed over Aken.

Hercule…was he alive? He knew they had their differences, but Hercule was still one of them, one of Harlow. And…

The fear submerged under a flood of rage, and Aken charged at Ellefsen with a snarl.

Ellefsen straightened, one hand pressed to his side; he thrust his other palm outward.

Rocks lifted from the ground in a spray of dirt around the clearing and then flung with force towards Aken.

There were too many to dodge, so Aken raised his left forearm to block and the armored fist to shatter the rocks coming at his head. The obsidian gauntlet extended and wrapped up his right arm to the elbow.

"Persistent little bug, aren't you?" Ellefsen's lips curled. "But how many rocks can you break through before you get squashed?"

Pieces of boulder sailed at him as if thrown by a giant. And the fragments of those that his fist shattered lifted again and flung at him from behind.

Bruises and welts pummeled his body as he failed to deflect all of the onslaught.

"Set me free!"

Aken forced his way forward, trotting into a run, smashing his fist through two more large rocks.

Just as he came within reach of Ellefsen, a tree uprooted and the trunk caught Aken in the chest—flinging him across the clearing and into the crescent boulder wall.

His head spun and he coughed, spitting blood and shifting onto his knees. Just feet away, Cy met his gaze for a brief moment, worry filling those lilac eyes.

The trunk came at him again, and this time Aken lunged his fist into it, breaking the tree in half.

Both halves flung away.

"You'll never be a match for him at this rate, little me. Take more power!"

Aken tried to resist, but nothing else was working. His body ached as it Healed. He needed to get within arms-length of Ellefsen and break through that force field!

The vines and thorns wrapped around Aken's mind; fire sung through his veins. His replica grinned darkly back at him.

With a new burst of power, Aken shot forward—dodging huge rocks and another tree, using some as footholds, hopping onto a boulder, a tree, and lunging into the air where Ellefsen levitated.

He grabbed for the man's leg.

Ellefsen vanished in a swirl of leaves. He reappeared several feet away, tossing a boulder at Aken's back.

But he'd been expecting that. Aken turned midair, grabbing the boulder and vaulting on top of it, jumping off and reaching Ellefsen before the man could react. He grabbed him by the ankle and dangled in the air.

The lesson on Touch.

Aken felt with his spirit-hand, seeking for the core of energy inside Ellefsen.

"Stop it!" Ellefsen thrashed, trying to kick him off. He hurled more rocks at him.

Aken ignored the pain, the beating, his spirit-hand latching onto Ellefsen's core and pulling the *essence* from him.

"You vempar leech!"

He could feel the power starting to drain from Ellefsen, and for some reason the guy wasn't able to use his vanishing trick while Aken gripped his foot.

A massive chunk of the boulder wall wrenched free and slammed into Aken—tearing his grip from Ellefsen's ankle and smashing him to the ground in a heap of rubble.

The world became pain and gray rocks.

He could hear Cyrus cry out.

He coughed out dust and gasped for air, and forced his body to move and claw his way free of the rubble, his body Healing faster than it ever had before as the Pureblood power thrummed through his veins.

Ellefsen landed, his back not standing quite as straight. He watched as Aken got free, streaked in blood from Healed wounds. "Who knew Pureblood power could be such a nuisance? But I suppose I should expect nothing less of the False Guardian." He smirked.

There was a rustle of noise off to the right—three criminals had appeared, headed for Cyrus and Hercule.

"I've no more time to waste on you," Ellefsen stated. He motioned with his reddened palm, and two swords rose free of the criminals' belts and into the air, directed by his power. The blades flew like arrows and struck through both of Aken's upper arms, the force of the impact knocking him to the ground and pinning him there.

Aken roared in pain and anger as Cyrus was forced to face the oncoming criminals alone. He channeled bursts of lava to thrust into the air around Cy like a protective barrier, even though he knew the act was useless—the simple *essence* lava unable to burn the men through their force fields.

He pushed against the swords pinning him to the ground— black silver—striving to break free before it was too late and they took Cy.

"Use more power. More!"

Aken pushed against the fiery agony, and the blades slid free of the ground as he hoisted himself into a sitting position. He grabbed the hilt of each blade with his opposite hand and pulled them out of his arms, blood streaming down.

But as soon as he did so, Ellefsen summoned the blades back and readied to stick them through Aken again.

The teleportal hung open in the air, and the criminals were dragging Cyrus towards it.

"No!" Aken turned to stop them, trying to reach Cy in time, even as the swords flew at him again…

And then a gust of wind rose around them all.

It flung the swords aside, pulled Cyrus free, and knocked the criminals backwards, rolling them across the forest floor like dolls—their force fields useless against the powerful gust.

The wind rotated, scattering leaves in waves, and Master Nephryte landed in the clearing near Cyrus, his midnight cape fluttering.

Ellefsen's gaze widened a fraction.

"First, you pretend to be caught. Then, you have the Masters called away during the Hunters Race?" spoke Nephryte, his arms out, the wind now a rotating wall encircling the clearing. "I suppose you think yourself terribly clever."

Ellefsen's lips drew into a smirk. "I don't suppose it but *know* it."

Ropes of wind rushed forward to wrap around the young man.

Ellefsen snapped the fingers of his raised hand and he disappeared, a thick swirl of leaves in the shape of his outline replacing where he had been.

Nephryte made an angry sound and hurried forward, scanning about the trees and the sky for any sign of him.

But Ellefsen was somehow gone—again.

The criminals, however, were still there, and caught up firmly in ropes of wind.

"Aken-Shou, are you all right?" he heard the Master say, unease in his undertone. The rotating wall of wind died down.

Aken shut his eyes. No, he wasn't. The replica of himself was laughing, gripping his hand through the cage, the vines and thorns holding him tight and not letting go. He tried to pull free, but the power raced through him, clawing to take over his mind.

"Aken! Come back to us," called an echoing voice from somewhere.

It made him think of Cyrus.

He tried to fight back, keep control of his mind, and the replica cackled, working to undo the cage's lock.

He couldn't stop him.

He couldn't...

Then there came a beam of light, bright as white sunshine, and it cut through the haze down to him.

The vines and thorns around him shrank and retreated, and

the replica backed away into the dark recesses of the cage, moaning.

Aken lifted his head to the light. Was it his imagination, or were there white feathers floating within that light?

He reached his hand up to touch a feather…

…And came back to himself, surrounded by trees and a gap of blue sky overhead.

"Aken!" Cyrus, at his side, flung arms around him in a hug.

His chest was breathing hard, but other than that, he felt okay. The Pureblood power no longer sang through his body, and the obsidian armor was gone.

"It looked like you were losing yourself," Cy said, lilac gaze worried.

Aken rubbed his head. What had that light been? What had called him back? "Was it you?" he asked. "Did you bring me back?"

Cy's mouth opened, hesitated…

"You have the Pure Light. You really are the Swan, like he said."

Cy turned his head away, avoiding Aken's gaze; but then he clenched his gloved wrists suddenly to himself and cried out in pain.

"Cy? What's wrong?" Aken looked down in alarm.

Cy's hands were shining white around the fabric, as if light were trapped inside them and trying to break free.

The great well of Pure Light, what Zushil had found inside Cyrus—was it overflowing?

Cy hunched over, tugging the gloves off, pain distorting his features.

Without thinking, Aken grabbed Cy's arm. He used the same method of Touch to reach for the power and try to draw it out.

The power was at once an explosion of beauty and pain.

A flood of energy attacked Aken's hand, starting to burn and then melt his skin, flakes of it peeling away. His Healing struggled to keep up, barely keeping his hand from falling apart. He gritted his teeth against the searing agony and thrust his other hand to the ground.

Energy shot up Aken's right arm and traveled over into his left arm and hand, where he then released it into the ground through his palm with a burst of white light.

Plants sprung to life, shooting up through the soil from his hand—ferns and flowers and berries filling the whole clearing.

Aken couldn't hold on any longer and he let go of Cy, panting from the agony.

The light had faded from Cyrus's hands, and the redhead now shakily held his palms up, inspecting them. "The pain...it's stopped."

They looked from Cy to the colorful garden of plants around them for a silent moment.

Hercule was just starting to wake, and Master Nephryte helped him up. "Cyrus, Aken-Shou, follow me," he ordered, a worried sternness in his voice. He dragged the unconscious criminals along behind them.

Aken took Cyrus's hand, and the gloves, and hurried with the Master through the forest.

25

Master Deidreem deftly caught and re-tossed his deck of cards. They would be nothing but curious cards with metal edges in anyone else's hands, but in his they became flying weapons, with edges sharper and cleaner than most knives, a purple glow of his *essence* wrapped around each one. Three criminals were cut down—cards passing through their force fields as easily as a blade through butter.

Already the cards were curving their way back through the air to his ready hands for another catch and toss.

A distance away, to the right, Master Eletor spread out both palms before him. Flashes of lightning channeled forth, coursing along the forest floor like fingers, seeking to fry the enemy. A distance to the left, Master Seren-Rose's body glowed. Her *essence* took on the shape of a giant glowing snake around her, and she sent the snake through the forest with her as she ran, its mouth gaping wide to swallow up one of the criminals before he could flee, fangs biting down.

Master Brangor had been the first to charge into the fray,

sprinting in headlong and striking left and right, waving his arsenal of mismatched battle axes. Each had a long chain attached to the handle's end, letting him throw axes into out-of-reach enemies, and then, with a tug of the chain, yank the axe back to his hand. "It's an art form," he had once called it.

Deidreem sniffed; as if waving about filthy axes could ever be considered art.

Earlier, as requested, they had all gone to meet with the Grandmaster. But when they arrived, the head of the Draev Guardian League had no idea why they were there, nor anything about having requested their presence. They realized the truth, then, and hurried back to the Hunters Race, only to find that they were too late; they spotted an injured student as he stumbled out of the trees.

Now, Brangor tossed two axes here, threw three over there, while wielding a pair of short-hafted ones in his thick hands. He roared and shouted with each stroke that he carved into the fleeing enemy.

Deidreem found it a wonder that the man could wield anything smoothly at all, having thick sausages for fingers. He gave a look of disgust, and re-tossed more blade cards, neatly slicing through two criminals, while he traveled smoothly over the loamy ground.

The forest finally fell silent as they ran out of enemies to finish off. Then the Masters had to go about their next task: locating injured students and transporting them back for medical treatment.

Dr. Zushil and a crew of medics arrived on scene not much later, at Principal Han's urgent call, and began to treat those who were in serious condition. The field at the forest's edge quickly became a swarm of activity.

The golden pixit came flitting across the grass to Han's side, and she went into the cage to hide.

He made calming sounds to soothe the troubled creature.

—✍

Cyrus let herself be led around tree trunks and underbrush, holding onto Aken's hand. She stared blankly at the soil and mix of mosses beneath her footsteps.

Cyrus the Swan. A reborn princess and hero. She jerked her head in a shake.

She didn't want this. She didn't want the Swan's tragic past to be *her* past. She didn't want to have past lives that she couldn't even remember living, and a fate of forever being hunted.

And if the Swan *was* her, reborn, then didn't that mean the evil Emperor had also come back to life, to finish what he'd started? That's what Principal Han had told her the legend said. Were the Impure Nights somehow connected to the Emperor?

Did she have time to worry about a hidden enemy, when she had the White Ghost on her tail right now?

Mamoru's voice cut through the forest, calling out to them. The group paused as he came trotting around a sunken boulder and reached them, concern written all over his scarred face.

"Are you both okay? You look a mess, Aken." He looked them over with an up-down scan.

Aken shrugged at his ruined clothes. "It's no big deal."

Mamoru then noticed Hercule, who had fallen unconscious again and was now being carried by the Master's wind Ability.

"We ran into the White Ghost," she explained to him.

Mamoru exchanged a look with the Master, a meaningful look that she couldn't interpret.

"You charged in and attacked without thinking, again, didn't you?" Mamoru chided and pulled a twig from Aken's hair. "When will you learn? I could swear the both of you haven't changed a bit since—" He stopped himself abruptly and didn't finish; instead, he gently patted Cyrus on the back. "Are you really okay? Both of you?"

She knew what he meant: the trauma. The experience of battle and seeing fellow students die. She bit her lip and realized that she was shaking.

No, she wasn't okay. How could she be?

She didn't need to answer, though. Mamoru pulled her and Aken close, wrapping an arm around each, a hand on the back of their heads, and hugged them to his chest. The tension inside her eased a little and she let the teardrops fall.

"I don't...feel well..." Aken mumbled after a while, and he slid down to his knees, his features going pale.

Mamoru touched his back in concern. Master Nephryte went to his side, feeling Aken's forehead with his palm. "It's the anemia. You've lost too much blood," he concluded.

He lifted Aken with ropes of wind to carry him, and Aken protested weakly, "Don't carry me like a crook. I've gotta keep my dignity..."

The Master huffed and shook his head. But he lifted Aken and placed him on his back, piggyback style, instead. "Will this suffice your dignity?"

"I guess. Thanks," Aken mumbled, eyes closed.

"Just don't drool on me if you fall asleep," Nephryte warned.

A smile tugged at Cyrus's lips. They looked like an older brother carrying his exhausted younger sibling. A sweet yet comical sight. She needed something to smile about right now, even if tears were not far away.

"The things I do for this kid," the Master mumbled under his breath. "Mamoru, I need you to find Zartanian, Lykale and Bakoa for me."

The older boy nodded and hurried off.

❧

Lykale dusted off his pants, paying close attention to getting a dirt smudge off his knee, then brushed his shirt and straightened it. Medical teams were scouring the forest and making their way past. He frowned and ignored them, perching his broken pair of glasses atop his nose. "Well. That could have gone better," he muttered.

"Could have, could have," repeated a purple, flower-like pixit floating in the air above his head.

"You don't have to repeat that."

The pixit made a wispy giggling sound through its sharp teeth.

A warm breeze rustled the canopy, and he raised his hands, feeling the air rush between his fingers. His right hand still ached.

"*Shoo*, go hide. I don't want anyone seeing you." He motioned, and the pixit gave one last giggle before floating up to the canopy leaves.

His uninjured hand went to the lock he wore around his neck, clutching the metal, and he closed his eyes for a brief moment. Then he made his way down the mossy slope, skidding over the loamy soil.

Near a rotting fallen tree he spotted a blue hat and rustling plumes.

He ventured near and found Zartanian alongside the hat: his back against the trunk, a dazed look on his face. His saber lay fallen by his hand, bloody; nearby were two bodies of convicts.

"Zartanian? Hey." Lykale patted his cheek sharply.

The boy's head jerked and he stammered, "They wanted to kill us...I took their lives... I... Elijob, d-don't leave me!"

Lykale frowned. The boy was in shock.

Well, it *was* his first time in a real battle of life and death, after all. But who was this Elijob person?

Oh well. It didn't matter right now.

"Zartanian, you need to pull yourself together. The fight is over. The criminals are gone. Everyone in Harlow is safe."

The raven-haired boy blinked, regaining some focus back to reality. "Lykale?" he whimpered.

"Yes, everything is—"

The boy fell forward, pressing his head to Lykale's chest as sobs raked through his body.

Lykale blinked and looked down at the curly mop of hair pressed against his shirt. Despite himself, he felt a pang of pity, and gently patted the boy's back. "Shush, everything's fine now. Really, there's no reason to drench me with your tears. You'll get over this soon enough, and be the stronger for it, I promise."

The boy didn't move.

Footsteps trotted nearby, and Lykale spotted the red highlights in Mamoru's hair before the guy appeared around a scraggly bush. "I have Zartanian here," he called over to him.

The puppeteer slowed and gave him a nod. Just then, Bakoa landed on the ground in a swirl of sand and took on his humanoid form.

"Bakoa!" Mamoru went to him. "Are you all right?"

Bakoa offered a smile, maintaining his positive attitude. But the elder knew better than to be fooled by outward appearances. It was usually the positive and comical types who were hurting the most inside.

Mamoru gripped his shoulder. "Are you sure you're okay?"

Bakoa slightly turned away, his cheerful mask failing. "Yeah...it's not the first time I've fought."

That was the only answer he gave.

Bakoa shifted his legs to sand again and glided up. "Is Harlow okay?"

Mamoru nodded. "Everyone's accounted for, now."

"Then we should look for other people to help." Bakoa flew past him, weaving his way through the trees.

Professor Kotetsu cupped a hand over his mouth, holding back the flood of tears threatening to gush out as he ran through the forest, passing people by, navigating through the ambush's aftermath.

'She has to be alive... Oh, Lord God, please let her be alive!'

He reached a wide-open space of field, where one student had pointed him to. And there, a pale form lay motionless in the grass.

Kotetsu collapsed to his knees beside the body, Cherish, brushing her hair aside and holding the back of her head in his hand. He checked for a pulse, the deep beat of a vempar's heart, and watched her eyelids flicker.

She was alive.

"Cherish! My little sister..."

She was in a terrible state. Her limbs hung limp and bruises bloomed all over, despite the protective body suit she'd worn for the race.

'No, oh no...she used her full Ability...'

The groan he tried to hold in escaped. How dire must the situation have been for her to go this far?

Ever so carefully, he scooped her unconscious form up in his arms.

26

Thunder rolled in the distance like the grumblings of waking giants. Churning clouds filled the afternoon sky, looking as if rain might break out at any moment, though not a drop had fallen yet. Perhaps the clouds were too angry to shed tears for the dead, while shovelfuls of dirt slowly buried each casket, the soil a soft blanket over cold wood, the last blanket their bodies would ever have.

There were mostly silent tears, but now and then a sob or whimper could be heard among the family members and students, a sea of black dresses and suits, veils and top hats. All of Draevensett was present at the cemetery. The gathered assembly watched the rhythmic motion of the gravediggers' shovels, a confirmation that those comrades and loved ones would no longer return home. Flowers and photos were before each of the seven caskets.

Cyrus recognized one of them: the ruddy boy with a bow who had tried to save her.

Her fingers gripped the rim of the top hat held in her hands.

She glanced sidelong at Aken, and at Master Nephryte standing silently beside him.

The Master kept a comforting hand lightly on Zartanian's shoulder, the boy's head slumped forward, raven-bangs shadowing his expression from view.

Zartanian had been taking it hard. To her, it felt like there was something more hidden beneath his sorrow. The Master told him he didn't have to attend the funeral, but the boy said he wanted to show respect for the fallen. His shoulders shuddered now and then, though his legs stood firm and determined.

Aken gripped his top hat in hand, silent as a statue. Cyrus felt her lip tremble and another tear roll down her cheek while speeches were given and the names read out. Aken's hand moved to hold hers in a gesture of support, and after a moment, her fingers entwined his, squeezing tight.

White roses were tossed as a final gift of farewell. Stray petals caught by the stormy breeze swirled together, carried beyond the cemetery hill and the cold gravestones to travel on to unseen places.

The raven, Corben, watched the scene through liquid black eyes from his perch in the single walnut tree behind the assembly, its branches curled as if reaching for the heavens and pleading for the lost souls.

At the funeral's end, they all bowed their heads one last time. The statue of an angel was erected at the head of the seven graves, a symbol and reminder of their sacrifice and a prayer for their rest. Cyrus gazed up at the serene stone face and the detailed feather wings trailing down, the Draev Guardian coat-of-arms at the pedestal's base.

She couldn't let this tragic scene happen again.

Never again.

"How could this be allowed to happen? *How?*"

Master Nephryte's fist nearly cracked the wall's surface inside Principal Han's office, the only space of wall not covered in shelves, preserved beetles and whatnot.

Lady Seren-Rose, seething in quiet anger herself, lightly touched his arm. "Your temper will not solve the problems at hand, Nephryte," her tone soothed.

"She's right. Don't fall off the deep end, just yet," Eletor added.

Deidreem made a sound through his nose.

"These students," Nephryte spoke through near-to-grinding teeth, "are God's precious creations. It's our responsibility to care for them, raise them, teach them, keep them safe..."

"Here he goes again," Deidreem grumbled and rolled his eyes to the side.

Nephryte faced one of the Chief Commanders of the D.G. League, the one who was responsible for checking the race's site and who also happened to be Master Brangor's eldest son. The stocky young man's expression held uncomfortable guilt.

"And yet we failed them!" Nephryte continued. "How could you not detect such a large ambush? You scanned the area before the Hunters Race began, didn't you?" His tone demanded an answer.

"I am sure the White Ghost took many measures beforehand," Seren-Rose said quietly. "His powers are strange. No one was expecting something like this, and certainly not so near the capital city. You cannot blame them for failing to notice something that none of us were looking for." She flicked a glance up into his eyes.

The commander bowed his head solemnly to the principal, to his father, and to the Masters. "You have my deepest apology, and my word that this will never happen again, not under my watch."

Brangor's frown was a deep and serious trench, but he clapped the back of his son's shoulders and mumbled, "That's how life is, lad," he told him. "I know you'll do better next time."

Eletor shrugged his palm up in the air and asked, "Just what *is* this White Ghost person we're dealing with? Do we know anything about him at all?"

The commander shook his head. "We're still looking into it... But whatever race he is, he's not of our lands, nor of anywhere commonly known."

A moment of silence passed through the large room.

"Nephryte," Seren-Rose whispered near his ear, "Do not blame yourself for what happened, either. It wasn't your fault. We were all deceived by that man's tricks."

The tension in his shoulders gradually eased beneath her hand.

He knew she was right, but it was hard to let the anger dissipate; he wanted someone to punish for this pain and heartbreak.

The group discussion continued for a while longer, detailing new security measures to be put into place, before the commander and his men took their leave.

"Just one moment, before you all go," Han spoke to the Masters, once their meeting had concluded. "The list of newly requested missions from HQ has arrived for you to sort through. I know you may not exactly be in the mood for missions," Han acknowledged, "but it is part of your job as Draev Guardians, and they must be carried out for the good of Draeth." He hung the long parchment up on a nail in the wall.

Nephryte was, indeed, too angry to think about missions, but he made himself look at the list anyway. One in particular caught his eye: a long trip to deliver a letter from the king to Salmu Baris.

Hmm. Could he use this in some way?

An idea gradually took shape in his mind. And with a head bow, he left the room.

～૭

Once it was his turn, Nephryte entered through the doorway into Viceroy Deciet's grand office chambers—a series of rooms made of curves and sharp arches and red furnishings—over at the royal palace.

"Master Nephryte. What brings you here?" rasped Deciet's deep voice from behind a dark, ornately carved desk.

"This mission." Nephryte handed over a copy of the mission request form. "To deliver a letter for the king to Salmu Baris. I will take on that request, along with my students in Harlow."

"Really?" Deciet's thin eyebrows lifted in surprise. "If that is what you wish, then I will not bother to question you. Although, it is highly unusual to bring young students along on such a mission." His gaze trained on Nephryte, his sickly pale fingers steepled at his chin.

When Nephryte did not give any further explanation, Deciet rose. "Wait here one moment." He moved with an unnerving grace and vanished through a door on the left, leading into a series of side rooms, to retrieve the king's letter.

While Nephryte waited, he scanned some books on the shelves: old and rare copies that only the wealthiest could afford.

He spotted a copy of *The Three Bladeers* lying closed on the desk. His hand went to the blue cover. This was a first edition, and a gilded one at that. He'd been wanting to find a copy for years.

He ran his fingers along the blue leather and gilding. He opened to a page where the title was inked like an exquisite piece of artwork.

When he ran his thumb to flip through more pages,

something pressed between them glinted: a small, flat-sided key.

Nephryte looked from the odd key to the desk. He didn't hear Deciet returning yet, so he got on his knees and searched around.

There was a narrow drawer underneath the desk with a small keyhole. He tried the key.

It opened.

Normally he wasn't one to pry into other people's belongings, but there had always been something about Deciet he didn't completely trust, something lurking behind the viceroy's outer mask.

He would just take a quick peek, see why a locked drawer was needed. No harm done.

Perhaps some of Aken-Shou's bad behavior was rubbing off on him?

He pulled the drawer open; it slid out without a sound.

Inside were folded bits of paper and a notebook. He took one of the scraps of paper out for a quick look.

The Bloodres have eliminated the person who was causing you trouble, My King. They are proving their usefulness, as I knew they would.

Nephryte's pulse quickened. The Bloodres—they were Aken's parents.

Have eliminated...

Did this mean the Bloodres were being used for their powers, for the king, back when they were still alive?

He shook his head. This didn't make sense. Viceroy Deciet had told him, and a select few others, that the Bloodres were murderers who had to be executed.

But this...it sounded, instead, like they were being used as assassins by the king.

Footsteps came, and Nephryte swiftly put the note and drawer back into place. He had just placed the key back inside the book when Deciet entered.

"I forgot you have a love for literature," rasped Deciet, seeing his hand on *The Three Bladeers*.

"Yes. If I ever retire, I will be a librarian," Nephryte replied, keeping his pulse in check and pretending to admire the leather copy on the desk.

Deciet strode over to him, his long fingers extending a sealed envelope for him to take.

Nephryte took the envelope, taking care to keep his expression indifferent.

Deceit nodded slightly, his silky black hair rustling over the lacy collar of his fine tunic. "Safe travels, Master Nephryte, for you and your students."

"Thank you, Viceroy."

As Nephryte left the palace, he let out a troubled breath and contemplated the note's message.

Was it from the viceroy, or someone else?

If the Bloodres had been the king's forced assassins, then that would give everything a whole new meaning. They were never bloodthirsty murderers, but instead had been working to please their king.

Which left the question: Why had Nephryte and a team of Draevs been ordered to execute them?

He had believed Aken's parents were evil, believed he was protecting the citizens of Draeth from them. But now...

A headache began in his right temple.

The king had used the Bloodres, and then thrown their lives away...

And he had helped.

"I can't be thinking about this right now," he whispered to himself.

Their current threat was what he had to focus on, protecting Cyrus, if she was truly the Swan of legend.

"Deal with one thing at a time," he murmured under his breath.

"What do you make of this White Ghost, my dears? Has anything been learned of him?" Leader asked the gathering of Impure Nights. His slow pace circled the black meeting table, each footfall made with intent and grace.

One of the members spoke up. "I did some digging, Leader, and it seems that not long ago the moonlight faeryn was kidnapped and rescued. There was a Draev student mission carried out to save the child, and the kidnapper turned out to be the White Ghost himself."

Leader drummed his fingers on the back of a chair as he passed by, his many rings clacking. "This person, the White Ghost, must be aware of the Oracle's valuable knowledge," he concluded. "His actions are interfering with our plans, whether he is aware of us or not."

Another member—one who dressed flamboyantly—sat upright in his chair as if just realizing something. "Could he be after the Swan?" he exclaimed. "Is that why he wanted the Oracle, same as us? What if he's already discovered who and where she is, and he gets to her first?"

Leader paused his pacing to rest a cold gaze on the member.

Adelheid rolled her eyes. "Duh. You only just now realized that? What do you think we've been discussing since this meeting began?"

The member ducked his head under his colorful hat and muttered something she couldn't hear.

"I want the Ghost's interference put to an end," rasped Leader's deep tone. "And I want the Oracle safely in our grasp." He turned in place with purpose and his unnerving stare bore into Pueginn from across the table. "You failed to collect the Oracle once. Should I presume to trust you with such a task for a second time?"

Pueginn pushed up from the chair with haste, his rotund stomach bumping the table, and bowed. "Please, Leader, I would be most honored with this second chance. I will not fail you. I swear it!"

Leader regarded him for one calculating moment. "Very well." He popped the fingers of his left hand, one by one, slowly. "Be sure to not disappoint us again, Pueginn."

It was quiet inside Nephryte's private study within the tower room. The walls were too thick for spying vempar ears to listen through, and so, it was there that he chose to meet secretly with Mamoru, this time determined to get answers from him.

"Lord Mamoru, *please*, you must tell me," Nephryte half demanded, half pleaded to the scarred boy. "After all that has happened, I must know. How can I help keep her safe if I don't know what it is that we're up against? The White Ghost is already convinced of who she is. So, tell me truthfully: is Cyrus the reborn Swan Princess or not?"

Mamoru's arms were crossed as he paced the circular tower study. He hesitated mid-step, rolling his left heel. "...Yes," he finally admitted, quietly, as if it pained him to do so.

Nephryte let his shoulders relax, though he had been hoping for the answer to be *no*.

"She still has the same face, the same eyes...even Aken is nearly the same as he was back then," Mamoru continued.

"You knew them personally?"

A smile tugged at his deep scar. "Very much so." His gaze took on a faraway look, as if viewing scenes from the past. "The Swan and her guardian...the help they gave me..." he quietly reminisced.

Nephryte laced his fingers together methodically. "Thank you for being honest. I know it must be difficult to reveal such things."

Mamoru gave an appreciative nod.

"About the White Ghost: do you know who he is, or *what* he is? You've lived through more than any of us have. Surely you must know something?" Nephryte pried.

A shadow crossed Mamoru's features. "I didn't catch a glimpse of him myself, but based on the descriptions, I believe he is of the Formakt, also known as a breed of shapeshifters. I had hoped never to see them in our world again. They live in a separate realm; sort of like a world within our world, I suppose? It's a bit complicated."

"Shapeshifters," Nephryte mused. "Great. Dealing with an opponent who can alter their appearance into anything humanoid definitely makes our situation worse."

Mamoru raised an eyebrow. "You know of the Formakt?"

"Not much." Nephryte shrugged with his hand. "I've happened across a couple of references in the Book Keepers Library. However, it seems that our common history books fail to mention that race's existence." He looked pointedly at Mamoru.

Mamoru lowered his gaze, his smile guilty. "I had felt it wise that we not remember them, and had hoped that by removing all knowledge of their existence from our records, it would ensure we wouldn't interact with their kind in the future."

Nephryte grunted. "Clearly that didn't work. Any ideas as to why a shapeshifter would be here now?"

"It's hard to tell... The Formakt sometimes banished their criminals into our realm. He could be one of them."

"How kind."

"Ha. I hope that's all it is, to be honest. We had bad dealings with the Formakt in the past, during The Purge, and I'm sure they still bear a grudge against us."

Nephryte mulled over that piece of information. "There's a group of mixed bloods that I know of. Some of them claim to be descendants of rogue shapeshifters, and they're currently living as a troupe of performers—and secretly as assassins for hire."

"Oh? And you're just now telling me this?" Mamoru cocked his head to the side.

"I didn't know it would ever matter, and I didn't really understand what the Formakt were... But Bakoa is related to them, which is how I learned about their troupe."

Mamoru blinked in surprise. "Really?" He shook his head. "I'd like to hear more about *that*...but later. My point, now, is that the White Ghost is not someone we can easily handle— even with your monstrous Ability." Mamoru tipped his head back, his gaze tracing the tower wall and a spiral staircase as it wound up and up into the distant shadows. "Which means Cyrus can't stay here. She must go into hiding."

Nephryte straightened. "Hold on. She's finally found a place where she can belong. I can't just take that away from her."

"Then, what? Wait until that white monster finds her again?"

Nephryte tapped his chin with a bent finger. "In a way, maybe that's *exactly* what we should do."

"He's too smart for a trap."

"Yes...that's why it won't look like one. A mission request recently came to Draev headquarters, from the king himself; there's a letter he wants delivered personally to the sultan of Salmu Baris. I've been wanting to do some research in the Book Keepers Library there, anyway, and now is a perfect excuse to go."

Mamoru raised one maroon eyebrow at him.

"If the White Ghost has ears in Draevensett, he will follow our trail. He doesn't have the convict escapees for his lackeys anymore—we finished them off. So, I'll lure him away from the city, isolate him, and take him out myself before he has a chance to react."

"Or he'll try to blend in with Harlow, and kidnap Cyrus the moment you turn your back," countered Mamoru.

Nephryte clenched his finger against his chin. "He'll try to do that regardless of whether we wait in the city or not. It's too crowded here—there's too much going on; I can't keep track of everyone in Harlow every second of the day. We need to leave…" His lips slowly drew into a smirk. "I know what he'll try to do—and he won't get away with his tricks *this* time."

27

It was crowded inside the infirmary, with every room occupied and every hallway bustling with activity and bickering visitors. The past several days had been the busiest the staff had had since the war. There were more patients than Doctor Zushil could manage—and most of them just worriers and whiners complaining about wounds that would Heal on their own. "Stop whining, already!" he snapped. "It will Heal when it Heals—be *patient*!"

Cyrus crept past, with Aken in tow. The doctor was too busy yelling at Doughboy—bandages wrapped around both his thick arms—to notice them sneaking by. If he caught them again, he would throw them out and shout: "No visitors but family allowed!"

Aken urged her to hurry. "Go go *go*!"

By the time Zushil must have noticed movement out the corner of his eye and turned to look, they had vanished inside one of the curtained rooms.

The first patient they came across was Malfred, a Tathom

boy. He lay there stretched out on a white bed, wrappings covering his limbs and one thick patchwork around his collarbone.

"Wow, can he breathe in that?" commented Aken.

Denim, seated glumly beside the bed, was munching on an apple from a gift basket. He half-turned, ready to tell-off whoever had entered. When he saw it was *them*, the glare in his expression became haughty. "What do you Harlow losers want?"

Behind the snarky tone, Cyrus could sense guilt being held back. Denim must feel terrible for not being able to protect Malfred—though he wasn't about to let his feelings show in front of them.

"Hmm, let's see," thought Aken aloud. "If every member of Harlow is safe and sound, not stuck in a sick bed like your group, then doesn't that make us winners and *you* losers?"

Cyrus jabbed him with her elbow. "We came to check in on everyone. How is he?" She indicated Malfred with her hand. "Will he Heal up soon?"

Denim shifted his gaze to hers, and the haughty sparkle diminished a fraction. "Doc says it'll be a while before he's his old self again. He got hit hard, trying to keep the team safe."

Cyrus handed him a daffodil from the wrapped bundle she carried in one arm, a cheerful yellow for the vase on the bedside table. "Tell him we wish him a fast recovery, when he wakes up."

Denim looked surprised, even startled, but he took it.

As she turned to exit the room, Aken surprised them both when he mumbled, "Hope he gets better," before ducking out.

She heard Denim faintly murmur back, "Worry about yourself."

There were fading red marks on Aken's arms from the black silver blades that had stabbed him. Rumor had gotten around about how they had both faced the White Ghost and how Master Nephryte had rescued them.

She shoved the memory to the back of her mind, and she and Aken finally reached Cherish's room next door. Oh, what a sad sight the girl made! If Aken said Malfred looked bad, it was nothing compared to the casts and neck brace holding the fair aristocrat together.

"Cherish..." Cyrus exclaimed in a whisper.

"Whoa," Aken silently mouthed.

Professor Kotetsu was there at his little sister's side, his chair scooted as close to the bed as the frame would allow. A book of fairytales sat open on his lap, which he'd probably been reading to her.

"Ooh!" his voice chirped in delight as they came in. "Cherishy, your friends have come to see you! How sweet."

Cherish blinked awake, her eyelids crusty, and offered them a weary smile. "Cyrus, Aken, I'm so glad you weren't seriously hurt. I hope everyone else is well?"

Cyrus nodded. "They are; we checked in on them." She placed the bundle of daffodils in a vase on the bedside table, replacing other flowers that had wilted.

Cherish tried to see the vase without moving her head. "You're so kind to bring me flowers, and they're such a cheerful color."

Cyrus faltered. She kept forgetting that people saw her as a boy. What was she thinking, giving a girl flowers? "Yeah, it's, well, I'm handing out flowers to everyone—no big deal."

Aken gave her a funny look.

Kotetsu nodded deeply. "Yes, yes, flowers are most special. One of the world's greatest mysteries and most pretty things! Except for my little sister, of course." He leaned close to Cherish, as if she were still a baby. "Cuz you'll always be the cutest wittle thing in the whole wide world!"

Cherish put on a long-suffering expression.

"So," Cyrus switched topic, "what's the diagnosis? Will you be fully Healed and back in school soon?"

The girl gave a light laugh. "I wish. But I'll have to be able to sit up on my own, first."

Cyrus swallowed, embarrassed to have asked.

"I really look pitiful, don't I? But I did this to myself." Their confused expressions trained on Cherish. "I'm a Metamorvis, the transformation type; I call my Ability *Ethereal Tiger*. It's strong, but the toll that it takes on my body is the price I pay for using it."

"And how brave you were to use it, my darling," Kotetsu interjected. "Your body is too weak to handle such great energy, and you can't Heal from it because of your disorder." He rubbed his head against hers affectionately.

Cherish would have pushed him away if her arms weren't bandaged. She fixed her gaze on both her and Aken. "Don't you go acting like I'm an invalid and treating me like a child, now— my brother does that quite enough already, no thank you."

Cyrus couldn't help but grin at that. "We won't; *promise*."

At least Cherish was feeling well enough to talk and laugh, even if she couldn't move much.

But it frightened Cyrus how close they had come to losing her.

❧

Inside Draevensett, Hercule glared down at the blue faeryn child, who had made it his game to sit on Hercule's foot and cling to his leg while he tried to walk.

Why on eartha did *he* have to be the one to look after the child while Aken and Cyrus were out? He had more pressing things to do than babysit!

Hercule spotted Marigold coming into Floor Harlow's corridor, arms full with a basket of fresh clean towels, shirts and...his underwear.

He gave a start and hurried towards her, the child-weight on his leg making his gait awkward. "I told you I would wash those myself, Marigold."

"Oh. You still have anxiety about me washing your undergarments, milord?"

His face flushed red. Marigold could be painfully frank at times. He nervously shushed her. "Don't say such things out loud, *please*! And hand those over." He speedily snatched the basket from her, and he hurried to carry it back to his room. "And would you kindly remove yourself from my foot?" he directed down at the child. "Don't you have wings hidden under your jacket? Go fly around the school or something."

Apfel pouted. "I can'ts fly yet. Thanks for remindings me, Grumpy."

He halted. "Grumpy...?"

Marigold sucked in her lips.

"Oh, the poor faeryn child can't fly, either?" spoke Lykale's voice. The older boy came out of his room, and Hercule noticed a burn on his hand that was still Healing.

"What do you mean by *either*?" Hercule questioned.

Lykale shook his head, as if it were obvious. "Don't you have eyes in that thick skull of yours? Marigold, here, can't fly—not with how wilted her wings have become."

Hercule looked from him to her. "Wilted? What do you mean? Her wings have always been like that."

"Ha! You mean you really don't know?" Lykale's aqua gaze became both smug and bitter at the same time. He could hear Marigold shift her feet uncomfortably. "When a faeryn is held in captivity for a long period of time, unable to travel the forests and be free, their once vibrant wings begin to wilt—withering like a rose on the vine, until they can fly no more." He made a fluttering motion with his other hand.

Hercule's jaw fell slack. "What?" He turned to Marigold. "Is this true?"

She kept her head lowered, staring at the floor instead of meeting his gaze.

"I wouldn't just make something like that up, kid." Lykale grunted, displeased. "I'm a scientist, remember? I always get my facts straight. You've probably never seen a faeryn outside of captivity, have you?"

Hercule grimaced. "Captivity. You make it sound as if they're miserable, caged animals."

"Aren't they?"

Hercule stared up at him, shock written in the set of his jaw.

But Lykale's lips curved slightly upward. "Fragile butterflies caught within a vempar-spider's web; their only fate to be trapped within slavery before they ultimately wither away and die."

Hercule dug his thumbs into his palms. Was that really how Marigold had felt, all this time? Was she a trapped butterfly?

His gaze drifted to her wings, so green and lovely yet drooped for as long as he could remember...

He thought back to the first day she came to the mansion, five years ago, the faeryn girl who he had been so mean to as a child. He regretted that; he always would.

But Lykale was right, he had never seen a faeryn fly, never seen Marigold even able to.

"Just because school's been canceled for the day, it doesn't mean you should stand around and gossip." Mamoru halted as he came out the single bathroom across the hall, a towel draped around his shirtless neck. He must have come back from his daily run and showered. "If you have nothing beneficial to talk about, then I suggest you end the conversation."

Lykale's smirk quirked. "Gossip, is that what you call it when you inform someone of the truth?" He adjusted the glasses on the bridge of his nose.

Hercule watched uneasily as Lykale continued past them down the corridor; he added one last remark before heading to the stairwell: "Perhaps the noble should stop standing around and go fold his underwear, instead of holding them up on display for us all to see."

Green-striped silk underwear was spread out on top of the laundry basket he was still holding. Hercule blushed furiously and scurried back to his room, steam curling out his ears.

Little Apfel let go of his leg, rolling on the floor, laughing. "I likes Lykale—he's funny!" He bumped into Mamoru's foot and sat back up. "And Mamowru! He's like a bossy mama, buts smart and kind."

Mamoru ran a hand through his damp, thick hair. "Well, thanks, I think?" he said, while Marigold hid her grin behind a hand.

———

Cyrus narrowed her vision, concentrating, focusing on the twelve pins lined up and waiting before her. In one quick motion, the bowling ball flew from her metal-wrapped hand, careening down the long strip of floor to bash into the wooden pins at the far end—*Bm-bm-bm-bm-clack!*

Nine pins fell down.

"Woohoo!" Aken cheered from his seat at a table booth.

She flexed her hand. The pain had vanished from her wrists since the battle—since Aken had syphoned that bit of energy away. She could sense that the pain would return, but for now, it was nice to feel normal and not have to be so careful with her hands. Coming here to the bowling café was a great idea.

Bakoa came up beside her, ready for his turn, a grin on his eager face. She put aside her light bowling ball—meant for children—and Bakoa took up the heavy one that only vempars could throw.

"Win us more points!" she told him.

"You got it!" Bakoa bounced on his heels, pumping himself up.

When he threw, the sleek bowling ball sped away, true as an arrow—and hit straight through the heart of the cluster of pins and knocked all but one flat.

Aken let a potato fry fall from his mouth in surprise.

"Woohoo!" Bakoa danced about. "I did it, oh yeah, I'm the King of Bowling."

Cyrus fist-bumped him. "Way to go, Bakoa!"

Aken smirked. "Yeah, yeah, keep bragging. Here's your reward of fries, Your Kingly Bowlingness." While Bakoa took the plate of fries, Aken pushed off from his seat, next. "All right, my turn. Let me show you how the real pros work!" He took the ball, and he made the heavy weight spin while balanced on his index finger.

"Ooh, that's cool." Bakoa watched and munched.

While Aken was proudly showing off, however, the bowling ball was snatched from his finger by a Holsome twin.

"He sneaks! He steals! He throws! *Aaand* he strikes!" the twin hollered as he sent the stolen ball flying into the pins: all twelve noisily flattened.

"Score!" Jack raised both arms and high-fived Victor.

"I should've known. The Un-Holsome twins," Aken's tone dripped with sarcasm.

"Oo, ouch." Jack flinched at the insult. "I do believe he made a rather bad joke about us, dear brother."

"Quite so, and poorly done, too." Victor feigned disappointment. He went to Aken's side and leaned down to whisper loudly in his ear, "I could give you some tips on how to make better jokes, you know. You desperately need help."

Aken ducked forward, grabbing back the bowling ball before Jack could toss it again.

"Stop butting in! I have a duty to perform for Harlow here."

"Duty?" Victor, chin in hand, tilted his head with a bratty smile. "So many things I could say right now, so many jokes…"

"…Yet so little time!" Jack finished.

Before Aken knew it, the ball had vanished from his hands again.

"Think you can be much of a challenge for us?" Victor spun the ball, perfectly balanced on his pinky finger.

"We're known as the bowling masters." Jack grinned mischievously. "The infamous Alley Beasts, who are feared by all the bowlers of Draethvyle!"

"A bowler has yet to appear who can defeat us," said Victor. "So, what do you think, young chaps?"

"Want to give it a try? Dethrone us, if you can?" finished Jack.

Cyrus shared a look with Aken, who then pointed at their smug faces, "Challenge accepted! Bring it on, evil twins!"

Minutes later…

…Team Harlow was being clobbered.

"Flying Chariot Ball!" Victor shouted, slamming pins down.

"Magical Unicorn Kick!" Jack's bowling ball zigzagged speedily across the lane, ricocheting back and forth between both barriers and taking out every row of pins.

"Power of Dance!" Victor threw, the ball spinning like a ballerina and kicking pins over.

Aken, Cyrus and Bakoa were left to bite the dust.

"I can't believe this!" Aken gnawed angrily on a fry.

"So unfair, dude," Bakoa sniffled despairingly.

Cyrus made one last attempt at a strike, planting her feet just right and gauging the angle, before finally throwing with all her might, and…

The ball landed in the gutter.

Silence reigned.

"Alley Beasts. I guess the title wasn't an understatement,"

Aken muttered.

The door to the bowling café jingled open.

Apfel, wearing his large cap, came skipping up to them, giving Cyrus a quick hug. "You losing the game alreadys, Goldilocks?" Apfel said disapprovingly up at Aken, who patted the child's head roughly.

Hercule came up behind and punched Aken in the shoulder. "That's for dumping this kid on me. Now *you* babysit." The nobleson looked worn out and pushed to the brink, with bags under his eyes and his usually combed hair unkempt.

Aken rubbed his shoulder.

Zartanian also came into the bowling café, looking tired from sword practice.

"My, my. What a bad father," frowned Victor.

"Quite so, dear Brother," said Jack, observing Apfel.

Aken grimaced. "He's not my child!"

Apfel put on the most pitiful expression, chestnut eyes big and glistening, and he snuggled in the seat between Cyrus and Bakoa. "He's a mean papa. Never cares abouts me, and is always leaving me alone."

A wave of pity sounded throughout the bowling café. Then laughter at the look on Aken's face.

Cyrus had to turn away, her body shaking with held-in laughs.

A Răsărit accent growled, coming from one of the nearby table booths: "Thees loud cheet-chat ees very much annoying me."

Cyrus noticed Aken visibly swallow; the prince hadn't settled his score with him just yet.

"I suppose what they say is true, oh Brother," said Jack, with a shrug.

"Yes, quite so," agreed Victor. "Harlow is made up of nothing but snot-nosed kids with rotten tempers and throwing skills worse than an old grandma—and add to that: bad parental behavior."

Jack nodded. "Very much the runts of the school."

A spark flashed in Hercule's golden eyes. He marched forward, taking the bowling ball from the twin's hand, and the dangerous glint in his gaze made everyone move aside to let him step up to the platform.

"Kids? Runts?" Hercule's tone growled. His hand, holding the ball, flashed yellow with fire, and the bowling ball became a mass of flames. "I've had enough of these insults. Blasphemers to the name of Harlow...shall perish!!" he roared.

The fireball left Hercule's hand in a fast throw, speeding towards the pins.

All the wooden pins shattered on impact, and the pieces went sailing through the café. People ducked and took cover under tables. Aken pushed Cyrus's head down just in time to avoid a flying chunk. Instead, it hit Bakoa square in the forehead before he could turn into sand. "*Gwah!*" he collapsed.

The twins hugged each other, their faces wide in mock fear.

Once the debris settled, Hercule lightly dusted off his shirt, satisfied, his pent-up anger now quelled. Chin in the air, he surveyed the booths of gawking people.

The Holsome twins straightened as one to salute.

"For throwing the world's fastest and most deadly strike in all of bowling history—" began Victor.

"—We acknowledge you, Hercule, and bestow upon thee the grand title of..." continued Jack.

"...Fireball Striker!" they announced as one.

Hercule stood straighter, combing a hand through his pearly hair.

Aken muttered out the side of his mouth, "Is that really something to be proud of?"

Harlow and some others applauded. But Tyomnii grumbled,

the noise disturbing his peace while he sipped at a melon smoothie. His ominous figure rose from his seat like a dark reaper. "Thees drama...ees very much annoying me," he said, and the black scythe was in his hand. "Let me drink my smoothie een peace!"

Those at the tables nearby scurried away from the weapon's reach in a panic.

Heion grabbed the shaft. "Tyomnii-sama—remember your anger management lessons!"

The prince and kitsune tugged on the scythe, back and forth, until the café owner nervously begged them to stop scaring his customers and go outside to cool off.

While everyone else was distracted, Hercule grabbed up Bakoa's jacket from a chair. "I need to borrow this," he told him.

"That old thing?" Bakoa asked, turning in his seat, a fry in hand.

But Hercule had already left.

⌇

Hercule shrugged on the jacket. It covered the Draevensett coat-of-arms on his shirt, and the poor quality made him look the opposite of a noble—which was exactly what he wanted.

He needed a break from Harlow and school and the endless drama that came with it. Right now, he just wanted to do some commoner shopping and enjoy a peaceful rest of the day.

He took his time leisurely picking out licorice snacks, and purchased some honey lotion for his hands, which dried out easily. With the shopping bag slung over a shoulder, he strolled along the river walk, watching the waterfowl below: mallards and pintails paddling close to the narrow stretches of stone docks down along the water's edge, where small boats unloaded goods.

Mother would throw a fit if she knew he went shopping alone! The heir of a Noble House, without servants following his every footstep, doing such commoner activities. Even using honey lotion, instead of the expensive and imported lotus flower oils that Mother swore by, would be enough of a shock to make her faint.

He enjoyed this bit of freedom and disguise, doing things for himself.

He chewed on a freshly baked bread roll—equally as delicious as those made by the Dragonsbane's personal baker back home.

He looked up from watching the ducks and ahead spotted the kitsune and the prince, now calmed and broody. Their backs were against the elegant stone handrail overlooking the river, the sun warming their faces, while they shared a large hot pretzel between them.

Hercule hesitated and considered taking a different route back. But then Heion caught sight of him and waved.

It was too late to turn back now. He would not let himself be seen as shying away from his rival. He smoothed all emotion from his face and pressed onward.

"Ah, Hercule-sama." Heion shifted against the rail to face him, her silver-and-red hair gathered back in a band. She gave an apologetic bow of the head. "*Gomenesai*. Please forgive our rude behavior earlier at the bowling café. Tyomnii-sama is not a very..." she tried to find better words, then gave up with a shrug, "...social person."

"Shut up," said Tyomnii, chewing on a salted piece of pretzel.

Instead of cowering at the prince's words, Heion glared, her ears turned flat. "Don't you tell me to shut up, after all I do for you." She thumped the back of his head with a hand, and he choked on the pretzel.

After a cough and a sulky look, Tyomnii said no more, instead making an irritated sound and turning his head the other way.

Hercule couldn't mask his speechlessness. Heion *was* a slave, right? The Sivortsova falcon-and-scythe Mark was on her neck.

Now that he thought about it, he had rarely ever seen these two apart. Of all the other slaves and servants the prince could surround himself with, instead he chose a single kitsune? There had to be more to this, a hidden reason…

"Someone has to keep him humble; it was part of our agreement." Heion's amber-brown eyes smirked knowingly at Hercule. "We've known each other since we were little; much like you and Marigold-chan, I suppose. Circumstances brought us together, and now we are tied by the string of fate." She waved her pinky as if there was an actual string there.

String of fate. There were rumors about House Sivortsova and their Legendary Weapon *Tyrving*. Dark rumors—about what it did to its wielder and those close to them…

"You get along well with Marigold-chan, don't you?" the kitsune pried. "Is she special to you?"

Hercule came out of his thoughts and focused on keeping his cheeks from coloring. "…In a way…" He cleared his throat and tried to change the subject. "The school feels different. Have you noticed it, too? Ever since the ambush, everyone has been more focused, more unified…"

Heion dipped her head. "Suffering brings us together in many ways, doesn't it? Hardships forge the strongest of bonds. You can connect because you have both felt the same pain. You understand what the other person has endured, and they in turn understand you." She brushed back her loose bangs. "Lord God Himself suffered to understand our pain."

"Hold on, you believe in Lord God?" Hercule questioned. "I thought all of the royal household had to serve the Church of Draeth and its three red goddesses."

"Yes. I am not permitted to attend any church but those of the goddesses, and so, I do not attend any at all."

Heion's ears drooped backwards.

Hercule knew that feeling. Most all nobles followed the Church of Draeth, the prestigious religion, even though it was based on false superstitions and empty promises. Father had been furious when Hercule refused to attend that church anymore.

"Heion," he asked, and her ears tilted towards him. "Why do you think Lord God allows tragedy? Why do such bad things happen?" His thoughts went to the ambush, the students fighting to survive, and the somber scene at the cemetery.

The kitsune's expression turned a few notches solemn, and she broke off a piece of pretzel. "Lord God gives us the freedom to make our own choices. We are not mindless puppets that He controls. The White Ghost made a choice to attack. The Draev Guardian League made a choice not to question whether the person they had captured was the *real* Ghost. Principal Han chose not to postpone the Hunters Race, despite the possible risks... When we make poor choices, we have no one to blame but ourselves for the consequences."

She tipped her head back to eye a large cloud drifting above the rooftops and gargoyles and briefly blocking out the sun. "But you know, Hercule-sama, sometimes good things are born from tragedy. It can bring us together. It can open your eyes to realize how much your family means to you, and that people—not things—are more important."

A warm breeze blew his hair into his eyes, and Hercule combed it back. He wished he could say that family meant a lot to him, but...

"I should get going," Hercule finally said.

Heion bowed her head. "Of course. See you at school, Hercule-sama. Tyomnii-sama, say something nice, or at least wave. Why must you be so stubborn?"

Hercule continued along the sidewalk while she reprimanded

the prince. On his way back to the academy, he thought about his own poor choices over the years...and the consequences.

He gazed down at his palm, remembering the dragon claws replacing his fingers—the dark secret that he could never let anyone know.

28

The finishing touches were made, and Aken stepped back to let the new clay swallow grow to its full size. He surveyed his masterpiece, hands on hips, looking pleased with his work. "Well, what do you think?" he asked them.

Cyrus came close. Bakoa cocked his head from side to side.

It was beautiful, a more refined sculpture than the previous swallow, its black feathers detailed and liquid eyes more alive. It felt softer to the touch, too.

"It's your best work yet! Very life-like," she said, and Zartanian nodded his agreement.

Aken blushed at the praise, rubbing the back of his head with a hand and grinning. "That's not even the best part. Look at the new feature I added!" He turned the swallow so they could see its claws. The claws stretched and hooked around Aken's shoulders from behind, like a harness. "I have wings!"

He did. The bird attached to his back like a pair of wings.

"But how is that any better than before?" asked Bakoa.

"Because this way I won't risk falling off, and I don't have to use my hands to hold on. I can use Limitless two different ways, now."

"I wants to fly! I wants to fly!" Apfel hopped up and down. He tried to grab at a wing, but Aken kept turning and moving the bird away.

"Not just anybody can use this, Apple. Only *I* can make it fly." He patted the pouting child's head, and he shrank Limitless down and pocketed it.

Cyrus's stomach chose right then to growl, and everybody looked her way.

Her face went red. "...Is it dinner time yet?"

Bakoa guffawed.

"Should be." Aken grinned.

Bakoa trotted on ahead of them up the sloping schoolgrounds. "I want steak! And gravy and mashed potatoes, or maybe a meat pie? I hope they put more salt on it this time," he chattered.

Cyrus almost gagged at the memory of his love for salt, and her stomach stopped growling.

⌐

After dinner, Aken flew alone up to the rooftop above Floor Harlow, near the tower that rose from the rooftiles there—the one that also served as Master Nephryte's study. He perched on the edge of the roof and watched as the sun sank beneath golden clouds and flocks of swallows cried overhead, speeding past him like small daredevils.

The scene brought back memories of the many times he had sat on the roof of his family's dilapidated house and watched the changing colors of the sky and the fearless swallows who soared, back when he longed to grow wings and fly with them...

Those memories felt somehow lonely, now.

He let his chin rest on his bent knee, and his thoughts turned to the scarlet princess he'd once seen in the starlight orb. The hunchback had said the small glass orb would help him find the reborn princess. He tried to picture Cyrus as an older female with long hair...but it just felt weird.

Was that really who Cyrus had once been, in another lifetime? The Swan, who his Pureblood race had betrayed?

The very thought stung...

"Keeping alone with your thoughts, are you?" asked a voice. "Careful, you might hurt yourself with all that thinking."

Aken snorted at the comment, and Nephryte glided over on air to land beside him.

"I haven't been thinking nearly enough," Aken replied. "If I had, maybe I would've questioned why my mom always made me drink a glass of berry juice every day. And why you always do the same."

Nephryte paused before sitting down on the roof's edge.

"It's not berry juice, is it?" Aken stared ahead of them into the sunset. "It never was."

Silent seconds crawled by.

"I wasn't sure how to tell you," Nephryte finally admitted. "I didn't want you to feel any more different from everyone else than you already do."

Aken closed his eyes. So it was true, then, what the caged person inside his head had told him.

"I'm a real monster..." Aken murmured.

Nephryte's finger reached, pressing down on the tip of Aken's pointy ear so that it bounced back up.

"Hey!" Aken swatted his hand away.

The corners of Nephryte's lips quirked. "A real monster wouldn't care about anyone else but himself—and I know that's not you."

Aken's facial expression still sulked.

"From what I've been able to research, Purebloods need

more than the *essence* of others to live on because of how powerful their own *essence* is. And...well, blood provides more raw energy."

"No wonder everybody hated us," Aken muttered into his drawn-up knees.

"Well, there's that, and the fact that it was a Pureblood who ruined the world and caused the Swan Princess to die."

Aken turned his head to give him a glare, and Nephryte tried not to grin.

"So, do I dare ask where the blood you've been giving me comes from?"

"From me."

Aken made a show of gagging. "No wonder it tasted sour."

"Haha, such a sense of humor. But I'm a prized specimen, I'll have you know. Your tastebuds are simply not sophisticated enough to recognize it."

Aken almost cracked up.

But the blood in the medicine tablets... The caged replica had said it came from Cyrus.

"You're bonded to that Cyrus, now. That's what happens to Purebloods. Did no one ever tell you? You live off the blood of others, until you come across someone special—and then, it's only their blood that can sustain you."

Aken wanted to ask, but part of him also didn't want to know, didn't want to hear the words. Instead, he watched the swallows dip and twirl through the undersides of the clouds.

"Anemia, my foot. How long were you going to let me believe that?" Aken muttered.

"It *is* anemia, in a way."

Aken gave him a look.

Nephryte coughed into his fist. "Well, at least it's an explanation that Harlow can understand."

Aken winced. That was a good point.

"I used that power again," Aken spoke after a moment, almost a whisper. "Am I in trouble?"

Nephryte tipped his head to the sky. "I haven't heard anyone accuse you. And other than me and Cyrus, I don't think anyone else from Draevensett was around or conscious to see you. So..." he shrugged, "we'll pretend it never happened." He lowered his gaze back to him. "But only because the situation was dire. You understand, don't you? That power isn't something you should rely on. You've already seen what the consequences can be, how dangerous it is. Focus on strengthening your lava Ability so you won't be tempted to use it again."

Consequences...

They were more complicated now than ever.

The replica was lurking, waiting for the chance to take over his mind if he reached for that power again...and he couldn't let that happen.

But the prince's words also echoed through his mind as a warning: *"Pureblood ees dangerous, but ees also a part of you. Learn to control eet first, before eet controls you... Power does not lie dormant and quiet. Eet veell find a vay out. You must gain control..."*

Which was the right answer? Fight to gain control and risk losing himself in the process, or lock it all away for as long as he could?

"Come," Nephryte finally said and rose. "There's something I need to speak to you and all of Harlow about."

⌐∘

Cyrus held out the inside of her left arm. Master Nephryte had carefully painted an ink symbol of the sun on her skin—a likeness of Floor Harlow's crest—just as he had done for each student in Harlow, including Apfel. The special ink quickly dried.

"Stay together in pairs, from now on," he had told them.

"And don't trust a member who doesn't have this symbol. It is possible the White Ghost might try to slip in among us."

Cyrus shuddered. Could Ellefsen really infiltrate Harlow and pretend to be one of them?

The atmosphere in Harlow's study room that night was somber, with each of them lost in their own thoughts. The Master gathered them around and gave comforting words, and he read them a story long past curfew—just as he had done the first night after the Hunters Race, when no one could sleep.

"Master?" asked Bakoa, once he closed the book. "How come your Ability worked, even when everyone else's bounced off those force field shields?"

Oh, yeah. She'd been wondering about that, too. She lifted her head to listen to his answer.

"It was a battle of which energy was stronger," the Master replied, his fingers laced together above his knee. "My *essence* was strong enough to overpower the shields' energy—as was the other Masters'. That is what being Draev Master rank means: the power of our *essence* is far above average. But I am sure that the shield surrounding the White Ghost, himself, is much stronger. What was around the criminals was more spread out and thin. It couldn't have been easy for him maintaining something like that around so many people..."

"Who is he? *What* is he? What kind of power was he using?" Aken asked, laying upside down on the leather sofa, his legs hooked over the back.

Master Nephryte's gaze trained on the empty rose marble fireplace before them. "There's not much we know about his kind, except that they are an ancient race of shapeshifters who wield something akin to mind powers."

Zartanian gripped his hat in his hands. Apfel rolled about the carpet, only half listening, and playing with his greyhound pup.

"Why was he attacking *us*, though?" pressed Bakoa.

Cyrus chewed her lip as she listened. It was because he wanted *her*. The Swan's power. The power that had sprung to life a garden in an empty clearing. But Harlow didn't know that.

She shuddered, rubbing her wrists. They were aching a little under the gloves again.

"It seems he has a deep hatred for vempar kind," the Master said, leaning forward to perch his chin on his clasped hands, his elbows propped on his knees. "According to Cyrus, he wants to exterminate our race, especially the Draevs. I need all of you to be alert and keep on the lookout for anything suspicious."

Cyrus glanced away, surprised. He wasn't going to tell them that it was because of her?

But she supposed the fewer people who knew about the Pure Light power inside her, the better. She just hoped the Master knew what he was doing, and what she should do next. Little Apfel was still at risk, too. If the White Ghost could use him to find the Swan, then so could the Impure Nights…

The Swan. Was she finally starting to admit it to herself?

'Just because I might have the Pure Light inside me, it doesn't mean I have to be her,' she told herself stubbornly.

"Wonderful," commented Hercule from the other sofa. "First humans, now shapeshifters. Is there anyone else who wants to join the kill-all-vempars club?"

He said it with such sincere sarcasm that Cyrus cracked up.

Master Nephryte rose from his chair. "I'm not even going to look at the clock to see how late it is," he said. "But I do need all of you to be well rested for Harlow's next mission."

"Next mission?" Lykale asked from the far table, a curious eyebrow arched.

"Yes. We're going on a road trip," he said with a smile. "To Salmu Baris."

Crickets chorused softly in the late night, and bats left the steepled towers to glide above the grand school and its grounds, the inhabitants within deep in the land of dreams.

A door in Floor Harlow's corridor quietly began to open.

Dim moonlight spilled across the floor from the windows in the opposite wall.

His footsteps were light across the rug as he carefully made his way down the corridor. He rubbed his hand, which occasionally still throbbed.

Which room was it, again? He couldn't afford to get this wrong.

He squinted in the dark. Yes, this had to be the one.

His hand went to the doorknob.

"Sneaking about in the dead of night, Lykale?"

Lykale gave a start, drawing back from the door. He adjusted his glasses and faced the accuser: Mamoru, who narrowed his eyes at him suspiciously from beside one of the windows, standing just inside the shadows.

"You offend me. I do not *sneak*."

Mamoru didn't say anything, he just kept watching him.

"What? I've been having problems, all right?" Lykale gave an irritated sigh, as if reluctant to admit such a thing. "I haven't been sleeping well since the whole…incident with the Hunters Race. I thought a walk around the dorms might help."

Mamoru's gaze flicked to the door. "That's not your room."

Lykale blinked, took a step back and scanned the door. "It is…oh? You're right. Ha, how funny. I really am feeling out of sorts, aren't I?"

He backtracked down to his door under Mamoru's quiet observation. "Ah, here it is!" Lykale then made a show of rubbing his forehead and yawned. "Well, maybe I've worn myself out enough to fall asleep now? I hope."

He opened the door and went inside.

Mamoru remained where he was, leaning against the decorative bat-wing window frame.

"Goodnight. Careful not to stay up too late," Lykale said as he closed the door.

29

The next day, after classes, Harlow spent time packing. With it being a road trip, and on foot, there wasn't much they could bring, but it still took time to decide on what things they might need.

Zartanian was the first to finish, and he hurried out to the practice fields to get in one last round of sword practice. The events of the ambush had left him shaken, but with the support of Master Nephryte, the school, and his friends, and much time spent in prayer, he was starting to feel better.

He unsheathed his prized rapier, and could feel through the hilt how swiftly the narrow blade cut through the air—the quick movements of the rapier much cleaner and faster than the saber. But this beautiful blade was dangerous blood silver, one of the Legendary Weapons, or so Master Nephryte had once told him. It had been hidden away in Zartanian's parents' house for years, unknown to anyone else, until Nephryte discovered it while helping investigators to clear the place out. He kept it secret and gave it to Zartanian.

He admired the dark, silvery pommel and basket handguard, the deep red of the blade's edge. He still wondered why a Legendary Weapon would have been hidden in their house, and what it could mean.

He had only just started to grow confident enough to hold the priceless weapon unsheathed. He wouldn't take it with him on this trip; the saber would work better for his skill level and pose less of a risk. He wasn't ready for anyone to find out a Legendary Weapon was in his possession, anyway, especially since he wasn't of any noble blood.

"Zartanian!"

He quickly set the rapier in the grass, trying to hide it, before turning to see who it was.

A Harcourt boy—the same one he'd helped during the ambush—trotted up to him. "That's your name, right?" the boy asked him, his hands fidgeting together. "I've been meaning to thank you for…for saving my life, back then."

Zartanian recalled the criminals coming at them. The fear. Then the calm that had washed over him as he fought.

"I'm ashamed, but I was so scared, that I could barely move." The boy glanced down. "You did the opposite, though. You were brave—like a real hero, a real Draev." The boy's expression then beamed at him and he bowed his head. "Thank you!"

Zartanian stood speechless.

The boy trotted off before he could respond or deny that he was anything like a hero.

He called him brave? *Him?*

Like a real hero.

The corners of Zartanian's lips lifted slightly.

Elijob would have been thrilled, grabbed his hands and leaped about and said that their goal to become heroes like the Bladeers was one step closer.

Oh Elijob, if only he really could share in this moment...

He sheathed and hid the rapier beneath a bush, picked up his saber and started going through the forms, trying to be lighter on his feet.

"I hear you are going on a long mission, student Zartanian?"

He turned from slicing the saber's edge through the air.

Sir Swornyte's angular features looked a touch more grave than usual, his hair still neatly slicked back and precise, as always. "Remember the lessons I have taught you." His intense gaze pierced downward at him. "And be sure to return safely. There is still much for you to learn before you can go gallivanting off on your own."

Gallivanting, was that meant as a joke?

Zartanian tried not to stutter and held the saber flat across his heart. "I will be responsible and act honorably as an apprentice of Sir Swornyte and as a student of Master Nephryte." He head-bowed, promising. "I will do my very best!"

The swordsmaster inclined his dark head. "I accept your promise, and will hold you strictly to it, young apprentice." He raised his own saber and shifted his stance. "A swordsmaster can never have too much practice. Face me, and show me what you have learned."

Zartanian moved his saber swiftly forward and to the side to meet the approaching blade.

❧

"Let go of my leg, Apple!"

"Nevers."

Aken shook his left leg, trying to shake off the faeryn child clinging to him like a leech. "You're killing my blood circulation! I need legs, y'know. They're kind of important."

Then Apfel cried out like an upset toddler, "*Uwaaah!*"

Now Aken's ears hurt worse than his leg.

People around Central Plaza's fountain were staring.

"What did you do to make Apfel cry?" Cyrus demanded, walking over.

"Nothing!" Aken shied away from Cy's metal fist. "All I did was say that we're leaving soon, and that he'll have to stay with somebody else while we're gone."

Apfel's blue face was melting in tears beneath the too-big cap.

"You poor thing," Cy said sympathetically. "You'll be so lonely without us." Apfel let go of his leg to snuggle into Cyrus's embrace. "Maybe we should bring you with us," Cy suggested. "Would you like that?"

Apfel nodded brightly.

Aken's jaw dropped. "You gotta be kidding me. Bring that little imp with us on a road trip?"

"He doesn't have any family or friends but us. You should know what that feels like."

Aken bit his cheek. "Apfel still belongs to the baker. We can't just take his slave out of the city on a whim. And with the Mark, he'll sense him leaving."

Cy's lilac eyes widened. "I forgot about that…" he admitted. Then Cy's eyebrows drew down and grew more determined. "In that case, we'll have to gather Harlow together and buy his freedom!"

For the second time that day, Aken's jaw dropped.

The next hour was spent collecting money from Harlow members, who each added what they could, and from other random students around Draevensett who felt pity. By the end, what they'd gathered still wasn't enough. But they had saved the *best* person for last, and they found Hercule studying outdoors, beneath the giant oak that grew against the school's south wing.

"Again, you're treating me like a piggy bank?" Hercule looked up from his history book at them.

Aken shrugged. "Yeah, pretty much."

Cyrus elbowed him in the gut.

Hercule rose and regarded the blue faeryn child, running a hand through his pearl-gray hair. "What will become of him once he's free? He can't stay in Draethvyle without an owner."

Cyrus's shoulders sagged. They hadn't thought that far ahead.

"Well, he's not safe living in this city, anyway. Who knows who else might come after him?" said Aken.

"True..." Hercule lifted his chin in thought.

Aken bent down to the little faeryn, resting his hands on his knees. "Say, Apfel, do you have any family you remember? Maybe back in Bergvolk?"

Apfel's face clouded over. "My papa was in Bergvolk," he murmured into his coat collar.

"Maybe during this road trip, we can find him."

Apfel looked up, suddenly hopeful. "Really?"

"Aken, we can't promise that," Cy rebuked him. "Do you have any idea how hard that will be? Besides, we're going to Salmu Baris, not Bergvolk. We're not crossing the sea."

Aken waved it aside. "If he's looking for Apfel, he'll be on our side of the sea, where most slaves are brought. We have to try. Like Hercule said, he needs a home." He bent down to the child. "If your dad is out there, I'll find him!"

"Promise?" Apfel hesitated, his chestnut-red eyes glistening.

"Promise. Now, let's go buy your freedom!"

❧

Apfel's body cringed, his small fingers curling into fists against the fear and brief piercing pain against the Mark on his neck. It was over in a flash; the owner of the small bakery released Apfel, turning the child over to a waiting Cyrus, Hercule and Aken. The Mark like ink melted away from his skin, as if it had never been.

Taken up into Cyrus's warm embrace, Apfel gingerly felt at the spot on his neck—no pain or blood—wondering if it really had gone.

The bakery owner fingered his leather wallet greedily. It had been easy enough for Hercule to convince the man to sell the faeryn to him, especially after dangling gold coins under his crooked nose.

Aken gave a wink. "Mission accomplished."

Apfel was now a free person and could live somewhere safe, wherever that may be.

Cyrus thanked Hercule profusely, and Apfel sent shy smiles up at him.

The dragon-eyed noble maintained his neutral expression, though Aken could tell he was secretly flustered on the inside, glancing away and pocketing his hands.

❧

"Freeee! I'm free, free, free!"

Apfel exclaimed over and over, skipping about, his too-big jacket flapping around him. Hazfel yapped and jumped, wagging his tail excitedly, mimicking his friend's cheer.

The child paraded around Draevensett's ground floor with Cyrus, like a spunky bundle of joy that couldn't be suppressed. Some students in the commons hall who heard him laughed and gave the child a thumbs-up.

Cyrus found the gesture uplifting. After she had earned herself some respect from these students, maybe they were starting to view other races in a better light? There were plenty of grumps and snobs who would forever stare down their noses at them, of course, but still...

They were standing in the colonnaded walk that encircled the moon courtyard when Denim came by. "I hear someone's got their freedom back. Congrats, little guy." He fist-bumped the child.

Wow, that surprised her. Was Denim actually starting to improve as a person?

"I bet you'll grow up to be someone cool, too," Denim continued. "You've got way more potential than that dunce blond. Just take my advice and steer clear of losers like him."

Uh, never mind. Maybe she had hoped too soon.

Aken made a fist. "You really wanna start this again?"

"Then tell me you didn't flunk our last math quiz."

Aken's lips thinned, and he turned his head away. "Math doesn't count."

Denim's smirk filled with smugness.

The puppy suddenly bounded out across the courtyard's cultivated grass and knocked over one of the decorative flowerpots, yapping.

"Hazfel, don'ts dig up the dirt!" Apfel scurried out after him. The puppy next lunged for the water fountain, splashing and creating a soaking mess. Apfel shielded his face with his jacket while trying to grab the pup's collar.

Cyrus chuckled as she watched them.

"Pastries, pastries, get them while they're fresh!" someone called out.

Around the next bend in the colonnade came the Floor Earnest boy, Mathias, carrying a tray full of sweets and pastries. Adelheid strolled leisurely ahead of him, as if he were following in her dainty footsteps. She turned around, picking up one treat after another off the tray while she walked.

Bakoa bounded over to gather a handful of deliciousness. "This is awesome! Dude, you're the best teen baker I know."

"He's the *only* one you know," muttered Aken.

"You mutter too much," said Bakoa, and he shoved a cannolo into Aken's mouth.

Aken would have protested, but the cannolo was creamy and delicious, with a hint of hazelnut.

Mathias brought the tray over and they each took from the assortment. Cyrus took a lemon curd tart with candied orange slices and gold leaf on top, and Zartanian went for the cream-filled croissants.

"Thank you for the compliment, Bakoa. I'm still new at this, though, and have a long way to go. The extracurricular pastry class that I'm taking has been very instructive," the boy replied.

Aken waved him near. "Say, Mathias. Where'd you get your hands on chocolate?" He turned over a shortbread cookie dipped in the sweet brown stuff.

Mathias brushed a lone hair strand back from his forehead. "Draevensett has made an arrangement with House Carolus, who owns land on a southern island in Diviso Sea, where cocoa beans grow. In other words, we'll be getting chocolate more often."

"Really?" Bakoa exclaimed from beside him, his eyes twin pools of delight.

Cyrus glanced from Mathias to frilly Adelheid, who was busy gorging herself on candied fruit sweets. A baker and a gorger; they worked well together. But how did that girl manage to stay so skinny?

"Hi there, cute red." Adelheid, in her high heels, came to pause at Cyrus's side, a half-eaten éclair in one hand. "I hear word that you grew up in a human town. That must have been something, trying to fit in with them and all, hm?"

Cyrus wasn't sure how to respond. "Uh, yeah, you could say that." She fidgeted with her fingerless gloves.

Adelheid rested an elbow on Cyrus's shoulder. "Say, were there many humans with red hair in your town? Any girls who seemed...unusual?"

Cyrus swallowed, unnerved. "I'm sure there's red hair in any human settlement. Why do you ask?"

The girl shrugged her petite gray shoulders, a secretive smile on her lips. "Simply curious, is all," she replied.

Apfel's fingers snatched a custard tart, his sleeves wet from pulling the puppy out of the fountain, and Denim nonchalantly grabbed a pastry cone full of cream. "Yo, Doughboy! Free snacks!" he called out.

The colonnade walk trembled as the huge boy emerged from a doorway.

"Hey! No fair, he'll empty the tray in one swallow!" Aken protested.

Doughboy scratched at his big belly. His nostrils flared as he sniffed the sweet aromas in the air. "The cream, the crunch of pastry—it's calling me."

The big boy came lumbering towards them like a hungry bear.

Adelheid left Cyrus, grabbed the tray, and tilted it so that the rest of the tarts slid into her open mouth, one by one.

By the time Doughboy reached them, the tray was empty. She licked her lips, handed the tray back, and strolled off into the courtyard, looking self-satisfied. She started polishing her nails, oblivious to the silence and their stares.

"Where does she pack it all? She's short and skinny as a toothpick," Aken voiced what they were all thinking.

"I didn't get any…" Doughboy mourned.

~⌒~

"You're leaving?" Worry sketched Cherish's voice, once Cyrus had told her the news. She was still recuperating in the infirmary.

Kotetsu skipped back into the room with a bagful of cinnamon doughnuts and drinks, offering some to Cyrus and Apfel.

Apfel took his share eagerly, munching and slurping, seating himself at the edge of the fluffy white hospital bed. She and the faeryn had managed one final visit before nightfall.

In the morning, Harlow would be on the road.

"Not that I'm worried—of course I'm not worried," Cherish hurried to add. "I know what a strong boy you are, Cyrus."

Cyrus swallowed. "Thanks," she managed to say. "Get well soon, okay? You'd better be all Healed up and moving by the time we get back!" She said the last part teasingly, knowing it probably wasn't realistic.

Cherish's pale face split a smile. "I'll do my best! But likewise, you take care of yourself out there. I won't forgive you if something happens; I mean it."

Cyrus laughed.

It was nice not to be surrounded by testosterone, for a change. Maybe, someday, she could reveal the truth to Cherish...

"I'll do my best, too," Cyrus assured her.

~⁊

Once the white curtain swung closed, and her friends were gone from her sight, Cherish's face fell and her shoulders slumped.

"Missing the redhead already, hm?"

She turned her face back toward her brother, who was still slurping at an iced coffee like an overgrown kid. "I never said that. Stop saying I have a crush on him! I don't anymore. It's just that I greatly admire him."

"Uh-huh. Is that what the youngsters are calling it, these days?" He giggled.

"Brother, kindly shut up."

How could she explain the worry she felt? Harlow going out on a long mission so suddenly, after everything that had just happened...

Something was wrong—something that Cyrus wasn't willing to tell her.

She clenched the white sheets and drew them up to her chin.

～౨

The sun made its descent west of Draevensett's towers and past the Backbone Mountains, coloring the horizon a brilliant crimson and glazing the atmosphere golden. Hercule waited by the front courtyard fountain, pacing, until he spotted the faeryn girl whose glossy braid was like spun shades of gold. She vanished around the corner of the academy's servant quarters.

He crossed the courtyard, quickening his stride to reach the corner where she had vanished.

He reached out and managed to catch her shoulder just in time before she could disappear inside a narrow backdoor.

"Marigold, wait!"

Her head turned. Surprise showed through the blank mask she often wore for the slave role she played. She shifted to face him properly, ready to curtsy. But Hercule spoke first, halting her.

"We—that is, Harlow is going on a road trip tomorrow." He swallowed, straightening his shoulders. "I need you to come with us. I mean, I would like for you to come with us, if you can. If you have time." The last bit came out a touch insecure and nervous, despite the noble outward appearance he tried to maintain.

Marigold's brow crinkled, perhaps confused. She gave a small curtsy, bobbing her head once. "If milord wishes it, then of course I will follow. I follow wherever you go."

He moved as if to protest her calling him "milord," then relented, knowing it was useless.

Her wings… He couldn't help but notice how slumped they were, now. It was all his fault, keeping her captive all these years.

"When a faeryn is held in captivity for a long period of time, unable to travel the forests and be free, their once vibrant wings begin to wilt—

withering like a rose on the vine, until they can fly no more," Lykale had said.

He couldn't let that fate be Marigold's.

"Okay. I mean, good. Great! Fantastic," Hercule said and stuffed his hands in his pants pockets. He gave an awkward nod before turning to leave. She frowned again, as if he were acting strange, and he nervously swallowed. "Goodnight!" his voice squeaked, and with that, he decided to hurry away before he embarrassed himself any further.

'What the heck is wrong with me? I never act this ridiculous!'

His stomach felt full of butterflies or clawing fingernails. He wasn't sure which.

Back indoors, Hercule brooded during a dinner of grilled lamb and fried vegetables, thinking about faeryn wings and what it was he would have to do. It would be the hardest decision he had ever had to make...but it would be done.

During this road trip, he would finally give Marigold the one thing she longed for most...

As Hercule finished dinner and headed back upstairs to Harlow's floor, his sensitive hearing caught the low whisper of voices: Cyrus speaking with Mamoru.

Hercule peered from around the stairwell doorway, and right away he could tell that something wasn't right. Cyrus was asking Mamoru if he felt well. And the older boy was shaking it off, saying he was fine.

But Hercule could see it too: Mamoru's face turning a pale shade of green, a furrow in his brow, as if his body was struggling against something.

The older boy patted the small half-human's shoulder reassuringly. "Some food just didn't agree with me, that's all. I'm sure I'll be right as rain in the morning. Goodnight, Cyrus."

"...Okay. Goodnight."

30

The next morning, Mamoru didn't show up for breakfast.
Instead, he lay in bed with a sickly green tint to his skin, and Dr. Zushil arrived on the Floor with his bag of medical supplies to examine him.

Cyrus waited near the doorway. She could tell Mamoru was trying not to clutch his stomach in pain.

"Hmm, this is most unusual," said the doctor, analyzing a chemical vial solution of Mamoru's spit. "It seems you have ingested some dwarf blood."

Cyrus lifted her head. Dwarf blood?

"Even a small sample of it will make a vempar sick, and a heavy dose of it is the equivalent of having the flu," Zushil furthered, while she and the other Harlow boys listened. "And this was a heavy dose, indeed. How did you accidentally ingest such a thing?"

How indeed. They had all taken food from the same platters at dinner, last night. How could it have missed all of them and ended up *only* on Mamoru's plate, or in his glass?

He must have been singled out, and the taste disguised somehow. But who would want to poison Mamoru? What was there to gain?

"I won't be able to draw the dwarf blood from you with my fangs," said Zushil, "Not without making myself as sick as you. You will have to take medicine, instead, and rest."

Cyrus placed a damp washcloth on the boy's forehead beneath his already soaked bangs.

"I wanted you to come with us," she murmured.

Mamoru's hand moved to rest on hers for a moment against the washcloth. "I'll recover...don't worry," he said between twinges of pain. "Keep each other safe and...stay alert."

Cyrus gave him a nod that she would.

Mamoru motioned with his hand for Aken, and she stepped back.

"Yeah?" Aken came over somberly, his right hand gripping his elbow.

Mamoru gestured for him to lean close, and he whispered, "The White Ghost did this...he must be here. Don't let Cyrus out of your sight..."

She felt a chill run up her spine.

Aken nodded firmly and clapped Mamoru's arm.

Her gaze went to Bakoa and Hercule, who were waiting by the door. Did they still have the inked sun on their arms? She tried to see without being obvious.

"Are Lykale and Zartanian still asleep? We should wake them," said Aken.

～๑

After the students had left the room, and Zushil prescribed Mamoru medicine and departed, Nephryte moved to the side of the bed.

Mamoru struggled to keep his eyes open from the medicine's drowsy effect. "*He* did this..." he said in a whisper.

"Why target you, and not me?" Nephryte wondered.

"I switched our glasses at dinner, at the last second…to be on the safe side."

Nephryte's brow furrowed darkly. "It was meant for me, then. He doesn't want us to leave the city."

Mamoru closed his eyes instead of nodding.

"Rest." Nephryte gave his chest a pat. "And look after things here while we're gone."

"…Take the Oracle with you."

A corner of Nephryte's lips lifted. "I was already planning to."

⌒ჱ

When Cyrus and Aken passed by Bakoa's room, the sand boy was taking things out of his backpack and mumbling:

"I don't know if I should bring these pants. And what about these shirts, will they be too thick? Aw, man! Why is packing *so* hard?"

"You packed yesterday," Aken said.

"I *know*, but then I changed my mind. Maybe I won't need this vest? But my other vests are too hot."

Aken shook his head.

At that moment, Lykale came out of his room, slinging a backpack over his shoulder. "I overslept. Is there any breakfast left?" he asked them.

"Yes, some pancakes. But Mamoru is sick; he won't be able to come with us," Cyrus informed him.

"Oh…" Lykale made a regretful expression and fingered the lock at his neck. "That's a shame."

Cyrus took a quick glance down at his arm: the inked sun was there. Lykale moved off towards the Master's dorm flat and kitchen.

Cyrus went over to Zartanian's door next and knocked.

She waited, but no answer came.

Aken pushed open the door before she could stop him…and they both peeked inside.

The room was dim, with the curtains drawn, the fabric curved like giant bat wings.

Cyrus ventured inside. The place had a gothic yet pretty feel to it. A chandelier hung from the ceiling instead of oilpowder lamps, a pretty thing of silvery metal and candle holders the shapes of roses and thorns.

Something *thumped*.

It came from a long, oddly shaped box set close to the shadowed windows.

Wait… She looked more closely. It wasn't a box at all, but a coffin.

"*Eek!*" she yelped and bumped backwards into Aken. "There's—there's a—a—" she broke off and pointed.

Aken swallowed. "Is this why he doesn't like people coming in his room?"

"What's he keeping in there?" she exclaimed under a whisper.

Aken shook his head.

"Go find out!" She pushed him forward.

Aken stumbled and caught his balance. "Why me?" he whispered, staring wide-eyed.

She gestured emphatically towards the coffin for him to keep going, not using words, in case something might hear her.

Aken looked from her to the coffin, then slowly made his way forward, step by step.

He reached the dark, polished wood, and she watched as his hands moved to touch the lid…

A scream came from inside the coffin and the lid shot up on its own.

Cyrus shrieked.

Aken fell over onto his backside.

They both stared wildly at the thing now sitting upright in

the coffin. Then the dim light through the curtains revealed the thing's silhouette.

"W-w-what's going on?" came Zartanian's timid, trembling voice.

The silhouette, with small antlers...it was just him.

Cyrus stopped crouching. Aken coughed into his hand and pretended to gracefully stand up off the floor.

"Um, hi, it's us." She gave an apologetic laugh. Her gaze drifted down to the coffin Zartanian was sitting in. "Were you...sleeping in a coffin?"

"What the heck, is that a mattress in there?" Aken leaned forward.

The shy boy took on a defensive posture. "S-so what if it is?"

"You seriously sleep inside that thing?"

"...Maybe."

As they both continued to stare at him, he furthered. "It feels safe," he admitted. "I slept in boxes and confined spaces a lot as a child. No one can find you or hurt you..." He trailed off, as if he had said more than he meant to. Then he shook his head, and he hopped down out of the coffin bed.

"Safe?" Aken guffawed. "From who, the Boogeyman?"

Zartanian made a frown.

There must be a reason behind his odd habit, Cyrus thought, so she punched Aken in the arm. "Stop being insensitive."

"Ow. Insensitive? How was I being insensitive?"

"We won't tell anyone, Zartanian, don't worry," she promised. "But we did come to make sure that you're packed and ready—we'll be leaving in a few minutes. You can grab some breakfast, if you hurry."

Zartanian nodded appreciatively and picked up a blue backpack from beside his old-fashioned closet.

After another ten minutes, the Harlow group was finally

ready, and they all assembled down in Draevensett's white-and-silver marble foyer. Their footsteps echoed off the white vaulted ceiling and delicate columns.

Cyrus was surprised to see Marigold joining them, bringing her own backpack and wearing a frilly, green travel dress. Judging by the questioning looks of the other Harlow members, they were surprised to.

Hercule gave the faeryn a nod and a rare smile.

They followed Master Nephryte out, and Cyrus waved to the marble statue of Protector Draev as they left, his extended hand this time feeling like a gesture of farewell instead of a greeting.

Bakoa mimicked the gesture. "Bye, Protector! Bye, school! Bye, peers and classmates who don't like us!"

Apfel followed with them, the greyhound pup dancing around him. "That's right, Hazfel, we're goings on a real adventure!" he told the dog. "And we'll finds Papa!"

Cyrus looked from the child to Aken. She hoped they could keep that promise.

Outside the academy, and past the grand iron gate with its curling rods, the sun drifted up from the eastern horizon with a warm, misty glow and the blackbirds sang their morning chorus from the tops of chimneys.

Master Nephryte looked to each of his students—Mamoru the only one of them missing. He carried a leather pack around his shoulder, the important letter from the king tucked somewhere inside.

He held out his arm, and they each did the same in a circle: the inked sun was still present on each of them.

"All right. It's time for your first mission outside of Draeth Kingdom," he announced.

They raised their fists to the sky with a cheer, and with that, their journey began.

"What? Harlow's left the school already?" Pueginn exclaimed.

Adelheid kicked her legs back and forth, perched on the low limb of a tree and sucking on a lollipop. "That's right. The little Oracle is going with them." She giggled. "If you hurry now, you can catch up to them."

Pueginn stomped his feet. "You could have given me a warning sooner! Now I've no time to prepare!"

Adelheid watched the man, who reminded her of an oversized and un-cute penguin, as he hurried out of the park. "Better not fail this time," she called after him. "You won't have any excuses left."

$\sim$

Huntter made it to the edge of the woods. Just ahead, Draethvyle City rose above the grasslands with its many steeples and sharp spires.

He'd been nearly caught three times, now, by Draev patrols during the early hours of the morning. There were more roaming about than usual, and they all seemed to be on high alert.

A worried thought came to him that something must have happened while he was away.

Was it more Corpsed? Was Cyrus safe?

He had to hurry and make sure!

He pulled up the hood of his cloak, over his cargo jacket.

Voices approached from beyond the trees.

Huntter ducked behind the nearest tree trunk wide enough to hide him, and then quieted his breath, listening.

The voices were unusually loud—nothing of stealth about them at all. So then, it couldn't be another Draev patrol. But what *was* it?

"You're really making us walk the whole way? Come on!" said one of the voices. It sounded oddly familiar.

Huntter muttered under his breath, "Stupid vempars, so confident that they can be loud in the woods and not get attacked…"

He edged his head around the tree bark, just enough to see the group coming through the woods.

Wait a second. He recognized that tall vempar, a Draev Master.

"Just use your wind Ability and fly us there!"

Huntter looked to the speaker. It was *him*, that idiot blond, Aken! And next to him walked Cyrus…

Huntter frowned in thought. What on eartha was going on? They each carried backpacks, as if for a long trip.

But a trip to where?

At least Cyrus seemed to be well…but where was she off to?

Curiosity got the better of him, and Huntter decided to change his plans and follow after Harlow's trail.

BONUS
STORY:
NEPHRYTE

1

I *was young when we lost our parents. Old enough to feel their loss—to know that no one would read me stories or make the same waffles that I loved—yet not old enough to process why they were gone, that they had been killed by an ancient Corpsed roaming the forested area they were researching.*

My brother was seven years older than me, and after losing our parents, he did his best to take their place, watching over me, even though as a teenager, with his own trials and responsibilities, he had no one to take care of him.

The small house in our parents' name now belonged to us. A shabby, creaky and weathered dwelling—with many cracks that would leak in the cold night air during winter and freeze me in bed. It hadn't felt as bad when our mother and father were still around, but the warmth and glow that their presence always gave was gone, and there was only a cold loneliness to replace it.

"Julian, my feet are cold."
Nephryte shivered under the blankets while his older brother

got out of bed, grabbed a pair of socks from the drawer, and crawled back under the covers. He passed him the socks, and Nephryte worked to slide the worn fabric over his feet.

"Couldn't you have done that before getting into bed?" Julian's teeth slightly chattered.

"I was too cold to think," murmured Nephryte. He huddled closer to his brother for warmth. The makeshift fireplace wasn't giving much heat against the winter chill that crept in through the cracks. Oilpowder heaters were too expensive for them to afford.

"Julian?"

His brother sighed. "I'm not going to get any sleep tonight, am I?"

Nephryte swallowed what he had been going to say.

After a while, his brother shifted so that he was facing him. "What is it? I can't sleep wondering what it was you were going to ask." The faint glow of the fire outlined one side of Julian's face.

Nephryte hesitated. "I'm forgetting Mom and Dad's voices," he said. "They're so faint now, just an echo in my memories...but I don't want to forget them."

Julian's features saddened for a moment. "You won't forget," he told him, meeting his gaze across the pillow. "I can hear them in your voice, and in mine. In the way we speak, and in the words we choose to use—they're a part of us."

Nephryte shifted his gaze in thought.

"Now, try to sleep, will you? Think of someplace peaceful and warm, and count fireflies."

Silence passed.

"My feet are still cold," whispered Nephryte.

Julian closed his eyes. "Fine. Put them on my legs and freeze me to death."

Morning dawned rosy outside the windows the next day, and Nephryte eyed the fried eggs that his brother set before him—a stark contrast to the waffles Mom used to make. But flour had to be saved for baking bread, now—not spent on luxuries such as waffles.

They had to make their small savings from Mom and Dad last for as long as possible, at least until Julian could find a stable job.

"Enjoying those eggs?" asked Julian, washing dishes at the sink, across from the table.

Nephryte had been poking at the rubbery eggs with a fork, but now started shoving them down his throat, trying to ignore the slimy taste. "*Mmff*. The best eggs I've ever had."

"Yeah. Sure they are." Julian smirked over his shoulder. He put down the washcloth and came over to the table. "Don't worry. Things might change around here soon," he told him.

Nephryte eyed his brother suspiciously between chews.

Julian's smirk widened. He lifted his hand towards the plate he had left on the counter.

As if by magic, or unseen wind currents, the plate rose off the counter and floated towards him.

Nephryte dropped his fork in shock. "You..."

"That's right! Elemental Manipulation. I first felt my Ability back when we...became orphans, but I couldn't get it to work again. Then, just this morning, I moved a cup without being near it."

Nephryte's expression widened as he started to realize what this could mean for them.

"I'm going to enroll in Draevensett Academy," said Julian. "And earn an allowance that can support us!" He finished his own plate of eggs in three swallows, then went to fetch his coat.

Nephryte followed him to the door. "This is...I mean, this is amazing!" he was saying.

Julian wrapped a scarf around his neck. He motioned to Nephryte, and when he came near, Julian pressed down on the tip of Nephryte's pointy ear with a finger so that it bounced back up.

"Hey, cut it out!" protested Nephryte.

"I'll be at the academy, waiting for their decision. I might not be back until tonight, so you'll have to fix your own dinner. There's some leftover bread you can toast." Julian flashed him a grin. "Pray for me, okay?" And with that, he hurried out into the wintery day.

Julian was accepted into Draevensett that very day, and given an allowance as a parental guardian to take care of me. He also chose to stay in our rickety house instead of moving into the school dorms, so I wouldn't be alone. Our food improved, our clothes improved, and we could finally keep warmer during the winters.

Brother worked hard to get the best grades; and he kept me company during after school hours, bringing me along with him on his errands. I didn't realize it at the time, but it must have been hard for him. Sometimes I wonder if he ever even had the chance to grieve...

Around that time, he discovered Pordenone Chapel, and he had me come there with him every Sunday morning. It was Julian who introduced me to Lord God.

I really admired my brother, his calm and tranquil spirit. I let my hair grow to my shoulders, just as he had done; his was a darker shade than mine. His work and training made him grow strong and lean, and he gained the unsought attention of many girls. I laughed every time he tried to get away from them.

Julian found new goals he wanted to pursue, as well. He wanted to become a Draev Master and help change vempar society—to fix the relationships with other races and put an end to slavery. They were such lofty goals, but I supported him with all my heart.

Years passed, and by the time I turned twelve, I was desperate to awaken an Ability of my own. I wanted to be brave like my brother, and go on adventures and important missions, and also be able to support myself.

So, every day after school, I tried to make one awaken.

I imagined the air, the wind, moving at my fingertips.

I tried and tried, until...

Nephryte found a secluded spot in the alley between two run-down factory buildings, a place which had lately become his practice yard. He positioned a can on top of the trash bin there, then stepped back until he was a distance away.

He imagined energy flowing through him, as Julian had once described.

With his face set in determination, he reached out his hand, fingers curled.

He strained his energy, willing the can to move, to float—to do anything at all.

But the minutes passed by, and the can just sat there—mocking him.

"*Grr!* Move, you stupid hunk of metal!" Nephryte growled, thrusting out his palm again.

Still, the can wouldn't move.

Nephryte was tempted to go over and kick it.

"Golly, you're being awful mean to that there can. Did it do something to offend you?" said a voice from above.

Nephryte looked up with a start.

A boy peered down from an open window in the left-hand building and gave him a wave. His black wavy hair was long and curly at the ends, tied back.

"Who are you? I didn't think anyone came around this place," Nephryte asked slowly.

The boy edged out of the window and shimmied down a pipe—losing his grip halfway and falling, hitting the alley ground with a grunt and a wheeze.

The boy righted himself dizzily and flashed a toothy grin. "That's the same thing I was thinking! Name's Gandif, by the by."

Nephryte's brow wrinkled. Who was this odd person? He looked about the same age as himself. "I'm Nephryte," he replied.

"What're you trying to do to that poor can, Nephryte?" Gandif asked, waltzing over to the object and bending to peer at it from different angles.

Nephryte released a frustrated sigh. "I'm trying to wake up my Ability. I *must* have one, since my brother does!"

"*Mm*, that's not a guarantee though, from what I hear."

Nephryte's hands made fists. "But I *have* to have one! I can't afford not to. I...I'm tired of being a burden to my brother. I want to serve a purpose and help earn us a living."

Gandif looked from him to the can. "And hurting a perfectly good can is going to do that for you?"

Nephryte gave him a flat look.

Gandif chuckled. "I'm only teasing. But hey, is having some special power really the answer to all your problems? I mean, I've got no Ability—nor any chance of ever waking one up. So, does that mean I can't serve a purpose or do anything great with my life?"

Nephryte's jaw went slack. His mouth opened and closed like a fish trying to think how to respond. "That's not... I wasn't trying to say that."

Gandif sauntered over and thumped his chest. "Instead of being a burden to your brother, I think you're being a burden to yourself, too," he told him. "That's what happens when you think you've gotta have power."

Nephryte let the words sink in, and slowly he nodded. "I suppose I have gotten a bit carried away…"

Gandif shrugged his shoulders. "Long as you realize it now, and not later!" He turned on his heel, facing the can. "Now, if I was trying to wake up some powerful inner force or whatever, I imagine that instead of forcing it out, I'd more…how you say, coax it out?"

Nephryte cocked his head. He'd never thought of needing to coax it out. But, well…nothing else had been working. He faced the can again, closed his eyes, sucked in a breath and let it out slowly. He opened his eyes and reached out his hand towards the can, this time more calm, more focused.

He imagined the energy, the *essence*, inside him reaching towards the can, coaxing it out of his fingers to glide across the air.

The air shimmered and shifted.

He blinked in surprise, and he kept willing the energy towards the can.

And then…the can moved, tipping over just enough to fall and roll off the bin.

As the metal clanked against the ground, Nephryte stared and his mouth gaped. "I…I did it. I did it!"

Gandif clapped his hands. "Yay, you moved a can. Not sure what that's going to accomplish for you in life, but yay."

Nephryte jumped up and down. "I did it, I did it! I can go to Draevensett! Oh thank you, Gandif!" Without thinking, he gave him a hug.

"Ah, okay. You're welcome. I'm just a slave, though, nothing great."

Nephryte drew back and looked him up and down: Gandif's clothes were clean, but they weren't exactly nice. Nephryte, in his poverty, appeared wealthier by comparison.

"Slave? But…you're vempar."

"*Mostly*, but not completely. My mom's half human." Gandif's worn shoes scuffed the ground. "But I've got it better than most slaves do, so I'm told. They call me a servant, since I'm technically a citizen of Draeth 'n all, but I feel no freer than a slave."

"…Well, whatever you are, I'm grateful for your help," said Nephryte. "Let's be friends. If you ever need anything, just ask." He held out his hand.

Gandif considered, then, with a toothy grin, took it. "Never thought there'd be a day when I had friends. Nice to meet you, Nephryte!"

～

Brother was already an official Draev Guardian by the time I enrolled in Draevensett, and he was working towards his goal of reaching Draev Master rank. He was proud of me, but also made sure to point out that it had nothing to do with my Ability. He loved me for me—not for whatever power I could wield.

In his spare time, Julian encouraged me through my ups and downs, and he tried to get me to be more sociable and make friends. I hated that last part, at first. But I knew he just wanted what was best for me; he didn't want me to be alone, in case something ever happened to him.

After all, it's dangerous work being a Draev Guardian…

Draevensett Academy was just as intimidating on the inside as Nephryte had expected it to be. He'd seen the grand towers and outer exterior walls when coming to visit Julian, but going into the white-and-silver marble foyer and the halls of vaulted ceilings was a whole other experience. He gazed up at the large statue of the Protector and the grand cape rippling behind him bearing the Draev Guardian coat-of-arms. It was all truly awe-inspiring.

The principal placed Nephryte in Floor Earnest, given the crest of a gryphon with its claws ready to strike and wings outspread, the same Floor that Julian had been in.

Nephryte wandered through the corridors of the Floor Earnest dorms, admiring the fanciful window tracery and painted ribbed ceilings and the polished floor tiles. So focused was he, that he nearly ran into someone just coming out of a room.

"Excuse me!" he apologized, head bobbing. But when he beheld the person, his breath caught in his throat.

It was a girl, with thick black hair and cute freckles dotted across her cheeks and nose. She was almost as tall as him, but kept her shoulders slouched.

Their gazes met before she glanced down at his wrinkled shirt. "Are you new here, too?" she asked him.

He stammered and nodded. "How'd you know?"

"The Draev coat-of-arms sticker goes on the back of your shirt, not the front."

"Oh." He looked down and peeled it off.

"Here." She took it, slapping the image onto his back.

He coughed from the impact, and when he turned back to her, she was laughing. Her teeth weren't positioned just right, so when she laughed it made a wheezing sound. "I'm Seren-Rose," she finally said.

He grinned at her. "I'm Nephryte."

He felt secretly overjoyed to be on the same Floor as Seren-Rose. There was something just so cute about her. And when their Floor group was called to gather on the practice fields, out back, he moved to stand beside her, offering a small smile.

She smiled back.

A boy came up on her other side, wearing an Arah-style patterned vest, his hair a modern mullet and his smile full of confidence. He nodded to Seren-Rose.

Nephryte's cheer diminished. Who was this brazen person?

The Draev Master of their Floor did roll call, and when he said "Eletor," the boy answered.

"Present!"

"Nephryte."

"Present."

Eletor looked his way, leaning around Seren-Rose. "Another newbie? He looks weak and skinny."

Nephryte grimaced, and the other boy smirked back at him.

The Master had each student demonstrate their Ability before the rest of the group, and Nephryte did what he had practiced and made a gust of wind lift his feet up off the ground.

There were sounds of awe from the other students as they watched him hover in the air.

Nephryte landed back down, his head held high with pride.

"Eletor, you're next," said the Master.

Lightning crackled between the boy's hands, and he made it dance in a mesmerizing arc above their heads, a bridge of flashing white.

The group was even more impressed with that, including Seren-Rose, and they applauded loudly.

Eletor turned in place, spreading his arms wide as if to soak in all their praise. "It was nothing, really," he was saying. "I should be able to do much more than that, soon." He flicked a haughty glance in Nephryte's direction. "After all, lightning has more battle power than wind ever could."

Nephryte's hands clenched into fists.

～

The next day.

"*This* is the first mission we get?" said Nephryte as he, Eletor and Seren-Rose combed through the streets of Downtown, forced to work together as a team. "Finding a lost pet pig?"

He didn't mind being teamed up with Seren-Rose—*he secretly enjoyed it*—but why did the Master have to add arrogant Eletor into the mix?

Seren-Rose shrugged her skinny shoulders in response to his complaint. "We're inexperienced. We have to start somewhere," she said reasonably.

Eletor tossed the photo of the pig aside as they walked. "Who even keeps a piggy for a pet, anyway?" He made a face.

Seren-Rose used her *essence* to Leap on top of a short building.

Nephryte flew himself up, looking down between the alleys that they passed.

"It was last seen somewhere around here—" he began.

Something suddenly let out a squeal, cutting him off.

"*Ah*—there's the porker!" shouted Eletor.

Nephryte hovered above as the pig—wearing a frilly pink collar—came running out of one alley and into another.

When the path came to a dead end, the pig was trapped, and he swooped down into a dive to grab it.

At the same time, Eletor came at the pig from the ground.

And they both collided.

"*Gah*—!!"

They fell to the ground in a heap, and the squealing pig trampled over them and ran out the mouth of the alley and into the busy street.

"You—you made us lose the pig!" Nephryte exclaimed as he scrambled to get up.

"Me? You were the one who ran into *me* and made me lose the porker. I would've had it if it weren't for you! Stupid wind boy."

Nephryte glared, his hands fisting.

Eletor glared back.

"I dare you to call me that again."

Eletor leaned forward and jutted his chin out. "Stuuupid wind boooy," he repeated with emphasis.

"Hey, guys, I caught the—" Seren-Rose peeked into the alley, having caught the pig on a leash, just in time to see Nephryte fly at Eletor.

The fists of both boys met, creating a storm of wind and lightning that immediately filled the alley space.

Seren-Rose quickly backed away with the pig, her hair whipping across her face by the sudden wind.

Nephryte lashed out with currents of air, slamming Eletor into walls. Eletor's lightning crackled and made burn streaks across Nephryte's skin. They grabbed and punched at each other, each trying to knock the other down. Their shoes scraped across the cobblestones, and they each had a fistful of the other's shirt in their grip as they threw their weight around.

Nephryte made a fist of air to punch him in the jaw, and Eletor's right hand came at his face, sizzling with electricity.

And then Nephryte felt hands grabbing both him and Eletor and pinning them both to the ground like caught animals.

"Is this how you behave on your first mission? Like children?" spoke their Master's booming voice above their heads. "Is that how you want to be treated now, *hm*? As children? Because that can be arranged."

Both boys were then hoisted to their feet in shame, bloody and bruised. Nephryte turned his face away, not wanting to look anyone in the eye, and he rubbed his nose.

Their Master had them both in an iron grip and he pulled them along by the wrists with him back towards Draevensett. Both he and Eletor hung their heads and sulked the whole way back, while nearby pedestrians stared and whispered. Seren-Rose followed slowly behind, her expression clearly embarrassed for them.

Both boys were then carted before Principal Han, entering his office room of beetle specimens.

"He's the one who started it! Came charging at me like a lunatic," Eletor told the principal.

Nephryte stammered in rage. "How dare you! You were the one calling me names! You've been a jerk to me since the day I got here!"

"Your wind slammed me against the wall!"

"Your lightning burned my arm!"

"Would you prefer a punch?"

"Bring it on!"

"Enough," the principal's voice boomed, and a warning glow of green *essence* wrapped around him in the shape of deadly beetle pincers. "I can see there is much underlying tension between the two of you. Now, sit down." He indicated the chairs before his desk.

They reluctantly obeyed and glanced unnervingly at his *essence* pincers until he let their glow fade.

The principal then proceeded to give them a lengthy lecture over an hour long. His beard swished over his red stole as he paced behind his mahogany, insect-legged desk, recounting to them the rules and responsibilities of what it means to become a Draev Guardian.

Near the end of the reprimand, he looked each boy in the eye. "Do you now understand why missions, even menial ones, are important?" he asked.

They both nodded glumly.

"And why teamwork is so vital?"

They nodded again.

"Will there be any more name calling or squabbling between you?"

Eletor made a face at Nephryte when the principal wasn't looking, and Nephryte stuck out his tongue in return.

Principal Han heaved a sigh, as if knowing without having seen. "I see this is going to take more work..." he muttered.

"Very well. You will both be on kitchen cleaning duty starting today, until your behavior improves."

"What?!" they both exclaimed.

And so, every day after school, both boys had to trudge over to the kitchens and clean pots and pans, getting their clothes and feet soaked in soapy wetness while they worked.

It was exhausting and gross, but the long hours spent stuck together eventually forced them to talk.

It turned out that Eletor wasn't as confident as he pretended to be, and he had only picked on Nephryte because of how easily he had fit in with the school and how people had accepted him. Nephryte hadn't thought about it, but because of his brother's work as a Draev, a lot of people were nicer to him and willing to give him help when he needed it. That wasn't something Eletor had.

"I shouldn't have lashed out," Eletor finally admitted.

Nephryte stared down at the greasy pot in his hands. "I didn't exactly hold my temper, either. It wasn't very Draev-like behavior."

Eletor held out his fist. "Truce?"

Nephryte fist bumped him. "Truce."

And after that, they were finally able to start working together as a team—and their punishment washing dishes soon ended.

Some days later, when they walked across the moon courtyard, Nephryte pointed to a section in the highest floor of the school dorms and asked, "What Floor is that, up there? Across from Tathom?"

"That was Floor Harlow. There used to be five Masters in Draevensett, back when the school had a whole lot more students," Eletor explained.

Nephryte summoned a wind current and glided up the spiral walkway levels. He hopped over the balustrade and landed on the fifth floor, before Harlow's entry door. The painted wood bore the emblazoned crest of a beaming sun and a falcon flying through it.

"Harlow..." he said, his fingers running over the crest.

It made him feel sad that the place wasn't in use, that it no longer had a purpose...

"I want to reopen Harlow, one day," Nephryte decided out loud.

Becoming a teacher or mentor wasn't something he had ever considered before, but...he felt drawn to Harlow, for a reason he couldn't explain. As if an invisible force was pulling him towards it, telling him to bring the Floor back to life.

Eletor had run up the walkway, and he now stood behind him, shaking his head. "Sounds like more trouble than it's worth, if you ask me."

Nephryte's lips drew up. "Well, I didn't ask you, did I?"

He glanced at the sun crest one last time before turning to leave, a newfound goal in his heart.

2

Nephryte gingerly sat on the operating table, trying not to bump any of the spine stingers that coated his arms and back.

"Really?" said the doctor. "You attacked a spine hornet hive?"

Nephryte felt ashamed of himself. Both he and Gandif had been exploring a small space of reserved nature, which also happened to be the backyard of some noble's house, when they had stumbled upon the beehive.

Gandif had been convinced that they were honeybees and wanted to get some of the tasty honey.

Nephryte obliged him, using his wind Ability to shake the hive and drive the bees back. Unfortunately, the bees didn't behave quite like how he had expected them to, and a mass of the insects swarmed out and came straight at them, avoiding the currents of wind he desperately threw at them.

There followed a lot of yelping and jumping in pain. Spine hornets were the worst of all bees to be stung by.

Nephryte had managed to fly himself and Gandif away, but not before the evil insects had waged battle and left hundreds of stingers in their skin.

Nephryte then hurried them to the infirmary, where they now sat on tables, waiting for the numerous stingers to be pulled out, one by one.

"I wouldn't say *attacked*. More like shook it up a bit," said Gandif, from the other table. He yelped as a stinger was yanked free.

"Zushil," called the doctor. "Handle the other patient for me, will you?"

A boy with stood-up black hair came into the room, brushing the curtain aside. He adjusted his glasses, looking Nephryte up and down, then glanced over at Gandif. He couldn't have been much older than them.

"This is my apprentice. He's well trained," explained the doctor while he worked on Gandif.

Zushil picked up surgical tweezers and began work on Nephryte's arm.

Nephryte bit back the pain.

"You thought you could take on spine hornets, did you?" commented Zushil. "What a bunch of idiots."

Nephryte grimaced at him. "We're not id—*ouch!*"

Zushil snorted disapprovingly.

"You look like you hate everything. Or is your face just stuck like that?" Nephryte shot back.

Zushil yanked out another stinger, pulling another yelp from him.

"Can't you be more gentle?" Nephryte glared.

"Can't you be less annoying?" Zushil retorted.

Nephryte shook his head. "How can you be training to be a doctor? Doctors are supposed to be nice, comforting; they make you feel better."

"No, they're supposed to keep your sorry self alive. Would you rather have someone who helps your emotions, or someone who's going to save your life?"

Nephryte opened and closed his mouth.

"Well, you could still learn to be a little nicer," Nephryte finally muttered, then yelped again.

Once all of the stingers were out, the doctor left for a moment.

Zushil began putting things away and cleaning.

"Say, you look like a smart fellow," said Gandif, scooting to the edge of his table. Zushil backed away, a look of distrust plain on his face. "Might you know what this flower is?" Gandif took from his pocket and held up a small purple flower with petals like narrow spikes.

Zushil gasped and snatched it. "A rare *star-needle*, a variety of *coughs weed* not found in this region." He then looked up sharply. "Where did you get this?"

Gandif grinned. "It was nearby the hive. I thought it looked pretty."

Zushil's gaze narrowed. "You weren't in a park. This flower doesn't grow wild here. It must have been imported by someone rich."

"Oh, is that right?" Gandif scratched his chin. "You know a lot about plants, don't you? Would you like to come see the flower plant for yourself?" he said with a twinkle in his eyes. "You'd be surprised what all we find in the upper-class gardens! Enough to make anybody who loves plant life drool."

There was a flash of eagerness in Zushil's gaze. "I've studied books and depictions, but...to see the real plants themselves would be..."

Gandif slapped him on the back. "Join our club, and you'll get to feast your eyes upon all sorts of grand, illustrious botany!"

"Club?" Zushil became a bit wary.

"If you can call it that. We're the only two members right now," said Nephryte, off to the side.

"It'll be three if you join!" said Gandif. "Our goal is to explore the unknown and make exciting discoveries!" he stated grandly.

Nephryte rolled his eyes. "You're too afraid to leave the city, Gandif. How can you explore the *unknown* while being stuck here?"

"I never said I wouldn't go outside the city. I just…don't want to walk through any untamed forests, that's all. There're things worse than spine hornets out there in the wild…" Gandif shuddered. "But anyway, there's plenty to explore right here, especially in rich people's collections. Did you know, that blue mansion down at the corner has a whole room full of crystals and geodes? Every color you can possibly imagine!"

"You sneak into people's houses?" exclaimed Zushil.

"No. I pretend to clean chimneys, and they let me in."

Zushil shook his head, glancing skyward. "What ridiculousness have I gotten myself into?" he muttered.

Zushil couldn't resist the chance to study rare plants, and so he joined our little club. When I went on missions to different parts of the kingdom, I always made sure to bring back specimens for him—which in turn made him feel indebted to me.

Gandif was always on the hunt for something to explore, in between his servant work, and would get us all into trouble along with him: such as uncovering a smuggler's plot, crashing a noble's Christmas party, sneaking into the palace just to see what the king's restroom looked like, and so on…

Julian couldn't complain. I had friends and was being social, just like he wanted, though I don't think he knew half of what our little club got into. He did, however, soon manage to place a new burden on my life…

"Babysitting?" Nephryte exclaimed. "Are you serious?"

"Yes," Julian stated, and he dragged Nephryte along with him by the elbow towards the Outskirts.

"Why? I don't need this! I have enough work between school and missions. I don't want to babysit some brat on top of all that."

Julian rolled his eyes skyward and exhaled. "That way of thinking is *exactly* why you need to do this. You've been raised like an only child, and dare I say maybe even spoiled. It's time for you to see how the other side lives and think about what you can do to help them. And who knows, what you do might be able to change someone's life, one day."

The streets turned from pavestone to dirt when they left the city walls and entered the Outskirts. The difference in poverty was immediately clear. Nothing anywhere was clean, and homeless people crammed the shadows of corners and alleys.

Julian stepped up to the door of a rickety wooden structure.

Nephryte gazed up at it, feeling as if the thing would blow over if a strong enough wind came through. Was this really supposed to be a house?

"These parents are poor, and they desperately need a babysitter. No one else is willing to help them out," whispered Julian. "Be polite, and smile."

"I'm always polite!"

Julian knocked on the door, and they entered.

The woman who greeted them was a pretty blonde, and she looked just as sweet as an alligator ready to bite your face off.

Nephryte tried to duck behind Julian.

"This is my brother, who I mentioned earlier. He'll be babysitting for you today." Julian stepped aside, introducing him.

Nephryte swallowed and straightened his back.

The woman looked him up and down like a slab of meat.

"I see," she said. "I suppose he'll do."

She gestured for Nephryte to follow as she strode into the room on the right: a small sitting room with a rug and sofa. There, on a creaky chair, sat a child in a diaper, sucking on a milk bottle, hair bright sun-blond and eyes blue as the sky.

The child's head turned up when he came in.

"This is Aken-Shou." The woman picked him up and practically shoved him into Nephryte's arms. The child blinked large eyes up at him, as if curious who this new person was. "Diapers are in that cabinet. Milk in the cool-box. Use whatever you need."

The woman was already slipping on a jacket and heading for the door.

"Wait—but—I mean—I can't just..." Nephryte stammered.

"You'll do fine." Julian winked at him.

The woman had already left.

Nephryte felt on the verge of panic. "But I don't know how to take care of a baby!" He looked down at the child wearing nothing but a diaper.

Julian smiled. "Then this will be a good learning experience for you. Don't worry, he's not fragile. Just make sure he's fed and cleaned."

And with that, Julian headed out.

"Wait!" Nephryte chased after him to the door, then was forced to watch as his brother strolled off down the dusty street.

He stood there in the doorway for a long minute, until the child started to cry.

Nephryte went back inside and rested his head against the door. Great. This was just great. Why was Julian punishing him like this?

He realized the child was shivering. "Are you cold?"

He carried the child back into the sitting room. He put him on the floor and found a blanket to wrap around him.

"Aken-Shou, was it? Just sit there and be good. Okay? Can you do that for me?"

Aken tugged the blanket this way and that, inspecting it. Then he rolled across the floor with the blanket, wrapping himself up like a taco.

"No, no, you'll suffocate!" Nephryte panicked and took the blanket away.

Aken's hand reached out as the blanket pulled away from him. Then his face squinted up and he started to cry.

"Oh seriously?" Nephryte groaned.

He gave him back the blanket.

"Don't be such a cry baby."

Oh. That was where that phrase came from.

Aken stopped crying and tossed the blanket up and down.

Nephryte sat on the floor, his back against the sofa. What was he supposed to do now?

He glanced at a worn clock on the mantle. Two hours. What was there to do for two whole stupid hours?

Aken started scooting across the floor, moving more quickly than Nephryte would have expected.

"Hey, where do you think you're going?" Nephryte chased after him out the room.

But when he reached the doorway, the child was gone.

Nephryte froze, his pulse racing.

Then he saw the basement door there, open.

With a jolt of panic, he dashed forward and grabbed up Aken before the child could fall down the steps into the darkness.

Nephryte's heartbeat hammered, and he held the child to his chest, trying to calm down.

This brat. Didn't he know any better? Were children really this ignorant of danger?

Oh crud, this babysitting was going to be awful!

Nephryte shut the basement door and brought him back to

the sitting room.

Just as he was about to put Aken on the chair, something started to smell—very badly.

"Oh no…"

It took twenty minutes of gagging before Nephryte figured out how to clean the mess and put a new diaper on the child. When he was done, he finally flopped onto the sofa, completely exhausted.

Aken crawled across the floor, heading to the open door of the bathroom.

Nephryte heaved a weary sigh.

"Here, do you want to play with this?" Nephryte used a wind current to move a wooden toy duck around, making it roll on its wheel feet.

"Ooo!" Aken chased after it.

Nephryte made the duck fly up and dip back down like a real bird. Aken giggled, trying to catch it.

When the child finally tired out, Aken sat back and watched the duck, waving his hands and feet about.

Nephryte chuckled. Such a simple thing could fascinate the little guy.

Aken yawned. He crawled over to the sofa and tried to climb up, his small arms unable to pull his own weight.

Nephryte laughed. "You want up here? Are you going to be good now?" He lifted him up under the arms and set him beside him.

Aken bounced on the sofa, then crawled into Nephryte's lap.

"What? You want more food? I refuse to change your diaper again, so it had better not be that…"

He cut off as the child curled up and snuggled against his chest.

Aken closed his eyes, thumb in mouth, and began to drift off to sleep.

"Oh...that is unfairly cute," Nephryte admitted, looking down at the peaceful child, warm against him. He brushed some of the blond bangs back.

Poor kid. He used to think his house was in a bad state, but it didn't compare to *this*. Everything looked old and ready to fall apart. And that mother was so cold. Did she ever play with Aken, or make sure he didn't hurt himself? There clearly weren't any child safety measures in this place. Even if they were vempars who could Heal, that didn't mean injuries couldn't hurt.

"What am I doing, scolding the parents already?" he thought.

The little rascal had stolen a piece of his heart, somehow. But he was a cute rascal, and not that badly behaved but just neglected. He needed more playtime to get rid of all that pent-up energy he had.

The next evening, Julian made him babysit again.

Nephryte complained and brought his homework along.

He stared down at the child on the floor waiting for him. Aken clapped his hands, as if he remembered Nephryte.

That softened him. And shucks, that child's smile was brighter than the sun, chasing away the shadows in his heart.

"You have to be good now, you hear? I've got lots of homework to finish, so I don't have time to play much," he told the child, who blinked obliviously up at him.

Nephryte sighed and got out his books.

He gave Aken a new toy, a wood-and-fabric bird, and made it fly about the room while he worked. The child eagerly chased after it, crawling, trying to stand, falling, then crawling faster.

Once he finished with homework, Nephryte set up a record player he had brought over, and he soon got a catchy beat playing. Aken tried to grab the tube where music sounded from, and Nephryte quickly pulled him away. "Stand out of the way, now. I have to practice my dance routine."

Aken watched as Nephryte moved his feet into different positions, moving across the floor. A turn here, a dip there, following the music. The child giggled.

"What? You think I'm not good enough? Well, I dance for myself, not for an audience. So, consider yourself privileged to see what no one else ever will."

As he continued to dance, Aken stood up on his feet and tried to sway to the tune, like Nephryte was doing. And he fell over.

Nephryte let out an involuntary laugh.

Aken tried again to copy his moves, sweeping an arm out when Nephryte did and turning in a circle with him.

Nephryte grinned at his efforts.

The next evening, Nephryte returned, and many more evenings after that. He pretended to grumble and complain, when really he was starting to enjoy their time together. And it didn't feel like long before Aken was learning how to walk and repeat the words that he heard.

But Nephryte also learned that Aken's family were no ordinary vempars. He overheard some of the neighbors gossiping that the Bloodre family were Scourgebloods, the last of their kind.

That explained why nobody else was willing to babysit Aken. The news did unnerve Nephryte, he couldn't deny that, but the family had been granted permission to live here in Draeth. And besides that, Aken himself was an innocent child.

During another evening, when Nephryte was getting ready to head over to the house, Julian arrived home early. "Oh, Julian! You're back from your mission."

Julian nodded.

Something was wrong. Nephryte paused while tying his shoelaces. He could see it in his brother's eyes, the way his smile didn't quite reach.

"Julian?" he asked carefully.

His brother removed his jacket, hanging it up by the door, and went over to the cool-box, getting out food. He exhaled heavily, staring at a frozen chicken. "...I guess there's no point in hiding it, is there? The whole city will know soon enough."

"Know *what?*" Nephryte asked slowly.

Julian turned from the counter to face him. "War is coming."

A chill creeped across Nephryte's arms and down his spine.

"The goblins are now invading our continent, and all of Draeth's forces are gathering to prepare."

No. Not now. This couldn't be happening *now*, not after losing their parents and finally making their lives stable again.

They would take him away. They would take Julian away from him!

"Brother..." Tears made his eyes blurry.

Julian drew near, hugging an arm around him. "My Draev squad is being called out to the west, to help defend our borders."

Tears ran down Nephryte's cheeks.

"Hey, I'll keep myself safe. Don't you worry, okay? With this Ability, no goblin will be able to touch me." He sounded so reassuring, so confident in that.

He hugged Nephryte closer.

"I'll come back to you. I promise."

~

Nephryte made his way to the rickety house in the Outskirts.

Little Aken saw him come through the door and he waved his arms and ran to him, hugging Nephryte—or rather, his leg.

Nephryte picked him up, spinning him in the air. Aken giggled, stretching his arms out like wings.

"I bird!" Aken said.

"*Haha*, that's right. You are a brave bird who flies up to the highest clouds!" Nephryte indulged him. "But watch out for the bats!" he warned, and made Aken dip down and up and curve around as if to avoid them. The child giggled all the more.

Later, when Nephryte got around to practicing his dance routine, Aken could almost keep up with him, though in a clumsy, cute childish way. And they were both worn out afterwards.

Nephryte gazed out the room's back window, which was open and looked out onto an alley and a bright moon above.

"Up, up," said Aken, reaching his arms up for Nephryte to lift him.

"What, you want to see the moon?" Nephryte picked the child up and sat him on the windowsill in front of him, keeping an arm around him so he wouldn't fall. The cool night breeze rustled their hair and brushed across their cheeks.

Aken's large eyes took in the full moon.

"That's the moon."

"Moom."

"Moon," he corrected.

Aken watched it with open, pure fascination. He pointed at dots around the moon. "Mooms?"

"Those are stars."

"Small."

"Yes, they're small because they're sooo far away. But the moon is close to us."

"Fly me to moom!"

Nephryte laughed. "I wish I could! I'm sure it'd be interesting up there. But you know, Aken-Shou, outer space seems like a cold and empty place to me. Why go there when there's so much life here to explore and people to cherish?"

He pressed the tip of Aken's ear down so that it bounced back up, just like his brother would do to him. Aken swatted at his ear, giggling.

They watched the night sky together, the stars twinkling brightly tonight despite the nearby city, and a night bird swooped across the moon, fluttering its arched wings.

Nephryte tried to freeze this moment in his mind, this perfect moment when the storm had not yet hit, with little Aken happy here at his side.

What would the future bring? He wanted these happy moments to last... But war was a force that relished in tearing things apart.

~

It was around this time, when the Goblin Shadow War began on our continent, that I found child Cyrus in the woods. I wished I could keep her, but knew I had other responsibilities of my own. I was still a student, and if the war grew dire, all Draev students, no matter how young, would be called to do their part. And so, I let her go back to the humans.

Two years passed as the war raged on. And then, the day that would forever change my life came.

I was fifteen. I can still see it so clearly in my mind, as if it had happened only yesterday...

The overcast sky thickened, threatening to rain, and thunder growled through the clouds and rumbled the ground. Nephryte was waiting for him to come home, standing at the open window and watching the storm.

Julian was supposed to be on his way back. It was his squad's turn to take a break from the fighting and return to Draethvyle.

Why wasn't he here yet? His finger tapped nervously on the windowsill.

An uneasy feeling rippled through him, as if something in the world had gone wrong, and cold sweat beaded his temples.

Since the rain hadn't hit, several neighbors were out on the street and talking in hushed voices.

Nephryte strained his ears to listen.

"There was an incident, that Draev boy said. Between two Draev squads and a force of Argos Corps," spoke a heavyset woman. "They were supposed t' be working together against the goblin army—crazy, isn't that? But something must've got the humans angry. The Argos started attacking them, and the Draevs had t' scatter! Can you believe it? Getting into a skirmish when there's a war t' be fought! I dare say, there were many dead because of it."

Nephryte hopped out of the window, not even bothering to use the door, and flew until he reached the speaking woman.

His focus on her intensified. "Which squads were they? Did they make it back? Tell me!" he demanded.

The neighbors speaking with her startled away from him. "Not sure, boy," she told him, a tremor in her tone, and she took a step back. "But it happened near the settlements west of here."

"That's where my brother was!"

Panic welled inside him. He lifted himself into the air on currents of wind and flew, hurrying toward the Draev Guardian League's headquarters, the thunder rumbling over his head like an ominous warning.

Surely, someone at HQ would know if Julian was safe!

Inside the grand structure that made up the League's headquarters, Nephryte asked around, wandering the hallways, and was pushed aside by other Draevs and told to get lost and go back to the academy.

But Nephryte persisted. And when Master Brangor spotted him making a ruckus, he came over to explain the situation to him:

The squads of Draevs and Argos had been under a temporary truce to work together and battle the goblins. But then, something happened between two of the groups and a fight broke out. Julian and others had tried to stop it.

"I'm sorry, lad, but things happen when tensions are high. And between old enemies like us and humans, those tensions run *very* high—truce or no truce."

"What are you saying? What happened to my brother?" Nephryte pleaded, hearing the desperation in his own voice.

Brangor shook his red-bearded head. "Not everyone's been accounted for yet, but some bodies have been brought back."

Nephryte's entire being stilled at the words.

"They're down in the Morgue Hall, if you want to check."

Time seemed to stand still as Nephryte hurried to the long building, his hair a wet, tangled mess as the rain finally broke out. He forced the heavy doors to the Morgue Hall open, water streaming down his tunic.

Inside, rows and rows of the dead were laid out on tables, black sheets masking their faces.

Trembling and breathing hard, he made his way down the rows.

From the hands and feet that were visible around the edges of the sheets, most bodies appeared to be around a week old, but the last row looked fresh—and caretakers were still tending to them.

Nephryte paused; he couldn't make his feet move forward, to look, to see if...

He swallowed and finally pressed onward. Glancing at each table he passed, his eye caught on a long-fingered hand similar to his own.

He halted there...and he knew. *He knew.*

"Julian...?"

The face beneath the black sheet... He drew the fabric aside.

There rested the kind yet tough face of his brother, his eyes closed as though asleep.

It didn't seem real. Julian should wake up, any moment now, and tell him not to cry and that everything was going to be all right...

But he wouldn't. He couldn't.

Julian's soul was gone.

He'd wanted to help other races. To change things. To make the world a little bit better...and *this* was what the humans had done to him in return.

It was hard to recall exactly what happened in those moments; Nephryte collapsed to his knees on the floor, all his strength gone, a soul-wrenching groan tearing him apart.

"How could they?" he was shouting. "How could they do this? HOW COULD THEY!"

He had never understood what blinding rage was until that moment.

Rage took over every fiber of his being, a tempest that could not be controlled. His vision couldn't see anything but the wicked humans responsible for his dear brother's death.

He vaguely recalled leaving the city, soaring over the walls, west, in the direction that the wicked humans would be. He wanted to find them, those murderers...

And find them he soon did.

"You were supposed to be fighting the goblins!" Nephryte shouted from above their heads, landing on top of an oak tree before the group of Argos he had come across in a meadow. He stared down at them, his veins bulging with fury.

The humans regarded him, some looking confused, others holding their gunswords in defensive postures. They didn't seem to care about a word he was saying, nor about what they had done to his brother.

"How could you be so evil!" Nephryte spread his hands forward. The air around him swirled, funneled, and moved faster.

Faster. *Faster.*

The branch he stood upon broke apart, and he hovered in the air, trees around the entire meadow now falling over from the force of the wind. The humans struggled to cling to the grass and shrubs and not be swept away.

The winds of tornados formed from Nephryte's hands, their funnels like the mouths of giant eagles screeching for revenge.

"You killed my brother!!" he screamed, and he unleashed the tornados filled with his rage.

All became destruction as the winds ripped up everything they touched, tossing Argos and trees like scattered toys, debris filling the air.

When the whirling winds began to slow their rampaging spin, a wave of exhaustion slammed through Nephryte's body and his vision cleared.

And then, he realized what he had done.

He had never formed a tornado before, but that wasn't what he stood gaping at right now: it was the destruction left behind that shocked him to the core and brought him back to his senses.

The humans were scattered forms amidst the churned rubble and vegetation.

He'd destroyed them.

Destroyed everything.

But they deserved it...didn't they? After they had betrayed the truce and killed his...?

Face wet with tears, Nephryte retreated, flying as far away from the scene as he could.

His mind was a numb blank, on the verge of breaking apart. He soared across the landscape, approaching Draethvyle and its sharp, rising towers.

He tried to calm down as he landed in the Outskirts.

What had led him here? Was it already evening?

That's right; the Bloodres would be expecting him.

He had to act like everything was normal. He couldn't let people find out that he had just…that he'd…

Drying his face on his sleeve, he entered the worn house when Aken's mother let him in; she hurried herself out, without barely a word to him.

Strange how she always seemed to be busy, with someplace to go. She never talked about what job she had.

The moment the door closed behind him, Nephryte sank to his knees. And there he broke apart.

He wasn't sure for how long he sat there on the floor, weeping.

Little hands touched his knees, and he lifted his face.

"Don cry, Nefite," said Aken, his small brow furrowed. He patted Nephryte's knees as if to make it all better.

Nephryte scrubbed at his eyes. "Oh Aken, my brother is gone…and I've done something terrible." He wiped his runny nose on a sleeve. "I…I'm all alone, now. Alone. Julian's gone… What am I going to do?"

Aken crawled into his lap and gave his best attempt at a hug around his middle.

Another sob racked through Nephryte, and he held Aken close.

For a long while, I believed I was alone.

But then I remembered Lord God, and the church brother had brought me to, and the friends that he'd had me make. Life would be different, yes, but I was not alone.

When I returned to school soon after that incident, the D.G. League was there waiting for me. Members of a scouting party had seen me— seen what I'd done—and they wanted to use my newfound power.

I became known as the ace in the hands of Draeth Kingdom, a hero to vempar kind, while the humans referred to me as the Tempest Slayer—a fitting name, and a reminder of my deepest regret.

While vempars praised me, inside I felt only shame over that incident of rage and regret for the lives I'd taken—a regret that I would never let myself forget.

The king quickly put me to work in the war, using my Ability with wind—which was far stronger than my brother's had ever been—to drive back the goblin armies.

It wasn't much longer before the goblins were finally defeated by our forces, and they retreated back to their homeland across the sea. At last, the nightmare of war was over.

I was able to graduate from Draevensett Academy, and at age eighteen I became the youngest vempar to be promoted to Draev Master rank.

I went on many travels for missions and brought back rare plants for Zushil. Sometimes I met up with Gandif, during his crazy attempts to do work as a bounty hunter—his newfound career. His fear of traveling through forests had diminished, due to an encounter with a certain faeryn—but that's all a story for another day.

Seren-Rose and Eletor worked hard to catch up with me, soon earning their Draev Master ranks as well. They, too, had done work during the war and had earned much respect.

I couldn't visit Aken-Shou anymore—I hadn't seen him since the months before the war ended. Work kept me too busy. But I planned to create a home for Aken, once he was old enough, so that he could be free of his cold parents and become my little brother.

There had always been something unsettling about the Bloodres, something secretive. I rarely saw the father, and the one time when I did, there'd been something red stained on the hem of his pants... They never did explain to me what sort of work they each did.

Years passed, and I remembered my goal to return to Draevensett and reopen Floor Harlow. I was ready. This would also be a chance to give Aken a new home. Whether he had an Ability or not, he could live with me in Draevensett, free of worries.

Or so I had hoped...

The old Masters at the academy had decided to retire from the school and pursue other Draev careers, and a group of young Draev Masters waited in hopes of taking their place—Nephryte among them. Master Brangor was the only old member determined to keep the job until his death.

Nephryte quickly applied for one of the open positions.

"I have two conditions," he told Principal Han, before the man could approve. "I want to reopen Floor Harlow, and I want to choose the students who will be under my care, even if it means I have to go out and search for the right ones."

The principal arched a bushy eyebrow at him. "In other words, you want to recruit your own students? I don't think anyone's ever asked for such a strange thing before."

"Well, I've never been normal."

Han gave an acknowledging chuckle. "There's certainly truth in that. I remember when you were a student here, and you were quite a handful at times..."

Nephryte glanced to the ceiling. "I'm begging you not to remember those times. Please, for my sake, pretend they never happened."

Han chuckled all the more, his wrinkles creasing. His gaze shifted from Nephryte down to the application form on the desk, then back. "Very well, go and hunt down some students for your Floor Harlow, Master Nephryte."

Han gave his signature of approval.

3

"**G**andif, I don't see why you needed to call me all the way out here. Do you have any idea how hard it was finding this place?" Nephryte said. He rested his hands on his hips and observed the old mansion before him, hidden away in the eastern fringes of Lesser Magica Forest. The trees here didn't stay ever-green as most of Magica Forest did, but they still loomed high. "I never would have found it without an aerial view."

Gandif flashed him a toothy grin from beneath his wide-brimmed hat.

Because it was on the fringes of the forest, the faeryn hadn't bothered the place. And unless someone was purposefully looking for the mansion, they would pass right by it unawares; its color scheme blended in with the surrounding foliage like magic.

It was unsettling, though, being in the woods, feeling like he was in the middle of nowhere, and yet finding a grand house.

"What is this even doing out here?" Nephryte said quietly.

"It ain't the middle of nowhere," Gandif told him, pronouncing his words in what he believed to be bounty hunter speak. "There're ruins about this whole area. Almost as if there was a little community or somethin' here, long ago."

Nephryte shook his head. "Again, I ask: why am I here?"

"Well, y'see, I stumbled upon this place by accident and—seeing as how it's so nicely tucked away from the world 'n all—I was thinkin' what a great hideout it would make."

"And?"

Gandif looked down at his hands and fidgeted his fingers together. "And I'd like yer help in makin' sure it's safe and not…occupied by somethin' dastardly."

Nephryte stared blankly at him for several seconds.

"What? Yer the one who's got fancy powers. Nothin' can hurt *you*. But Clover would kill me if I fell into a trap 'n died."

Nephryte rubbed a hand over his forehead. "She would kill you if you died, hm? How does that work exactly?"

Gandif spread his arms wide. "Just help an old friend out, will you? Like during our adventure club days."

Nephryte shook his head. "Fine. Let's get this over with." He strode up to the mansion doors.

The old doors creaked open, and a mouse went scurrying past his boot. Behind him, Gandif gave a spooked yelp. The foyer waiting inside met them with layers of dust and pollen and cobwebs.

Nephryte coughed, waving a hand, and blew open some of the windows, though most the window glass was already broken and letting in air—explaining how pollen had gotten indoors. Shafts of light from cracks in the vaulted ceiling highlighted furniture spread about the space, some of it still in surprisingly good condition.

There were books and objects inside glass-sealed shelves. And everything seemed to be encased airtight in a thin layer of *something* yellowish and transparent, like a layer of preserving sap turned amber.

"Golly, what is this stuff?" Gandif poked at it.

"I'll take the left wing, you take the right," said Nephryte, moving to the doors on the left side of a grand staircase.

He looked inside each room that he passed, ventured down a twist of hallways, up a set of stairs, and came into a dark corridor on the second floor. So far, the ceiling and walls were still intact. "I would have brought a lampstick if I'd known this was what I would be doing," he muttered under his breath.

He felt his way through the dark gray space while his vision adjusted. Something his hand bumped against made a clicking sound, and a hidden door swung open from the wall. He paused, peering inside to a narrow staircase leading down into darker depths.

Curious, he made his way down the marble-slab stairs. It was a long descent before the stairs ended at a stone path, and the air chilled as if he had gone deep underground; the walls around him changed from wallpaper to rough, tan stone.

He followed the path, feeling with his hands along the walls, until the space opened up and took the shape of a catacomb. He breathed on his fingers to warm them.

Lights flickered to life in sconces along the walls, somehow triggered by his movement. The path led him into a chamber. The stone floor scraped under his boots, thick with old soil. Moth-eaten tapestries hung about the circular space, and shadows shifted in the flames of light.

He jumped when he saw a large shape against the far wall.

A sarcophagus sat atop a dais, a piece of grand and detailed stonework layered in centuries of dust. This underground room was a crypt!

Winged lions and ancient letters were engraved across the front. Nephryte drew near, his brow creased, but he couldn't decipher the words.

Who could be buried here? Clearly someone important. Perhaps the owner of this mansion?

His fingers itched to slide the lid off and take a peek.

Well, nobody else was around. No one to care if he touched an ancient object that scholars would no doubt want to have in their hands. He would be careful.

He used ropes of air to gently lift the lid and slide it aside.

He glimpsed scarlet silk bedding and a scattering of white and red rose petals. And there, lying as if in a deep sleep, was the body of a perfectly preserved boy, wrapped in a red silk robe. Olive skin smooth as wax, maroon hair uneven around his head and cheeks, and a cruel scar tracing down from his right eye.

His appearance seemed so alive. Nephryte leaned closer.

Alive, almost as if...

Nephryte placed his palm against the boy's chest. Doubting that anything would happen, on a whim, he channeled some of his *essence* into the body.

...Nothing happened.

He ceased, and analyzed the body for a while longer.

Then, the boy's eyes snapped open.

Nephryte jerked back with a yelp, and almost fell backwards onto his backside.

The boy sat up in the sarcophagus. He lifted his arms and hands, and studied them as if surprised they still worked. He flexed his fingers and turned his head about, eyeing the chamber around him. Then his gaze rested on Nephryte, who got up off the floor.

Nephryte wasn't one to believe in ghost stories, but...what the heck was this? He kept his Ability ready to attack, his palms open.

The boy regarded him sleepily. "Was it you who woke me?" he asked.

His ears were pointed, bat ridges along the insides—a vempar, so…maybe he wasn't an enemy? Unless this was a ghoulst who had taken over the body.

"Yes," Nephryte answered cautiously. "Who are you? How long have you…*been* in there? How are you alive? Are you a ghoulst?"

The boy's lips quirked upwards. "Ghoulst? Last time I checked, no. Red blood still pumps through my veins, if you need proof."

He pushed a sleeve of his thin robe up.

From where he stood, Nephryte scanned the veins pulsing on the arm the boy exposed. They appeared to be normal.

"I recognize that coat-of-arms." The boy nodded to the back of Nephryte's shoulder cape: the Draev Guardian symbol there. "So, it's a fellow Draev who finds me? That's nice." He stretched his arms, checked himself over as if for wounds— which there were none—then he climbed out of the sarcophagus, landing with a *thump*. "You may call me Mamoru," he said, once he stood before him, barefoot.

Nephryte stared at him openly, unsure what to make of all this. "My name is Nephryte. Are you the owner of this place?" He gestured around them.

"Yes. Though I fear to see how it has changed over the years since I've been asleep Healing."

"Healing?"

Mamoru walked around the stone chamber walls and the damaged tapestries. "Tell me, what year is it?"

Nephryte hesitated. "It's 2012 After Disaster."

Mamoru's gaze on the wall widened for a moment. "Has it been *that* long?" He looked down at himself. "And it's made me *this* young?"

"Young…?" Nephryte repeated. "Do you mean that you somehow aged backwards?"

Mamoru exhaled slowly. "Everyone I knew is gone…" He touched an image on a wall tapestry: a worn depiction of what Nephryte guessed to be the Twelve Legendary Knights.

Nephryte looked from the wall to him. "Were you one of *them?*" he asked, incredulous.

Mamoru's gaze took on a distant glaze. "Yes… And I suppose I'll have to trust you with this secret, since you are the one who woke me." His glance cut sideways to him. "You have the look of a trustworthy soul about you."

Nephryte bowed his head, still trying to wrap his mind around what was happening. One of the Legendary Knights—here, and alive in front of him?

Mamoru glanced about and then started down a path out of the chamber and through the catacomb. Nephryte followed.

After walking a windy series of inclining turns, the boy triggered a hidden door to open in a stone wall, and the light of day flooded over them.

Mamoru stepped out into daylight, onto a carpet of moss that now grew over a sunken patio floor. He lifted his palms, closed his eyes, and breathed in the surrounding forest air and its scents.

Mamoru then made a surprised sound. "This place really *has* changed! Everything else is gone… The mansion is all that is left."

Nephryte came up beside him. "Well, a good many centuries will have that effect on a place."

Mamoru turned back around slowly. "Nephryte. I must ask you never to speak of this mansion and of finding me here. No one can know who I am, that I'm still alive."

Nephryte opened his mouth. But before he could give an answer, Gandif came bursting out of a side door and spotted them.

"Hey!" He came rushing across the grass, tripping over his

own legs. "What's this? Was this hooligan sleepin' in my soon-to-be secret hideout?" he demanded to know.

Nephryte facepalmed.

Mamoru regarded the bounty hunter, and his lips quirked. "A secret hideout? Is that what you have planned for my house?"

"*Your* house?" Gandif blinked.

Mamoru let out a hearty laugh at the man's surprise, and he wiped his sleepy eyes with a thumb. "It's fine. I won't be living here anymore, anyway, from the look of things. Just make sure you don't trash the place, nor tell anyone else about its existence. Deal?"

Gandif's jaw hung open, dumbfounded. "Uh...deal."

Mamoru surveyed the wooded area, his back straightening and chin lifting, his aura and stance like that of a warrior. "Take me to Draethvyle, Nephryte. I wish to see the city again and see how our people are faring."

Nephryte's gaze narrowed at the loose silk robe the boy wore: thin, like something you would put on after a bath. "All right...but you might want to change into something that resembles actual clothing, first."

Gandif burst out a laugh. "That's for sure! *Heheheh*. Walkin' around Downtown dressed like that'll give people the wrong impression!"

Nephryte narrowed his eyes at the bounty hunter. "Give him one of your outfits. I know you have some stored away around here. You're practically a hoarding squirrel."

Gandif's laughter died. "...Eh?"

After learning about my mission to find students for Floor Harlow, Mamoru insisted that he be included. It was the perfect opportunity for him to enter the Draev ranks and help the city and kingdom that he loved, while still keeping his identity a secret.

And so, Mamoru became the first member of Harlow.

⟿

Nephryte plunged into his search for more students. He didn't want just anyone in Harlow, but wanted those who had no other place to go, those who were damaged and needed guidance, those who Lord God would lead him to.

In Principal Han's office, he found a discarded application that none of the other Masters seemed interested in. The name on it was Lykale. He could guess why there were no willing takers: Lykale's Ability was with chemistry and knowledge, not a classic Armavis type who wielded a weapon, and he was already fifteen years old.

But being different was what he wanted Floor Harlow to be. And it didn't seem that Lykale had any family.

He took the application.

Floor Harlow now had two students.

Nephryte stumbled upon Zartanian next, while the boy was on the run from his wicked father. He had endured much trauma, and yet Nephryte sensed a strong will inside him, a boy who wanted to leave the past behind and become something better.

Nephryte accepted him into Harlow.

Bakoa he had discovered in the Arah Sands city, Salmu Baris, during one of his trips to visit the Book Keepers and their grand library. Keeper Ekur knew Bakoa, and he was worried about the boy and the Ability he had awakened.

Nephryte searched the area until he found Bakoa, and he eventually persuaded him to come back with him to Harlow.

It was after that that Hercule Dragonsbane's application came to Draevensett. Principal Han let him know about it first, before the other Masters had a chance to snatch the talented boy up.

Nephryte looked into his background, spied out Dragonsbane Mansion—as well as gathered information from

Butler Lynk—before he decided that Hercule was just as much in need of his help and would fit in with Harlow. Although his parents would be more than a pain in the backside to deal with, later on…

Floor Harlow was finally being transformed into something like a home. And very soon, all that was left to do was to bring in Aken-Shou, as he had promised he would.

⟿

The morning when Nephryte was planning to go get Aken, he received an urgent call.

The viceroy had called for a meeting with Nephryte and a select few others, to give them the details for a secret mission from the king.

Nephryte didn't think too much of it until he entered the viceroy's office chambers. Eletor was there, among other powerful Draevs—and he knew then that this mission must be a serious one for them to need this much force to carry it out.

"As you may recall, there was a crime spree this past year across Draeth, and the culprits were never identified. A most recent murder, however, has finally revealed those who are responsible," Viceroy Deciet informed them, standing before the gathering inside one of his ornate, red office rooms. The lace at his cuffs trailed down his sickly pale hands, clasped behind his back. "The body that was discovered had been drained of blood. And there are only two such creatures left in existence who would do such a thing: Purebloods, the Bloodre family."

Shock jolted through Nephryte like a stab to the heart. The Bloodres—Aken's parents.

"We have obtained their fingerprints in secret and have been able to link them to a series of other crimes, as well." Deciet cast a folder down on the desk, revealing images and documents which detailed the incidents.

Deciet took a seat and laced his fingers together, resting his elbows on the grand desk. The shadows of his hollow eyes and cheekbones deepened. "It is clear that they have broken their oath to live as peaceful citizens in our kingdom. Our most gracious king had given them a chance at a new life here— accepting these Purebloods when they should have been destroyed. And yet, they have broken their oath and insulted our king's kindness." Deciet raised his chin and cracked one of his fingers. "Now, it is with a heavy heart that the king is forced to order their execution. Master Nephryte, you and those here are the only ones capable of defeating a Pureblood, providing you work together. This mission has been placed upon you. Terminate the Bloodres and end their killing spree."

Nephryte couldn't move.

The red stains, their strange behavior, their rarely being at home...is *this* what Aken's parents had been doing? Committing brutal crimes in their kingdom?

"Execute...but what about their son? He's still young," Nephryte argued.

"He's a Pureblood. He will only become one of *them* if we let him live. It is best to end things now."

Aken. Little Aken? The child whose smile was as bright as the sun? Who watched the moon and the stars, filled with wonder? Who had tried to comfort him when he needed it most? End that sweet little child's life?

Nephryte's hands became fists. "I refuse to execute a child, nor let anyone else do so. The sins of his parents are not his!"

"Master Nephryte," said one of the king's council members present. "Are you going against the king's orders?"

Nephryte held his chin high, determination storming his features. "I will not let that child die." His tone was a fact, and a dare for anyone to challenge him.

After a moment of silence, Viceroy Deciet flexed his wrist

and motioned to him. "You know of the old tales concerning Purebloods, the destruction that they once wrought, and why The Purge came about. What would your solution be, then, to protect our kingdom from such a threat?"

Nephryte's chin lowered a fraction in thought. What could he say that would convince them all?

"I vow to take responsibility for him, starting now," he declared. "My Ability is strong enough to overpower a young Pureblood. I will watch over the boy; and if, as he grows, he shows signs of becoming the monster that you all fear he will be, then I will deal with him myself. But no one else is allowed to harm him."

Deceit flexed his fingers as he considered this, and the council members began to argue with one another over whether such a risk should be permitted.

But Deciet finally inclined his head, his gray gaze fixed on Nephryte. "You are this kingdom's ace. If letting you take responsibility for the boy will appease you, then may it be so. I know you will not break your vow." He waved a hand in dismissal. "The parents cannot be spared for their crimes, however. Go, and carry out your mission."

It was the worst mission I had ever been forced to play a part in.

I couldn't let Aken-Shou be anywhere nearby when it happened, and so I opened the window to let out a pet sabercat I saw he'd been keeping, in hopes that searching for the animal would keep him busy all that day.

And it did.

I waited until he left the city, and then the plan was carried out.

We moved swiftly. There was no room for error or else we all would have been killed.

I bound the parents with ropes of air, with the force of tornado winds, as Eletor and the others attacked. A Legendary Weapon was used—weapons made of blood silver and capable of felling a Pureblood.

To cover up the scene and any evidence, we made it look like an isolated human attack and let the explosion and fire burn everything away. I had never felt more horrible, thinking of what Aken would go through. And I couldn't bring myself to face him for a while afterwards.

But when I did finally go and locate Aken, and saw those same sky-blue eyes again, I was reminded of the little child and the home I wanted to give him. Needless to say, it wasn't easy getting Aken into Harlow. He'd become quite a troublemaker, and I felt mostly to blame for it.

I should have made time to visit him back when he was little, even when I was busy with Draev work. I shouldn't have let him grow up and forget all about me. Maybe he would have turned out differently if I had, and he would have had an easier time with life... I will never know, now.

But that kind and wonder-filled child was still there somewhere inside him. I could see it, and I wanted to nourish it and make him into the person I knew he could become.

Scourgeblood or not, I believed Lord God had an important role for him to play in this world, and I would see it through.

EXTRA BITES

LAUNDRY PROBLEMS

"Today is the day I finally do this for myself, before Marigold can!" Hercule declared to his reflection in the mirror.

With a bagful of dirty laundry in his arms, he quickly snuck out of his room. "I'll wash them in one of those steam washers, recently installed in the school."

Yes, today he would do his own laundry before she had a chance!

"Milord Hercule."

'Oh no, Marigold!' He winced, clutching the bag to his chest.

Refusing to turn and look behind him, he instead took off at a run, determined to reach the laundromat before she could stop him.

"Milord? Milord! Are you running from me?"

Marigold's footsteps quickened after him. He panicked, running faster.

"Is that laundry you are holding, milord?"

Down the stairwell and through a series of hallways, Hercule zipped through a pair of wide, swinging doors and into the long laundromat room. He made it just in time, stuffing the bagful of clothing and underwear into a steam washer, pouring in soap and switching it on.

Marigold arrived moments later, finding him there leaning against the machine as it slowly rotated inside, a victorious and pleased look on his cool face.

Marigold looked at him, then at the machine, her expression blank. "Oh no…"

She was an honest person, so when she murmured those words, his smile shifted into worry.

"What do you mean, *oh no?*"

When the machine finished washing, she pressed a button that made it turn off. She waited for him to open the lid himself.

Hercule reached his hand inside and pulled out the first item, which happened to be a pair of underwear—it had shrunk to a small size fit for a porcelain doll.

Hercule stared at it, stretching the fabric between both his thumbs. Not only was it small, but the water had somehow dyed it pink…

In fact, all of his clothes were now shrunken and pink.

He stood there silently, mortified.

"The material of your clothing is delicate, the colors touchy and prone to bleeding," Marigold stated frankly. "That is why I wash them by hand, and by color, milord."

Hercule hung his head in shame.

"What the heck is that?" Aken came around the corner, laughing and pointing. "You wear pink baby underwear?"

Other students, who came to pick up their clothes from the laundromat, also started laughing.

Steam poured out of Hercule's beet red face. He shot a stream of fire that made Aken retreat, and then he grabbed up his laundry and ran out.

So much for trying to wash his own clothes! Now, he needed to go shopping!

THE LEGENDARY WEAPONS

"Heion, where are all of the Legendary Weapons now?" asked Cyrus.

"Most of the Weapons are still lost," Heion explained. "They were passed down through the descendants of the Legendary Knights, who are the twelve Noble Houses. But across the years, whether due to thievery or disasters or scandals, only a few of the Houses still have their Weapons."

"That doesn't make much sense, though. How could they lose something so valuable? Aren't the twelve Weapons almost like national treasures?"

Heion shook her head. "I won't pretend to understand it, either." She patted the katana on her desk. "No one really has an answer, so much time has passed. House Sivortsova still has theirs, *Tyrving* the scythe, and we also have *Sakura* the katana. There is no solid proof of who *Sakura* had once belonged to, and so the royal family keeps it, lending it to whomever they choose. I carry it now to defend the prince—not that he needs much protecting."

"Do you not have an Ability, then?"

Heion shook her head. "The power to summon a storm of petals comes from *Sakura* itself. And I can only wield it because the blade chose to bond with me...so to speak, even though I'm not a vempar."

Cyrus pondered that. "Another ancient mystery, hm?"

AN OLD FRIEND IN THE PAST

Child Aken held the old leather Bible in his small hands, the same one that the blue hunchback faeryn had given him. He flipped through the mysterious pages, taking in the scrawled words and wishing he knew how to read. He was having trouble learning in school, and it was the poorest of schools.

Aken took the book with him outside, hiding it under his coat. He navigated through a series of grimy dirt streets in the Outskirts until he finally reached the spot where a certain wrinkled peasant sat huddled: an old vempar who was close to reaching his age limit.

Aken hopped up to the senior sitting on a rickety upturned bucket and roasting chestnuts in a can over a pitiful fire.

"Hey, Gramps!" said Aken, even though they had no blood relation.

The elder's face creased into a smile. "Aken-Shou. What've you been up to, ya rascal?"

He was the only person Aken knew who didn't judge him for being a Scourgeblood—whatever that word meant, Aken didn't yet know, except that it made people scowl and avoid him.

"What you got there, lad?" he asked, and Aken eagerly showed him the book. "Oi my, what a pretty thing t' find. Didn't steal it, did ya?"

Aken's child cheeks pouted. "No! A stranger gave it to me." His brief indignation vanished, and he regarded the elder. "My parents'd be mad if they knew I had it. I heard 'em say people should stay away from believing in things. I don' understand why. What's wrong with readin' this? What's it about, anyway?"

Gray eyebrows arched high on his old friend's wrinkled forehead. "Somehow I ain't surprised those parents of yours'd say that. *Heh*, what don't they hate?" Gramps muttered something under his breath, and Aken cocked his head. "Ah, what I mean to say is, don't let your parents' hate become *your* hate, lad." He shifted to warm his fingers over the sizzling can, gaps of missing glove fabric exposing his skin to the cold.

"So, what's this book, then?" Aken pressed.

Gramps regarded the spunky child. "You remember what I told ya before, hm? About Lord God, the person who created all that we see, touch, hear 'n breathe in this world?" He pointed upwards, "Even them shiny lights called stars, way up there beyond our reach."

Aken let his head tip far back, looking up at the sky and nearly toppling backwards.

"He made us, too, and gave our souls life." Gramps reached to tap Aken's chest with a bent finger. "That there book," he then pointed at the Bible, "contains His history 'n teachings, words to all the peoples, and the path to Heaven."

"Really?" Aken's rosy cheeks beamed against the chill of winter. "The path, like a map or somethin'? But I don' know how t' read yet..."

"I'll read it for ya." The old vempar lifted the book from his small hands. "Where do ya wanna start?"

"At the beginning, of course," Aken responded like it was obvious.

"Oi, this'll take a long time t' read! Ya know that, right?" Gramps fingered the thick, heavy book.

"Then I'll keep comin' back, every single day, until you finish it," Aken said determinedly. He shuddered against a cold gust of air and shuffled closer to the weak fire.

"You ought t' pay me for such hard labor, ya rascal," the old timer mock chided him.

And so, days, then weeks, passed by with Aken listening to Gramps' crackly voice each evening as he read chapter after chapter from the old book. Weeks became months, and he read through into warm spring and hot summer days, colorful fall and freezing winter nights. It became the thing Aken looked forward to most in his hum-drum life.

On the next wintery day, Aken gathered chestnuts to toss into the can and roast. He peeled and plopped the finished ones into his mouth while he listened to Gramps, the heat burning his tongue.

"I don' understand complicated words," Aken grumbled after a while. "How can this person, Jesus, be the path to Heaven? I thought roads and boats are what take you places. How can a person do that?"

His elderly friend chuckled. "The same way I could take your hand 'n lead ya to Draevensett—that's what it means. He takes those who trust in Him up to Heaven when their souls depart this world." He spoke out the side of his mouth, and he wrapped his worn coat tighter around him. "A forever home awaits up there, where you'll finally belong 'n where you'll be loved. There's nothin' can beat that!" He chuckled, though it came out more as a cough.

"So…does that mean anybody can go there?" Aken asked. He really wanted to see Heaven, it sounded like such a wondrous place, and he wanted to meet the Creator.

"That's right, Aken-Shou." The elder tapped his finger on a page. "But Lord God's book, here, says there's somethin' you've got to understand first."

"Like what?"

"Just one simple thing."

"What?" Aken grew more exasperated.

"Understand that sin has separated us from Lord God and must be paid for."

There was a long pause of silence. "What the heck are you sayin'? What's sin?"

"Watch your language." The elder gave him a mock accusing look, as if he should already know these things. "Sin be the bad inside each of us, when we do and say hurtful things and tell lies. Sin separates us from God."

"Separates?" Aken carefully asked.

"Lord God must punish sin—punish the bad things we've done—and Hell is the place for that punishment."

"Punishment...?"

"But fear not, lad!" the old timer chirped. "Jesus made a way to save us from that."

Aken scratched his head. "How?"

"As the Son of God, He has the power and holiness able to cleanse us from sin. Jesus became a mortal and sacrificed His life, taking on the punishment meant for us," replied the elder. "He died for us, took our spot and paid the price of all our sins."

"He died?" Aken stared at him, wide-eyed. Stars appeared in the cold twilight sky above them, and off to the side, a pair of peasants pretended not to be eavesdropping on their conversation.

Gramps nodded. "He did. But death couldn't hold Him, and so He came back to life. After all, He is God 'n couldn't stay dead."

"So...what now?" Aken looked around at the chilly night and the slow bustle of people on the streets.

"It's simple, really. All ya have t' do is trust in what Jesus did for you; believe in who He is as the Son of God, and build a relationship with Him. *John 3:16* summarizes it nicely."

Aken lifted his head in time to see the fiery tail of a shooting star cross the sky between the rooftops, winking out of existence as quickly as it had appeared. "So...then...?"

"Jesus is the one who brings you to Heaven—nothing else, and no one else, can."

"That's it? Nothing else?" Aken pondered.

"Nothing else, says His book, plain 'n simple."

"So, I don' have to do good stuff and be perfect?"

"Silly lad, you'd better not go misbehavin' because I said that."

Aken shook his head with a grin.

"Good works can't save ya. No matter how much good you do, it can't wipe away the stains from the wrongs you've done. Only Jesus's sacrificed blood can do that." The elder's wispy eyebrows drew inward, and his forehead wrinkled like leather. "But good works are how we serve Lord God 'n show our thankfulness and love. Yes, we should strive to do all the good things we possibly can."

Little Aken nodded, trying to understand it all. "You're saying that trusting in Jesus is what saves us. Not doing good things?"

Gramps's aged hand patted the top of his head. "That be it, lad. Plain 'n simple!"

Aken scooted away from the hand, static electricity now making strands of his hair float about.

The elder leaned back on the bucket, propping his back against the wall behind them and resting his achy spine. "Sin is corruptin' this place, y'know…we have t' keep resisting its temptations. Jesus saved our souls, but our bodies still age and die from sin's curse."

Aken's gaze turned down to the fire, watching the ember flecks glow. "Will there ever be no more curse or death?"

The old man's neck creaked with a nod. "Accordin' to the book of *Revelation*, which we ain't read yet, yes."

The old timer stood up then, wobbly, and stretched his creaky joints. "Welp…it's about that time for some good ol' sleep! Best be off home, lad, before your parents notice." He winked. "We're halfway through the book of *Matthew*. A few more months 'n we'll be done with everythin'!"

Aken grinned, holding the Bible. "Yep! Thanks for explainin' confusing stuff to me."

The elder waved, coughing and chuckling into his hand. "See ya later!"

That was the last time that Aken saw the old timer and got to read with him.

Gramps passed away...

He would never forget him, nor his kindness toward a rascal like him. He knew, at least, that he would see the old man again in Heaven. But even so, he really wished they could have finished reading together.

MUSIC CLASS

For Music class, students were required to either choose an instrument for study throughout the year or take voice lessons. For those too dreadful at either playing music or singing, Professor Sir Swornyte punished them with the task of learning the accordion.

"Here's the dull sheet music for you lazy failures." Sir Swornyte tossed a stack of stapled sheets to the talentless lot in the class, then pulled out accordions from the closet, tossing them to Aken, Bakoa, Denim, and several others.

"As for the rest of you," Sir Swornyte eyed the group, "continue with your lessons. Off to the practice rooms with you!" His clapping hands shooed them off to separate rooms, where they would hone their skills at violin, piano, cello and other sophisticated instruments. Zartanian, among them, rose to leave and practice the organ.

Sir Swornyte nodded his chin to Doughboy. "I am especially pleased with your hidden talent in soulful cello music. And your gift for opera is quite superb. You truly have the voice of a baritone meadowlark. I will bring the sonnet *Fallen Flower* for you later today."

Both Aken and Denim blinked at the rotund boy for one long moment.

"Since when did you get into opera?" Denim demanded.

"Dude, soulful cello music?" Aken made a face.

Doughboy replied with a classy smile. "There are many layers to an onion," he said, and he slicked back his short hair with a hand.

The music professor paused at Cyrus's desk. "As for you…" He stared down his nose. "Any talent with instrument or voice? Trying out for the school choir is an option, if you're not the lazy type like those sloth-brained oafs over there." A sour frown swiveled toward Aken, who was now yanking at his accordion's handles, and Denim, who furiously ordered the thing to play instead of wheezing out air as he pumped its bellows, and Bakoa, who kept dropping his on the floor.

Cyrus had never been in a choir. It sounded fun—more fun than listening to these boys squeal accordions. "I don't know any instruments, so I'd like to try for the choir," she said.

"Good, very good." Sir Swornyte raised his chin. "If you pass the test, you may join. If not, your fate will be among these sloths. Follow me to the auditorium!" He moved briskly, and those who were in choir followed him out, Cherish wheeling alongside them.

"You're leaving us?" Aken exclaimed. He reached out a pleading hand, but Cyrus gave him a smile and a wave before slipping out the door: "Sorry, but choir sounds more fun!"

Betrayal split his face in two, and he let his hand drop.

"Well…if it makes him happy, I guess." Aken sniffled. "I shouldn't be selfish. I can't keep Cy to myself forever. He's gotta learn to fly on his own."

"What are you, a parent?" Denim spat.

"Ohhh, the tragedy of a lonely soul~" The accordion in Aken's hands puffed and squealed notes in what he imagined to be some old sea chantey. "Bobbing alone as the sea waves roll, a sailor's lonnnely life for me~"

Bakoa trotted over. "Don't be lonely, buddy. You've still got me!" He wrapped an elbow around Aken's neck in a hug.

"I was joking, let me be lonely!" Aken tried to fend him off.

—⁓

Draevensett's auditorium was a beautiful work of trefoil arches and high-vaulted ceilings, the rib supports making a crisscross pattern overhead, decorated in gilded designs. Rows of tiered seats led down to the wide stage. Stained-glass windows glowed a rainbow of colors in the daylight, and bat-winged sconces of lit oilpowder ringed the walls. The students' voices, as they entered, resounded throughout the large space and slender gothic columns.

Sir Swornyte handed out sheet music, which he expected them to memorize and perfect during the next two weeks. Cyrus had to tip her head back to meet his unfeeling gaze. Whatever went on in his mind was impossible to read beyond the angles of his harsh features and cleft jaw.

Besides being a talented musician, he was also one of the best swordsmasters in Draeth Kingdom, or so she had heard. Apparently, he was the one training Zartanian in the sword arts.

His skin, gray as a storm cloud, made her think of Master Deidreem and Adelheid. Were they somehow related? She couldn't explain why, but the very thought of them sent a chill running through her bones.

Cyrus cleared her throat before trying to sing the short ballad that was the entrance test. Her voice started out timid, and she fought not to let fear get the better of her as she sang, up on the stage. Sir Swornyte tilted his head back and forth, listening, thumbing his chin.

At the end, he stated there was potential, but that, at the moment, she resembled a broken bag of pipes. She would have to practice, practice, *practice*. "The key to perfection, young student, is always practice."

From the side, Cherish applauded encouragingly. "I think it was a lovely try, Cyrus. High and clear."

Cyrus's mouth twitched. High? She completely forgot that a high voice could give her gender away. What a dunce she was! Thankfully, a young boy with a high voice wasn't that uncommon.

"Yes, we are in need of more voices that can reach the higher octaves. Few boys are capable, and even fewer as they grow." Swornyte nodded to himself again while Cyrus sweated inwardly. "You have an oddly high voice. We must put it to use before puberty cruelly snatches it away."

She swallowed, hoping she hadn't just made life more complicated for herself. Maybe playing the accordion didn't sound so bad, after all...

STRAYPATH

Floor Harlow's adventure continues in book three of the Draev Guardians series!

COMING SOON

Get the latest details, extras, and the FREE prequel to Strayborn: *Storm & Choice* at www.eerawls.com

And follow the **newsletter** to be first to hear about new releases, bonus content, and sales!

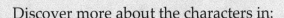

Discover more about the characters in:

DRAGONS & RAVENS | STORM & CHOICE

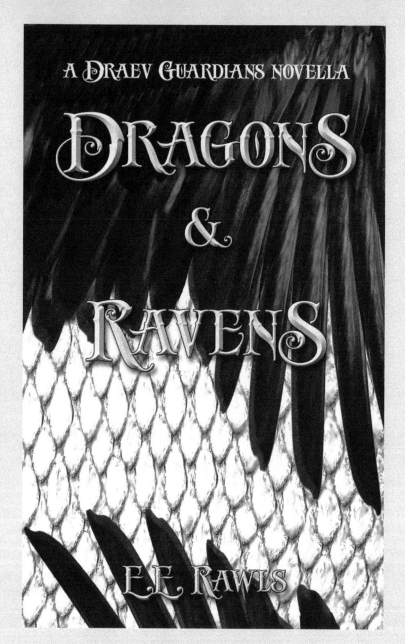

Dragons & Ravens

How did Hercule and Marigold first meet, and what is the secret he's so desperate to hide? Who is Elijob, and what drives Zartanian's goal to become a great swordsmaster? Find out this and more in the first Draev Guardians novella!

OTHER BOOKS

THE ALTEREDVERSE

Books in the *Alteredverse* are standalone tales that take place in our world, at different points in time, and they often feature the humanoid Altered Ones (read **Portal to Eartha** for the origin story of the Altered)!

They can be read in any order. Some books take place during our time, and some far into the future. To see the full Timeline of events, and where each book fits, visit:

eerawls.com/alteredverse

Suggested reading order:

- *Frost, Winter's Lonely Guardian*
- *Portal to Eartha*
- *Beast of the Night*
- *Madness Solver in Wonderland*

Turn the pages for a **sneak preview** of
Portal to Eartha!

How You Can Help

Reviews help boost a book on retailer websites so that it'll be found by more readers, which in turn helps support the author. *If you read Strayblood and want to share it with others, please consider leaving a review on Amazon and Goodreads* —this makes a huge difference for indie authors like me! It doesn't have to be much, just click on how many stars you want to rate the book, and maybe add a sentence or two on your thoughts.

AUTHOR

E.E. Rawls is the product of a traveling family, who even lived in Italy for 6 years. She loves exploring the unknown, whether it be in a forest, the ruins of a forgotten castle, or in the pages of a book. Her brain runs on coffee, cuddly cats, and the mysterious beauty of nature while she writes. *All thanks to God, who makes her able.* To learn more about Him, visit **AnswersInGenesis.org/good-news**

Visit her online at **eerawls.com** and join her newsletter for updates and extra content—you'll also get the Draev Guardians prequel: STORM & CHOICE

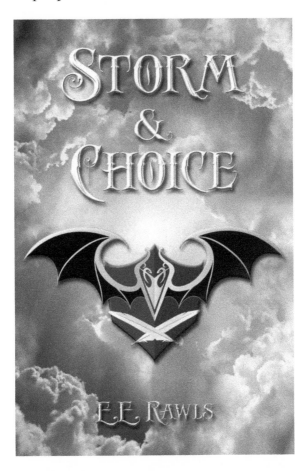

P orta L

to

E arth A

1

Sweat trickled down her brow as she concentrated on the knife wound.

Sixteen-year-old Lotus channeled a flow of life-energy down her arm, through her hand and into the wound pressed beneath it. The super-cells unique to vempars seeped from her palm and began Healing the damaged flesh.

After several minutes, she withdrew her hand, and the burly, gruff man sat upright, twisting to eye the now-gone stab wound in his side.

"*Mirakuru*, it's really gone. Just like magic!"

She hated doing this.

"That's right, *chinpira*. Now get back to your job," said Shiro, her bodyguard—or more accurately, her jailor. He pulled the thug by the elbow and shoved him out the door, before letting the next man who stood in line enter the room.

Not as long of a line today—thank goodness. Healing these undeserving wretches of the underground world never got any easier on her conscious. But she was the property of the Kuro Mafia, here, in Fukuoka City. Brought and bought for only one reason: to make a profit off her vempar gift of Healing.

The mafia's thugs and followers were Healed of injuries acquired from their dangerous work and odious deeds, while others, not related to the mafia, who heard the rumors of Healing came pouring in for the service—and paying a hefty sum to get it.

Even after years of doing this, she still couldn't get used to seeing nasty gashes and bullet wounds, and having to knit together almost-severed appendages.

"Get your head out of your thoughts, Lotus."

Shiro's impatient growl made her rise and bow politely to the next customer, before seating them down on the bench. This man had a blade wound across the chest that had become infected.

She sucked in a breath, then started in again on the only work she knew how to do.

Lotus yawned into her elbow and finished washing her hands in the medic's room. It was late morning and time for her shift to end. Shiro tapped his shiny heel against the wall behind him, waiting.

The mafia's crew—or whatever you wanted to call them—did their dirty work from dusk into the early dawn hours, which meant that her day consisted of night hours as jobs went wrong and people needed Healing.

"Spending an hour cleaning those nails isn't gonna make you pretty," Shiro said.

"No, but it lets me forget what I'm forced to do for a living every day," she muttered.

"A living?" He laughed at that, coughing on a cigar. She was no better than a slave—she didn't make *a living*. "Before you go making me choke and die of laughter, you ought to know I'll be away on another job, starting tomorrow, for a few weeks." She dried her hands. "Another fella's gonna be escorting you around."

"A substitute jailor? Who knew they did that?"

"Heh. Careful, he may be too much for even your sense of humor to handle." Shiro tossed the cigar and stamped on it. "Ready?" He went out the door before she could answer, and she trotted after him.

The underground district was quiet at this hour. Lotus tipped her head back at the ceiling's swirling metal patterns and dimmed lights. The series of tunnels and stores had once been an underground shopping mall, but now it was the place of dark business dealings, ruled by the mafia. She rarely got to go outside the tunnels—the customers came to her, here, where she could be secured.

What shade of blue was the sky, again? Memories of the rice paddy farm were faded, what grass felt like beneath her feet a distant life belonging to someone else.

She and Shiro passed walls of glass windows filled with illegal merchandise and halted at the exotic butcher's shop. "Oi, Karlo!" Shiro kicked the metal base of the register booth, making it clang.

A rotund head peeked out from the back. The man grumbled something in Japanese, and after several minutes emerged with his live catch for the day: a tied up wild boar and three caged hares. Lotus glanced down with pity at what would be her victims.

Rotund Karlo kept a noticeable distance between himself and

her as she bent down, reaching her hand to touch the boar. It wheezed and growled but couldn't do much tied up. In a way, the animal was like her, except she wore a tracking collar.

The boar's body pulsed with energy, and she drew that life-energy into her palm, soaking it up and replenishing her own body with it. Vempars needed life-energy to survive; but when she took it from animals, it made her nauseous and weary.

When she lifted her hand, the boar was dead, and Karlo hauled it back into his butcher shop where it would become tomorrow's specialty. She turned to the hares, doing the same, and hating herself all the while. Caught animals had no chance to run, no chance to survive.

Shiro was tapping his foot impatiently.

Done, she sank to her knees as her stomach fought off nausea and her head spun. After a while, the feeling faded, and they continued the tunnel trek, up to one particular store lined with bars like a jail.

Shiro unlocked the door before navigating through a series of rooms inside, stopping once they reached hers. She yawned as he locked the door behind her, then she flopped onto the platform bed and stiff pillow.

Lotus fished for the miPod under the blanket and plugged the earphones in her ears. A button made the thin, folded frame open and turn on. Scrolling through the air inside the frame, she found the latest soothing dubstep album and let the light techno drift her away into sleep.

"The members of the Society were the last to leave, and they left behind clues for those Altered who had chosen to stay behind, should things grow worse one day and they, too, needed to flee. This is said to be one of those clues."

Dad's words.

The pendant with its dangling crystal rotated, light reflecting off its numerous facets, the green metal leaves cupping it like a flower.

"A map lies somewhere inside it: showing the way to the portal for any who seek to escape this world."

Escape this world…

Lotus sat up, awake, shoving the blanket aside and blinking in the darkness.

She reached for the nightlight, then slumped back against the wall, touching the pendant that dangled beneath her shirt, always kept close to her heart.

"A map to the portal…is it real? Could there be such a thing?" she spoke aloud to the dark. "If there really is, will you show me, Lord God?"

She watched her faint shadow on the wall, the crystal rotating on its chain.

Who was she kidding? She couldn't escape the Kuro Mafia. They made big money off of her Healing and had put a tracking collar on her neck to keep it that way. Even if she did somehow manage to get away and lose the collar, she'd need to find sources of life-energy every day to stay alive; and she'd have to escape the notice of other humans who might kidnap her, as the mafia had.

It wasn't just one group or one city that was the enemy—the whole world was full of enemies eager to kill her or use her.

She understood that now, what her parents had been protecting her from.

Was it that day in the village, watching the circus perform, that had sealed their fate and allowed the wrong people to find her and her family?

"Dad…Mom…" She let the tears wet her cheeks.

Dad would have told her it wasn't her fault, that all things happened for a reason. But she would always carry some guilt in her heart.

The crystal was smooth between her fingertips as she rolled it back and forth, except for one facet that rubbed bumpy along her thumb—centuries of encrusted grime, probably.

"Is this all my life will ever be?"

Trapped. Used. Shouldering guilt.

She tried to recall the serene night sky and myriads of stars back at the farm, the moments of stargazing with her dad and chasing fireflies with her mom.

Portal to Eartha

Future Japan.
A clue to a secret portal world.
The only hope for Lotus, an Altered girl with the gift
of Healing, on the run from the mafia…

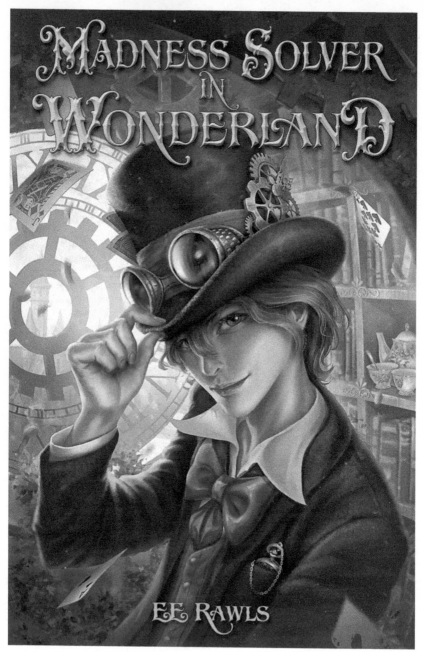

Madness Solver in Wonderland
"It's a crazy ride trying to keep the peace between both
Wonderland and Earth, solving mysteries, but somebody's
got to do it—and unfortunately that somebody is me.
Welcome to my nonsense life!"

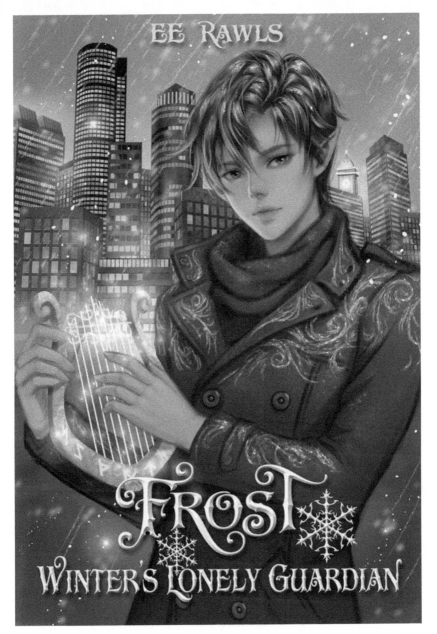

Frost
Winter Guardian and current resident of Boston.
For centuries he's watched over the winter seasons, and
now he longs to end his work and move on from this
world. But for that, he needs a replacement...
A Jack Frost retelling and snarky teen sweet romance!

Beast of the Night

A one-armed, practical girl. A rude lord hiding a curse. A dark secret with the town's fate hanging in the balance…

A Beauty and the Beast retelling with an Austrian twist and a new breed of curse.